WHALERS

A TALE OF BOATS, GIRLS AND INTERNATIONAL INTRIGUE

BOOK 6 IN THE FIREBIRD SERIES

IAN DOLBY

DISCLAIMER:

This is a work of fiction. While names, characters, businesses, events and incidents are the products of the author's warped imagination, places and locales are as correct as possible, but are used in an entirely fictitious manner. Some characters are a composite of several personalities the author has encountered in his travels across Australia as such richness of true-life character could not be ignored. However, any resemblance to actual persons, living or dead, or actual events is unintended, accidental and purely coincidental.

The opinions expressed by the various characters in this story are deemed appropriate for their role and should not be assumed to be those of the author. I ride bikes and embrace the right to freedom of the open road on two wheels for everybody.

Published in Australia by Silverbird Publishing

First published in Australia 2022
This edition published 2022
Copyright © Ian Dolby 2022
Cover design, typesetting: WorkingType (www.workingtype.com.au)

The right of Ian Dolby to be identified as the Author of the Work has been asserted in accordance with the Copyright, Designs and Patents Act 1988.

Dolby, Ian
Whalers — Book 6 of the Firebird Series
ISBN: 978-0-6487179-3-5
pp386

ABOUT THE AUTHOR

I was born and raised on the Gold Coast, Queensland where my extended family always had boats. My love of sailing came from this background and developed through a series of racing catamarans that in turn led to the purchase of an old 47-foot wooden, engine-less, monohull yacht that had been built in Ireland in 1905 and had taken part in the Dunkirk evacuation. I lived on this boat at a marina in Rushcutters Bay, Sydney Harbour for several years and my engine-free adventures on this wonderful old boat may one day appear in writing.

The love of flying dragged me away from the boating scene, and after 38 years of glider, aeroplane and helicopter flying, I have retired to live in country New South Wales with my partner, who is my Chief Editor, and our two cats. While my writing has evolved from a part-time hobby to become a full-time occupation, it is no less enjoyable while the story lines keep coming to mind.

*Thanks to all my readers who keep asking for more books.
It keeps me on my toes and out of the pub.*

*Thank you also to Rita, for your boundless enthusiasm and
encouragement. It is much appreciated. Thanks again Jen.*

CONTENTS

CHAPTER 1...

I'm Harry Stevens, an Australian ex-SAS Major. The 'ex' part was due to a medical discharge from the Service following a bit of a dust-up in the Middle-East, when I stupidly let myself get shot by a not-so gentleman wielding an AK-74.

Discharged and rehabilitated, I was at the stage of wondering what the hell I was going to do with my life, when a timely phone call from a sleazy lawyer revealed I had received a sizeable inheritance from my wildly-eccentric but revered uncle. It was this which allowed me to buy into the lifestyle of my dreams; that of living on a 60-foot catamaran, moored on the Gold Coast.

Following the high-profile fallout from an abused-wife rescue operation I'd naïvely got talked into, I'd been recruited by the Australian Commonwealth Police to be an undercover operative posing as a wealthy playboy living on a yacht. It was a tough gig, but someone had to do it! Since then, while sharing my boat with my two cats, Jasper and Krazy and my lovely lady, Sandy Thomson, a serving Queensland Police Inspector, we've been involved in five major operations, all concerning maritime-related crime. After our second operation, two more crew had joined us, a giant South African ex-mercenary named Alex Chetty, and his lady, another ex-mercenary, Brianna Welsh.

This sunny morning, we had just left Lord Howe Island with three additional crew aboard, having just completed a harrowing, but highly lucrative operation which had three peculiar, and largely unrelated elements. Uncut gem smuggling, Australian native reptile smuggling and a psychopathic killer and rapist who happened to be the resident police presence on the beautiful and tranquil Lord Howe Island. While sorting out the killer was the initial mission, we tripped over the smuggling operations purely by accident.

The lucrative part came about because part of the deal with my employers, was that my deliberately lavish and decadent undercover lifestyle was to be self-funded as much as possible. Apparently the Australian Treasury bean-counters balked at paying the taxpayer's hard-earned to fund such an obviously self-indulgent lifestyle. I had trouble working that one out, since they were perfectly happy doing exactly the same thing for most of the so-called leaders of our great country. Go figure!

Still, no complaints, since their double standards meant I got to keep any valuable assets like cash, gold and gemstones which I happened to trip across or seize in the course of taking down the bad guys. I even had that more or less in writing!

On several occasions and purely by chance, my team and I had been spectacularly successful at accumulating high value, liquid assets; the operation we had just concluded being one of them. This accounted for the fact we were headed for the tax-haven of Port Vila in Vanuatu to make a rather large cash deposit into our already fat numbered bank accounts.

If it seems peculiar that the Commonwealth Police appeared to be condoning the seizure of assets belonging to criminals, then recall this highly practical approach to crime-fighting had started in the US of A, and had been wildly successful.

As well as the cash, we had with us what promised to be a superlative collection of stolen, smuggled gemstones, representing the final drop in the waters off Lord Howe by a container ship. With no-one left alive to lay claim to them, we gladly gave them a new home.

Having wrapped up that particular den of thieves and murderers, we were also officially on leave, with nothing more to look forward to at the moment than some intensely satisfying retail therapy; namely, the purchase of a new boat in South Africa.

It has been said that the amount of satisfaction derived from retail therapy is proportional to the amount spent. Therefore, I should be jumping out of my skin, because I was dropping around $10 to $12 million, less the trade-in of my existing boat.

The only challenge we faced involved sailing this boat the nine thousand nautical miles to St Francis Bay, South Africa to collect the new one. And that was after we'd made our cash deposit in Vanuatu!

As crew on our lengthy journey, we had the expert services of the giant South African ex-mercenary, Alex Chetty and Brianna Welsh, his partner who was much more expert with a frying pan than a gun, plus a new boating convert in the shapely form of Kelly, the ex-wife of the recently deceased NSW policeman who had been such a bad boy. She was with us for recovery reasons.

Also joining us for this portion of the long voyage, at least as far as Darwin, was the Fleet Commander, Royal Australian Navy, Rear-Admiral Alan Stallman and his daughter, the lovely and highly-competent Hillary, who mostly ran the Navy from behind the scenes. I had come to know Alan on a personal level through a previous operation, where his professed love of sailing had led me to promise him a cruise on my boat, *Firebird*. Of course, my two cats were along; the large, mystical and enigmatic Indonesian jungle cat, Jasper, and his little female side-kick, a black dynamic bundle of domestic house cat called Krazy.

Jasper's uncanny ability to understand human speech and to defend his territory and 'family' to extreme levels made him a fearsome bodyguard, as many a misguided bad guy had discovered to his terminal regret.

Our trip plan was that after the Vanuatu visit, we would drop Alan and Hillary off at Darwin on the outbound leg, but the old sea-dog kept making noises about wanting to go all the way. I'd told him to wait and see how this first portion of the trip went. Naturally, as the current Navy Fleet Commander, he couldn't just take a month off to go sailing. Or could he? We had just about every modern communication device known to man on board, so it was entirely feasible... perhaps.

Since only Sandy, Bree, Alex and myself were familiar with the boat's systems, we had to bring Alan, Kelly and Hillary up to speed so they could help with watch-keeping duties.

Being a multiple Sydney-Hobart entrant, Alan took the least time to work out the systems, but as Kelly and Hillary were happy to look after the catering, Bree got a break from galley duties. Since my watch policy was there were to be at least two persons on deck at night, I made sure Hillary and Kelly were accompanied by either myself, Alex or Alan on night watch. This gave everyone a decent amount of undisturbed time in bed.

With the watch bill sorted, we lightly danced across the low swell, a steady breeze blowing from the starboard beam, the sun turning the spray of droplets lifting off our bows into a sparkling rainbow display. Hillary and Kelly were entranced and lay on towels on the trampoline netting, watching the water sliding past underneath and calling out when the occasional dolphin was enticed away from feeding, to effortlessly race ahead of our slender bows.

They were soon joined on the netting by Sandy, who like me, had been ashore too long and loved being back at sea. Unfortunately, both she and Kelly carried the burden of being severely brutalised at the hands of the now deceased Lord Howe killer cop, and both had the physical and mental scars.

However, she had recovered sufficiently to be comfortable taking her top off and just wore a brief bikini bottom. When I saw them talking and laughing, I wondered how long it would be before Hillary and Kelly followed suit. As it was, it didn't take long until Kelly, then Hillary went below to change.

From the time of leaving Lord Howe that morning, Alan had insisted on hand-steering for a few hours, keeping a steady course to the NE for our next waypoint, the southern tip of New Caledonia. By 10:00, however, before the girls had even discovered the joys of laying on the trampoline netting, he decided he needed a rest and turned the aiming duties over to my ever-reliable autopilot, George. It interfaced with Charlie the chart plotter which told it where to steer and between them, they had proven to be a reliable system, saving me many tedious hours standing at the wheel.

With the radar giving advance warning of ships likely to be a hazard, and the forward-looking sonar to warn of lost containers mostly under the surface, I was able to keep watch and do other important things; like look at three lovely half-naked ladies!

Kelly was similar in build to my Sandy, and in many ways, apart from hair colour, they could have been sisters. I was surprised and delighted to see Hillary was also keen to strip down; especially with her father aboard. She was quite slight in build, although bigger in the chest than was apparent with clothes on and looked so good, my depraved mind wondered what she'd look like without her pants as well.

As usual, Bree refrained from stripping off, but was happy to keep everyone hydrated and fed. There was much laughter from them when Jasper and little Krazy cat went forward for some attention, and since Krazy hates getting wet, she was kept busy dodging the spray being lifted by the bows as the breeze slowly built. She cuddled in beside whoever offered the most protection and was happy tickling sensitive bits with her whiskers.

Just after morning tea, I noticed the swell was becoming longer and higher, so on a whim, I checked the weather synoptic situation, and noted a small low was forming east of the French colony island of New Caledonia. It wasn't big or deep yet, but needed watching, as it was the obvious cause of the strengthening east wind which was giving *Firebird* such a fast and easy run to the north-east.

Alex and Bree joined me in the cockpit where we were able to chat about precious gems without offending the Admiral's sensibilities.

'What's the latest on the auction of the treasure and gems, Harry?' Bree asked.

'I don't really know, I'm afraid. I haven't given it much of a thought with all the excitement on the island, so perhaps I should call Mr Jacobs. He needs to know we have some new items.'

'Perhaps it would be worthwhile you flying back to the Gold Coast to deliver them in person?' she sagely suggested. 'After we've been to the bank in Vanuatu, we could spend a few days playing tourist while you do the business end of things. I'd be happier with them off the boat and into safe, expert hands.'

Since Alex and Bree had signed on a permanent crew, I'd noticed Bree had become more interested in the business side of running the boat and crew, and had taken on the task of managing our investments and loot disposal. She didn't speak a lot, but when she did, I always paid attention. Her ideas were always to the point and well-considered.

In this case, I nodded thoughtfully. 'Good suggestion. It would fit nicely with our schedule, but I might just call Mr Jacobs to see if he's going to be available.'

Taking a long, careful look around, including the three lovely ladies on the trampolines, where Sandy had removed her pants to improve her all-over tan, I took the SatPhone from its charger on the chart table and resumed my seat in the cockpit.

Jacobs Fine Jewellery, this is Miriam. How may I help you?'

'Good morning, Miriam. This is Harry Stevens. How are you both?'

'Oh, Harry! Wonderful to hear from you. I have much to tell you, but firstly, I must say my grandfather is not so well at the moment, and is confined to bed. He's a terrible patient, so I've had to employ three nurses to be with him day and night while I run the shop and sleep. Since we have been handling your fascinating merchandise, our humble shop has become very busy. It would seem our reputation for having special gems and other exotic items for sale has spread widely. I've had to employ two assistants to look after routine trade in the shop, and one experienced manufacturing jeweller for the back-room. I'm afraid the extra work has been all too much for Zaydee, but he's getting better now he's started relaxing.'

'I'm glad you are doing so well Miriam, but sad Mr Jacobs is laid up. But as you say, it will be for the best when he relaxes more.'

'Thank you for your thoughts, Harry, I'll pass them on to Zaydee. But here I am prattling on about our problems; how can I help you?'

'I wanted to come to see you in a few days, if it's convenient. I'm afraid I have some more stones for cutting. I expect that these will be the last of the uncut stones.'

'Ahh...Zaydee will be excited when he hears the news. May I presume these stones are very special?'

'Indeed so, Miriam. The situation in which we acquired them suggests this, and although I've learned a lot from you and Mr Jacobs, you're the best ones to judge.'

'No problem, Harry. When do you wish to visit?'

'Well, we're at sea at the moment and expect to be in Port Vila, Vanuatu around midday on Sunday. To allow for some bad weather we might run into, may I visit you next Tuesday afternoon?'

'You do lead an exciting life, sailing all over the Pacific Ocean. But there is no problem with your visit, Harry. Any time of the night or day that suits. We also need to discuss the auction, if you can allow enough time?'

'Sure can. I'll stay overnight with Dave and Corrine on their boat. Perhaps you would like to have dinner with us that night, because they'll be interested to hear the auction details as well.'

'It might be better for you all to have dinner with us Harry, as Zaydee can't travel yet. It will be good to have the extra time to discuss your options. Also, before I forget, Teresa Rubens has been busy and has cut about 25% of the stones you left here last visit. She had to get some help in, but your work has prompted her to move more quickly in setting up her new business. She's been complaining about all the hard work, but I know she loves what she's doing and is having a wonderful time. She's in raptures over the quality of the stones you have supplied. She will want to talk to you about them as well, so perhaps I'll invite her to dinner as well?'

'That'll be great. I'll see you on Tuesday afternoon then. Bye for now.'

'Bye Harry. Be careful.'

I disconnected and looked at Bree and Alex. 'Well. There we

have it. Fly out on Tuesday early, back on Thursday midday, with all the info on the auction, cutting and our new stuff.'

I called our travel agent on the Gold Coast and had her book my flights, then made another call to Dave and Corrine, bringing them up to date on things, including dinner with Miriam and Mr Jacobs on Tuesday night. I mentioned I needed a bed for two nights on *Seeker*, their 100-foot Italian sports cruiser with the ridiculous amount of 10,800 horsepower that could push it up close to 80 knots on calm water.

With all that organised and discussed, I checked out the girls, delighted to see Kelly had removed her pants as well. I was pleased to see that where I'd applied the magical healing green goop to her bruises, they had mostly faded. There was nothing wrong with her other bits either. Hillary was showing some discretion and had left her pants on.

A check on the sea state showed the wave height had risen some more, and the wave spacing was lengthening. The wind had veered in a clockwise direction, which suggested the low had perhaps intensified and moved south toward us, although still well to the east of our position.

Cursing myself for being weak when it came to the ladies, I strolled for'rard and sat down beside them. Sandy promptly laughed and said to Kelly, 'See? Told you so. You owe me $10!'

She laughed back, but said, 'You're right, but you do know him much better than we do.'

'Yeah, sorry about that.'

When I looked puzzled, Hillary, who made no attempt to cover her lovely chest, stopped giggling long enough to say, 'Kelly and Sandy made a bet how long it would take you to come forward after Kelly took her pants off. She almost lost, because you were on the phone a long time, but you came good just in time.'

I grinned back at the trio, 'I'm glad I'm so predictable, my love-lies! But since you ladies insist on taking your clothes off, what else could I do?'

Sandy had a sly grin on her face and I could imagine what she was thinking. I'd hear about it later, I was sure.

'Anyway ladies. Enjoy the sun while you can; I'm afraid we're in for a bit of a blow. We're doing our best to outrun it, but we still might get some strong winds and big seas for a while. The good part is that it'll push us on our way a lot faster for a while, but if it gets too strong, we'll toss the Jordan drogue over the stern.'

Hillary sat up, forcing me to look at what that movement did to her chest. 'I heard one of Dad's mates talk about a para-anchor, but not a Jordan drogue? What is it?'

'If we have the need to keep running with the wind and waves, although slowly and under control, the drogue is a very long line of mini-parachutes or fabric cones, connected to a heavy nylon line attached to the sterns. It has a strong braking action which helps keep the sterns straight onto the seas and stops us surfing down big waves. The para-anchor is just a big parachute which stops us dead in the water. Anyway, you'll know when to come inside.'

'Can we help with anything?' asked Kelly.

'Nah! Just stay there looking decorative as long as you can. It won't be nice when it blows up, so make the most of it.'

She looked me up and down, then cheekily commented, 'Looks like you are already!'

In the face of their combined laughter, I haughtily retreated to the safety of the cockpit, where I discussed with Alex what I wanted to do. We dug the bag holding the Jordan drogue out from its locker under the cockpit floor and attached the bridle to the strong points I had already installed at each stern.

As we were setting up, Alan appeared, woken by the increased motion, and the sound of the girls shrieking occasionally when they were being sprayed with cold water.

'Bit of weather brewing, it seems?'

'Yes, Alan. It's a small, deepening low, lying east-north-east of us and seems to be moving south. We're getting the drogue ready just in case, but we'll keep running fast before it as long as we safely can.'

'Good plan. Do we need to reef yet?'

'Yeah, that was next on the list. I want to take in the screecher and half the main. The wind seems to be increasing a lot more now.'

As we secured the boat for the coming blow, the girls finally decided they'd had enough and came aft. For a moment, as Alan stopped cranking the winch for the screecher furling, I wondered what he was staring at, until I saw neither Sandy nor Kelly had bothered to dress and Hillary was still topless.

'About time you woke up, Dad,' she said with a big grin, as they all squeezed past him to get into the cockpit.

His eyes followed all three into the saloon, mumbling almost to himself, 'My little girl's all grown up!'

'She certainly is,' I agreed happily. 'It's all Sandy and Kelly's fault. They've corrupted her.'

'No, no! They're just fine like they are. Lovely young ladies; absolutely no problem there at all.'

I grinned to myself, thinking the Rear-Admiral must be relaxing somewhat if he was that keen to perve on the crew.

The breeze was already a strong breeze, but then slowly climbed the scale into a Force 8 gale, but since it stayed almost directly behind us, our boat speed lessened the apparent wind speed and what we felt was barely a fresh breeze equivalent. Nevertheless, we were doing 19 to 22 knots and because the seas weren't too high yet, there was little danger of being overpowered, while we were making good speed and distance away from the storm centre.

Alan volunteered to man the wheel and I could see how much he was enjoying hand-steering at such speed. The thought occurred to me that the new boat would normally cruise at these speeds and under the right conditions, would be much faster again. I rolled the big mainsail down some more which just left the small piece of main and the inner staysail to drag us along and although the speed dropped slightly, we still made around seventeen knots, with the boat riding more comfortably.

The swell was getting up now, two to three metres, and with the wind blowing the tops off the waves, showering the cockpit with spray, I rolled down the rest of the main, letting just the staysail drag us along. Speed dropped some more, but the motion steadied enough for Bree to serve tea and coffee in the saloon.

Actual weather reporting had the storm centre still moving south, which was now off our starboard quarter and a good 80 nautical miles away with the distance increasing all the time. The winds briefly snuck up to Force 9, or a strong gale, but running before it in a fast catamaran with narrow hulls which tracked straight, it didn't seem that strong. Two hours later, when spray stopped blowing so much, lunch was served in the cockpit. The wind had dropped to Force 7, although the seas were a little higher, but we still rode comfortably.

We couldn't tear Alan off the wheel, because he reckoned it was the most fun he'd had in years.

Consequently, the Jordan drogue remained in its bag, unused.

CHAPTER 2

That piece of excitement over and done with, the first night watch for several of our new crew was an anticlimax, with a near-full moon laying down a glittering, silvery highway for us to sail along. All the clouds had disappeared along with the setting sun and the sparkling array of stars overhead was stunning. I took the first watch until midnight with Kelly and she was surprised we didn't have much to do except brew tea and coffee and nibble on snacks Bree had left in the oven.

'But aren't we supposed to be doing something?' she asked wonderingly. 'I mean it's night and we're sailing quite fast on the ocean.'

I chuckled at her concern. 'Relax. We just have to be here in case one of the systems plays up. Otherwise, the autopilot steers, the chart plotter tells it where to go and the radar lets us know if another boat or ship might become a danger. If the wind changes direction too much, we'll have to adjust the sails, but that's about all. Sit back and enjoy the ride.'

The general peace and quiet of night at sea allowed me the time to get to know Kelly better. It also gave her the opportunity to unburden her soul of some of the hurt and torment she'd been suffering for years.

We were joined by little Krazy cat who mainly wanted to play, since her main source of amusement, Jasper, was down below sleeping with Hillary. He'd taken quite a liking to her since his usual cabin had been occupied by Alan. By the end of the watch, Kelly was more relaxed and started asking questions about the functioning of a big cat. I promised more tuition tomorrow night before she went to join Hillary in their shared bed, while I waited for Alex and Alan to relieve me. I'd put them together to get Alan more familiar with our watch routine, since the Navy used the more usual four-hour cycle as they had more crew to draw upon.

Friday morning saw the sea reduced still further, and the wind back down to moderate breeze level with all sail hoisted. We had quickly run away from the influence of the storm system which allowed the trade winds to re-establish, making the sea surface choppy for a while, but keeping boat speed up without the need for a noisy engine. The different routine of being at sea under sail was quickly established as the crew became used to life underway.

As always, boat maintenance took up some of my time, but the way *Firebird* was designed and built, this was kept to a minimum. Still, I made the rounds of the whole boat each day looking for signs of critical bits threatening to break. The ladies shared cooking and housekeeping duties, which still left plenty of time for them to convene on the trampoline netting for more chatting and tanning. Jasper spent time with them until his black fur soaked up too much heat.

I took the opportunity to call the Bank of Vanuatu and after identifying myself, made arrangements to deposit a large quantity of cash with them on Monday morning.

The manager I spoke with was delighted to be doing more business and arranged for an anonymous van, driven by a trustworthy employee, to meet us at the public wharf on Monday morning.

SATURDAY

Kelly and I took the same watch, but I was up early anyway as we skirted the messy shoal patch which marked the most southern point of the French island, and changed course more to the north; direct for Port Vila. With the typical sea haze, there wasn't much to see and even radar had little to look at. Our arrival at the laid-back town that was the capital of Vanuatu, was now estimated as 12:00 tomorrow, Sunday.

I had several long chats with Alan about his sailing experiences in the Sydney-Hobart races, which he'd entered seven times. He also spent an hour each day with Hillary, the Internet and the SatPhone, keeping up with the running of Australia's Navy.

The rest of the time, he was happy to steer, look at the sunbaking girls, often at the same time, and sleep, which made him an undemanding crewmember.

After her ordeal at the hands of the late, un-lamented Darryl, Sandy took time to get over it. Despite being happy to strip off on the foredeck, she still was edgy about being touched.

Even being a professional police officer apparently didn't render one completely immune to being traumatised by a serial rapist and psychopathic killer. I think Kelly was recovering faster than my lovely lady was, so I didn't push her for a resumption of our usual level of intimacy.

On the other hand, Kelly's beaming smile and irrepressible humour was a delight at any time. Jasper seemed to want to be a part of Sandy's healing process and spent a lot of time sitting close beside her, his black-furred head resting on some part of her.

So, apart from my slightly desperate shortage of nookie, I was happy with the way the crew had settled in, as well as our rapid progress.

The final leg to Port Vila was 450 nautical miles and the trade wind kept our average speed well above the standard fourteen knots I use to normally calculate approximate trips times. The highlight of the leg was an encounter we had with a small pod of whales.

It was just after lunch, when Jasper started mewling loudly and running back and forth between the bows and sterns. I was at the chart table looking up the Port Vila procedures and the best place to anchor, when Kelly alerted me.

'Hey Harry! Jasper's going nutso about something. Is he okay?'

I followed her out in time to see him run from stern to the bow, making an excited barking sound, almost like a small dog's yap. Nothing was visible around and the radar was clear. We were travelling at seventeen knots, beam-on to the wind and a small 1.5 metre swell. I climbed up on the cabin top, and could see his attention was mostly focussed on our starboard beam. He followed me up onto the cabin top, slipping a bit on the smooth, glassy surface of the solar cells packed side by side, with only a narrow walkway in-between the rows.

Standing beside me, he was almost prancing with excitement, although for a few minutes, I still couldn't see anything. Suddenly, only a few hundred metres away, a plume of spray shot into the air, followed by two more big ones and several much smaller ones. The short and sharply-swept back dorsal fin suggested they were humpback whales; perhaps two or three adult females and three or four calves.

'Whale-ho!' I gave the time-honoured call, which sounded a bit silly as soon as I uttered the words, but it brought all the crew out to take a look. Jasper scared the crap out of everyone by cutting loose with one of his jungle-cat yowls, so loud it hurt my ears and easily reached out to the whales who stayed cruising on the surface.

Then as one, the whales sank from sight, and while the humans gave a sigh of disappointment, Jasper gave another drawn-out, spine-tingling yowl. Apart from the endless, uncaring waves, the sea remained empty, as if the whales had never been. I continued looking to where they should surface again, but nothing showed.

That was until Kelly poked me in the ribs and hissed, 'Harry! Turn around!'

As I did, Jasper trotted to the other side of the coachhouse, making a series of funny little sounds. What attracted Kelly's attention was the bizarre sight of a huge slab of white pectoral fin towering over the side of the boat, while its owner eyeballed us from just a few metres away. Her huge, expression-filled eye seemed to radiate a mixture of curiosity and intelligence as it turned back and forth to calmly inspect the boat and the cluster of humans standing on it.

The other attention-grabbing feature about Jasper's new friend, was that she was easily the length of *Firebird* which was 18.3 metres. Another scary sight was that while she was content to swim on her side looking at us, half of her huge tail fin was also out of the water, gently waving in the air. Which meant there was around 4-metres of incredibly powerful muscle sweeping slowly to and fro, at times coming perilously close to our stern. Two other huge bodies were staying close to her, with four small, sleek calves carefully corralled between them. I recalled reading humpbacks normally spent the summer in the Antarctic, but maybe a late birth or two had kept this small family group in northern waters.

Jasper was standing at the rail, alternately mewling and making a much softer yowl, when the big female alongside us started singing! They weren't supposed to do that while on the surface, and the sounds were quite musical, but at this range, were almost deafening! They meant something to Jasper, as he stopped his own sounds to listen to her, then replied when she stopped.

As a form of conversation, it was impressive and something I'd have thought impossible. After a while, the mother sank down a bit, then used her huge pectoral fin to gently shepherd two of the calves right up beside our hull, as if showing them to Jasper. Naturally, Krazy cat was right in there, standing between Jasper's front feet and in serious danger of falling overboard. I quietly asked Alex and Alan to reduce sail to about 25% of normal, making it easier for the whales to stay alongside.

That helped the small pod stay with us for nearly an hour, with the other females also pushing their calves up beside the boat to be inspected. Fortunately, with a creature easily 60 feet long, there would be no repeat of Jasper's performances when he'd nuzzled the orcas and the crocodile on the stern platform. Finally, the whales sped up, swam two fast laps around us, then moved ahead of *Firebird* before raising their tail flukes out of the water several times in what could be construed as a farewell wave.

The magic of these majestic leviathans lingered for the rest of the day, with Jasper alternately prowling around grinning broadly or sitting right up in the bows scanning the waves ahead, hoping for a return visit.

Saturday night's watches passed uneventfully and as the trade wind direction held steady, no sail changes or even adjustments were necessary. Because we were getting close to Vanuatu, several ships came up on radar, and the lights of several more were sighted closer. Passenger ships in particular, were easily distinguished by the blaze of light from every cabin, so the entire side of each ship more closely resembled a horizontal high-rise building than a ship. Just one solid mass of white light.

SUNDAY

I was up at dawn as usual, and the first thing I checked was the chart plotter's assessment of our progress. To my delight, the steady trade wind had done its job and we'd gained two hours, making our arrival time as 10:00 local, so I suggested that everyone make sure their passports were handy.

As it happened, our entry into Vila Bay was quite uneventful, with the Harbourmaster directing us to a quarantine buoy, but then asking for the Captain to report to his office ashore with all crew passports and boat documentation. He was a genial gentleman and happily stamped all our passports, granting us a thirty-day stay. I also negotiated a mooring position reasonably close to the main wharf, adjacent the centre of town. He didn't require any payment, but happily accepted a small donation to the local kids charity.

As the Harbourmaster had advised, we tied the dinghy up at the private jetty belonging to a waterfront hotel, where I paid a small fee at the reception desk for the privilege of having a degree of security for our RIB.

After re-locating to our assigned mooring, we tidied the boat and ourselves and went ashore. Jasper was a bit miffed to be left on guard, but I promised him and Krazy that I'd take them for a run on the deserted beach on the other side of the bay later on.

Seven was a big load for the RIB, but we managed to stay dry. We also noticed a large, white cruise ship tied up at the cargo terminal at the protected southern end of Vila Bay.

I wanted to find the bank, so we'd know where we were going in the morning. It wasn't far, being in the Rue de Paris, which was the next street up from the waterfront. Then we found a hotel with an open-sided bar fronting the street where a local gentleman in a brilliantly-coloured shirt was singing a wide range of songs from all eras. He had a terrific voice, the beer was cold, the small crowd friendly and happy, so we stayed a while or three.

Sometime later that afternoon, we fumbled our way back to the boat. I was heading for bed, when Sandy kindly reminded me I'd promised to take the pussies for their beach run. I managed to refrain from saying some rude words, loaded the RIB with my pair of four-legged beach-runners and headed for a spit of scrub-covered land which only had a couple of tracks leading to it, plus some good-looking beaches.

While the pussies ran and played in the sand, I stripped off and went for a swim to freshen up. The warm, salty water helped clear my foggy head, so I let myself air dry, rounded up the cats and returned to *Firebird*. I didn't bother to dress, which made it easier to hose off on the swim steps, but as I pulled shorts on, I found I had been under the amused scrutiny of Sandy, Kelly and Hillary. The cats were the only ones who didn't laugh at my nude condition!

CHAPTER 3

VANUATU, MONDAY

At 10:00 the next morning, we were waiting at the hotel's wharf, when a smiling young man in neat casual dress, introduced himself, with ID and written credentials, as being from the National Bank of Vanuatu and he had a van available for us. Alex, Kelly and myself, had come ashore in the dinghy, along with ten innocuous-looking cardboard cartons of cash.

The bank dude's hand trolley helped transfer our load quickly to the van, before the short drive to the bank's service entrance where a prominent security guard was on duty to assist us transfer the boxes to a counting room. We were invited to watch the counting process from outside the secure room, but as the bank weighed the contents of each carton before counting and showed us those figures, it was a bit like watching paint dry, although Kelly was fascinated and stayed glued to the window. Alex and I accepted the offered tea, coffee and danishes.

The count came out at AU$2,350,000 which was about what I had in mind and it was double-checked by the weight since all the cash was in hundred-dollar notes.

We sat down with an account manager and arranged for new account in the name of Kelly Fitzgibbon to be opened, letting her provide her details. The accounts were numbered with complicated passwords I could never remember, but Kelly seemed to have no problem with the string of unrelated alpha-numerics.

The rest of our crew already had accounts with the bank, so it was an easy matter to deposit mine and Kelly's share into our accounts, then place the rest in a trust account until authorisation was received from each account holder for the transfer of their share.

When it came to splitting the booty, I had decided to just split everything equally amongst everyone involved with any particular loot grab. It was much easier to work out that way, since there was plenty to go around and usually more to come. To cover maintenance, Bree insisted the boat always received one share, and she'd already established an account for that purpose.

With all the paperwork done, Kelly and I found a coffee shop called Jill's Café, which promised they'd be happy to feed a hungry boat crew, so Alex took the dinghy back to pick up the rest. The café service was at island pace, but that didn't matter to us and late breakfast became brunch, then happily became early afternoon as we celebrated the first infusion of funds; courtesy of Mr Xavier. Comfortably full, we wandered the streets, enjoying the laid-back atmosphere, while the ladies loved buying colourful, lightweight wraps and shirts at the clothing shops which are such a feature of the town.

The rest of the afternoon was taken up with swimming from the pretty little beach where I'd taken the pussies yesterday. Bree packed drinks and some nibblies and this time Jasper and Krazy weren't left behind.

It was a fun afternoon where the same three girls got naked, Hillary included, prompting a bit of grab-arse and wrestling. All were receptive to some body contact, and even Sandy seemed to be getting over Darryl and Lord Howe, so I had high hopes of a bit of productive cuddling that evening.

Hillary was the surprise, seeming to relax more than ever and provided more delightful eye candy.

TUESDAY, GOLD COAST

I had an early start next morning, and Sandy ran me ashore to be at the airport on time. She made sure I had the three sets of stones; two from the last delivery and the strange collection of apparently rocky rubble from Xavier's original stash we'd found in the Foley's safe. The flight left on time and after going via Sydney, landed me in Brisbane at 13:30 that afternoon. I caught a train outside the terminal for the 60-minute ride to Nerang, where Dave and Corrine met me for the short drive to the now-familiar little shop in the Queen Street Mall, Southport.

There had been some changes since my last visit, with the counters manned by two briskly competent ladies in their late thirties, who later proved to know the gem business extremely well. Myra Henry was a tall blonde and Lacey Kerrison, a brunette of average height. Both were smart, cheerful and had been head-hunted by Miriam from one of the largest gem dealers in Queensland.

Miriam greeted us warmly with a hug and led the way through to her private office which had been created from one of the numerous store rooms in the back of the shop complex.

'It's wonderful to see you all again. Especially so soon. As you saw, we have expanded considerably since your last visit. We found that due to the large quantity of exceptional gems you have been bringing us, word about a 'mysterious supplier' spread to the extent that I couldn't keep up with even the walk-in trade, and Zaydee wasn't able to do more than a fraction of the new jewellery commissions we started receiving, so we hired the best away from some of the major outlets in Queensland. We can afford to pay them well, so they're happy to be in a small, but prestigious shop which caters for a select clientele.'

I nodded admiringly, 'It is impressive, Miriam. But how is your Grandfather?'

She gave her usual radiant smile, 'He's driving the nurses nuts! We both live above the store, so I hired three nurses to be with him on shifts, but he's a difficult patient. Apart from that, he's recovering well, but the doctors say he can only work one day per week. Now you're here, he's coming down to see what surprises you've brought us this time.'

I grinned, 'I do have what appears to be some very unusual stones, including some which look like nothing at all and probably are just that. We nearly chucked them in the bin! Nevertheless, I hope to be able to spark Mr Jacobs' interest with at least some of our offerings.'

We chatted about the new shop staff and arrangements for a few more minutes, before Mr Jacobs shuffled in with a gorgeous young nurse in tight jeans and a T-shirt, fussing along behind him.

'Harry!' he exclaimed, holding his arms wide open to me. 'My dear friend. And the lovely Corrine and her David. It does my old and failing heart good to see you again, and to know you have brought me something to excite my interest. I feel I know you all well enough now to have hugs with all of you!'

'Not too much excitement Mr Jacobs, please,' the nurse said, but the old man just flapped his hand irritably at her and hugged each of us in turn.

After we returned delicate hugs with the frail old jeweller, I said, 'Wonderful to see you again, Mr Jacobs, but I'm afraid I can't guarantee no excitement. I do have some particularly unusual offerings this time.'

'Excellent! That sounds like the Harry Stevens we have come to expect to liven up our dull days.'

There was a beautiful wood table in Miriam's office, with a sheet of black velvet cloth already spread out, and set right under the heavily-barred window. Mr Jacobs sat in the prime seat with Miriam beside him, the basic tools for gemstone inspecting carefully laid out before them.

The nurse apparently wasn't used to this level of activity from her patient, and continued to fuss around, until Mr Jacobs politely told her to go and do something useful.

Undeterred, she calmly retreated to the other corner where a battered old leather sofa lurked and sat carefully, ready to spring to his aid.

'Now Harry, titillate my senses, if you please.'

From my small backpack, I produced the bag which clinked and looked and sounded like it was full of marbles. 'I think these are just white diamonds,' I commented dryly, tipping the bag upside down on the cloth.

The old man carefully poked a finger at several, making them clink off each other, before he sighed, seized a loupe and started a detailed inspection of the inside of the largest dull, white rock, peering through one reasonably clear facet of the stone.

Attracted by the clinking, his nurse couldn't help herself and wandered over to stand between Dave and me... a decidedly distracting position at best!

While we were both engaged in a close scrutiny of Nursie's generous proportions, Mr Jacobs sat back, passed the stone to Miriam and pronounced his verdict.

'Superb Harry, absolutely superb. I would need a microscope to be more certain, but there don't appear to be any inclusions, at least down to loupe magnification level. That by itself makes this a very special stone, quite apart from its size and basic shape which should cut with minimal wastage.

It is difficult to judge an uncut stone for clarity as the cutting process itself may induce some flaws, but all of them appear similar in quality and should cut to around 20 to 30 carats each. Then there will be many smaller chips to offset the cost of the cutting. I couldn't begin to estimate the return these would bring at auction, but as we've said before, it would be unwise to put these on the market all at once.'

I responded, 'I understand. We risk flooding the market and depressing the price.'

'Precisely! Although with the big auction pending, there is one approach we could possibly take. I could put out strong suggestions that I have been offered a parcel of outstanding diamonds of large size and unusual clarity, possibly Internally Flawless grade.'

I looked puzzled. 'But what would it achieve that the auction wouldn't?'

'Ahh...It reaches a different audience! One that constantly keeps its ears and eyes open for hints of a special offering; in other words, private collectors. They don't like auctions as any item processed through one becomes too well known. A true collector loves to swap and trade with his or her peers, and these thirteen will have enormous trading power. Although I must say it would be a rare collector who could afford to buy the 'Firebird Thirteen' as a single parcel.'

I chuckled at his description. 'I do see your point, Mr Jacobs, but what sort of money would be so difficult for the truly wealthy?'

He gave his gentle trademark smile, 'As a package, we could possibly realise $80 to $100 million with the right buyer.'

That set me back on my heels and Nursie looked like she might need resuscitation herself, if the delightful heaving under her shirt was any indication.

'That's quite a lot of money in anyone's language,' I commented dryly.

'Yes! It certainly is. However, we have an auction to look forward to soon and we must discuss that.'

I coughed into my hand, 'Ah...Mr Jacobs. I'm afraid these diamonds aren't all. I have a few more stones I'd like you to see.'

That caught his attention like nothing else. 'Of course, my dear Harry. How silly of me. We've had this very same conversation several times before. Naturally you have kept the best until last, as usual. Please, do carry on. You have, as always, my complete attention.'

I dug out the roll with the coloured stones. 'I'm not sure if these are really good, but they sure are pretty.'

As I spoke, I laid out the pretty coloured stones; the blue, the green, the amber, the deep purple, the steely-grey, the red/orange, the intense yellow with a slight orange tinge and my favourite, the blue/green or teal one. All seemed about 20 to 25 carats in size to my untutored eye.

It would seem I'd done it again to Mr Jacobs, as he sat and stared for moments, before stirring the beautiful stones with a finger.

'Good grief! Rather amazing, Harry. To see so many coloured diamonds in one place together is to realise a lifetime's ambition.'

'Really? I wasn't sure if the coloured stones would be worth much.'

He gave a dry laugh. 'Worth much? Ha! The value of these eight could eclipse that of all the other magnificent stones you have already presented. Their rarity and size are what makes them so valuable, quite apart from their sheer beauty. I have never seen a green with colour that deep or intense in a diamond, while the yellow and the blue/green are almost unique.

These might be impossible to auction!'

'Um...what do you mean?' I asked, a chill running down my spine as I dreaded his answer. Maybe, I briefly thought, the girls might like one each on a chain around their pretty necks.

'I mean,' he said, leaning back precariously in his chair to stretch his back, 'these are so rare and valuable, it would be difficult to find enough persons to publicly bid on such stones. Once again, to draw out the serious, cashed-up collectors, I would recommend the more subtle approach the same as for the whites.'

'But won't that affect the prices at the auction coming up?'

'Not really. As I said before, while the wealthy collectors follow auctions to see what stones are in circulation, they don't normally go through with the bidding process. They are also the best buyers if the stones don't have a publicised history or provenance, and if I'm not mistaken, these stones are from the same source as the last lot of amazingly beautiful uncut gems?'

He raised his eyebrows in question.

I nodded, 'Yes, you are right. I don't mind saying they are basically stolen stones, but I didn't steal them and can guarantee that no one is able to, or will ever try to lay claim to them.'

Nursie's beautiful blue eyes were wide open at all this money talk and the sight of the beautiful gems, so unable to help herself, she stepped forward, almost mesmerised by the display. 'May I hold one, please?' she almost begged.

There was no reason not to, so I picked up the biggest one, a beautiful deep red colour with a hint of orange.

After staring in awe at its beauty for a few moments, she asked, 'Please correct me if I'm wrong, but from what you've said, this diamond, when cut properly, could be worth several million dollars?'

Mr Jacobs smiled gently and raised his hand, palm upwards.

'More?' she asked, 'like maybe $10 million?'

'At least,' he confirmed. 'That particular stone is unique; perhaps much more, and there will be no shortage of interested buyers.'

Nurse looked at the pretty, coloured lump of translucent stone in her hand, murmuring like a mantra, 'Maybe ten million. Maybe much more! One small lump of crystallised carbon has that much power?'

Which I thought was an extremely insightful comment. Almost reverently, she put it back with the others and reluctantly stepped away.

'So, Mr Harry. Once again, we need to call Teresa to have a look at these stunning new offerings.'

Miriam looked up, 'Already done, Zaydee. I also took the liberty of asking her for dinner as well, as the time is getting late. We have naturally allowed for the three of you.'

'Excellent, and thank you,' I replied politely. Although in reality, my interest was stirred more by the prospect of again meeting the pretty, but feisty little lady gem cutter with the huge reputation.

After Miriam had placed both sets of stones into padded trays, we went out to the shop to find Myra and Lacey had just chased the last of their cashed-up clients and walk-ins out of the door and locked it. Both ladies looked tired, so Miriam invited them upstairs to have a post-work day drink before they went home. Peter, the backroom jewellery maker, was also invited to what was apparently a regular de-briefing session, a practice I wholeheartedly endorsed.

CHAPTER 4

Upstairs, Mr Jacobs disappeared to his rooms to get tided up, while an assortment of delightful smells drifted from a spacious kitchen which opened off the dining/lounge room dominated by a large table. Another attractive girl in tight leggings and a T-shirt was doing food stuff and waved cheerily at us.

'Hi guys! I'm Gina. I do the night shift and take over from Patty who does late morning to now. Terry relieves for either of us when we have a day or two off. But I love to cook, especially for more than two or three, so this is great. It's just basic roast pork, roast vegies and greens, but it's looking good so far. Even the crackling has crackled. Won't be ready for another 30 minutes at least.'

The last comment was directed at Miriam, who replied, 'No problem and thank you Gina. We'll be having at least one extra guest if that's alright, and you can slow it down a bit more if you can. We'll do the de-brief over drinks first.'

'Okay,' the cheerful Gina replied, 'how about one hour from now?'

'Perfect! Thank you.'

Mr Jacobs re-appeared, while Nurse Patty gave Gina a quick update on Mr Jacobs, then left, her shift complete. I noticed Miriam had placed the two trays of gems on the table, both covered with a deep blue cloth, so I placed the old cigar box on the table beside my Sat-Phone which looks like a fat mobile, and took a seat.

Miriam appeared with a selection of beers, wines and a small glass of scotch for Mr Jacobs. Everyone helped themselves as Myra, Lacey and Peter started a quick rundown on the day on the shop floor. It sounded to me like business had increased dramatically recently and Jacobs Fine Jewellery might need a bigger shop sooner rather than later.

Miriam must have caught what I was thinking, when she leant over and said, 'Mainly thanks to your incredible series of amazing gemstones passing through our humble store, business has picked up so much, we'll have to expand soon. But I recently bought the small shop next door to allow for that. We'll just expand sideways.'

The day's de-briefing completed, Miriam announced Teresa was arriving at any moment to inspect the new batch of uncut stones, and invited the staff to have a quick look. As all three were qualified gemstone assessors, they were keen to look at the contents of the trays, and loupes were dug from various pockets before going through the collection.

Not having seen one of my offerings before, they were suitably amazed, so I pushed the old cigar box into the middle of the table and diffidently said into the silence, 'I have also come across these other stones, rocks or whatever they are. They don't look like much, and probably aren't, but they have been locked in a safe for many years if that's any clue to their value...'

Myra was closer and opened the box, peering at the seventeen coloured stones cushioned by soft cloth inside.

She did look puzzled for a few moments, before passing the whole lot to Peter.

'This is more in your line, Pete. I've not had much to do with minerals and semi-precious stones.'

He took the box, had a cursory look, and was about to pass it to Miriam, when he did a double-take and picked out one of the large-sized red crystals that was a perfect hexagon in shape and looked as if it had already been roughly cut.

He peered through his loupe for a while, turning it back and forth. Then he put it carefully back in the box with its mate.

'If I'm not mistaken, those two large hexagonal crystals are Red Beryl. That stuff is incredibly rare and although one famous stone is just over 9 carats, it has been the only one of its kind. Most known pieces are not more than 2 or 3 carats, while each of these here has got to be around 30 carats. This is amazing!'

'What's it worth per carat, Peter?' Miriam asked.

He tossed his hands in the air and shrugged, his chubby face gleaming with excitement, 'Who knows? With the usual small 0.5 to 2 carat bits, it sells for about $10 to $15K per carat, but in this case, probably more like $30 to $50K per carat because of the sheer size and rarity.'

He took a breath, then added, 'And that value of around $30K plus, is as they are, in their rough, as-found, shape. Carefully cut and polished, much more. Quite amazing!'

The red beryl must have inspired him for he sat down, grabbed a fresh beer off the tray and looked the collection over again. Talking almost to himself, he said, 'Now if these were Red Beryl, then maybe the other ordinary-looking stuff is rare as well. Let's look at these other two red stones.'

The ones he dug out looked like pieces of red quartz and were a deep red with the faintest brown tinge. After a close examination with his loupe, he smiled with deep satisfaction.

'I believe I have unravelled part of this particular mystery.'

'And that is?' asked Miriam, although Mr Jacobs and everyone else were following the conversation closely.

'I know nothing about this collection of items, or where they came from, but it would appear they are minerals, which have been collected on the basis of their extreme rarity. I just identified Red Beryl, which is possibly the 8th rarest mineral on earth, and now these two intensely-coloured red stones which look like pieces of quartz, are in fact, Painite!'

'You sound quite excited about it,' Miriam said. 'What's so special about Painite?'

'Once again, rarity!' was his short answer. 'It's so rare, there are just 30 known examples worldwide, and none are over 2.5 carats in weight. These would be around the 15 to 18-carat mark, uncut.

Their value could be a minimum of $50,000 to $60,000 per carat, but given the size, maybe a lot more.'

He worked through the rest of the collection, naming Alexandrite, Serendibite, Grandidierite and Taafeite, summing up with, 'All are extremely rare, are hard enough to allow cutting and polishing, and would produce incredibly rare, unusual gemstones. Their value is tied to their extreme rarity, so I would strongly suggest you target specific collectors like you intend to with the other stones.'

A buzzer sounded softly and Miriam got up to activate a back-door video viewer.

'It's Teresa,' she announced, pressing the door release and moments later, the pretty, dynamic young woman, radiating an aura of raw energy trotted up the stairs. She kissed Mr Jacobs, then to my surprise, hugged and kissed me as well.

'Hello Harry,' she said in her sexy, husky voice which made my spine tingle. 'It's really good to see you again and we have much to discuss, but apparently more important matters must keep us from that for the moment.'

Given my general state of nookie deprivation, what I thought was suggestion in her words renewed the tingle running up and down my spine, but I told myself I had to behave and gestured to the trays of gems and the little cigar-box beside them.

'I do have some interesting stones for you to look at,' I said, as Corrine, reading my thoughts as usual, smiled broadly at my discomfort and winked.

Hastily, I continued. 'I hope you'll be able to take on the job of cutting these, like you have the others I brought you. Although, if you could cut the lovely blue/green/teal coloured diamond so there are a few sizable 'off-cuts' and keep them for me, that would be really good!'

She smiled, 'You certainly gave me a lot of work with the last batch, Harry. I've had to hire two more cutters at great expense to cope with the project. But it is exciting and we are getting through them. Now what do you have for me tonight?'

I let Miriam show her what I'd brought and the moment she laid eyes on the stones, Teresa was all business. The tray of diamonds received a careful scrutiny, before she gave her initial assessment.

'Because of their Internally Flawless grade, and basic shape, I suggest I make the largest, single stone possible from each piece of rough. If you agree?'

We all duly agreed.

She nodded briskly, 'Perfect! I think these stones will cut so well, there will be a flood of wealthy buyers all trying to give you ridiculous amounts of money.'

That called for another round of drinks, although Myra, Lacey and Peter took it easy, before Miriam uncovered the tray of eight coloured stones. Her fresh wine was promptly forgotten, as she fairly pounced on them, loupe in eye. As she peered, she muttered fiercely to herself, until she replaced the last one and pushed the tray away.

Looking around, but holding the gaze of Miriam and Mr Jacobs, she said, 'Quite amazing to once again find such a collection in one place. I would love to find out the story behind both lots of stones.'

She flicked her gaze to me, 'An unsubtle hint Harry, to tell your favourite cutter everything.'

Miriam laughed, 'Good luck with that, Teresa. He won't tell us!'

Teresa then said to me, 'I'm sure you already got this from Hiram and Miriam, but these stones are almost unique. The red/orange lump is almost certainly a red diamond and by far the biggest known example. I can't even guess at its value. Probably as much as some fool with too much money is prepared to pay. The green looks like a superb emerald, but as a diamond, it's worth many times more. The yellow and the teal are superb examples of intense and even colour saturation, and as with all these coloured stones, I'll have to consider the shape of each one carefully to make the most of them.'

At that point, Miriam pushed the old cigar box toward Teresa. 'What's this? Not more?'

'These are a bit different,' Peter offered. 'I found them... interesting!'

As Teresa looked at each of the eight different types of rocks, her first comment was, 'These aren't gemstones. I'm not even sure they're hard enough to survive cutting. What the hell are they?'

Therefore, Peter led her through them, adding the carat value as he went. Once he'd finished explaining, she was more than willing to tackle the cutting and polishing.

'They'll make interesting stones,' she commented, 'and very pretty. But not in the same class as the others. Without knowing their history, I'd say they were collected years before these other gems.'

That perceptive judgement showed her sharp mind, as did her next question. 'Are these legitimately owned by you, Harry? That is, do we have any reason to prepare a visit from the police?'

Mr Jacobs and Miriam had a good chuckle between themselves for a moment, until Miriam said, 'Sorry, Teresa. We should have said earlier, but Harry *is* the police. And Commonwealth variety, at that.'

Teresa slung me an appraising look, as if seeing me for the first time. 'Oh? You really are full of surprises.'

I shrugged, Miriam giggled, and the shop crew looked intrigued.

'To answer your question,' I said into the silence, 'as I said earlier to Mr Jacob and Miriam, while these stones were originally stolen, it wasn't by me, and I can guarantee that no one can lay claim to them, nor will anyone ever be looking for them.'

She took my word at face value and nodded acceptance.

Mr Jacobs asked, 'Will you take on these new stones, my dear?'

Her stern look faded, 'Of course, my old friend. I have no doubt the results will be the peak of my career, given the quality of the material, but please understand that I cannot work to a time scale. There is too much at stake to rush the job and risk shattering a flawless stone.'

'Of course. That is understood and I'm sure Harry would want nothing less than the best result.'

I agreed wholeheartedly, before Miriam suggested we stop looking at stones and eat.

Gina's cooking was superb and she joined us for the meal which was a relaxed affair with lots of talk and laughter when I related a few of the funnier stories from my travels over the past couple of years.

After dinner, we got around to discussing the much-delayed auction of all the loot from our Indonesian operation.

'What's your schedule, Harry? Are you going to be able to get to the Auction House in Sydney next Monday to see the televised results?'

'No, sorry, I can't. I've got to get back to Vanuatu where we head west with one stop at Darwin, then across the Indian Ocean to South Africa.'

That raised a few eyebrows, until Corrine suggested, 'If the Auction House will give you the URL of the broadcast site, you can watch it live on-board wherever you are, Harry. Or maybe there's a Skype hook-up available in case you need to make a comment or two. Dave and I will be there as representatives. There's plenty of time before we have to meet you in Darwin.'

I looked at Miriam, 'Sure. That'd work for me. What about the hook-up? Is it possible?'

She gave a soft laugh, 'Harry! With the unique and stunning collection of gems and gold pieces that you're putting through this auction, the Auction House owners will do anything you want. I'll make sure you get all the details of the hook-up.'

That wrapped up the evening, so while Miriam made out descriptions and receipts for all the stones, I arranged for Corrine, Dave and myself to visit Teresa's cutting workshop in the morning. It was a lovely evening, but I was glad to get back aboard *Seeker* with Dave and Corrine where we could talk further without worrying about being overheard.

Next day was a learning experience in how precious gems are cut, faceted and polished when we visited Teresa's small, neat workshop. With Dave and Corrine's approval, I decided to tell Teresa the story behind the origin of the gems, including the ones we had lifted off Terry Williams, Paula Henderson and the pirates.

Even cutting the story as short as I could, it still took some time in the telling and we ended up having lunch with her, and left in the early afternoon with a wide-eyed Teresa showing renewed enthusiasm in the project, despite the extra workload. She also promised to keep three or four sizeable off-cuts from the blue/green/teal diamond for me.

CHAPTER 5

VANUATU, THURSDAY

Next morning, Dave and Corrine drove me to Brisbane airport in plenty of time to check-in. With assurances they would be checking in on the auction on Monday evening and meeting me in Darwin in about ten days, we parted.

My flight was direct this time, and nearly three hours later, I was stepping out into the heat and humidity of Vanuatu's Bauerfield International Airport where I was greeted enthusiastically by my lovely Sandy who seemed a great deal brighter than when I left, even though it had only been a three-day separation. I brought her up to date with all the happenings, and suggested either of us should tell Alex, Bree and Kelly in private so we didn't put the Admiral on the spot.

I also learned the crew had been active in my absence and had covered all the touristy stuff and spent a lot of dollars on the beautiful island, but now were keen to get going.

'Well, that's an easy fix,' I commented cheerfully, 'because I'm happy for us to pull up anchor as soon as we're back on board.'

After dumping my gear down below, I briefly told Alan I'd been disposing of further proceeds of crime, and left it at that. He appreciated I was protecting his position, rather than being deliberately evasive.

Sandy was sticking close which suited me, and told me she and Alex had visited the Harbourmaster to tell him of our plans to depart as soon as I returned, with Darwin as our next port. 'He was very helpful and quickly sorted the paperwork,' she said, 'so we're free to go.'

'That's excellent, however,' I added more quietly, 'I'm even more keen to take you down below while Alan has the wheel and get suitably re-acquainted.'

She pretended outrage, 'Really? How could you think of such a thing when the sun is still almost overhead?'

I grinned, 'Easy, so why don't you go on down and I'll point Alan in the right direction!'

She patted me on the bum, cheekily checked the front of my shorts, smiled happily and disappeared below. I plotted a course to the north-west straight for Cape York.

'There's nothing on the way to run into, so steer or leave it to George.'

'I'll stay on the wheel for a while,' he suggested, 'then I'll fire up George.'

'Yep. Good plan. If the breeze holds like this, it'll be comfortable sailing for the next day or two.'

I left him to it, thoroughly enjoying himself hand-steering. I took note that Kelly, Hillary and Bree were up for'ard on the tramp netting, Alex was doing something mechanical down below, so I headed for our cabin and my dear Sandy. Prudently, she had closed the overhead hatch since the three girls were just ahead of it, but had opened Alan's cabin hatch for some welcome flow-through ventilation.

It was a gentle, delightful and lengthy romp on a quiet afternoon, getting to know each other again after the dramas and abuse she had to put up with on Lord Howe Island.

I was enjoying being with Sandy again too much to enquire how Kelly was recovering, deciding to save that for a later time. I think we were both surprised by our appetites and it was late afternoon before we rolled apart for the last time, then headed for the bathroom.

Up top once again, I scanned around to see we were in open waters.

'No traffic?' I asked Alan.

'No, all quiet. Breeze steady over our port quarter, 10 to 12 knots over the ground with all sail set and pulling nicely.'

I grinned at his report, noted that the ladies were still flaked out on the foredeck, two unclothed and one sort-of clothed in a minimal bikini.

After a while, the girls moved back off the foredeck and went below to clean up before getting dinner ready, so I let Alex take over the watch.

FRIDAY

The night passed peacefully with moonrise at midnight. It was especially welcome by creating another silvery seascape across the carpet of the low, rolling swell and occasional small breaking wavelets which chuckled at our retreating sterns, then swallowed our small wake.

I ventured to ask Kelly how she was getting on with Hillary and things in general.

'Oh, just great! She's a lovely girl and terribly smart, although she doesn't like to make out she is. But to hear her and Alan discuss the occasional business, she knows the Navy better than he does sometimes.'

'No problem sharing the cabin?' I asked carefully.

She laughed. 'No silly. Girls don't mind doing stuff like that. I know most guys would freak out being asked to share a bed with another guy, but it really doesn't matter to us. We've had lots of talks and she's been really nice. I told her what had gone on with Darryl – all except the blue-ringed octopus bit, that is.'

'I'm glad about that. Sometimes I feel we're straining Alan's official standing a bit too much, so I'd hate to try to explain that little incident to him.'

She laughed at the thought, which I reckoned was the healthiest thing I'd heard from her. To be able to find something funny about any part of the Darryl saga was a great achievement. I didn't want to get any more personal than that, so I just said, 'Well, it's good to see you recovering so well. Boat life must agree with you and the bruises seem to have faded completely.'

She giggled, 'I knew you'd notice. And it seems Sandy has recovered as well.'

I blushed slightly, 'Yes. The few days' absence seems to have done wonders.'

She gave an evil grin, 'It certainly sounded like it for most of the afternoon! It's a wonder you lasted so long. We were making bets to see if you could do it again, but you always did.'

'Cheeky buggers...we were trying to be ever so quiet.'

'Ha! You two be quiet? Never!'

I filed that mental note away and let the subject fade, since Kelly was content to sit beside me watching our bows run down the endless parade of waves. Almost as entrancing as watching a warming fire.

SATURDAY

With no particular time schedule to follow, we sailed the whole time and the winds proved mostly co-operative, so the four-and-a-half-day journey was peaceful without the engines being used once. The batteries were kept topped by the mass of solar panels covering the cabin top, as well as the wind generators.

Monday night, or more accurately, Tuesday morning, 02:00 came around and Sandy and Hillary were able to set me up with a Skype connection direct to the Auction House in London where it was 11 hours earlier in the day. My only other experience of an antique and precious gem auction had been a couple of years earlier, when the room was quite intimate and maybe fifty bidders were present. This time the sheer size of the crowded room was a big surprise; looking like at least two hundred bidders present. Waitresses were bustling about with drinks for the obviously well-heeled clientele.

Hillary had downloaded an auction program with an inventory list and we saw, as Mr Jacobs had suggested, the auctioneers had included some major art works as a starter, with the 'Mother Blue' as the finale.

The auctioneer, who introduced himself as, 'Bond...Peter Bond,' drew a good laugh, and was a short, older man with a very dry sense of humour. Contrary to the cut and dried delivery manner of most auctioneers, he was conversational and funny. Within moments, he had told a slightly off-colour joke which got the crowd laughing again and bidding for the paintings was brisk. Apparently, happy people can be coerced into parting with their money more easily.

Finally, the program moved onto our items, and what was listed as 'The Pirate's Treasure Chest' was introduced by Peter Bond with a short history of roughly where it was found and how it had been pirated from ship seizures and wrecks over the last 100 years or so.

In an unexpected move, initially the huge collection was offered up as one item, but no one poked a hand up, so Mr Bond moved onto the first of the main items, the solid 22 carat gold, ten-place dinner setting weighing 35 kilos.

Bidding was immediately brisk, but it was knocked down to a major American museum for the princely sum of US$3.5 million.

That raised a few gasps in the *Firebird* saloon.

Next were the assorted gold items like crosses, chalices, mugs, jugs and jewellery pieces. The Auction House had split these up into the beautifully-crafted gold utensils as sub-lot A, and the jewellery as sub-lot B.

Sub-lot A bidding finalised off almost as quickly as the dinner setting, selling to a phone bidder for US$1.9 million. More gasps aboard.

Sub-lot B was different with an increased level of interest, but as the bids soared past the US$3.5 million mark, most dropped out. Then it was down to just two phone bidders and a tall, handsome young man in the third row, who despite his youthful looks, had the air of being the main man and not just a trusted executive assistant.

He held a slight smile on his face as though he had all the time and money in the world and it was this superior attitude which caused many a muttered conversation between the phone bidders and the Auction House employees whose job it was to pass all the small nuances of bidder's body language on to their clients.

Then two shaken heads from the bank of telephone bidders and the hammer fell to the handsome young man for the sum of US$4,900,000.

Gasps were mingled with a few well-directed 'Bluddy 'ell's!' And a few, 'Who is that guy?'

Hillary had stayed to see what all the fuss was about and being the efficient PA she was, whipped a calculator out and came up with a total so far of US$10,300,000!

'Divide that by eight if you would, please Hillary?' I asked, noticing Bree crying on Alex's broad shoulder with even him looking a bit misty-eyed.

'It comes to US$1,287,500 each, for eight people.'

I grinned, 'Yep! That'd be Alex and Bree here, then Jane, Rick, Terry, Gillian, Roger and Jill. We have two new millionaires in our midst with more to come in the future.'

Alex came up beside me and grasped my hand, 'I don't know what to say, Commander. I shall never understand why such riches have fallen into our laps, but we are happy to seize the opportunity as you have often said. And it's all because of you and Major Johns... and we'll be forever grateful.'

Bree threw her arms around my neck and hugged with surprising force, a flood of tears taking the place of words, while I made a mental note to call Roger and Jill at the end of the auction. If they weren't awake, then they needed to be.

The show of gratitude was interrupted by the Skype connection where an Auction House employee was murmuring, 'Commander Stevens? The jewels are coming up in two minutes, Sir.'

I thanked him, belatedly realising he could see us as well as we saw him.

Then Peter Bond was back and with much hype and talking around the lack of providence of the six 30-odd carat, flawless rubies, the bidding closed with three buyers taking two stones each. The total was US$9,035,000 for an average price each stone of just over $1.5 million.

I thought that once again Mr Jacobs had been proved correct when he said the value of rubies could be quite high if they were flawless.

Our auctioneer then had a lovely time building the drama for the penultimate 'Lot of the Auction', by relating the tragic and heart-rending story of the 'Columbine Stones'.

'One hundred and fifty years ago, a ship left Colombia with many souls aboard who were immigrating to India because of the harsh and primitive conditions existing in Colombia at the time. After crossing the Pacific Ocean, the ship passed through the Indonesian Archipelago, but pirates lured it onto rocks in a storm. Many of the crew and male passengers died trying to drive off the pirates and save the ship, but the women and children were taken ashore where the pirates had a large camp.

The pirates became drunk on the small cargo of brandy carried on the ship and for many days, all of the female passengers, regardless of age, were repeatedly raped until they died. The boys were then subjected to a similar fate. Their bodies were strung up and used for target practice or hacked apart with machetes. There is some evidence of cannibalism, but this cannot be proved as few of the local tribesmen would talk of that.

A journal was found which belonged to one of the women, where she described six flawless emeralds, three each of two different cuts, being the net worth of a wealthy, extended family. The stones were meant to re-establish the family with new homes, businesses and a new life in India.

The description of the stones was highly detailed, they were named after the ship carrying the passengers and the description matches precisely the ones you are bidding for here today. A copy of the original newspaper report is attached to the back of your catalogue.'

There was a stunned silence throughout the room at the conclusion of the story; a rustling of pages, and more than a few damp eyes needed wiping.

Brisk bidding was the best way to restore spirits and Mr Bond was good at that, as the numbers echoed swiftly around the room, finally slowing to a halt at US$5.35 million paid by an anonymous collector.

By now, Sandy was clutching my arm, trembling with excitement.

Then our Mr Bond put his story-teller hat back on, by relating the tale of the much stolen, huge blue diamond.

'In the 16th century, a large, pure blue diamond of some 93 carats, was found in India, and quickly made its way into the collection of the local Maharajah. Although largely left uncut, it had a few basic facets ground onto it to pretty it up, but was not properly cut until the 18th century, after parties unknown stole it from the Maharajah. It re-appeared in the possession of a Dutch trader who had acquired the stone under dubious circumstances. Presumably to conceal its origins, he commissioned a cutting. He had the large stone cut into six smaller stones of just over three carats each, and one larger one of 42 carats. None of the stones have ever been sighted in public since.'

He paused dramatically, glanced around his captivated audience, before saying, '

Around eighteen months ago, The Auction House was privileged to be able to offer for sale, six flawless blue diamonds, the colour and intensity of which caused a new classification to be issued and adopted world-wide. There was informed speculation at the time, they might possibly be the missing six stones from the original 93-carat monster.

Today, the stories and speculation have been resolved, as we offer the final piece in our showing today, the missing 'Mother Blue' which weighs in at precisely 42 carats!'

Lights and two close-up cameras were focused on the magnificent stone, sitting in glorious splendour on a bed of white silk, its image projected in huge and exquisite detail on the wall behind his lectern. As a number of gasps and a lot of murmurs rose from the audience, I realised the 'Mother Blue' had not been listed by name, just a cryptic, 'TBA'. It was a most unusual and unprecedented break in auction tradition, but in this case a most effective one which caused a flurry of discussions on phones as potential buyers grovelled to higher authorities for guidance and/ or additional funds.

Over the top of the hubbub of noise, Peter Bond's dry voice said, *'We make no apology for the omission of detail about this final Lot, but we will pause the bidding for fifteen minutes to allow for an escorted inspection of the Lot by serious bidders only.'*

As a number of men and women held their paddles up to signify an inspection was required, the noise level rose further. 'That man's a bloody genius.' I said to the saloon at large, a big grin stitched on my face. 'The place is going nuts over that rock.'

Finally, peace was restored and once all were seated, the bidding was opened at a paltry US$10 million. However, it swiftly raced away from there through 20, 30, 50 with hardly a pause, while several financially impoverished bidders fell defeated. Finally, as the bidding moved slowly past an eye-watering $70M, two more bidders dropped out leaving two phone bidders and the handsome young man in the third row, with the enigmatic smile. Then the gavel dropped a last time, with the stone becoming the property of the young man for the record-breaking sum of US$83.5M.

Sandy was trembling so much, she sat abruptly on my knee, the only seat close-by, and was speechless for a few moments, before asking quietly, 'Did we just make a half share of.....?'

'A$94.49 million my dear, which comes to A$47,275,000.'

'Bloody hell! And there's more to come from the uncut stuff. Are we becoming seriously wealthy?'

I nodded cheerfully, 'Yep! 'Fraid so my darling girl. We'll have to take lessons in how to behave seriously wealthy and not mix with the cretins.'

Following congratulations from The Auction House rep, I closed the Skype channel and joined the others sitting around the cockpit table, NQ teas in hand, quietly celebrating.

Sandy looked at Alan, 'What happens when Navy personnel inherit or legitimately win large sums of money?'

Alan shrugged and hand-balled that one to Hillary.

'As an inheritance or a legal lottery win, they can do as they wish,' was her reply, 'but this might be a bit close to illegally gained. Off the record, didn't you say you had opened bank accounts in Vanuatu for everybody who had a share in the various, ah... 'spoils of war'?'

'Yes, that's right.'

'Well, I'd be putting tonight's result straight in those accounts if you've got access. You can let them know on the quiet, but I'd let the dust settle a little for now.'

Sandy nodded, 'That's good advice. We'll do just that.'

Although sitting beside them, Alan held fingers to his ears and pretended to 'hear nos'sink', as Sgt Schultz would have said.

I made contact with Dave and Corrine and found they too were delighted with the outcome of the auction. Or should that be income?

Sandy and I drafted up a cryptic email for Petty Officer Jane Glen, who with Leading Seamen Terry Boone, Gillian Smith and Richard Jackson, had been with us on the operation when we acquired all the loot which had just been auctioned. Bree had Jane's email address, so we got her to send a simple, 'Hey. Let me know if you get this email. I've got some stuff to tell you.'

When she replied the next morning, I had Bree ask if Jane had phone access. The answer was yes, but limited and not private, so

I drafted up another email for Bree to send, saying, 'Check your island bank account in 24 hours. Auction of Indonesian items went very well. Tell the others to keep very quiet or there may be official problems.'

CHAPTER 6

The much-anticipated landfall of Cape York came up after lunch on Tuesday and when the subject of the giant crocodile inevitably came up, I tried to put my foot down and sail on past.

I mean, really...two visits should be enough for any cat. Yes? Apparently not, as we had three crew who were intrigued by the stories about Jasper and his huge mate, which seemed to have grown somewhat in the re-telling.

So, to keep the peace, I relented and to Jasper's obvious delight, we put into the narrow, shallow creek located just two and a half kilometres west of Cape York at the end of a sandy, curving beach. Neither Alan, Hillary or Kelly had seen much of Jasper's mystical side, apart from the whales, and the sight of him prancing around the deck like a kitten, merowling and mewling, was enough to make them start to believe in the other adventures.

Once anchored in our usual place, the whole crew wanted to go ashore for a walk on solid land, even though it was getting close to sunset, so we all ferried ashore in the dinghy, Jasper and little Krazy included. While the humans walked and scuffed in the sand, the pussies romped and played, until Jasper suddenly stopped in mid-play and gave one of his fearsome howls. It was the one that echoed off the cliffs of the little headland, raised the hairs on the back of my neck and gave everyone else goose bumps. He stood still while Krazy jumped on his back and settled into her travel position on his neck. She had her claws extended to hang on, as her mount trotted off up the creek, dodging around a large patch of mangroves.

I tried to call him back, but it was a waste of breath, so Sandy and I led the charge after him.

Fortunately, he didn't go far, just a few hundred metres to where the mangrove patch allowed access to the creek again at a small beach where there was a break in the vegetation. We caught up with him, standing at the water's edge making softer calls and looking out across the creek.

'There he is Commander,' Alex spoke quietly beside me and pointed straight out to the deeper water against the opposite bank.

As usual, I couldn't see anything and it wasn't until the others had quietly come up behind us, when I saw the usual four lumps, looking like seed pods, seeming to drift on the current like four walnuts. Except in this case, they stayed in a perfect rectangle and moved slowly toward us.

'We might just want to step back a little bit if he's going to come ashore here,' Alex suggested.

Alan, Hillary and Kelly were getting very nervous at this point, with Alan saying, 'Harry. Even I know that really is a crocodile and it's coming this way. We're in its territory and I know this isn't a good place to be, so can we just get the hell out of here?'

'Hang on a minute, Alan. Let me check with Jasper. He'll know if it's his mate or not, and I reckon he wouldn't be standing there if it isn't.'

That earned me a very odd look from the Admiral, but he bravely stood his ground while I stepped forward and said to Jasper, 'Is this your friend?'

He didn't even turn his head, but he did huff loudly, which was good enough for me, so I stepped back to Alan, who had Hillary and Kelly hiding behind him for protection.

'All good, Alan,' I said cheerfully, 'it's Jasper's mate alright, so we'll be okay if we just give them room.'

He looked at me as though I had two heads, as he remarked, 'Frankly Harry, he can have all the room he wants. In fact, he can have the whole bloody beach! I'm not much of a judge of crocodiles, but I'd say those bits sticking out of the water a long, long way back behind his eyes must be his tail.'

I managed to look puzzled, 'Well, yes, of course they are, Alan. It's how he swims.'

'Now you're being a smart-arse! My point is that those tail bits would have to be at least five metres behind his eyes, and the tip of the tail is still underwater. That makes him a seriously huge croc and I'd really rather not offer him a human sacrifice!'

I laughed. 'Actually, he's well over six metres long, the last time we had a chance to get a good look. But back up if you want, so long as you keep watching. You really don't want to miss any of this!'

To his credit, he stayed put, although neither he nor the girls were happy. They were reassured slightly by the way Alex, Bree and Sandy stayed back with them, apparently happy that I was the crash-test dummy who went down to stand near Jasper.

My big cat was quivering with excitement, his tail up, and little Krazy was also standing, although I was sure she had a full set of needle-claws dug in for balance, as the two nostril tips and two eyes drifted closer. The place we were standing was the inside of the bend in the creek and the water shallowed gradually, allowing the croc's enormous shadowy form to show just before his back broke the surface.

'Careful Harry!' was the call from Alan, since I was just two metres off to one side of Jasper who stood with his front paws right on the water's edge, still mewling quietly.

The croc didn't stop in the shallows and kept unhurriedly moving straight between Jasper and me, so I took another pace back. As the water shallowed, more and more of his colossal bulk rose into view prompting a renewed round of expressions of alarm and disbelief from the crew behind me. Then his whole head was exposed, easily a meter and a half long, his mouth open slightly as he took slow, deliberate steps forward. There were gasps from the girls when the huge snout and head poked right up beside Jasper and Krazy, then he took a few more steps until his entire front half was out of the water, forcing Jasper to back up the bank so he could crouch down beside one eye.

I noted the other eye was regarding me carefully.

I had turned to face the croc and copied Jasper by squatting down to get closer to his eye level, despite the agonised whisper of, 'Harry!' from Alan. I motioned slowly with my hand behind my back that they should all squat down, and from the corner of my eye, saw them comply.

Slowly, the croc turned his head toward me, opened his jaws a bit further, gave a quiet grunt, closed his eyes briefly, then turned back to lower his head onto the sand right beside Jasper.

I was stunned to realise I'd just been recognised and greeted by a seven-metre saltwater crocodile who was big enough to swallow me whole in one gulp!

Meanwhile, my beautiful, mystical cat had snuggled up beside the croc's snout, their eyes just centimetres apart. Jasper stopped with the mewling, but occasionally the croc would make a soft grunt... presumably of contentment. At that point, dear crazy little Krazy cat stretched her back, then delicately stepped across Jasper's head, onto the broad top of Mr C's snout and went for a stroll up his head, between his eyes, stopping at the start of his neck to scratch behind her ear.

She then picked her way down his neck between the array of stubby armour plates decorating his more than two metre long back, only stopping when she reached the water's edge about where his three and a half metres of tail started.

She wandered back up the exposed half of his length, all the way to the tip of his snout where she sniffed inquisitively at his nostrils, apparently tickling him with her whiskers in the process, since he snorted gently a couple of times, making her prance back a bit. She then turned around, adopted the Sphinx position, much beloved by all cats when they feel like being inscrutable, and locked her gaze on his.

Then Mr C closed his eyes and seemed to go to sleep.

I took the opportunity to stand and stretch my aching muscles, then stepped back to the crew, still huddled together ready for instant flight. Looking back briefly, I appreciated what a bizarre scene it was with the huge croc, half exposed on dry land, his tail dimly visible in the clear, shallow water. Stranger still, was the presence of the big, black cat crouched down beside his jaws and the tiny, silver-speckled, black one stretched out on his broad muzzle.

'This could go on for a while,' I informed them, 'so you might as well have your walk and go back aboard. I'll sit with them, but perhaps someone could come and relieve me in an hour?'

Surprisingly, it was Kelly who immediately volunteered. 'I'll stay here now, if you like. I don't want to miss any of this. It's like a miracle. However, if someone could bring a beach chair when you come back, that'd be good.'

'Okie doke. I won't be long.' As we walked quietly away, that was when I realised Bree had brought the video camera and had taped the entire encounter, start to finish.

'That's brilliant, Bree. I'll change batteries and tapes and come straight back. Nothing usually happens once they go into this sleep or trance mode.'

'No problem, Boss. It was truly amazing; even better than the last time. I don't want to miss it either, so I'll come back with you.'

To my surprise, her thoughts were echoed by the rest, so I suggested to Bree maybe we could start a fire well back from the communing animal trio and have a BBQ tea. That idea was even more warmly received, so back aboard, there was a general bustle to round up beach chairs, cooking and food stuff and an esky of drinks. Jasper and Krazy type food were thought of, as well as a frozen old leg of lamb well past its use-by date. It took two brief dinghy trips to ferry all the stuff and crew ashore and the girls set up camp well back from the croc and his companions. As Alex started the fire, Mr C lazily opened one eye, checked out the scene, then closed it again, apparently reassured by our presence.

A campfire BBQ was something we rarely did and was a great success as darkness settled over our secluded little creek and the smoke chased the whining mossies away. We even went so far as to have the traditional billy tea to go with the Bundy rum liqueur. After all, we were still just in North Queensland.

The NQ teas went well with the steaks, chops and potatoes wrapped in foil in the embers. I was sitting with my back to the water, as we were finishing off the last few succulent morsels, when Hillary gave a quiet little shriek and pointed behind me.

Turning around, I was startled to see the long snout of our friend, Mr C, as everybody was now calling him, emerging from the shadows just behind me. He'd approached in my shadow and moving slowly over the sand, was utterly silent.

What defused a potentially scary situation was the presence of little Krazy cat, still perched happily on his head, and with Jasper walking beside his overgrown friend. Half the crew started slowly backing up, but Sandy waved them down. The croc stopped with his snout beside my seat, opened his jaws a bit and gave what could loosely be described as a polite cough. When nobody reacted, apart from freezing in place, he did it again.

Then Bree gave a nervous laugh and suggested, 'Harry. If I didn't know better, I'd think he wants something to eat. Remember last time you gave him the old leg of lamb?'

'Damn! I bet you're right. I did toss an old leg in, but it's still frozen.'

'No, I fixed it,' she replied. 'I sat it near the fire earlier, so it should be fine now. Not that the garbage guts ever chews anything small! It just goes straight down.'

Moving slowly, she passed the large leg of lamb across, the croc's eyes following every movement. When I took it, he slowly opened those massive jaws with their frightening array of teeth and waited until I placed the three-kilo morsel onto his lower jaw.

Jasper must have taught him some manners, for he slowly closed his jaws to make sure nobody pinched it back, then politely turned away from the fire before lifting his head and tossing the leg to the back of his throat with two abrupt jerks of his head. Then it must have been wombat time as he slowly completed the turn and half-walked, half-slithered down the sand to the water's edge. Unfortunately for me, he'd forgotten about the three and a half metres and half a tonne of tail which described an arc behind him that neatly intersected with my chair, knocked it over and dumped me on my arse on the sand.

Krazy had bailed out before feed time started and was perched back on Jasper, watching Mr C slide silently into the water and disappear from sight. The relief shown by Alan, Hillary and Kelly was priceless to see, but then turned noisy as they all wanted to describe in their own words what we'd all just seen, yet couldn't seem to explain.

Alan looked at me with shining eyes, more like a kid with a new bike on Christmas morning, than an admiral. 'Harry. I know you and Sandy have talked about how Jasper can commune with other wild creatures, but this is way over anything I could have imagined. And not just for Jasper's part in this. The croc was actually acknowledging you as a person and behaving as though Jasper had taught it how to behave around humans.'

I shrugged, 'Yep. I know what you're saying, and I can't explain it either. Ever since Jasper started his whole 'Doctor Dolittle' routine, I've been at a loss to work out half of what he goes on with. However, I have noticed the more he does of this sort of thing, the better focused he's become at doing more. If that makes sense?'

It must have, for nobody looked blank. We finally packed up all the BBQ doings, doused the campfire and headed the two hundred metres back to *Firebird*. Jasper, with his little furry passenger, was happy to trot along with us and didn't seem to be pining for his big mate.

After having a chat with Alan and Alex, I decided we would let Jasper stand watch, so everyone could get a normal night's sleep. I told him to watch out for bad men and to wake me if there was trouble coming, which he would have anyway. I fired up the hot safety-railing system anyway, and both pussies knew to back off when they felt the energy field surrounding the safety rails. I took the precaution of digging out my favourite handgun, the Grizzly Mk IV .44 magnum pistol which looked like the venerable old 1911 Colt .45, but had nearly twice the stopping power.

As it happened, the night was quite peaceful and we all slept really well, undisturbed by drunk fishermen, greedy locals or friendly crocodiles.

CHAPTER 7

CAPE YORK, WEDNESDAY TO SATURDAY

I woke with first light as I normally do, stuck my head up through the hatch over the bed to have a quick look around, but saw nothing out of place, so I climbed up onto the foredeck and greeted the new day, in time-honoured fashion, with a long and satisfying pee over the side. The soft noise attracted little Krazy cat who scampered up to me then started prancing around making more noise than I'd heard her make for a long time.

I crouched down to better look her in the eye and said, 'OK. What's going on? Is Jasper in trouble?'

She bounced around even more, so without wasting time dressing, I walked aft to see Jasper perched near the top of the stern stairs, with Mr C's big fat head occupying the lower three steps. No surprises there!

Then I looked more closely and saw another slightly smaller head, tucked in close against his armoured flank. It must be his mate he'd brought around to meet Jasper and Krazy, so I quickly went forward and called down to Sandy through the hatch, then did the same to the others, before squatting down beside Jasper at the top of the stairs.

'Is that his mate he's brought to visit you?' I asked.

In reply, Jasper gave a quiet huff, not taking his eyes off the pair. Now I was closer and the light was improving, I noticed the smaller croc had her eyes open, making no move to swim away. The big one opened his briefly, registered my presence, then closed them again. The increased light level also showed the other croc was perhaps only six-metres long as opposed to Mr C's seven-metres.

From the faint scuff of feet behind me, I guessed the others had turned up, and I hoped someone was recording the whole thing. I'd probably have to send a copy on to Georgia and Beth, the two animal behaviouralists from Sydney Uni who came to see Jasper on Lord Howe Island.

There was a giggle behind me as well, and it was Kelly who said, 'I do hope Krazy doesn't decide to play with those dangling bits she's eyeing off, or you're about to get a bit of a heart-starter.'

I didn't catch on for a moment, then realised I still had no pants on from my first foray on deck, and a small, black cat was stalking what would appear to be a very tempting target! A minute later, a hand appeared over my shoulder holding my shorts, which I carefully put on, while being calmly regarded by the female croc.

With dangling temptations removed from sight, the small black fur-ball wandered down past Jasper and hopped nonchalantly up on Mr C's snout again. He opened on eye, checked her out, then closed it again as she strolled up between his eyes to the top of his knobbly head, inspected the female, then settled down in sphinx position, to watch her.

We quickly tired of the inactivity, since whatever might be going on was way above human understanding, and made a quiet withdrawal. Kelly set the video camera on time-lapse and propped it up on the deck where the whole scene was captured.

That made it about breakfast time, where we celebrated the fascinating double event with a lovely cooked brekkie of all my favourite things like sausages, bacon, beans and tomatoes.

We had plenty of time to discuss the events of the last 24 hours as well as enjoying the meal, before there was a soft coughing from the stern, the boat gave an all too familiar lurch, and our two huge visitors were gone.

Jasper looked a bit mournful, but didn't carry on, just sat on the day-bed and looked out over the creek as we made preparations to get going. Ten minutes later, with the admiral at the wheel, we punched through the small waves breaking on the sand bank across the mouth of the tiny creek, then turned left once we cleared the small headland.

Just before lunch, Bree had an email from Jane.

'Unbelievable! I cannot thank you all enough for doing this for us. I haven't told the others yet since I don't want to upset the routine while we're at sea. I'll tell them when we go on next work-break rotation. Some may want to leave the Service, but it's their choice. I'll be in touch as soon as I can talk privately. Thank Harry for me and give him a hug. I owe him everything! Love you guys!'

It was a little over two days travel ahead to reach Darwin, and since we could refuel there, I saw no reason not to make the best time possible. Therefore, to keep our average speed up, the engines were used any time the winds became fluky or light.

That stretch of our journey was pleasantly uneventful and even the weather was benign, although Thursday dawned grey with a low overcast and a few showers, which didn't develop into anything. I didn't bother with the Hole-in-the-Wall or any other diversions, and just pushed on.

We saw a few other sails in the distance, but that's where they stayed, as the sea-going routine kicked in again. With plenty of crew, there was enough time for everyone to sleep well, eat well and laze around.

Kelly continued to relax and Hillary reported privately that her frequent nightmares were greatly reduced. In fact, it would be hard to find a happier person and more willing crewmember, although we did notice, with a touch of amusement, that she and Alan were spending a lot of time together.

DARWIN

There were three unhappy people on Friday, around lunch-time, when we motored into Darwin harbour and nosed into the familiar Stoke's Hill Wharf, where I'd lined up a mooring for a couple of days. Our usual on-shore meeting spot was the excellent seafood restaurant on the wharf, where the panoramic windows in the bar gave us a great view of the water front and the busy Darwin harbour. Three US Navy ships were moored in a self-protective cluster at the western wharf, where last time, a huge white cruise ship had disgorged thousands of passengers.

Hillary had been busy on the SatPhone and arranged commercial business-class seats back to Canberra for her and Alan, who kept dropping heavy hints he'd like to be on the South Africa run. But Hillary, in her quietly effective way, shut down all his wild plans and steered him back into active control of the Royal Australian Navy. To his obvious disgust.

Dave and Corrine were due to fly in on Saturday afternoon, with Hillary and Alan departing in the morning, so we sadly waved them off in a taxi with repeated promises to keep them updated with all our news throughout the coming voyages.

Our reduced crew of five adjourned to the restaurant for some mood-uplifting drinks and a feast of fresh-cooked mud crabs with a side dish of crocodile kebabs marinated in mango and basil. It was a real spoil of a feed and we promised not to tell Jasper that the croc meat was succulent, white and tasty with a delicate flavour which didn't taste anything like muddy chicken. The mango/basil marinade seemed to compliment it perfectly and I fear we virtually waddled out of the place, just in time to meet Dave and Corrine as they climbed out of a taxi with their usual minimal luggage.

They unpacked in the stern cabin just vacated by Kelly and Hillary, and while Kelly moved her few items into the starboard bow cabin ahead of Sandy and me, we caught up on news.

'Top result from the auction, dude!' was Dave's enthusiastic response, starting a round of hi-fives. 'Another $47 mil each in the bank won't go astray, with heaps more to come from all those uncut stones which are being processed as we speak.'

Sandy and I agreed and I repeated my flippant comment that

we'd have to start taking lessons in how to act like most other seriously wealthy arseholes.

We spent two relaxing days in Darwin, or at least the girls did; out shopping each day and running around the extremely cosmopolitan city of Darwin. It was a fascinating place, and it seemed like every race from India eastwards was represented, although the habit of Northern Territorians drinking prodigious quantities of rum thankfully hadn't been wiped out. While the girls played, Dave, Alex and I checked the boat thoroughly and replaced anything which looked even remotely suspect. We refuelled all the tanks, bladders included and treated the engines to a full factory service, courtesy of the local Yanmar agent who was pleased to have the business.

MONDAY

Early Monday morning, with a nasty gusting wind, heavily overcast skies and a choppy sea, we left the security of our mooring and headed out into the wilds of the Timor Sea. The next possible landfall was Ashmore and Cartier Reefs where there were several small coral and sand islands. They were a good two days sail away, although our next scheduled landfall was Cocos-Keeling Islands some 7 days or so away. I always found it interesting, from a psychological point of view, that when one first sails away from land, there was a strong desire to keep the legs between landfalls as short as possible, but once the cruising routine was established, making landfall was the last thing anyone wanted. Human nature... hmmm.

In this instance, we'd have to deviate from our planned track to visit the lonely outlying specks of sand and coral which were so often the first landfall of refugee boats from Indonesia or SE Asia. I said nothing and no one else made noises about wanting to go roll in the sand except the pussies, so they got out-voted as we passed the reef complex at some point during the day on Wednesday. By then, however, we were making good time to the west-south-west, with a steady south-easterly breeze blowing up our left-rear skirts, making *Firebird* hustle along nicely at several knots above our normal average. The engines stayed quiet and looking at the weather pattern, it seemed the summer monsoon trough which should have been stirring up the weather right on our track, was running late and conveniently stayed north of us.

That meant we had a much-reduced chance of running into a cyclone, so at a briefing during the evening meal, I outlined the revised plan.

'With the monsoon trough still well north, we'll continue to have these dry conditions with a steady breeze and are making really good time. I intend to bend our track a bit further south so we miss the Cocos-Keeling Islands and keep pushing on. If we can avoid getting caught either by a cyclone or the doldrums, we could make the northern tip of Madagascar in twelve days.'

As everyone was happily in a cruising routine, and not in desperate need of a dry land fix yet, that plan was well received. We also were in the routine of having a daily briefing session at 17:00 when we all got together to have a couple of drinks before the evening meal.

The other 22 hours were at the mercy of the watch system and personal preference for off-watch activities.

Despite missing Alan, Kelly was settling in better all the time and it wasn't a problem having her passing through our cabin at odd times of the day or night. She'd often stop for a brief chat unless we were actively having a romp, although a couple of times she stopped anyway. Then there were many times when she sprung me in the process of getting in or out of bed, but it didn't seem to bother her and it certainly didn't worry me.

I always copped a cheeky grin on those occasions.

She and Sandy had become close from the shared Lord Howe Island traumas, and that helped her regain her easy manner and cheeky nature. Given my dear lady's past experiences in enjoying a bit of a fool around with other girls, I wondered how long it would be until she invited Kelly into our bed.

Our luck with the weather held and the breeze stayed strong and steady out of the south-east, speeding our progress toward Madagascar, with the only excitement being an encounter with a whale shark on Thursday morning.

I was just coming up on deck at first light to relieve Dave and Corrine, when Jasper started going berko up on the bows, running from one side to the other, mewling and occasionally cutting loose with his incredibly loud yowl which scares the crap out of the unsuspecting, and still sends shivers down my spine. He was staying more on the right bow, so Corrine and I wandered up to see a huge fin covered in pale spots slowly moving through the low swell, about fifty metres up ahead. A second, even taller fin about nine metres behind the first, lazily waved back and forth. I called back to Dave to douse all sail except the small inner staysail to allow us to creep up on what looked to be a whale shark. Either that or it was the mother of all Great Whites with a case of the measles.

We slowly and quietly closed in on the monster fish, and even as Dave steered us close alongside, it merely rolled on its side slightly to get a better look. Apparently satisfied with what it saw, it resumed sucking up vast amounts of plankton through the huge mouth that could take in a 200-litre drum, even though whale sharks were totally benign creatures and harmless to humans.

Dave had partially rolled the staysail in so we'd keep pace with the whale shark which was barely moving at a walking pace.

It was Kelly who pointed out an interesting fact.

'Harry? I just noticed our friend's nose is about level with our bow. Is that correct?'

I took a quick look, 'Yep, that's about right.'

'Well. I just went to the stern and its tail is well beyond the stern! If this boat is 60 feet long, then our friend is close to 70 feet long! Should we be just a little bit concerned?'

I peered aft and she was right. The tall tail fin waving lazily was well behind the stern and since the beautiful creature was tucked right in against the right-side hull, it was easy to judge the distance. 'No. No need to worry. It won't intentionally harm us, although I'd prefer it didn't give us a love pat with that tail.'

Kelly gave a nervous giggle, then jumped when the boat gave a gentle lurch as our visitor bumped a hull. I was glad Jasper refrained from doing anything too mystical with this gentle giant. I reached out and stroked the dorsal fin when it came close and was surprised at the rough texture of the skin.

Soon after, the school of plankton must have run out or moved, for the whale shark slowly submerged and headed away from our side. It would seem that whale sharks do everything in slow-motion.

We sighted the dorsal fin and the waving tail a few times in the distance, then it disappeared, to become the topic of conversation for the rest of the morning.

Sandy had shot some excellent video of the whole encounter, sending a preview of a few seconds worth to act as a teaser, back to our dear friends, Roger and Jill at the Chronic Pain Treatment Centre on the Gold Coast.

After breakfast, I was doing some maintenance jobs with Dave, when Sandy, who generally kept up with the internet news and media stuff I couldn't be bothered with, wandered up for'rard where we were greasing the anchor winch.

'Just got this off the 'net',' she said, flapping a piece of paper in my face.

'Yes, my darlink?' I grinned at her concerned look. 'What's the problem with the great unwashed world today?'

She planted a bare toe in my backside.

'Don't you 'my darlink' me! This is serious. It's a pirate advisory from the International Maritime Bureau for the Madagascar area. Apparently there are two new pirate groups operating out of North Madagascar and the islands between it and the African mainland. They're Somalis who have sailed south looking like refugees and hi-jacked a small ship to act as a mother ship, then in turn, hi-jacked all the smaller boats they need.

They are reported to be totally ruthless and have already killed several crews. I think it might be a good idea to not track via the north end of Madagascar. I'm a bit over pirates just now.'

I sat back, absent-mindedly wiping my greasy hands on my shorts in the approved fashion. 'OK. Let's see if we can do something about that. Hopefully, there won't be a problem to make a course change. Let me go consult the charts.'

Bree was serving a late lunch, so I sat down with some notes, having already altered course some 20° to port and re-trimmed the sails, with a south-east breeze still blowing, the new heading let us gain a bit more speed.

Halfway through the lovely feed, I announced. 'Okay. New plan. We won't be deviating too much from our original course for several days, so we can stay with the current that's going our way. The winds here should still be good for a while yet. Further west, we'll alter course more to the south-west to pass the small island of Rodrigues. If any problems develop between now and then, it's a good, safe place to call in.

The idea is to pass south of Madagascar to stay with a favourable current and more reliable winds, which should be in about 12 days' time. Otherwise, we avoid landfalls or sailing too close to any hard stuff, and should be at St Francis Bay about 4 days after that. It adds up to roughly another 16 days from now.'

Sandy leant over and gave me a quick kiss on the cheek. 'Thank you for that, my love. I know I'll be more relaxed now we are staying well away from the whole island.'

Oddly enough, no one was too concerned about the rough schedule I'd produced, which suggested we were all in cruise mode and just took things a day at a time. This would be the longest voyage I'd made away from land, which meant I had only very limited experience with the psychological aspects of long-distance cruising. I knew as we approached our scheduled landfall at St Francis Bay, there would be a feeling of mild panic and apprehension, brought on by the fact that the day after day easy and safe routine was about to change radically.

CHAPTER 8

INDIAN OCEAN, ST FRANCIS BAY, SOUTH AFRICA

At sea, most plans don't remain intact long, since unforeseen events usually conspire to introduce change, but for once, we had an event-free run. While we were still mostly heading west, there were a couple of days of storms and vicious squalls which charged aggressively across the darkening sea, from any direction and with little warning. They were the precursors of the monsoon trough starting to move south. The weather settled down once we turned south-west, and the extra speed boost from the strong south-going current shaved nearly a day off our timeline.

As I promised, we passed well south of Madagascar, then altered course more to the south to track direct to St Francis Bay. Part way across the Mozambique Channel, we received a curiously insistent weather warning about a cold front rapidly approaching from the south, which would result in a southerly wind change for 24 to 36 hours. My first thought was that all the warnings I'd received about the Channel were somewhat overstated. Even though we were well south of Madagascar itself, the strong, south-flowing current was only pushing us south of our track. Plus, at the time, we were sailing fast in a stiff northerly breeze, across a low to moderate swell.

They were, in fact, exhilarating conditions to be sailing a big cat at sea and it was just by chance I'd caught the report which was tacked onto a standard weather report for the whole area south from Maputo, Mozambique.

In itself, a cold front with a brief southerly change didn't sound like any sort of a big deal, but something I'd read in the Pilot directions for the Durban coast made the hair on the back of my neck prickle slightly, so I made an on-line consult about what the effects of such a happening meant to small craft. What I read was enough to make my hair stand on end, and I promptly went to wake Alex who had been on watch until 06:00.

Five minutes later, yawning and scratching, he was in the saloon, reading the reports and noting our position.

'What do you think? How bad can it get for us?' I asked.

The big South African frowned as he studied the synoptic chart. 'My apologies, Commander,' he said, still insisting after all this time on using my rank instead of name. 'This can mean very rough weather for perhaps two to three days. The south-going current is still flowing at 5 to 6 knots here and when we get a 30 to 40 knots southerly blowing against it, the sea will become very confused or even chaotic.'

I nodded, 'The sailing directions talk about short, steep waves, but that's typical of any wind against the current situation.'

'That's so, except that here, the conditions often lead to ridiculous wave heights. Sixty to seventy feet have been recorded by large ships, and when a wave that size is steep-sided and breaking, it becomes very dangerous. Even big ships are wary of those conditions, but small boats stay in port.'

I had come to completely trust and rely on Alex's seamanship.

'Then what's your recommendation?'

He looked at the chart again and read the weather report, before looking grimly at me.

'Reverse course immediately. We aren't too far into the main southerly current flow, so with this good northerly breeze which should hold for another few hours, we should be able to get out of the worst of what will be insanely rough water. But,' he cautioned, 'we will still get some very rough conditions for maybe 24 hours, so we should prepare for that.'

'Sounds like fun,' I joked, but Alex didn't share my warped sense of humour.

'This change will be with us within 5 to 6 hours, and the sea will be dangerous within 20 minutes of the change.' he said matter-of-factly. 'It is hard to say whether the parachute sea-anchor would be better than running before it with the Jordan sea-brakes deployed. Maybe with the short-pitch waves, the parachute would be better.'

Dave had the watch, so I called out and asked him to reverse course. With all sail set, it wasn't just a case of turning the wheel, but thanks to the powered sail control, within 5 minutes, we were beating a hasty retreat back to the east. Naturally the girls wanted to know what was happening, so I brought them up to date on the whys and wherefores and asked them to do their bit by securing everything down below, just in case.

In pre-voyage preparation, I'd already fed the main cable for the parachute sea-anchor around the side decks outside the guard-rail stanchions, where it was secured by a series of small cable ties. All we had to do to get ready, was connect the parachute to one end of the cable in the cockpit, then shackle the other end at the bow to the anchor chain.

When the parachute was tossed over from the shelter of the cockpit, it remained only to feed 20 metres of chain out to make sure the parachute stayed below the surface. The length could then be adjusted with a press of a button to keep the 'chute on the same phase of the wave train as the boat.

I've always had a deep-seated issue about retracing my steps, preferring to always look and move forward rather than back, but in this case Alex's advice proved to be excellent. We had an exhilarating sail for a few hours, before a low line of purple-black cloud, impossibly dark and dense in the bright sunshine, came boiling up over the southern horizon at a ridiculous speed.

At least the sailing instruments showed we had moved out of the worst of the south-flowing current, which I hoped would reduce the severity of the seas. We monitored the progress of the angry cloud-mass, becoming increasingly alarmed at the speed of advance, as well as the vicious stabs of blue-white tongues of lightning angrily attacking the sea surface, as well as arcing from cloud to cloud.

As if being bullied out of the way by the new bad boy on the block, the northerly wind had almost died away, so I looked at Dave and Alex. 'Let's get the parachute over the side now while we have some peace.'

They heartily agreed, so while we got it organised, I asked Sandy to collect all loose electronic devices and put them in the oven or microwave to protect them if we were struck by one of those nasty forked, electrical tongues.

As the breeze had slowly faded, we had already stowed the sails. Then with the parachute sea-anchor appearing to drift away upwind, its long nylon cable slowly paying out, we hauled down the long thin sausage that was the screecher and fed it into a bow locker. I also raised both dagger boards to allow the hulls to slide sideways if necessary, without tripping.

The next important job was to drop two thick sheets of copper overboard, with very heavy copper cables attached, one on the outside of each hull attached to the mast shrouds.

The idea was that a lightning strike would be fed down either or both mast shrouds to the grounding plates, while sparing the interior of the boat from misdirected bursts of electrical energy.

Inside, the ladies had secured everything which was loose or might become so, and had filled the oven, the microwave and the special Faraday cage locker lined with copper mesh earthed to the boat. By now, the roiling, ugly mass of cloud was close enough to hear the almost continuous grumble of thunder. I started the engines and backed away from the parachute, positioning it between us and the squall line, and tensioned the stretchy nylon cable.

The approaching front looked even more dramatic with the sun shining brightly on the black cloud mass, and Kelly had the video camera going, excited by the spectacle. A last quick check around topsides and we were ready for whatever might happen.

Minutes later, we could see in the distance, the amazing sight of clouds of white spray being lifted high off the ocean surface by the first, very powerful, squall gusts. Around us, all was still;

a perfect example of 'the calm before the storm'. In this case, the storm was just seconds away and it hit like a bomb exploding. The wall of white spray was the first to arrive, blotting out all visibility for a long minute, then the wind slammed into us with a vengeance.

I thought I'd seen some powerful storms in Bass Strait, but this made those look like amateur hour! The wind speed indicator wound up like a stop watch, going from zero to 60 knots in a couple of seconds, then reaching higher up the dial into new, scary territory.

I'm sure I saw the needle flickering around 85 knots for much longer than was reasonable, as the insane howl of the ferocious wind overloaded our senses and mostly drowned out the crashing of thunder, as a veritable forest of blue/white stabs of lightning blasted away at the water around us. I kept waiting for some sign we'd been hit, but someone was watching over us that afternoon for we escaped unscathed, despite the constant barrage of strikes, some within 20 metres.

I managed to herd the shell-shocked girls inside and slam the cockpit door, which did little to cut the noise, but a least gave the illusion of security. Outside, despite the sun being nearly overhead, it was totally dark and I flicked the red night-lights on before sending Sandy down to get some towels to dry everyone off and mop up the water on the floor. I found I was yelling into her ear to get her attention, as her eyes were fixed on the wind speed repeater dial set above the dining table, a look of fright on her face.

So, I looked. And shouldn't have! When I'd specified the instrument fit-out for the boat, I had the choice of maximum speed readout. Stupidly, I opted for the highest one, and apparently the 85-knot reading I'd seen a few minutes ago wasn't anywhere near the peak. The needle, hard to see in the dim red light, seemed to be happily pointing at 115-knots and holding steady for the brief time I was brave enough to look at it. If there was a Beaufort scale reading for that wind speed, I imagine it would be expressed in superlatives.

The noise level had risen above the insane level and was just an ear and mind-numbing scream which could be coming from the throats of a thousand demented banshees, and had the effect of physically battering the crew to the floor. Sandy and Kelly crawled under the dining table, where Alex was trying to comfort Bree, while Dave and Corrine at least had their heads up, looking out for what might come next. Jasper and Krazy were sticking as close to their humans as possible.

With the total external blackout, we couldn't see what the sea was doing, but by the lack of serious motion, it felt remarkably flat. I was sure that lovely condition wasn't going to last.

Thankfully, nor did the wind, soon dropping to more reasonable levels like what seemed an almost gentle Force 12 which was merely around 65 knots! Hardly enough to ruffle one's hair by comparison. The lowering of sound level allowed me to note that our speed through the water was now negative 2 knots, meaning the current was dragging us upwind, which in the circumstances, was a testament to the strength of the para-anchor and its fittings. Unfortunately, the dropping of the wind speed meant a corresponding rise in the wave height and soon we were surging up and down ever-increasing steep waves, although the parachute did its job superbly and held our head to the wind and waves, so the odd breaking wave merely thundered over the low deck, meeting little resistance. The effect was still dramatic when solid green water belted up against the armour-glass forward windows.

Alex was unfortunately correct when he had said the storm could last up to 24-hours. Although the worst of the wind had headed north, in its wake it left an extremely confused and lumpy sea. Waves ran in several directions at once and when two or more of these coincided, the result was a pyramid of water with near-vertical sides.

We just managed to miss the fun of being a 60-foot Christmas tree ornament at the peak of one of these monsters, when one peaked close alongside and dumped what seemed like half the Indian Ocean across the bows. We could only tell it was night by the clock readouts, and as is usual at sea, things seemed so much worse in the dark.

It was a long, long night. The instruments displaying wind speed and direction, as well as the GPS unit, indicated that in fact the wind was slowly abating, although it wasn't until after dawn the seas decided to settle as well and we three guys got to have all the fun of wrestling the para-anchor back aboard. More than an hour later, wet and bruised, we had the boat-saving device back aboard, where I rinsed it in fresh-water and stowed it in its bag.

With that aboard, we hoisted the staysail, plus a small portion of the main, and scooted off west again, straight across the still heavy seas. I left the dagger boards raised, allowing the odd breaking wave to simply shove *Firebird* bodily sideways, with no tendency to trip. No one became sick, although Kelly and Bree looked a bit green at times, but they stayed on deck, which helped, and soldiered on.

Three days later, at 14:00, we motored quietly in through the gap formed by the seaward breakwater arm and a substantial wharf in Port Elizabeth, South Africa. Our actual destination was just 54 miles further down the coast at St Francis Bay, but Port Elizabeth was the closest Customs entry port, so we were here first to do all the official paperwork.

At first glance it was a pretty town, but close-up it showed the black stains from the endless supply of coal-dust from the loaders that roared day and night, pouring the black stuff into ship holds. Anytime the winds blew, and they did frequently and hard, clouds of the stuff coated everything in sight in choking black dust. Still, we were here just to do the paperwork, then head down for St Francis Bay. The internet had proved most useful in regard to learning the procedure for clearing properly and we even had the correct forms to line up in quadruplicate on the desk of the Immigration official.

Apparently, the officials were supposed to visit the boat, but no one we spoke to could remember when that had last happened, so we all crowded into his office, while he laboriously churned his way through the piles of papers.

It wasn't encouraging to be reminded we had to do the same business all over again with the Customs gentleman in the next office. One interesting part of the entry procedure was that when it came to the listing of 'pets', there were no formalities at all. Apparently, pets are quite welcome in South Africa, provided they are listed as being healthy.

Finally, we were done, and I nominated Port Elizabeth as our departure port, even though all the sailing blogs said Capetown was a better choice. I had no desire to visit there, because once the sea trials in the new boat were complete, I intended we would head east for Australia without delay. With a whole list of restrictions in place for harbour entry at St Francis Bay, we stayed the night at Port Elizabeth and set sail in the morning, making phone calls to the Harbourmaster at St Francis and to the builders of the new boat, Southern Nautical.

They were delighted to hear from their latest customer and reported that while the new boat was completely finished, it was not in the water yet.

I found that news to be slightly alarming and my concern was picked up by Jan Kruger, the principal of Southern Nautical.

'Please do not be concerned, Mr Stevens. Our boat yard is in an industrial estate with a number of other builders and is several kilometres from the water. It is perfectly normal for us to finish our boats in our yards, then transport them by road to the water.

With your boat being the biggest to be launched in St Francis Bay, everyone is very excited. It is also the first of this design for Le Tromp Marine. But to ease your concerns, I can say your boat is complete, including the mast and rigging, which the riggers have left mounted. The fully-rigged boat has been standing in our yard for more than three weeks now, so the rigging has had time to stretch and settle in. The riggers have already made several small adjustments to take slack out, but the final tune will be on *the water after the first test sail. So apart from not actually being in the water, we have tested all systems as thoroughly as possible. Sails have been run up and down and the mainsail boom-furling system is working particularly well.*

I'm also proud to be able to say all other systems have worked perfectly from the start.'

'I'm very glad to hear it Mr Kruger, but how long will it take to actually get the boat in the water?'

'Please call me Jan, if you would. But to answer your question – as soon as you have looked over the boat, then approved and signed off on the fit-out as it is, the riggers can have the mast removed by late this afternoon. The boat is already raised on blocks with its special transport trailer in position, so all we need do is to hook up the prime mover and have the police escort us to the launch point at dawn.'

'I'm sorry Jan. I didn't mean to sound petty or pushy. Those arrangements will be just fine. We expect to be berthed in St Francis Harbour by 12:00 at the latest.'

'Excellent, Mr Stevens. I'll speak to the Harbourmaster to speed your arrival and will be there to pick you up myself.'

'Thank you Jan. See you then.'

I relayed the gist of the conversation to the crew, having to tolerate Sandy's knowing, *'I told you it would be alright!'* look.

From the tip of the sandy, scrubby land east of Port Elizabeth, the coast to the south fell away in a large, deserted bight mostly rimmed with a white sand beach, but I had no desire to linger or sight-see. That was even with two of the world's greatest surf breaks, J-Bay and Cape St Francis right next door to each other. Therefore, we made a straight-line course for St Francis Bay, a distance of 52 miles.

It was a pleasant, if nostalgic sail, as this would be the last in my lovely, reliable and comfortable 60-foot catamaran which had been my home for so many years and carried us through so many adventures.

Like a first love, an owner never forgets his first boat!

A strong easterly gave us a fast, but wet passage across the bay and was the reason for being able to call the Harbourmaster at 11:15 to announce our imminent arrival.

CHAPTER 9

ST FRANCIS BAY, SOUTH AFRICA

Jan's word seemed to have carried plenty of weight since our radio call was answered immediately by a pleasant-sounding woman's voice with the delightful, lilting South African accent. She provided detailed berthing instructions, adding that a man in a small work-boat would be meet us to direct and assist.

Her instructions were concise and clear and the promised escort led us straight to a vacant berth, with just a short walk to the shore.

A lean, fit-looking bloke in casual office gear took our mooring lines and expertly tied us up.

Leaping to conclusions again, I shut down the engines and jumped onto the dock.

'Jan, I presume?' I said, projecting an aura of happiness and confidence that my ill-gotten $12 million plus had been wisely spent.

He beamed in turn, 'Indeed, and if I may call you Harry, now we have met?'

He had a firm handshake and was about my height; lean, tanned and fit from running around boatyards all day, I presumed, and with a shock of thick, white hair.

He ran an expert appraiser's eye over *Firebird*.

'Lovely boat. I know the designers quite well and they have an excellent reputation. Those clients I mentioned are still very keen to see the boat as soon as possible. We need to make up a schedule so I can let them know when they can make an inspection. Perhaps we can do it now?'

'Of course, Jan. Come aboard, meet the crew and have a tea or coffee.'

Once seated in the cockpit, Bree offered to do the teas and

whipped up some sandwiches made with fresh-baked bread to go with it.

'We can stay with the schedule I outlined for today,' Jan said, diving into the tasty offerings on the large plate in front of him, 'and that will see your new boat in the water early tomorrow morning... if there aren't too many foul-ups.'

He said the last with a grin – the pragmatic result of too many launchings where things did go wrong!

'I must tell you, because of the size of your boat, we can't launch it here at the harbour.'

I must have looked concerned again, for he laughed and went on, 'When I said everyone is excited about the new boat, some of that has spread to the town council who are proud of the reputation St Francis Bay has gained for boat-building – catamarans in particular. Therefore, we have gained permission to close the main bridge and freeway on the north side of town for a short period tomorrow morning, but we must be early and have everything ready. Since this road is the only way in and out of town, our time allowed on the job is very short.'

I waited him out, then asked, 'Why exactly do you need the bridge?'

'Oh, sorry. The highway is the only road wide enough to fit your boat. Therefore, we have to crane it directly off the bridge into the shallow river, on the downstream side. All the lifting strops will be in place on the boat and the crane can be pre-positioned on the bridge ready to hook on and lift as soon as the trailer arrives. The crane only blocks one lane, but the wide, 11.4m beam of the boat will totally block the highway, so the police have asked us to make most of the move at 03:00 tomorrow morning. It'll be easier for us as well, since the highway is close to our factory. We will park the trailer just off the highway close to the launch site on the bridge, then wait for enough light to work safely which will be around 06:00. If all goes well, your boat will be in the water within 15 minutes.'

'I hope you have faith in the lifting strops and slings.' I said half-jokingly.

He smiled, 'All double checked.'

'What about the mast? Where can it be put in place?'

'Same place. With the boat in the water, we send the big crane away and bring in a smaller one to lift the mast off the truck and lower it into position. The riggers have everything sorted and it won't take long. Then, we motor around to this harbour for the transfer of equipment from this boat to your new one. I've already arranged with the manager to berth it alongside which should make the transfer much easier.'

'Thanks Jan. You've done wonders! Now, to be ready for the inspections of this boat, the only item we need assistance with is the transfer of the masthead camera. All other equipment, some of it 'special' as I mentioned to you once before, we can do ourselves and it won't hold up any inspections. Are you able to let me have two riggers to do the job?'

He nodded, 'No problem. They will be here when you have made your inspection of your new boat, then they will fit it to the new mast overnight. It'll be a lot easier to fit with the mast lying down. Anything else?'

'Not for now, thanks. I think we're ready to go, if you have space for the whole crew?'

He laughed, 'I did allow for it and brought the factory minibus. Everyone is welcome.'

The unworthy thought crossed my mind that for $12.5 mil plus change, I could have insisted on bringing the Aussie rugby team as well.

Fifteen minutes later, we were pulling up on the apron in front of a small office block, dwarfed by three huge sheds hulking protectively behind it. It appeared the whole complex was enclosed by a substantial fence, complete with razor wire and an enclosed dog run. Signs warning of lethal electrification and the danger to personal health were hung every few meters.

Grinning, I jerked a thumb at the impressive and daunting security. 'I guess you don't have much of a problem with casual break-in's?'

He laughed in return, 'No. Not anymore, but it's the usual problem in my country. When someone's desperate for food or work, they rarely think to just come to the front door and ask. I try to employ as many locals as I can, but there are limits. And as I mentioned, I'm very proud of my workforce and the standard of production.'

Although Jan was keen to show us around the factory, the large, concrete forecourt in front of the main shed was dominated by a truly monstrous catamaran. It filled nearly all the space and even with a low, sleek profile, it towered over us tiny humans standing on the ground. The black mast reached more than 35 metres above the waterline, which gave me a kink in the neck just trying to look at the top of it.

It was a shock when I belatedly realised...this was it! The new *Firebird!*

Like icebergs, all boats look much bigger when out of the water and this was no exception.

A string of doubts immediately ran through my mind. How the hell could just two persons handle this giant and keep it under control? Then I smiled – only one way to find out and that was going to be the fun part. Of course, the other truly stand-out feature of the monster was its all-over colour of Ferrari red. The only relieving colours were the bottom anti-fouling paint which was white and a yellow boot-topping trim line just above the bottom paint.

The whole crew were silent and totally gob-smacked, until Sandy uttered the definitive statement of the day when she said softly, 'Well, fuck me! Will you look at that? Is this monster really ours?'

Walking closer, I noticed the trailer aligned under the bridge deck with six hydraulic arms extended out to cradle the hulls with carefully padded and shaped supports. Additional supports sat under the hulls as a temporary measure until it was time to move. I had to admit the boat looked absolutely stunning, quite apart from its sheer size.

'You are pleased so far, Harry?' Jan asked anxiously.

'Oh yeah, mate; more like blown away! This is something else again. I thought the current *Firebird* was big out of the water, but this is a huge step up.' By now I was running my hands along what I could reach of the towering sides.

'The workmanship is remarkable, Jan. There's not a wrinkle or blemish in the layup or paintwork.'

He smiled, 'The crew are very proud of how well this first production 83-footer has turned out and they all loved your choice of colour. Such a pleasant change from the standard white.'

A set of mobile steps were lined up with the right rear boarding platform, and I took a moment to admire the name, *Firebird*, painted in yellow against the red transom with Southport, Queensland below it. The more I looked, the stranger it seemed to be looking at such a huge boat, fully rigged, sitting on dry land. Externally, it was fully-fitted out, even down to the new RIB to act as the official dinghy, which was a metre longer than the old one staying with the old *Firebird*. I had requested that the name had to be removed from both the old boat and RIB before any inspections were made.

The next couple of hours were spent going over the whole boat, starting with the highly automated sail handling gear. Jan wanted my approval on it first before he called the riggers in to start undoing everything so the mast could be lifted off and laid on its own long trailer ready for tomorrow's short journey. I had already marvelled at the relatively thin, black cords of carbon-fibre holding up the massive mast.

Jan noticed my wondering stare, for he said, 'I know, it looks all wrong. Even I am still getting used to it, but with this new type of rigging, you have a 70% weight saving aloft, a 50% gain in strength, and being thinner, has less windage than wire or rod rigging. Also, it doesn't stretch very much at all, nor corrode or fatigue. The carbon mast, the furling boom and the standing rigging are all the same New Zealand manufacturer. They are our usual first choice unless a customer specifies something different.'

Luckily, the breeze was light, so I had a lovely time hoisting the mainsail, unfurling and furling the other sails and sheeting them in and out. To my delight, I quickly discovered it really was as effortless and functional as discussions with Jan had indicated. Should there be a total loss of power, a hand-held electric driver like a large battery-powered drill could still be used to drive the mainsail furling mechanism, or we could even do the task more slowly by hand with a crank-handle.

The new helm station was set up the same as on the old boat, being under the cockpit roof on the left and raised above the cockpit deck to allow visibility above the saloon top. A full-width windshield with lift-up window frames stretched across in front of the helm, with a large sliding hatch overhead the double helm seat. This allowed the driver to stand on the seat with just head and shoulders poking out for better visibility when docking.

Once we had finished playing silly-buggers with all the buttons, Jan shooed us into the vast saloon, while he called up the team of riggers to start the task of de-rigging and unshipping the mast.

Meantime, we went through everything, making sure all the fittings and gear worked as best we could tell without being on the water. The amount of extra internal space was amazing as was the new cabin layout with five guest cabins plus a huge master with its own direct access from the saloon. Sandy was delighted with the space in the master cabin, including the way we could use the next cabin forward of our bathroom as extra space if we wanted. Otherwise, that cabin was a comfortable twin-berth space with its own access from the saloon and shared a bathroom with the next cabin for'rard.

Dave was the first to spot an anomaly with the drive system.

'Hey Harry? What's with the stubby sail-drive legs poking out under the hulls? I thought you were a fan of shaft-drive? And how come there's two legs, side-by-side on each hull?'

By way of explanation, I took him down into the port engine room, parked my bum on a blue lump of machinery the size of a 60-litre oil drum bolted to the floor, and propped one foot on a similar blue lump beside it. Waving grandly around, I indicated the neatly laid out equipment and wiring bundles. 'What do you see?' I grinned.

'An uncrowded and neatly laid out engineering space, but I was looking for the engine room.'

'Ha! You're in it!' cried proudly, standing up. 'I was sitting on two of the eight engines.'

He peered at the two lumps of blue machinery, then exclaimed, 'Electric, you sneaky old bugger! You've gone electric. Tell me more!'

I shrugged, 'To cut a short story long, a Scandinavian company makes and supplies the whole system with two coupled DC electric motors driving a short sail drive unit. There's a limitation on the amount of power each leg can handle, so I doubled up, making four sail-drive units and eight motors. We have a very large bank of the latest lightweight lithium batteries which are 25% the weight of lead-acid. There's also a large bank of even lighter super-capacitors for extra power storage. All battery banks are re-charged primarily by hydro-generation when we sail, and backed up by solar power and wind generators. The props are variable-pitch which makes them very efficient, and are controlled automatically by the system for re-charging mode, or by the throttles when we need drive power. When we're sailing and decide we don't need re-generation, the system parks them in the fully-feathered position for low drag.

We have two small back-up diesel generators for emergencies, but with so much stored power, we can run air-con, water-makers, induction cooking and electric everything without concerns, and mostly without using any diesel. Therefore, we'll rarely need refuelling and there's no engine noise. We saved a couple of tonnes in fuel tankage and saved the tank storage space, as well as the heavier weight of the diesel engines, so overall, the boat is lighter.'

Dave shook his head in wonder, 'I can't believe you didn't tell me, you rotten bugger, but I'm really keen to see how it all works.'

With Jan hovering expectantly, I moved on with the check-out inspection. I had asked for the same type of systems which had worked so well on the old *Firebird*, but being new and updated they were much better. Out of hearing of the workers, I quietly asked him about the series of hidden lockers I'd wanted built-in to the internal structure.

He gave me a conspiratorial grin, 'Ah, but of course. I do not wish to know what will reside in those padded lockers, but they are all as requested, and the cabinet-makers have done a superb job. The lockers are nearly impossible to find.'

Finally, I had to agree that as far as I could tell, everything was as good as I expected, and all systems appeared to work as designed. I signed a preliminary document to that effect and reluctantly let Jan take us on a tour of the factory where several cats of different sizes were being constructed.

The workers, black and white, male and female, were a happy bunch and seemed to work well together. Each waved or said hello as we wandered past, with Jan rattling off details about each boat they were working on.

We were introduced to the crew who had built our boat and they were very proud of their efforts and grateful for my genuine praise.

Then it was time for a last look at my new giant red baby before Jan bundled us into the van, and with two riggers and a paint shop girl following, took us back to the harbour.

Jasper and Krazy were pleased to see us, and Jasper drew some wide-eyed looks from the two riggers and the paint-girl, as they made ready to go to work. I could do the job myself, but they were a lot younger and more used to dangling around 22-metres above the deck.

I had to marvel that the new mast was another 14-metres higher again, so a trip to the masthead would be quite an un-nerving experience at sea.

To that end, I joked with the two riggers, 'You make a good job fitting the camera to the new mast, please. I don't want to have to climb up the new one to fix something. It's too bloody high for an old fart like me.'

They grinned and assured me the job would be perfect.

I lowered the dinghy into the water so the young lady painter could get on with removing the name *Firebird* from the transom. It was a sad moment since we'd been through a lot together, but I firmly believe in looking forward in anticipation of new opportunities, not backwards with regret over missed ones.

Keeping an eye on both sets of work, I noted my crew were all busy below packing their gear, before they started to sort out what boat gear was to transfer and what was to stay. We'd had many discussions on the long voyage over about what to keep, and it really came down to just some basic stuff like eating, drinking and cooking utensils, the booze supply of course, the hookah shallow-dive gear and specialised radios. I'd sent Jan measurements of the mounts for the radios, so it was just a matter of swapping them over. His instrument and electrical crew were going to tackle that tomorrow.

So otherwise, the old boat was going to be left ready to go, while the new one would be all-new with the biggest and best of everything. The para-anchor and Jordan sea-drogue which had done such a great job off the African coast were being left behind since they were too small for the much bigger new boat. With such a large boating industry, South Africa had all the best and latest gear available, and Jan had done a great job sourcing and fitting everything necessary. At my request, he'd included some gizmos which weren't truly necessary, but were nice to have anyway. It was exceedingly satisfying to be able to just order up the best gear without getting heart palpitations over the price tag.

The paint girl was finished well before the riggers had unbolted the camera assembly and carefully lowered it to the deck. The 25 metres of cabling still attached to it would need at least 14 metres of extension, so Jan had a young, but bright assistant, whose job it was to keep track of all the little details like this, and make sure nothing was overlooked. She had created a checklist which had grown to the size of a small book.

By the time darkness fell, much of the sorting and packing work was done, so after a clean-up, we trooped the thankfully short distance up to Mauro's Italian Restaurant which overlooked the marina. It proved to have such terrific food and service, we all pigged out and drank a bit more Chianti than was smart for those of us who were getting up well before dawn.

It was a sluggish and sleepy crew who turned out in the chill early morning air, and wandered up to the small people-mover van I'd hired to ease our transport problem. It was a treat to find that South Africa drives on the left, same as Australia, the UK and Japan. Luckily, it had a GPS navigator, so with Alex driving we were able to find the wide place on highway R330 where our massive new home constituted a long and very wide load, parked awkwardly across someone's driveway. At least it was off the road. Barely. Just past where the boat sat on its trailer, another much longer, but slender trailer attached to a smaller truck, held the 33-metre length of mast, with all the rigging and wiring attached.

With four police cars with two cops in each, two truck drivers and their assistants, Jan and several workers, plus a large number of rigging crew, made for what seemed like a cast of thousands. There was even a small crew from the local TV station to record the event. Jan had thoughtfully organised a coffee van to come out, so there was plenty of hot drinks to ward off the chill, and tasty things to eat while we waited for sunrise. The last two vehicles to arrive, just before 06:00, were a hulking 200-tonne mobile crane to lift the boat, and a smaller 60 tonne unit which had enough boom length to handle the length of the mast. Just the collection of vehicles was enough to slow passing traffic to a gawking crawl until the coppers went out to wave cars on.

It was still dark when Jan looked at his watch, blew a silver whistle, and like a well-organised military operation, action commenced. The police moved out to block off one lane on the downstream side of the bridge, followed by the 200-tonne crane which needed fifteen minutes to set up its outriggers. It was ready just as first light revealed our surroundings. Then, radios crackled and police blocked off both ends of the bridge. Truck engines roared into life, dogs barked and the proverbial baby cried in the house behind us as my lovely, huge red boat moved ponderously out onto the highway for its last short journey on land.

I couldn't fault Jan's organisation; obviously everything had been measured to the millimetre and timed to the minute.

The prime-mover stopped in just the right place, *Firebird's* hulls spanning the entire width of the bridge, right up to the guard rails with barely 0.5 metre to spare. The rigging crew swarmed aboard and in just a few minutes, had coupled the dangling cables from the crane to the strops which were attached to heavy fabric lifting sheets cradling the hulls in four places. Safety lines were also attached to the chainplates where the mast rigging would be attached.

More whistles blew, arms were waved and effortlessly, the 200-tonne Tadano crane plucked my beautiful boat from its trailer cradles and swung it precariously out over the drop to the unforgiving water below. More whistles sounded and the gleaming red hulls slowly sank from sight down toward the water. We spectators were leaning over the bridge railings and saw it ease gently into the water where more crew in two small power boats were waiting with mooring lines already attached to the bridge supports. This was to keep it in position ready for the mast to be lowered. Within minutes, all cables and strops were lifted back up, unhitched and the crane-crew were starting to pack up their monster. Ten minutes later, they fired up the motive engine and with a cheery blast on the airhorns, roared back into town.

Traffic immediately started flowing on one lane as the other smaller 60-tonne crane drove into position and started setting up.

The trailer with the mast was backed into position, strops already in position at several balance points. This time, several guy ropes were manned to help guide the mast into just the right position, but the crane driver was in superb form and almost without pause, the mast rose high in the air before descending smoothly to the boat where the lower end was fitted carefully into the mating socket on deck.

The rigging crew who had ridden the boat down to the water, swiftly made the necessary connections and lightly tensioned the thin black strings sufficiently to keep the hideously expensive piece of carbon-fibre, vertical for the motoring trip around to the harbour. It was only about a fifteen-minute task for the nimble-fingered crew, before the crane was released to start packing up, although before they did, Jan spoke to the operator and two soft fabric, one-tonne slings were attached to the huge hook, dangling just clear of the roadway.

Jan looked at me with a cheeky grin. 'It is a tradition with us, for the new owner and the boatyard owner to make the first voyage in a new boat. Therefore, I offer you a quick ride down to your new boat.'

Sandy started to burr up, but in answer, I grinned back at Jan, stepped forward and stood on the sling, holding the upper end with both hands. He quickly did the same and at a nod we were smoothly lifted above the bridge railings, swung out over the river then dropped swiftly down to deck level where we stepped off onto *Firebird's* deck. The crane hook and strops disappeared as Jan went to the helm station and started the engines. Except nothing happened.

That was until I realised the electric power system was utterly quiet and vibration free. The only sign it was working, was the boil of water at the sterns and the fact we were definitely moving under our own power. To say I was both entranced and excited was an understatement! Jan's crew had been busy down below, checking the bilges for any sign of water ingress, but all was good. The riggers kept checking their stays and shrouds, but they were smiling as well.

I was happy to stand back, as officially, I hadn't completed the signing-off process, and was fascinated to watch as Jan expertly weaved back and forth across the shallow river, dodging sandbanks. We slowly threaded our way along the last few narrow channels with bare sand showing just metres away on either side, before bouncing across a line of small soft-breaking waves marking the entry to the ocean. It was just 2.5 miles across the bay to the harbour, where we were met by the same work-boat as yesterday who guided us in, despite Jan's local knowledge. He expertly and soundlessly parked us stern-first into the double-wide berth beside the old boat where both Jan's and my crew were waiting.

Before he left, Jan promised to be back tomorrow morning to start sea-trials, where all systems would get a hard work-out to make sure everything worked properly. On the short trip down from the launch site, the riggers had been busy tightening rigging screws and checking mast bend, or lack thereof. As they were leaving with Jan, they pronounced themselves happy with the rig, but cautioned it would need a few days of sailing to settle everything down properly.

Jan's parting words, 'Enjoy your new boat, read the manuals and get used to all the extra space.'

We proceeded to do just that and the rest of the day was taken up with transferring all the equipment and utensils we intended to keep. We also avoided getting in the way of the cheerful electrical crew installing the radios and making what seemed like a vast number of connections from the mast. The masthead camera, weather instruments and radio antenna wiring looms were run through pre-installed concealed ducts to the chart table control station. We waited until they had finished hooking up and testing everything and had left for the factory, before we transferred the contents of all the special, hidden lockers to their new padded homes, which placed knives, hand-guns, sub-machine guns and shotguns within easy reach of most places on the boat.

Some more exotic items like a box of hand grenades and a bunch of tubes in the machinery which we had painted to look like spare cartridges for the water makers, but actually held HE rounds for the RPG-7 rocket-propelled grenade launcher, were either hidden in plain sight or tucked well out of sight. The launcher tube itself, now sprayed bright yellow and adorned with nonsensical nautical-themed markings, was posing as a piece of exotic plumbing in the port machinery room.

Being permanent crew, Alex and Bree elected to move into their new cabin immediately, having decided on the port stern queen-size one, while Sandy and I had the identical starboard one. Dave and Corrine grabbed the smaller port mid-ships queen, while Kelly said she'd prefer to take one of the starboard forward cabins. That still left three spare cabins, although the starboard forward two were on the cosy side with two bunks in each. Leaving the upper bunk in each folded down gave more cat-swinging space.

CHAPTER 10

ST FRANCIS BAY, SOUTH AFRICA

When it was time to visit our favourite Italian restaurant, I noticed Sandy had been busy moving the galley and pantry contents across to the new boat, and presumably hadn't the time to move our personal stuff across. Jasper and Krazy were having a wonderful time running from one boat to another and generally getting underfoot. Dinner that night was a real cause for celebration as the objective of all this money and effort lay gleaming redly within a stone's throw of where we sat. We were unfortunately even more in a party mood than last night, and well after dinner was disposed of, we weaved an unsteady course back to our various beds. No one wanted to sit up after a long and busy day, so lights were turned out almost immediately.

Except in our cabin and Kelly's next door, since this was the last night on the old boat and Sandy had apparently invited Kelly into bed with us. Both girls had the wobbly boot on, and were very prone to fits of the giggles at the slightest provocation.

I didn't know about the arrangement in advance, although the frequent whispering sessions should have alerted me that some sort of tomfoolery was planned. The other give-away was the lovely sight of both ladies getting ready for bed by wandering back and forth to the bathroom without any clothes on. Both were stunning examples of the female form, so it was no hardship to sit propped up in bed watching the parade of bare flesh where I, in turn copped my fair share of ribald comments about 'tenting the blankets'.

Kelly was the first to calmly climb up into the big bed, slid under the sheet and cuddle up against me. Suspecting a setup, I waited to see where my dear lady was and shortly after, she appeared and climbed in beside Kelly, who promptly rolled over to cuddle her, giving me a fond tweak on the way.

Amused, I watched them snuggling together for a few minutes until tiredness prevailed and I rolled over and went to sleep. There were numerous bumps, wriggles and giggling sessions through the night, but both ladies actually wanted to get some decent sleep, so at least I did too.

Since the next day was the first of the sea-trials, I was up early, leaving the ladies snoring softly. As I quietly dressed, the thought crossed my mind that if Kelly was to be a regular bed companion, it was just as well our new bed was a king, not a queen. Not that I was complaining.

The old boat's galley had been cleared of food and eating gear, so I climbed across to the new one, marvelling all over again at the vast amount of space in both the cockpit and the saloon. Designed as a proper ocean-cruising boat, there was a decent load-bearing bulkhead between the cockpit and the saloon with a pair of proper water-tight doors for access. Dave, nursing a mug of coffee, was comfortably parked at the ten-seater cockpit table, and Corrine had a batch of crumpets toasting in the galley. Bree and Alex soon joined us, and that was how we were when Jan trotted down the jetty, followed by his Girl Friday notetaker with several clipboards in hand, two workers and two riggers.

I left Bree to organise drinks and eats and went to stir the sleeping beauties who were still just that, so I pulled the sheet off them, grabbed a couple of shapely legs and shook hard, then gave them five minutes to get moving or they could stay in harbour for the day.

With flung pillows chasing me out of the cabin, I left them to it and retreated topside where Jan was laughing at Dave who was peering helplessly at the cockpit steering station instrument panel where two dinky little chromed shift/throttle levers had a simple key-operated on/off switch above each.

'OK you pair of smart arses,' he growled, 'how the hell do you get this thing ready to do motoring stuff?'

A grinning Jan reached across and turned both keys and the engine panel leapt into LED-lit life. He carefully explained how the motors were always ready to go and didn't need warming up or anything old-fashioned like that. He pointed out the battery gauges, which were at 85% and said, 'Like any throttle lever, just move the levers forward to go forward and back to go back. Move them further to go faster.'

Several open hatches around the cockpit floor and noises below indicated Jan's crew were hard at work, checking for leaks of any description and re-checking the function of everything now we were afloat.

The two riggers were checking the tightness of all standing rigging, but nothing had really changed overnight, because it would need the stress of sailing to settle the whole thing down.

Mooring lines were being cast off when Sandy and Kelly finally hopped across after carefully locking up the old boat. Both pussies were already aboard because they had spent the night on the new *Firebird*, getting used to the new smells and, of course, discovering which was the best bed for them.

Jan took the boat out with Dave, Alex and me peering over his shoulder, but moving under power was so delightfully simple; anyone could do it. It was just rather unnerving to move without any noise or vibration!

Once clear of the marina confines, the breeze was initially light over a low swell, which was perfect for discovering how a new boat will handle. And what a treat *Firebird* was! The huge sails were effortlessly raised by the electro-hydraulic motors at the touch of a button on the console, and their immense power was harnessed by more power winches driving the sheets. Even though there was a lot of room below, the racing heritage was soon proven as the fine hulls created minimal drag. This simply translated to a boat which was easily driven, as was demonstrated when *Firebird* slipped along with almost no wake at a steady 12 knots, while the wind speed was around 10 knots.

As sailing faster than wind speed is normally the province of the specialised race or record-setting designs, to say I was delighted was an understatement!

Alex understood and shared my excitement, going so far as to clap me on the back in congratulations.

Sandy gave Alex and me a strange look. 'What's with you two? Do you need to find a room, or did something just happen I missed?'

Alex explained just how special was the ability to sail faster than the wind, and as Sandy started to grasp the concept, we saw Jan was also very excited.

'The designers said the boat should be capable of this level of performance, but to see it realised, is bloody marvellous! This afternoon we may get a chance to let her stretch her legs a bit more in stronger winds, because there's another small front due.'

The rest of the morning was taken up with working every piece of equipment on the boat, either by itself or together with other stuff. The girls were tasked with cooking things using all the resources available, just as we were doing on deck with sail handling.

Jan called for our attention again as he pointed to another pair of gauges which showed power consumption. There was a small button marked, 'hydrogeneration' which he pushed, bringing a red LED on. After a few seconds, the numbers on the gauge moved swiftly from a minus to a plus reading.

'The pitch on the props have now been adjusted from low-drag feather mode, to deliver optimal RPM for our speed and the state of charge of the batteries and capacitors. It is all managed automatically, so when the batteries are full, the system will put the props back into the feathered position for minimal drag. Even when in full regeneration mode, the overall speed loss is only about two knots, something you'll hardly notice on this boat.'

I had to agree and resolved to spend more time reading the

manuals on how to work the boat, and less time playing with the ladies. For a short time, anyway.

At one stage, we closed the coast while the swell was still low and practiced anchoring well outside the surf line. We did it several times, making sure the automatic chain counter was reliable, and more importantly, that the Rocna 110kg main anchor I was trying out, behaved itself. It did as advertised, setting quickly each time, and held us steady even on short scope, but proper testing would have to wait until we encountered a strong blow.

By lunch time, there was a stiff northerly blowing and *Firebird* really picked up speed and wanted to fly. It was awe-inspiring to feel the huge power in the sails being transmitted through the mast and rigging to the hulls. After a final check and a few slight tightening adjustments, the carbon rigging didn't need any further attention. Even with the strong wind and the small swell, it didn't even look stressed. We were heading east because Jan wanted to try to pick up some of the wind-against-the-current waves further out. So far though, even with a one to two-metre swell, the very slender bows just sliced straight through the waves without any hesitation and little shock resistance, so the ride was a lot softer and smoother than I was used to. A lot faster too!

The downside was more spray was flicked up onto the trampolines, but we could all live with that for the gain of a better ride and more speed.

Lunch was served with the boat speed flickering around 25 to 27 knots, and the grin on my face was mirrored by Jan, Dave and Alex.

Sandy looked up from delivering a platter of sandwiches, 'You're doing it again. What's up with you lot this time?' she demanded good-naturedly.

'Look at the boat speed read-out,' I pointed at the read-out cluster above the rest of the instruments.

She did, blinked and exclaimed, 'Bloody hell! I thought we were still doing about 12 knots! I mean, we're hardly bouncing around and there's almost no heel angle.'

She looked out over the sterns. 'Fuckin' hell! You could water-ski behind this thing. Easy peasy!'

Jan looked amused by her concise and expressive assessment of the impressive design, so we sat down to eat and drink, while the new 'George' the autopilot, took care of steering out toward some rough water.

We found it about an hour later and it was almost like sailing into a concrete wall – low swell one moment, then just ahead of the bows, the ocean was going mad with steep-sided waves standing up, then toppling over with a roar and a mass of white foam.

'This is a good test for the automatic sail-handling set-up!' Jan cried out as the girls scrambled to rescue mugs and plates before we hit the maelstrom. He was the quickest to punch George off-line and hit the 75% Main and Furl Screecher buttons. Above and forward of where we stood in the cockpit, the main smoothly retracted 25% of its area into the enclosing shelter of the boom, while the screecher sheets were flogging loosely as it was rolled swiftly around the roller forestay foil. Well within a minute, the boat was de-powered enough to be safe and comfortable, and all without leaving the cockpit or raising a sweat.

'This is amazing! When I asked for some automation, I didn't think it would be anywhere near as competent as this.'

He smiled modestly, 'When you said you were prepared to pay for it, we were happy to oblige. The whole system was developed in-house. Because we have received commissions from several other builders for units like this one, you have received a substantial discount for yours.'

The boat was moving around a fair bit more in the steep waves, but it strode over or through most of them without any problem, although the foredeck got a good washdown which tested the sealing of the deck hatches.

Under Jan's guidance, I got to play with the sail handling panel and had a wonderful time varying the mainsail size; rolling the inner stay sail up, then letting it out again.

Our efforts gave the riggers a bit more work, but they were a cheerful pair and re-assured me this was just what was needed.

'It's settled down enough so you shouldn't have to adjust any part of the standing rigging for at least 12 months Mr Harry,' the senior man said. 'It's an excellent system for controlling such a big rig.'

Finally, Jan decided he and his team had enough data for later analysis and we turned around and headed west. Two hours later, basking in rounds of congratulations for a job very well done, we were backing into our berth, decks glittering in the late afternoon sun as the dying rays reflected off millions of salt crystals in a scintillating display of red fire. Jan and his crew gathered up all their equipment, thanked the ladies for feeding them and hustled ashore, still dictating results and required modifications to Girl Friday. He assured us he'd be back first thing in the morning to make the necessary changes and try them out again.

'I'd like to have the first inspection for your old boat tomorrow afternoon, perhaps about 14:00 when we'll be back from sea trials. Will that be alright?'

'Yep. No problem.'

After they left, I used the hose on the jetty and washed the salt off the gleaming red gelcoat and everything else I could reach with the spray. We ate again at our new favourite Italian restaurant where we were almost too well known and the wine flowed freely. The physical day caught up with us and cut short the celebration. Sandy and Kelly had moved all our gear across from the old boat, so we slept aboard the new *Firebird* for the first time.

Apart from the new bed, which had very welcome walk-up access from both sides, there was a whole new set of noises for me to get used to. It was also different sleeping right at the stern instead of almost at the bow, although it would be much more comfortable at sea.

New cabin and bed notwithstanding, I slept well and awoke

early feeling refreshed. It was just as well I did, because Jan and his crew were banging on the hulls at 06:30, bearing a stack of boxes of croissants to go with the coffee they consumed in vast quantities. At his gentle insistence we dropped the mooring lines at 07:00 and with my crew still sleepily getting their act together, we motored silently out of the harbour for a shortened repeat of yesterday's testing marathon.

'Remember our potential buyers are arriving at 14:00,' Jan cautioned, 'therefore we must finish this last series of tests in time. If all is well, you can sign off on the boat, make the final payment, and are free to depart. Even though I would like to be able to show you some more of our fascinating country, I know you are anxious to head back to Australia.'

I nodded, 'That's true Jan. We'd like to stay longer, but need to head back as soon as we can.'

It was a busy morning with a rapid-fire repeat of the tests from yesterday designed to re-check every system, although I was pleased the rigging didn't need adjusting. I lost count of the number of electric sail changes I made as we tacked and jibed and shortened sail, hoisted everything, then furled the lot all over again. We pumped the bilges, or tried to anyway, but the construction was so good, the bilge pumps complained about trying to pump dust. The only solution was to tip a few buckets of water into the lower depths of the bilges, just so they could prove how efficiently they could move water from where it wasn't needed, to where it belonged.

Finally, the last checklist was ticked and as Alex took us back in toward the port, I sat at the saloon table with Jan and signed off on reams of paper checklists. The final act was to go on-line through the satellite system to arrange a bank transfer of funds for the last payment, and the boat was fully mine.

Jan phoned ahead to the Port Elizabeth Authorities to expedite our clearance from South Africa, as I was determined to get to sea as soon as we could stock up fully for the long voyage back to Australia.

However, an idle comment by Jan about our homeward journey caused the germ of an idea to start forming in my devious mind.

He also made a practical suggestion.

'Tell me, Harry. Do you have cold-weather gear for yourself and the crew?'

I looked at him and cursed myself. 'Ah...I'm such a fool! Even though it's summer, we'll be dipping further south, so naturally it'll be bloody cold. No Jan, we don't have any serious warm clothing.'

He patted the air in front of me. 'It's not a problem. We have some of the best marine clothing stores in South Africa right here in St Francis. I suggest you postpone your departure for one extra day and the ladies be allowed to go shopping for all the crew. I imagine you also need to stock up on provisions?'

'Yes, we do, and that's a good suggestion. But how about our outbound clearance? You've just arranged it for tomorrow.'

He waved his hands dismissively, 'That's not a problem. You have 48-hours from when the forms are signed to actually leave. Tomorrow is Wednesday, so if you sail up there early, you can be back here in time to do some shopping, then you still have all Thursday free with departure on Friday.'

He made it sound easy, so that was the plan we would follow, but first, I had to tag along with Jan as we waited for the inspecting clients to arrive. Jan was to do the salesman bit, while I was the technical consultant. They were on time and proved to be a pleasant and enthusiastic American couple in their early 50s, named Don and Jeanna Akron. They were both fit and trim, especially Jeanna who looked 20 years younger, and were cashed up from selling their successful engineering business. They had the cruising bug, but like me, had already discovered the pleasure of doing so with the boat sitting flat in the water instead of leaning over at 45°.

Also like me, they appreciated the space and speed of a big cat and from the start, they loved the old *Firebird*. They were also impressed by the length of the delivery voyage and lack of any resulting problems.

I took them on an extensive tour, explained all the systems, showed them the detailed operating manual I'd put together, then took them for a sail. Happily, the breeze was still blowing quite hard with a low swell and was a great combination for my old boat to show her capabilities. Don and Jeanna greatly appreciated the way I'd designed the sail-handling and anchoring systems so one person could do everything without strain.

The Wi-Fi remote docking controller was something new and I showed them how easy it was to be able to stand anywhere on the boat and to move the boat in any direction.

Securely re-attached to the jetty, we sat around the cockpit table to talk deals.

It was clear they loved and wanted the boat, so a small amount of gentle haggling went on, and in the end the price we agreed on was hardly less than what I had in mind from the start. Namely, US$1.85 million. They made a 50% direct-deposit transfer on the spot, pending a surveyor's report and Jan made the arrangements.

He paused his phone call to the surveyor to say to the Akron's, 'If you want an out-of-water inspection, we will have to take the boat to Port Elizabeth, and it may be a couple of days before we can arrange a haul-out on a slipway.'

They were an impulsive couple and clearly hesitated to delay the sale any longer than necessary. When Jan saw that, he suggested the marine surveyor had an associate who was happy to do an underwater inspection in scuba gear. It wasn't as good as an open air one, but was cheaper and much quicker. They decided quickly and jumped at the chance to do the deal faster.

With the surveyor and his scuba-diving associate booked for the next day, they insisted on taking Jan and our whole crew to dinner.

It was a happy evening with much wine and laughter, although Don kept pumping me for information about the boat, and Jeanna did the same to Sandy. At some point, Jan suggested Don and

Jeanna go to Port Elizabeth with us in the morning on the new *Firebird* so the flow of information could continue. He would personally supervise the survey if they would accept it.

'That'd be wonderful,' Jeanna gushed, only slurring a little bit. 'There's so much to learn about our magnificent new boat.'

Luckily, both were practical engineering people and had already picked up most of what was necessary to operate their new boat. We adjourned to the new *Firebird* for a brief taste of NQ tea, before everyone fell into bed.

Our new good friends, the Akron's, together with a slightly hung-over crew, headed out of the harbour at dawn. The sail up to Port Elizabeth in the early morning light was a pleasure with a brisk westerly breeze blowing quite hard. It was our first chance to run the boat ourselves without Jan and his crew scuttling everywhere poking, prodding and testing to make sure everything moved when it should or didn't when it shouldn't.

The west wind didn't raise much of a sea, so *Firebird* moved easily and with wind speeds of 15 to 20 knots, we consistently saw boat speeds of 20 to 25 knots! Don and Jeanna were very excited, so I had to point out while their new boat was fast, it wasn't normally quite as fast as this. Which was to be expected with twenty feet more length and another few million dollars in carbon-fibre alone.

By the time we reached Port Elizabeth, I was a lot more relaxed about the handling of the new *Firebird* since there was no tendency to misbehave. It accelerated quickly and smoothly in gusts, never seeming to exceed 5° of heel, and even when the gusts hit us on the stern quarter, the slim bows didn't bury or nose-dive excessively. The all-carbon fibre construction made it incredibly stiff, and impressively, the 54 miles were covered in just 2.5 hours. Don and Jeanna wandered around while we were processed by Customs and Immigration, Jan's phone call doing wonders to speed the paperwork, and we were through in just 40 minutes. We met at a coffee shop, then back to the boat for another fast sail back to St Francis Bay.

Jan was waiting with the surveyor who presented Don and Jeanna with both a written and verbal report which gave my lovely old boat a clean bill of health. Don immediately phoned his bank to make the transfer of the other 50% of the agreed price and the deal was done.

They planned to spend the next couple of weeks at St Francis Bay settling into their new boat and Jan was going to help with the technical and sailing side and I was sure he'd sell some extra gear along the way.

Then it was time for us to go clothing shopping and Jan directed us to a huge, modern marine equipment store with a vast array of the latest wet and cold weather gear, from underwear and sleep-wear, right up to waterproof deck gear. We all went to make sure of getting correct sizes and I warned everyone to get the best they could find because we might be making a detour on the way home.

As always with this stuff, personal fit and comfort was the most important thing, but it was hard to go past the British Musto range, so most of the crew opted for that. The Australian brand Zhik were represented with their new Isotak X offshore jacket and pants and they certainly suited me.

While I was waiting for the girls to decide on colour schemes, I got an idea and turned it over a few times, prompting Sandy to comment with a grin, 'Harry's got his thousand-metre stare going, so we could soon be hit with a wild scheme.'

She pushed me for an explanation, but I held off until I'd spoken with Jan again. I even bought a selection of Gath lightweight sailing helmets for face and eye protection in strong winds and paid the eye-watering bill happily, knowing that everyone would need to be as well-protected as possible.

Then I took Jan aside and asked a few questions and he turned out to be a veritable fount of information, having visited the place a few years ago. My resolve hardened, so while in-store, I purchased a selection of charts and a couple of pilot books, refusing to let the others see what I had.

Back at the boat, Sandy bailed me up and refused to move until I sat down and explained what I had in mind. I knew I wouldn't get away with the surprise any longer, so over pre-dinner drinks, I laid out my idea.

CHAPTER 11

ST FRANCIS BAY, SOUTH AFRICA

Sitting around our much larger cockpit table, which failed to fill our huge cockpit, I spread out a chart and secured the curling edges with a few bottles. It was a good thing it wasn't a photo, since most of Heard Island is snow, ice and glaciers and I didn't want to frighten anyone off just yet.

'On our way back to Aussie, I thought it would be a terrific opportunity to see a part of the world few people have visited.'

Dave peered closely at the contour lines on the chart of the island. 'Hate to butt in, old mate, but that looks awfully like a bloody big volcano taking up most of the island. I don't suppose it's still active?'

'Funny you should ask Dave, but yes, it is very much so. It's called Big Ben and the island is Heard Island.'

Sandy leant forward, peering at the chart, 'Last time I looked at Google Earth, dearest one, Heard Island looked to be uncomfortably close to Antarctica.'

'Well, yes, it is sort of down that way, but 900 miles north isn't really that close. Anyway, I thought it would be interesting to go have a look. There's even a surf break called Satan's Shank, of all things, so that should be right up your alley, Dave, excuse the pun.'

That got a grin out of Dave and a poke in my ribs from Sandy. 'I guess I could find a good surfboard in this town along with a decent double-layer steamer wetsuit,' he commented. 'It certainly would be something to surf so far south. By the way, Harry, just how far south are we talking?'

'Ahhh....That'd be 53° south, I'm afraid.'

Sandy's eyebrows climbed up to her hairline, '53° south! And here we are....?'

'Ah...just on 34° south, about the same as Sydney.'

A thoughtful silence descended on the table, until Bree quietly spoke up and said, 'Well. It'll certainly be an adventure, so I guess we'd better stock up on some extra supplies. I think it'll all be very fuckin' interesting.'

It was probably the understatement of the month, but interest revived quickly and planning started in earnest, continuing on at the restaurant.

At one point, before everyone got too shit-faced, I said, 'It might be best if we don't advertise our plans too widely. Jan told me we should get permission from the Australian Antarctic Division to make a visit. Unfortunately, it takes 3 to 4 months to process any request, so most people don't bother. We can always claim we needed to shelter from bad weather.'

'Speaking of weather, dear one, just what is the weather like on Heard Island in summer?'

'Jan tells me it's much the same as in winter, except not quite as cold and with not so much ice around.' I was well aware that I'd dodged actually answering her question, and figured I'd let everyone drink more wine before I mentioned the perpetual gale-force winds, sub-zero temperatures and snow-storms. And that was the summer weather!

'Oh goody. I'll get to use my bikini again!'

Sometimes Sandy can be just a little bit sarcastic, but I was glad she seemed to be getting into the right mood about my surprise side trip.

Bree spoke up again, 'Tomorrow's our last shopping day here, so we need to extend the supply list. Can everyone let me know what extra you want in the way of food and drink. Personal stuff, you get for yourselves.'

I was coming back from the gents when Antonio, the restaurant owner, pulled me aside into his office.

Knowing we were about to leave in a couple of days, he had some disturbing information.

'I haven't had the chance to speak like this before, Mr Harry, but I have come to know and like you and your friends. For some time now, a number of newly-delivered boats which have sailed away from here with their new owners, have been found drifting, stripped and abandoned, crew either simply not there, or with evidence of having suffered extreme violence.'

'Very disturbing, Antonio. What have the police found?'

'Nothing, Mr Harry. In fact, they aren't trying hard because most times, the boats are found in international waters, so it isn't strictly their problem. Also, the missing owners are usually foreigners, so there's even less incentive to investigate. It has been the families of the missing who have stirred the small amount of police action.'

I looked at him thoughtfully and detected a gleam in his eyes. 'Is there perhaps some information the police don't have, and which might possibly be of use to me?'

In return he looked suitably thoughtful. 'That is a possibility. We southern Italians by nature are raised in an atmosphere of intrigue. We had Machiavelli and his teachings, for instance. It has occurred to me that if a capable person with an inquiring mind were to visit some of the ship's chandlers which specialise in selling used boat equipment, then perhaps a reason for the attacks might become apparent.'

I jumped in with....'which in turn, might lead to who is organising and directing these attacks. And that capable person might discover that the organiser was currently working in a business allowing him or her to keep tabs on new boat sales and delivery options.'

He beamed at me, as would a teacher with a particularly bright young student.

'That is a strong possibility, Mr Harry, and should such a thing be detected, the investigating person would be well advised to exercise caution, given the evidence of extreme violence being used.'

I nodded, almost to myself, 'Is there an estimation how many boats might have been taken in this manner?'

He scrabbled in a desk drawer, pulled out a piece of paper and consulted it. 'To date, 13 boats spread over 3 years.'

That raised my eyebrows. 'That many! But you say the families have been here? They must have wanted to know what happened to their loved ones?'

'Yes. We have had many such family groups visit. I overhear their discussions, but the police still say they have done all that can be done; they cannot find any evidence to follow up.'

'OK, thanks Antonio. If you think of anything more, please call me, anytime.' I handed him a card with both my mobile and the boat's SatPhone numbers then re-joined the others.

We finished our meal soon after, thanked the chef and as the place had closed and we were last again, they let us out the kitchen back door which was closer to the jetty anyway. There was a noisy party happening in a waterfront villa a few hundred metres away, but where we were parked, all was quiet and peaceful.

That was until Sandy led the way aboard. As she climbed the stern steps with Kelly just behind her, there was a snarl from Jasper and two dark figures darted from the other side of the table, heading for the jetty, the lead one roughly punching her in the shoulder so she spun around, falling heavily to the floor, taking Kelly with her. Bree and Corrine both quickly slipped back down the steps, while Dave, Alex and I were still on the jetty. Before we had a chance to do anything, there was a sickening, wet crunching sound, followed by a heavy thump which shook the whole boat.

A stifled cry of shock preceded another heavy thump and a loud groan of pain. I rushed aboard and flicked the dim nightlights on, to be greeted by the sight of my darling lady being helped to her feet by Kelly, a spreading red patch staining the shoulder of her shirt. Almost at her feet, Jasper crouched over one of two prone bodies, his jaws clamped over his face like the octopus-thing in *Alien*, a deep, angry rumbling coming from his chest. The other prone body was face-down in a pool of dark liquid and didn't appear to be moving. Or breathing for that matter.

I turned to Sandy who had been helped into a chair by Kelly, and peeled her shirt back from her shoulder to reveal a small wound just below her collar-bone where the bleeding already seemed to be slowing.

'That useless prick stabbed me!' Sandy said indignantly. 'Good thing he hit the leather strap of my carry bag.'

No one else was hurt, although the same couldn't be said for the two intruders. Dave and I rolled over the one who'd stabbed Sandy to find that Jasper had delivered his trademark love bite and torn out a large chunk of his throat. As a way to keep things quiet, it was a most effective treatment. The other idiot was alive, making little groans, but trying not to move as every time he did, Jasper shook his head like a shark, tearing even more flesh off. Blood poured from multiple facial wounds and flaps of various bits of face hung down to the deck.

'Okay Jasper. Release him, but sit on his chest please boy,' I commanded. He immediately complied, much to Kelly's horrified fascination, but the injuries were a bit too severe to recognise who it was. Bree, however, said in a shaky voice, after looking at the dead one, 'That's one of Jan's workers. He was on the boat when it was brought around from the launching. I fed them breakfast, the rotten buggers!'

Sandy kicked the dead body, 'At least this arsehole got what he deserves!'

I took a careful look around and Alex took my thoughts and said quietly, 'I'll just take a bit of a walk, shall I Commander?'

'Appreciate it Alex. There will most likely be a lookout or two. It won't matter what condition they're in. We're going to have to disappear them anyway.'

He nodded, 'That will be best.'

Followed by a questioning look from Kelly, Alex left, and for such a big man, he could move swiftly and quietly. No one else in the houses surrounding the marina appeared to have seen or heard anything, so I doused the red night lights and turned on the dimmable foot-level white lights.

Kelly already had the first-aid kit open and had dusted the small puncture in Sandy's shoulder with antibiotic powder and applied an adhesive dressing.

'Dear, oh dear!' Sandy whispered. 'Look at the mess on our brand-new deck.'

'Stay there,' Kelly said, 'I'll get a mop.' She and Bree attended to the blood, although on Bree's advice, they used the saltwater deck hose and flushed it all into the overboard drains, while Dave and I lowered the RIB into the water and positioned it against the stern steps. Before we moved the first one, Bree handed me two long-blade knives with razor-sharp edges, and an automatic pistol in good condition. I set it aside with the two knives to examine later, but first, I searched the pockets of the two men and came up with two wallets, car keys and a compact suppressor for the pistol.

With some difficulty, we dragged the dead body down the steps and draped him over the dinghy's side. By the time we were done, Kelly reported the second intruder had carked it as well. I managed to find an intact area where a pulse should be, but wasn't, so Dave and I repeated the first manoeuvre and tossed the faceless body onto the first, giving the girls a bit more saltwater hosing to do.

A soft hail from the jetty revealed Alex, with a slight, but limp body tucked under each arm as though they were two slabs of beer. Without ceremony, he dumped them onto the boarding platform and jumped down beside them.

'Stupid buggers! They were both having a smoke of yippee weed out the front of the restaurant, and by the pile of butts around their feet, they'd been there quite a while. But they were carrying these and they tried to poke me with them. I didn't like that.' From a back pocket, he produced two long, curved knives which were wickedly sharp, and tossed them onto the deck.

'Well, they weren't going to be showing us how to tie knots with those!' Dave drawled. Just then Corrine leant over the stern railing, 'Ah...boys? I think you're missing something?'

She nodded at the RIB, now bobbing violently against the stern boarding platform.

We looked and for a moment couldn't see what she was looking at, or why the RIB was bouncing around. Then, just under my feet came a thump and a broad head with a pair of un-blinking, expressionless black eyes, rose from the water, bit down hard with a soggy crunch, and with a violet shake of his fat head, dragged a complete body under.

'Shit!' was Dave's comment. 'I was going to have a dip in there this arvo to cool off. Rather glad I didn't. Does anybody recognise the clean-up squad....?'

Nobody did, until Kelly said, 'Bull shark! Very aggressive, fearless and determined. All the blood we've been washing into the water has brought them in.'

That was when I noticed two more fins curling around the back of the boat in excited, jerky movements.

'Bloody hell!' Dave exclaimed. 'Look mate. Let's just chuck 'em all in. It'll save us the trouble of taking them out to sea and nobody's going to see or hear a thing.'

'Yeah. Might as well, although there's only these two skinny buggers left that Alex picked up.'

The problem came when it was made obvious the two lookouts lying in an untidy heap at our feet were still breathing. That is, one was having a lot of trouble doing so, while the other was only pretending to be unconscious. We pushed the one who had a crushed throat over and he was immediately taken down by a bull shark, whereupon the last one gave us a hell of a fright by leaping to his feet and trying to run up the steps.

It was a pity Alex was standing on the third step!

The big man chuckled quietly, 'Looks like even those 'men in the grey suits' don't want this piece of garbage. What shall we do with him, Commander?'

I stepped up to be almost nose-to-nose with the local lad, but recoiled at the powerful stench of voided bowels, bladder and the usual BO.

'Can you understand me?' I asked quietly.

Although nearly gibbering with fear at the sight of three fins circling in the water just metres away, he nodded violently.

'Who came up with this idea to rob our boats?'

'Tre men at boat place, Boss. Two big fellas come here tonight… can't see 'em now. One more big Boss still at boat place. Doan feed me to dem big fishes, please Boss!'

I thought a moment, 'I'll let you go, but you must tell me about the man at the boat place.' Trembling violently, he nodded. 'I don't know much Boss, but him important man, in charge of erey'ting.'

My ears pricked and the hair on the back of my neck tingled. 'What 'erey'ting' is this man in charge of?'

He gave me a puzzled look as though it was something I should already know. 'The whole 'ting to sell the stuff off the boats to shops in town, Boss. Him good man to work for. Pay lot's money.' He babbled on describing the man, right down to the full, bushy moustache.

After a few pennies dropped into place, I figured there was little else to come from this low-level clown, but then an idea zipped into my brain. 'OK Alex. Hose this miserable sack of crap off, then tie him up, gag him and dump him on the cockpit floor. We'll have to keep him out of circulation tonight. I don't want this 'Big Boss' alerted before we go visiting in the morning.'

Alex was well practiced in securing prisoners and quickly found some large nylon cable-ties. His mouth was taped with a small hole for extra air, then with well-taped ankles, he was tethered in the middle of the cockpit where the deck was easily washed down.

He was then introduced to Jasper. I squatted down beside him, 'This is an Indonesian jungle cat. He's already killed two of your mates tonight and would love to do the same to you. He's going keep you company for the rest of the night, and if you try to call out or make any attempt to get away, he will bite you very hard! If you behave, he might leave you alone, so it's your choice. Live? Or die horribly. Do you understand?'

He nodded violently.

'OK. But remember, you only get one chance to do this right.'

We washed the rest of the stern down, including Jasper's bitey bits and the RIB, before we hoisted it back up against the stern. There still weren't any curious heads poking out of windows, so we tidied everything up and turned the lights out. But not before activating the super-charged electric fence controller which was wired into the safety rail system which ran around the entire boat. It delivered a current which usually wasn't quite lethal, but because it seriously messed up the heart rhythm, without immediate resuscitation, the victim usually died.

Kelly dosed Sandy up with Panadol, although she said she was comfortable. As Kelly helped Sandy down the aft stairway to the master cabin, Corrine silently passed me a thin chain with a metal disk attached.

'This was on the cockpit floor.'

I took it and peered closely at the embossed printing, dismayed to read, 'Southern Nautical staff'!

'Thanks Mouse. I'll talk to Jan in the morning.'

The rest of the night was peaceful, although Sandy did have a small after-shock attack of the trembles. Our prisoner had behaved, which was expected with Jasper glaring at him from half a metre away. He was hosed off again and given some food and water.

Kelly changed Sandy's dressing again in the morning with a rather sombre crew as spectators. The events of last night were analysed to put the action into perspective and by the look on their faces, no sleep was lost on account of the intruders, which I took as healthy.

Since this was Friday and our last day in South Africa, the girls planned to use our hired people-mover to hit the supermarket first, then do the rounds of the town for all the other items. Therefore, after brekkie, Dave and I called a taxi to go visit Jan at the factory, while Alex wisely decided to stay to look after the boat and our prisoner.

Jan was initially pleased to see us and asked about the run to Port Elizabeth. After going through that for a few minutes, I then asked him if two workers hadn't turned up for work that morning.

His fine brow furrowed, 'Yes, in fact. But how did you know? One is a leading hand and he's been reliable, so it's unusual for him to goof off.' Silently, I fished the neck chain out of my top pocket, the little red disc glittering in a stray beam of sunlight.

He took it slowly. 'Yes..... This belongs to a leading hand. That's why it's red. The others are white. How did you come by it?'

'Last night, two of your workers came calling, but they weren't looking for sparkling conversation. One was wearing this disk. They were starting work on dismantling the cockpit instrument panel when we arrived back unexpectedly after dinner. They had two lookouts, but one got in a fight with Alex, fell in the water and was taken by a bull shark. The other two encountered Jasper, my cat, and they too, are no more.'

Jan looked quite stricken, so I added, 'The last bit of information was for your ears only.

He nodded, 'I understand completely, but I'm devastated that my staff would do such a thing.'

'I'm holding one of the lookouts for now, and he's already dobbed in the bloke who's been organising these raids on new boats being sailed away by their owners or delivery crew. Because he's right here in your factory, he knows at any moment just who's launching what boat and when, as well as the departure schedule and crewing arrangements. There's another bunch doing the actual hi-jacking and wiping out the crews, so this bloke is responsible for the violent deaths of a lot of people who were customers of yours and the other yards in town. And all this so he could sell the stripped-out gear to the second-hand market in town.'

Jan looked aghast. 'But...but, I've bought stuff off those dealers when I've been caught short waiting for instruments and fittings!'

I gave a mirthless laugh. 'You were buying back stuff your former customers had paid you for. And they had just been killed for!' I added brutally.

Jan kept shaking his head in denial, 'But this is obviously a trusted man, Harry. Have you got a description?'

I passed on the description the lookout gave me the night before, including the tell-tale moustache.

'Oh, dear God! He's my production foreman. He's worked here for years. Why would he want to do something like this?'

'Opportunity, Jan. They see the gulf between the haves and the have nots and want to move over to the other side without putting in the hard yards to make it legally. I'm afraid with my background, I tend to see this sort of thing in black or white, and my crew feel the same. By the way, your ex-leading hand was carrying a gun and a knife last night and stabbed Sandy in the shoulder as he tried to escape.'

'Stabbed Sandy? Oh, no! This just gets worse! How is she? Is she alright?'

'She's okay. Her shoulder is stiff and sore this morning, but she's mobile. I have to ask; what would be your plans to deal with this ringleader who the look-out fingered?'

Jan looked shattered, 'I haven't had to face this situation before. Normally if a worker is caught stealing, which is the usual thing they get up to, I just sack them and call the police. But if the police come in now after all that's been going on, you'll be tied up in the investigation for months. I presume you don't want that?'

I regarded him evenly, 'Entirely correct, Jan. This mongrel has probably been running his murderous operation for a long time and it sounds well-organised. Is he at work today?'

Jan looked stricken and hung his head miserably. 'Yes, I was discussing schedules with him just before you came.'

'And of course, he's indispensable?'

'Yes. At least until I can train a new man. There are two leading hands who show promise, but they aren't quite ready yet.'

'Well, I'm sorry about your production schedules, but as I said earlier, we have this 'Eye for an Eye' policy which doesn't include watching and waiting while he and his associates get processed through your legal system. The fact he's arranged the murder of many of your ex-customers means he deserves what he gets.'

He finally looked up at me. 'I understand Harry. What's your suggestion?'

'Don't do or say anything for now. We'll go away and be back soon to collect him.'

'Should I ask what's going to happen?'

I smiled gently and patted his shoulder, 'No Jan. Let the professionals handle this one. But, do not let him leave under any circumstances.'

Dave and I jumped back in the taxi and were taken to the boat, where the girls were unloading the first lot of purchases from our hired van.

Sandy seemed to be moving almost normally, so I asked how she was and where they were at with the supplies.

'I feel a lot better,' she said, 'and this is the bulk of the supplies, but the booze and some odds and ends are being delivered shortly. What are you up to?'

Speaking quietly, I said, 'We've found the guy who organises the boat hi-jackings and crew murders, so we're just going to collect him and sort him out. It looks like he's been doing this to Jan's customers for years. It's been a nice little earner on the side for him for a long time, but he's not getting away with it anymore.'

She nodded seriously, 'Okay, but don't get into more strife than necessary... please.'

I just smiled, asked Alex to come along, telling him he could maintain his low profile by staying in our hired van, then called Jasper. I had Dave bring the van as close to the jetty as he could where there were the least number of people moving around, clipped Jasper's lead on his collar and said quietly as we walked back ashore, 'Try to look like a black dog, please Furball. Don't do any cat-stuff until I tell you. We're going to get the bad man who arranged for Sandy to get hurt.'

He padded beside me in silence for a few paces, then gave a loud 'huff' which always sounds like a big sneeze, and when he looked up at me, I could swear he was grinning. We only passed two elderly couples strolling around looking at the boats and licking ice-creams. One said, 'Hello puppy,' while the other couple commented, 'Nice dog.' In reply to that high-level social contact, Jasper wagged his tail, not easy when it's about a metre long, prompting one old dear to add, 'It's so good that you haven't docked his lovely long tail. Well done, young man!'

Once clear of them I said to Jasper, 'Nice one Furball. Great dog imitation, especially the tail wag. Maybe I should lay in a stock of dog food. You'd like some Pal wouldn't you? Lots of lovely, smelly farts? You'd drive Sandy nuts in a couple of days.'

He gave me what would pass for a glare from a human, then marched on ahead, nearly yanking the leash out of my hand. We were almost to the van, when we passed an elderly black man with a lined face just chock-full of character and life experience, not all of it good I guessed. He took one look at Jasper padding along, not quite in dog mode, and smiled, nodded and softly said something like, 'Ahh, yee!' stepping aside to let us pass, his eyes not leaving Jasper.

As I opened the van door, I looked back at him and as our gazes met, he gave me a slow nod, seeming to convey respect and understanding. I returned the nod and smile.

When Dave saw Jasper he grinned, 'Good one mate! I take it we're going to do a number on numb-nuts? The hi-jacking king of St Francis?'

I frowned at both men, 'Yep! Mass murder, betrayal of trust, attempted theft and causing physical harm to our lovely Sandy. That's enough to invoke the Jasper solution.'

CHAPTER 12

ST FRANCIS BAY, SOUTHERN OCEAN

After a few false turns, we finally managed to find Jan's factory, parking just around the corner of the office. A nervous Jan came out to meet us, especially when he saw the hulking form of Alex who can look extremely intimidating when he's not happy... and someone causing injury to Sandy made him very unhappy.

'I have Carlos in the office now. What do you want me to do?'

'Just ask him to come out to the van. Say the customer has a problem with a fitting and needs his advice on whether to repair or replace it.'

He disappeared inside and moments later, a Spanish-looking chap with the obligatory large moustache appeared. He looked fit, so I gave Alex the nod and he retreated further inside the rear section of the van.

'Good morning, Sir. I understand one of your mast fittings is causing you a problem?'

'Yes, Carlos. We took it off to bring it here seeing as you're so busy. It's just in the back on the floor.'

'Most considerate of you. Even with your boat finished, we're down two workers today, for some reason. No one has seen them. Anyway, let's look at this fitting.'

I stepped aside from the doorway, Dave stepped up behind him and gave Carlos a hard shove in the middle of his back which sent him straight into the clutches of Alex, who almost purred as he held him immobile in a crushing bear-hug.

'You come to me, you bloody murdering crook. Your man stabbed the Commander's lady and paid the price. Now it's your turn.'

Carlos's eyes were bulging with the pressure Alex was putting

114

on his torso and could only gasp, 'What's going on? Who are you? Let me go!'

Naturally, Alex smiled gently and increased the pressure even more and I heard what sounded like Carlos's ribs creaking.

'You be quiet, little man. The Commander needs to have a chat with you. We think you've been a very naughty boy.'

By now, Dave had reversed out of the carpark and needed directions.

'Head back toward the harbour, please mate. But when we hit the main road called St Francis Drive, turn right and just follow it to the end. Carlos has been working so hard he deserves some time on the beach. It looks like a lovely day to go swimming.'

In fact, it would be a crappy day on the beach with a strong on-shore breeze and a messy, choppy surf which wouldn't entice even the most die-hard surfer to get wet. As we drove, Carlos started to burr up again and I heard the word 'rights.' I turned in my seat, smiled at Carlos and said, 'Jasper?'

My big, black cat slid between the seats, then hopped up on one so he was at eye-level and about 150 millimetres away from a suddenly still Carlos.

'Ahh. There you are. Carlos, meet your worst nightmare. In a moment I'm going to ask you some questions and I want straight answers. No delay, no bullshit! Comprehendo, Senor?'

A nod was the reply.

'Excellent! Now, if I think you are being evasive, Jasper here is going to bite you... just once, each time. The first one will be just a light nip, although his fangs are very sharp. More lies or evasions and the bites will start... and they will be a lot harder! Anyway, I just need to chat to my mate up front for a minute, so you consider whether you fancy being truthful or whether you'd prefer to be in a whole world of hurt.'

Deliberately, I turned my back on the dead silence behind me, and in a conversational tone asked Dave, 'How did you get on finding a surfboard?'

He laughed, 'Aww mate. There's got to be ten thousand of the bloody things in this town. It seems like dudes come here for a surf and find it's cheaper to just leave the board behind when they go. Some were just lying on the ground at the surf beaches and the board shops have so many stacked up out the back, they just give them away.

I was going to buy a new one, but then I spotted a beaut mini-mal just the right size for me. It even has a bit of a gun shape as well, which is really cool and should be perfect for unknown waves in a remote spot.'

His enthusiasm was contagious, although the only gun shape I knew was the one you hold in your hands and has a trigger to help even up a fight. Still, the bizarre conversation served to keep an incredulous Carlos quiet.

We were approaching the end of St Francis Drive when Carlos started up again with the 'You can't do this to me' bit, so I quietly said, 'Jasper.'

His sleek head snapped forward, then back and a sizeable chunk of Carlos's left bicep was exposed to the air with a corresponding leakage of claret and a howl of fright and pain from the victim. I used my survival knife to slice a sleeve off his shirt to bind over it.

'Now that was a silly thing to do. I did say...'

'Harry,' Dave called from the front, 'the road sort of ends here. Where now?'

I leant over his shoulder. 'There should be a... ahh, there it is. Take that sand track. It should lead to another small clearing right beside the beach.'

Dave carefully drove down the narrow track curling through the low, wind-blasted scrub until we popped out into a small carpark set amongst the low dunes. It was just above a narrow strip of sand which bordered a rocky beach, presently being pounded by the messy, wind-blown surf. Better for our purposes, the small clearing was deserted since even legendary surf spots have blow-out days too.

'What are we doing here?' whined our captive, looking and sounding less like a crime boss all the time.

'We're going to have a little chat, my friend. I'm told confession is good for the soul and I want you feeling really good about yourself.'

'What sort of bullshit is this? I don't have to answer your questions!'

I shook my head in mock disbelief. 'Look around you, Carlos. Do you see any of your cronies rushing to help you? You're on your own now Sunshine, and my large friend with his arms around your chest hasn't even started to squeeze yet. And of course we mustn't forget Jasper who seems to like the taste of you. I know he wants more, since I sort-of forgot to give him breakfast this morning.

Now it's question time and I'm sure you remember the rules - I explained them a short time ago.'

Just then, my mobile phone rang and it was Sandy.

'Sorry to interrupt whatever it is you're doing, but we thought you should hear the latest. A police boat just came into harbour and was met by the Coroner's wagon. I bunged on an official attitude and was told a catamaran yacht had been reported adrift, not far off the coast. The Police found the boat had been stripped of all equipment, right down to pots and pans, sails and fittings. The owners and crew were all dead and the women had been raped repeatedly. There were three children as well, all female. The boat had sailed from here less than a week ago. I thought this info might help your decision-making. Bye bye.'

I looked at Dave, then at Alex and their grim expressions must have reflected my own.

Addressing Carlos I asked, 'Let's keep this simple. All I want to hear is that you're the person who planned this scheme, organised the crews to hit the targets you chose, then supplied the stolen gear to second-hand dealers. The names and addresses of you associates would be good.'

He looked blank for a few seconds, then said, 'Alright. What if I am the person you just described? What does it get me?'

I ignored his question and asked again about other principals involved in the scheme, including the names of the second-hand chandlery outlets.

He couldn't help but be evasive and paid the penalty, much to Jasper's delight.

Finally, we had several more names of informants at other boat yards, and also names of three second-hand marine gear outlets. I had to cut up most of his shirt to protect the hired van's upholstery, but there was enough information to turn over to the local coppers.

I gave Carlos a mirthless smile, 'There. Doesn't that make you feel better? Your soul must be cleaner, but it looks like your body isn't so you need to go and wash. My friend is going to help you out, then I want you to walk down to the water and go for a swim. The saltwater will be good for those bites, although I don't think fingers can re-grow. Still, let's not worry about that for now; you just get cleaned up. Oh, I nearly forgot. In case you think that running will be better than swimming, Jasper will be coming with you to the water's edge. If you try to get out, I'm afraid he's going to bite you again and this time it'll really hurt. Clear?'

He nodded sullenly as Alex almost effortlessly lifted him and shuffled out of the van, before marching him down to the little strip of sand.

I waved him seawards, 'Away you go. Cleanse those wounds. You'll feel much better.'

Faced with little choice as Jasper was nipping at his heels, he turned and limped slowly over the rocks and visibly shuddered when the first wave crashed at his feet. He turned to see Jasper standing just beyond wave reach, red-streaked teeth bared in readiness, then continued wading out into the surf. It appeared he could swim quite well and must have thought his best chance of survival was to swim around the nearby point and head back towards civilisation.

Under the right circumstances he might have made it, but he

must have forgotten the fact this area is renowned not only for wonderful surf, but is fairly teeming with sharks. Mainly bull and great white's, although it probably didn't matter which one took the first leg off, making it much harder to swim.

Belatedly, he decided Jasper was the lesser of two evils and clumsily turned for shore, but whatever was under him, had the taste and in moments, Carlos was a fading memory in a patch of pink froth.

Jasper returned and was roughly wiped down, while we waited to see if the brief scene had been witnessed, but no one came rushing out of the expensive houses lining the beach. We left, heading for the harbour, looking like just another van-load of frustrated surf-seekers and not drawing a single glance from the locals. On the way, I stopped at a car-wash and managed to rinse Jasper's mouth and face as well.

The same afternoon, while events and details were still clear in my mind, I wrote a lengthy, but anonymous note to the local police and had Dave and Alex check it for accuracy. Careful to keep fingerprints off the paper and envelope, at dinner that night in the restaurant, I asked Antonio to mail it for me when he had a chance.

'Someone left this lying around, Antonio. You don't know who it could have been.'

'Si, Mr Harry. Bene, bene! But may I also say, grazie, on behalf of all the ones who would have suffered had this scheme continued? Your meals and drinks for the evening are on the house.'

I fear we played up that night and Antonio and his staff played along with us. Accordingly it was a sorry bunch of piss-heads who slowly surfaced mid-morning to the sound of banging on the hull and Jan's voice.

'I just wanted to thank you for taking care of business Harry. Very few will know the good you've done here, but I've brought a few cases of our best beer and wines for you to remember us by.'

He started to get emotional, so I told him that Antonio was holding a letter for the police and he promised to make sure it got to the right person since his cousin was the local Police District Commander.

It was an hour later before we could safely head for sea and our Southern Ocean adventure.

CHAPTER 13

SOUTHERN OCEAN, FRIDAY

Those of us who hadn't been quite so over-indulgent last night, sort-of looked after the boat, while the rest went back to bed. I took the watch, which consisted of setting the autopilot onto a heading of 135°, set the sails to match and sprawled back on the starboard day-bed to keep an eye on our progress. There was the odd moment or two when I had trouble seeing through my eyelids, but in general, I was on the case. The south-west breeze was brisk, around 18 to 22 knots, and produced an effortless boat speed of 20-odd knots.

To stir my foggy brain cells, I called up the weather situation for the Southern Ocean we were driving down into at a shallow angle, and found we were going to have SW winds for quite a while, remaining in the 20 to 40 knot range, but the endless parade of low and high pressure systems around the higher latitudes, held the promise of some lively weather to break the monotony.

We would also have to adjust to the temperature drop, which would fall steadily down through the low-teens as we angled across the Roaring Forties, but would then edge closer to 0° C as we passed further south into the Fifties.

Based on our current rate of progress, Heard Island should be reached in just five days, and since this was Friday, we should be close by early Wednesday morning. By early afternoon, the crew were coming alive and I was relieved at my lonely post. Looking and sounding sufficiently pathetic, I was able to wheedle Bree into making up a big batch of savoury rissoles for a late lunch and they were superb – as usual.

Dave surfaced, looked around at our fast, swooping motion as we angled across the perpetual westerly swell which had become noticeably bigger since we'd left St Francis Bay, and commented dryly, 'Gets along alright for something that only has a few ratty bedsheets flapping in the breeze as a power source.'

Those 'few bedsheets' were made of mylar and Spectra laminate and cost a small fortune, but at least held their shape for a long time. Alex had already relieved me on watch and commented, 'The new boat moves very well, Commander. Fast and with a soft motion over the waves.'

'Yes. I didn't think there would be so much difference between the two boats, but I'm very pleased!'

The ladies even commented on the different standard of ride and motion, pronouncing it to be an improvement. Now we were at sea, everyone liked the extra space and the ease in moving around, although the vast expanse of the saloon needed careful movement if the sea was up. The two full-length strips of tempered glass set into the overhead were a great feature. They let in so much light, it made the saloon seem larger and allowed a good view of the huge mainsail and the towering black mast overhead.

As the day closed down and the dark curtain of twilight slid across the sky from the east, we were 250 miles on our way and the swell had lengthened and gained some extra height, but it was still comfortable travelling.

The disappearance of the sun also meant a sharp drop in temperature, sending the crew scrabbling in their lockers for tracksuit bottoms and wool layers on top. Dinner was also served in the saloon for the first time, with the cockpit doors closed. The wind was very consistent in direction, so the person on watch was able to eat at the table before being banished back outside. There was an inside steering station, but at night, it was safest to be outside so as to be able to detect a rogue wave or change in wind. The only crew members to relish the drop in temperature were the two pussies.

Both Jasper and Krazy seemed to grow fat-fur almost immediately and wanted to snuggle up to any warm-bodied human who'd sit still longer than five minutes.

Being in the stern cabin for the first time, I was made aware of the loud hiss and rush of water as we surfed diagonally across the larger waves and I thought of Alan Stallman who so desperately wanted to come on this leg of the trip, and how much he would have enjoyed hand-steering *Firebird* in these conditions.

Even Dave, who normally wasn't happy without 10,500 horse-power under his right hand, enjoyed his time on watch.

That was the way life went for the next few days as the miles ticked up more rapidly than I believed possible, and the temperature steadily dropped. A couple of times we were overtaken by one of the many Southern Ocean lows, and each produced a rapid rise in wind speed and wave height for 12-hours or so, but moved on quickly, letting us set full sail again. Another excellent feature of the new boat, was being able to quickly reef or completely furl any or all sails if a sudden squall snuck up on us.

As we dropped still further south, and even though we were getting what passed for milder summer weather in these parts, sudden squalls would charge up from behind with little warning, meaning we had to quickly reduce sail to just the inner staysail or a storm jib hoisted on its own stay. The huge main was either furled to barely a scrap or stowed away completely. I remained delighted with the handling of the bigger boat in such conditions and became confident that if necessary, two persons could safely handle it.

Naturally, just as we were due to make landfall on Wednesday morning, another sub-polar low chased up from behind and raked us with 60-knot winds, steep seas and driving rain which soon became sleet, then snow flurries. With visibility almost non-existent, and even the radar a bit fuzzy, we dropped all sail and deployed the Jordan series-drogue over the stern attached to a bridle.

The difference in motion was immediate and dramatic as the boat slowed to about 1.5 knots and the mad, headlong charge down the face of each wave was halted, to the great relief to the crew.

Now, as each wave reared up astern and the boat started to accelerate down its face, we could feel the brakes of the drogue being smoothly and gently applied, letting the wave pass harmlessly under the hulls. The chain weights on the far end of the long nylon line holding 180 small, fabric cones hung almost straight down as soon as the pressure came off it, ready for the next braking action. With our speed under control, there was no need for the on-duty watch to be out in the cockpit at all, so I decided they could keep watch inside the saloon where we had all the sail controls, instruments, radar and chart plotter. Additionally, we could steer manually either via a bluetooth hand-held joy-stick, or with the autopilot.

Outside, even with the superb cold-weather gear we all had, the wind-chill factor made it feel like -10° to -15°. Knowing our course would take us very close to McDonald Island, which lay some 30 miles west of Heard Island, I made sure the digital radar was properly adjusted to reduce rain and snow clutter, although at times it was still affected by the conditions.

After a couple of nervous hours, the chart plotter decided we were passing some ten miles north of McDonald Island, and this observation was backed up by two independent GPS units.

At 1.7 knots, we wouldn't be abeam Heard Island until the wee small hours of Thursday morning, so after consulting Alex and Dave, I decided we would try to haul in at least some of the 140-metre length of drogue streaming astern to speed things up a bit.

Due to the loads on the drogue line, the only time we could winch in a few metres was in the trough between waves, so with a combination of determination and an electric winch, we slowly cranked in the drogue line until the average speed indicator had crept up to 7 knots. We were still being held securely, stern-on to the waves, but now we could plan to be just north of Heard Island by late afternoon. Our increased speed allowed the steering to work properly, and I took the chance to head in closer to the island so we could gain shelter in Stephenson Lagoon on the east side of the island before it grew too dark.

I will admit to being quite nervous about closing in on Heard Island in bad visibility, since Shag Island and some associated rocky attachments were just six miles north. My anxiety was increased since the radar was still being messed around at extreme range by snow and sleet.

In a supreme act of faith in modern technology, I pushed on and was rewarded by the snow suddenly clearing as we reached a point just three miles north-west of Lauren's Peninsula, the north-western-most tip of Heard Island. Revealed for the first time, and appearing so close it seemed to be towering over us, we saw the utterly majestic beauty of Big Ben, rearing up out of the low-level, wind-driven sea mist in all its snow-covered glory.

I can't express the incredible impression the sudden appearance this volcanic mountain made on all of us; it didn't just dominate; it virtually was the entire island!

There was just a small skirt of flat land in a narrow rim around its base, which had the classic active volcano shape. Fortunately, to the east lay a couple of small harbours, including Stephenson Lagoon; the one I hoped we could get into.

The next couple of hours were very busy as we started the laborious task of winching in the rest of the drogue. I should have done this earlier, but had planned to head around into the dubious lee of the island if we hadn't been able to get a good visual or radar fix on the place in time.

Naturally, our speed picked up as the drogue shortened, but as we moved closer to land, the seas diminished a lot, although the wind blew just as hard; regularly gusting to 50 knots.

Under power and with sails tightly furled, we followed the coastline less than a mile off-shore. Big Ben really towered over us now, and the intermittent snow squalls which still blasted us weren't enough to sap my confidence. It was a pleasure to be out of the huge swell and I was hopeful we could make the 17-metre-wide entrance channel to Stephenson Lagoon without trouble.

Sandy came out to where we were still stowing the drogue, and said, 'Just before that last snow-squall came through, I thought I saw a big boat or small ship in against the shore-line. It was hard to see against the black rocks because it looked like it was painted black, but according to the chart, it would be in a rather exposed bay called Sealer's Cove.'

I looked, but a white wall of blowing snow-flakes blocked the view, and by the time it cleared, the view back across Corinthian Bay to Sealer's Cove was blocked by terrain anyway.

'Did it look like it was anchored?' I asked.

She shrugged, 'Hard to tell, I only caught a glimpse for a moment between squalls, but I was sure there was some smoke coming from the funnel.'

'Oh, okay. It must be a reasonable size to warrant a funnel, but we're not going to have a look. I'll be happy just to get into our lagoon and have a rest.'

'Amen to that, dearest. Sooner the better. A steady bed would be good for a change.'

I grinned at her. 'Does this mean you're interested in making better use of it if we're steady?'

She cleverly arched one eyebrow, 'Maybe yes?'

The time was approaching 16:00, the snow squalls were increasing in frequency and opacity, and daylight was starting to fade as we started the run-in to the narrow channel leading into Stephenson Lagoon. There was a much wider entrance just a hundred metres along from the one I'd chosen, but it was shallow with medium waves breaking all the way across, so I decided not to risk it. The channel of choice was narrow but deeper, and with the tide not doing much, I lined up the entrance from seaward. Driving straight between waves breaking on the shallows either side, we were soon in the short channel itself, the small island which divided the two entrances to the right and more shallow water to the left.

Moments later, we were in calmer water, although the wind still howled unabated around the flank of Big Ben, whose snowy slopes towered over the sheltered anchorage. It appeared that two glaciers fed the lagoon, although both had receded from the water's edge for the summer. Interestingly, there was a scattering of small ice floes about the harbour, and the depth sounder and the 3-D forward-looking sonar suggested most of the 16 km² lagoon was very shallow. There was plenty of water depth for *Firebird* to the right of the entrance where a small bay tucked up against the shore at the foot of the volcano promised calm water, but there would be no respite from the howling wind. The water surface downwind of our precarious anchorage was a seething mass of white foam as the howling wind ripped the top off any wave daring to try and stand up.

In fact, the wind had two shots at us. We copped it curling around the northern flank of Big Ben, as well from over the top, where it gleefully roared down the steep slopes to slam into us with squall gusts which hit 80 knots at times. The 'bullets' as the downhill gusts were aptly called, hit with a physical blow, fairly rattling the mast and rigging, making me glad I'd set two anchors close to shore in shallow water. It was the first real test of the new Rocna anchors, a brand I'd not used before, although the brief set of tests we'd made back at St Francis Bay had shown they worked superbly.

These conditions were a much tougher test, so once they were set with plenty of chain laid out, I set both the radar and the GPS anchor alarm which would alert me if we moved significantly from our position.

Everyone was too tired for a celebration, but we did unwind with a couple of drinks along with a selection of finger food Bree had whipped up in her newly-stable galley. A few NQ teas were also just the thing for a freezing windy night after Alex and I did the brief rounds of the outside deck looking for anything which might be working loose and could be plucked off by the screeching, prying gusts. All was well and *Firebird* didn't appear to have sustained any damage from the rough seas and winds.

As we defrosted in front of the hot air vents, Dave checked the synoptic chart for the next week and reported the intense low we'd just sailed through would be moving on, and we could expect several days of clear weather.

'The winds will drop a lot, but will still be strong. It'll be our best chance to get ashore and have a look around before the next low comes through.'

I nodded thanks. 'Okay. We'll have a think about when we leave. It might be wise to wait and leave with the next high, rather than fight those gales again. At least they don't take long to move through now we're parked up.'

'I love the scenery and I'm awe-struck by Big Ben,' Sandy commented, 'but I'm getting a bit tired of the wind.'

A heart-felt round of 'hear, hears,' endorsed her remark, although it was difficult to make out the words over the scream of another bullet shaking the whole boat like a terrier with a rat.

For the first night, I decided to mount a one-person watch, 4 hours on each, just to monitor the anchors and able to wake the crew should anything endanger the boat. I was conscious of our extreme isolation should anything go wrong, and apart from Sandy's sighting of a black-hulled ship at the other end of the island, we couldn't expect help in a hurry.

Even though I was tired, I evoked Skipper's privilege and took the first watch while the others disappeared to their beds like rabbits down a hole when a hawk comes calling.

CHAPTER 14

Around 22:00, the sky cleared and the wind moderated considerably, revealing a full moon which bathed the landscape in its pale, colour-leaching light. I rugged up and with the two pussies in tow, ventured outside to be greeted by the stark spectacle of an all-white Big Ben towering up west of us, with the white fingers of the two glaciers pointing at the lagoon.

It was stunningly beautiful, so when I went back inside, I fired up the masthead camera and let it run for a while, setting it to scan 360° every 30 seconds. I was sipping a welcome mug of Milo, when Alex came up to take over the watch, and commented on the brightly-lit landscape around us.

I made my full hand-over report, mentioning that I'd had the camera running and went to shut it down. My finger was reaching for the stop button, when something dark moved across the screen. I fumbled for the zoom control and tried to quickly revert back to manual control, but whatever it was had disappeared. I told Alex about it, lamenting that I was too slow to stop it in time, when once again he proved a tired mind doesn't function anywhere near as good as a freshly-rested one.

'Ah...Commander. Why not just replay the recorded footage? It'll definitely be on that.'

I sighed, 'Thanks Alex. When we get home, I think I'll go check into a nursing home. I've got no business being out here in this mental state.'

He laughed, 'Nonsense, Commander. You're just tired. Now, how about we replay the movie to satisfy our misgivings?'

So, we did and about five minutes from the end, solved the

mystery. As the camera panned slowly past the other side of the fifty metre-wide spit of land which separated us from the ocean, a black RIB with a centre console cruised slowly past, three big men standing where they could, but all looking straight at us. As it was a recording, I was able to run a zoom function, which didn't tell us much, except that the guys were big and wore neoprene balaclavas. There was something about their eyes that niggled at me, but then Alex did it again and said, 'Oriental!'

One minute later, the boat cruised past again, heading back the other way, to the west.

I tried to make something of their odd behaviour, but tiredness had taken hold and Alex sent me tottering down the rear set of cabin steps which led directly to the spacious master cabin. I was too tired to even contemplate fooling around, which must have been some sort of record for me, so Sandy let me sleep through and it was 10:00 when I woke, feeling refreshed and in a much more positive mood.

I felt in another mood entirely when Sandy wandered back in from the shower, hair still damp, so we decided to dry it naturally with body heat.

With that operation successfully completed, I went up top to greet the day and the crew, except while the day definitely was there, the crew weren't. Not even the pussies came to say hello, but then I looked to the shore and saw the crew and the kitties, walking or running up and down a narrow strip of rocky beach. They in turn, were watched by a pack of chubby little penguins with spiky, bright orange, punk-type hairdos. They had black faces, black backs and white chests and weren't in the slightest bit afraid. Even the pussies behaved; Jasper, with Krazy on his back as usual, wandering up to have a sniff before retreating with dignity intact. Strangely, Jasper didn't want to sit and commune for hours, but after the exchange of views, the little fellas waddled closer until they were crowding up against the humans with Jasper and Krazy mingling sociably.

Having encountered penguins once before, I could imagine the comments passing between the crew as penguins en-masse are incredibly smelly. Consequently, it wasn't long before the whole crew were back in the RIB and motoring the short distance to the boat.

That was when Jasper started running around the boat, bow to stern and back again, mewling softly. After the third or fourth lap, he stopped right up in one bow and let loose with his yowl; the loud one! Even with the wind still blowing, the hackle-raising sound echoed across the water, especially downwind.

'Uh oh!' was Sandy's cry. 'What's he calling up now?'

'There's all sorts of creatures down here,' I sagely replied, able to sound like a smart-arse with the benefit of prior knowledge. 'Whales, seals, orcas. Seals are likely, although I can't see a whale coming in here, it's too shallow.'

Jasper's activity continued until he stopped running from side to side and stood, quivering, staring down at the water from the port bow. We took this to mean imminent arrival time and slowly and quietly made our way forward. Kelly was in charge of the 4K Camcorder and had it running as she approached Jasper. At first there was nothing to be seen, but then a tall, sharply raked-back fin cut the surface, closely followed by a smaller one. Both were accompanied by a cloud of fishy smelling spray from a pair of blow-holes. The water wasn't clear like in the ocean, being coloured a light milky-green by run-off from the glaciers, so it was hard to see just who the fins were attached to.

'It looks like a mother and calf of something,' Sandy softly commented. 'Do they have dolphins down here in summer?'

'Good question, but buggered if I know. There's no vertical tail fin, so it's probably a mammal of some description.'

Nothing further happened for a few minutes, until a bulbous black, shiny head poked quietly out of the water just a few metres ahead of the bow. Jasper gave a series of mewling sounds and the creature responded with a rapid series of clicks and a few high-pitched, but faint squeals. It turned side-on to us and I suddenly remembered my previous research into the island.

'It's a pilot whale. They have the long-finned variety down here, so that's probably a cow with her calf.'

Sure enough, mother sank back into the water and lifted her baby to the surface. To our horror, the baby's left front flipper was caught in a long length of blue nylon fishing net trailing back to wrap around its tail. The baby made a few little squeaks of its own and let out a big breath.

Sandy spun to me, anguish in her eyes, 'Oh Harry... please! Do something. Quickly before she gets frightened off.'

By way of answer, I turned to Dave. 'Can you dig out the double steamer wet suit you bought in St Francis Bay? It might be a bit chilly in there.'

'Way ahead of you, bro,' he called already trotting back to the cockpit, 'but I'll do it. How about you get me a couple of survival knives tied to cord with a snap-hook on the end. And maybe a pair of wire cutters. That nylon net looks tough.'

He had the steamer suit stowed in a cockpit locker and quickly shed his clothes and dragged it on. A heavy balaclava over his head and a pair of heavy booties completed the outfit as I passed him a weight belt with only two weights and with the knives and wire cutter shackled on. A pair of flippers and a face mask followed, then moments later, he slid into the freezing water with only a slight whimper of agony, before heading for the bow. I hastened to launch the RIB, but it took a few minutes to release it from the spider's web of security lines. Alex was quickly there to help and together we pulled along the side of the left hull to avoid making any noise.

Amazingly, the mother was still holding her calf up and had let Dave start to cut the thick, heavy strands of nylon netting. The baby was distressed by the activity, and the unfamiliar human presence beside it, but mum was making sounds, presumably to calm him down. Jasper was still doing his mewling from just above, which may or may not have been helping. Alex and I held back until Dave needed a hand, as a soft cheer from deck signified the release of the baby's front flipper.

Somehow, the mother kept him quiet as Dave started hacking at the tangle around the tail flukes. He was making good progress, until Corrine called down to me, 'Dave's in trouble Harry. I think the cold has got to him.' We pulled the RIB further forward and sure enough, Dave was flapping about in a uncoordinated way.

Alex didn't need telling and heaved the RIB forward as without thinking, I slid over the side into what felt like hot water, except the cold was so intense, I couldn't draw breath. Still, it was only two quick strokes to grab Dave and help Alex drag him into the RIB. By then I managed to draw a breath and gasped to Alex to unclip the cutters from Dave's belt. He did and passed them over, then turned back to check Dave's condition. I only had two more strokes to reach the baby whale's tangled tail and conscious of everything going rapidly numb, attacked the netting in a frenzy. Large pieces started falling away, until the baby gave a violent flick of his tail which gave me a hard smack on my leg, and shot forward, net-free.

I was barely aware of Alex lifting me bodily out of the water and dumping me unceremoniously beside the prostrate Dave. A minute later, I was being hoisted out of the RIB by Alex again, stripped of my clothes and hustled below by Sandy and Kelly to a luke-warm shower. When I got my voice back under control, I asked, 'How's Dave?'

'Coming good,' Sandy replied, eyeing my white mottled appendages known as fingers and toes, which had so far resisted returning to their usual healthy pink.

'Then how are the pilot whales?'

'Really good, Harry,' chipped in Kelly. 'The mother swam off after the baby, but they didn't go far. I think Jasper must have called them back, because they're just slowly swimming around the boat making squeaking sounds.'

'We've got a bag of bait fish in the cockpit freezer,' I said, my voice still trembling, 'dig it out and toss them to the baby. See if he wants a feed.'

She grinned and hustled off as Sandy finally pronounced me fit to leave the shower. I was still shivering violently and she had to dress me in several layers of soft clothing. I needed to move, so went up to the saloon in time to see Kelly pitch a handful of frozen fish off the stern. In moments, two black fins had zeroed in on the feed and were busy making sure they didn't miss any. Two more bags later, the mother, with her calf alongside, made a slow pass by the sterns, splashed her tail twice, then the pair headed for the entrance, just 200 metres away. Jasper watched them go, then came to sit beside me as I hogged all the hot air blowing from the starboard vent. Dave was already parked in front of the port one, with Corrine checking on him occasionally.

CHAPTER 15

HEARD ISLAND, THURSDAY

My mind felt a bit fuzzy for a while, but after one of Bree's lovely hot lunches, albeit a bit late, I felt pretty good and it was even better to see Dave almost back to normal. That was until Corrine called out in a low, urgent voice, 'Harry! Visitors!'

Her tone of voice made it clear that it wasn't the neighbours calling around to welcome us. I moved to the chart table where I pressed a recessed latch and a concealed locker door sprang open. I passed the wicked-looking Mini-Uzi sub-machine gun and two part-loaded mags to Corrine and grabbed the Grizzly .44 magnum pistol for myself. Alex had found the Remington TAC-14 shotgun and Sandy appeared with her Glock 22.

Then I turned to see what had Corrine so excited, and spotted a black RIB with several big men aboard, racing through the wide entrance at high speed, before turning to head straight for us. There was no sign of weapons, but the speed of their approach didn't seem friendly as they broadsided to a halt right at the stern, wetting everything, then killed the motors. There were four of them, big men, and obviously Asian. The driver wore a pair of designer reflective sunglasses and didn't bother to remove them as he rudely called out.

'Who you? What you do here? What your business?'

I made a show of stuffing the Grizzly into the waistband of my thermal pants, hoping the elastic was strong enough to keep the whole lot from slipping down to my ankles. Fortunately it was, as I stood at the top of the stern steps, looking down at him. For a few moments, I just eyeballed all of them in turn, before addressing the driver.

'I don't think that's any of your business... mate. So how about you go back to where you came from and get on with whatever it was you were doing?'

He sneered, then pointed at the Grizzly which was still threatening to disrobe me.

'You got licence? No gun allowed here.'

I gave him my impassive look, waited until he started to show signs of being impatient, then replied, 'I think that's between me and the Australian Commonwealth Police, this being Australian Territory and me being Australian. But I'm betting you and your friends aren't Australian. And I reckon you don't have a permit to be here. So why don't you tell me what you're doing here?'

'You smart-arse man. You leave here very soon!'

'We'll leave when we're good and bloody ready, sport. There's too much to see in this beautiful place. Did you know that this island and the waters for 200 miles around are a sanctuary? No fishing, no shooting, no damage to flora or fauna allowed?'

He didn't look happy with my attitude. Most people aren't when I get in this mood, but he was the one telling us to leave.

Savagely, he punched the starter buttons and as the big 200 horsepower V-6 outboards burst into life, he revved them in neutral until they screamed in protest.

Over the din, he yelled, 'You leave... no trouble! You stay... trouble!'

With that parting threat, he engaged gears with a loud clunk, then angrily shoved the throttles hard forward. Intending to impress or intimidate us, the RIB shot forward, and as an exit line, it was a noisy and dramatic way to have the last word, but unfortunately, Sunglasses hadn't bothered to warn his crew what he was doing.

Two of the big men were standing just aft of the centre console, while the third was standing in the bow, and became a classic demonstration of Newton's first law of motion.

Four hundred horsepower abruptly applied meant the boat

accelerated very quickly, but three of the four men weren't ready for the change in motion. The guy in the bow was slammed helplessly and painfully back into the control console, then flipped over the top, spearing Sunglasses in the chest and taking him in a tangle of arms and legs right back until they hit the engines. Very hard!

By rights, the other two standing in the stern should have caught them, but they had been ejected straight over the low transom beside the screaming engines and were floundering in the freezing water, blood pouring from head wounds.

Sunnies and his bowman were still locked in an embarrassingly intimate embrace, jammed down between the engines. Naturally, he didn't believe in wearing a safety tether which would've cut the power if he went too far from the controls, so at top speed, which should be around 40 knots, the RIB shot away across the lagoon, hit a small ice floe, slid right across it, then hit the rocky shore at a shallow angle, sliding and lurching fifty metres along the glacier rubble, destroying the outboards as they ground to a halt.

We couldn't see any movement from the still-entangled couple aboard, so Alex and I re-launched our RIB, tossed in a first aid kit and some old towels, leaving Dave and the girls trying to toss ropes to the near-comatose pair barely keeping their heads above water, 20-metres off *Firebird's* stern. There was no way Dave was going back in the water for anybody or anything.

We didn't have too far to go to the wrecked RIB which had attracted the attention of our punky friends, the Macaroni penguins. The faded words '*Nissabe-Maru*' on the stern of the RIB proved we were dealing with Japanese, but Alex had already pointed that out, so I said, 'They're bloody rotten whalers! Did you get the smell when they first turned up?'

'Yes, Commander, I did. I am afraid it would explain why they want us to leave. Perhaps Sandy saw one of the catchers in Sealer's Cove.'

I gave him an evil grin, 'This little clusterfuck might give us the perfect excuse to go and find out. What do you think?'

His wide grin in reply was all the encouragement I needed as we reached the beached boat with the wrecked engines. The drive legs of the motors were bent and twisted, all the blades stripped off the prop hubs and tendrils of blue smoke were still leaking out of the overheated exhaust pipes. The hapless interlocked pair were stirring and after sorting them out, the tally was two badly lacerated heads, two broken arms and several deep lacerations to their legs and hands. After using nearly all the contents of the first-aid kit, we almost stopped the bleeding and strapped up the broken arms as best we could. I'm afraid I might have been just a tiny bit rough with Sunnies when I strapped his broken arm to an overhead canopy support strut. My excuse was that I couldn't find anything else to immobilise his arm and as he was only semi-conscious, he wouldn't notice the slight discomfort or lack of mobility.

It was too bad the strut was vertical and well away from a seat.

With a perfectly straight face, Alex asked why I chose to tape the limb to the strut up as high as possible, and accepted my perfectly logical answer that 'it seemed a good idea at the time, and might slow the bleeding'. When Alex carefully pointed out that there was no bleeding, I suggested that there might be before we got them back to base. He calmly accepted that twisted logic.

We left the two whalers in their boat and adding our bow line to theirs, dragged the badly damaged RIB back into the water. Alex pointed out several badly torn sections in the aluminium skin around the bow area which would let water in, but once again accepted my answer that if we towed them fast enough, the bow would be out of the water and couldn't leak.

This standard of reasoning almost made me out to be a caring rescuer.

To test my theory, we towed them back to *Firebird* at high speed and the bow did stay out of the water, thereby proving me correct. I made the assumption that the weak hand signals from Sunglasses meant he wanted us to go faster, but Alex suggested maybe Japanese hand signals are different to Aussie ones. Still, as he had slumped unconscious again, held up solely by his tightly strapped arm, he couldn't feel much pain, could he?

Dave and the girls had finally managed to retrieve the two swimmers and had bound up their head wounds. When I pointed out that both still had blue and white hands and fingers, Dave said he'd had to overrule the girls, who wanted to strip their wet clothes off.

'To me, they looked like men who would be offended to be seen naked by strange females, so I thought we should let them keep their own clothes.'

I nodded enthusiastically, 'Excellent thinking, mate. I think they'll appreciate it when they defrost later on. I mean, remember how painful it was for us to regain circulation under the warm shower. That wouldn't be good for them just now. There must be a doctor on their ship. He or she can look after them better than we can.'

Sandy gave me one of those looks, while Corrine grinned, openly displaying the Mini-Uzi.

One of the men seemed to be trying to say something, but he had trouble forming the words.

'Probably just trying to thank us for saving them, I guess,' Dave commented, patting the man on the head.

'It's all right, old mate. You just relax like your cobber here. See, he knows he should take it easy when he's had a nasty shock. We'll run you back to your ship soon.'

The man made a few more futile attempts to speak before he lapsed back into unconsciousness.

'There!' I said to Sandy triumphantly. 'He's much better off having a snooze.'

She glared at me, but held her tongue and went below to get me more warm gear, while Alex filled the RIB's fuel tank. As I pulled on more warm layers, I noticed the automatic bilge pumps on the Japanese RIB were running flat out, so we didn't have to worry about bailing the fool thing. While I dug out an old mooring line to use as an extension to their tow line, Alex swapped the TAC-14 short-barrel 12-gauge shotgun for one of the Glock 22s we had acquired which was the same as Sandy's official police issue, and shoved two full magazines in his pocket. I tucked the Grizzly into a more secure inner pocket, checked the towlines were hooked up, then we set off.

Overnight, the wind had abated a lot more and was down to a mere Force 7, or near-gale. Still, by staying close in-shore, the swell was manageable, although the towed boat was copping a rough time as Alex played with the length of tow line trying to make it better. Or was it worse?

Nevertheless, we still managed to make 15 knots which meant the trip to Sealer's Cove took just under 50 minutes.

Sandy's initial brief glimpse through the snow squalls had been spot-on although what she didn't see was that there were three black-hulled boats rafted up in Sealer's Bay and each had the ominous and hated harpoon gun mounted on a railed-in platform sticking out over the high bow. The bridge and accommodation were all forward, while the aft end of each boat was very low to the water and the deck was open at the stern. As we neared the outside boat, a large crowd of men gathered at the rails.

Dave nudged me and said, 'I don't know if you saw, but looking past the high ground into the next bay, I caught a glimpse of the bow of a much larger boat. Could be the mother-ship?'

I nodded, 'Yeah. I thought I saw something like that too. Okay, here we go. Standby for some fun and games.'

Even though they had a gangway, it was hoisted up to the railing and no move was made to lower it. We pulled in against the side of the catcher, Dave untied our mooring line and tossed the end of the Japanese boat's bow line up to waiting hands. Then the crowd of sailors parted and a tall, fit-looking Japanese man stepped up to the rail and in perfect English, said, 'Thank you for bringing our boat back. May I ask what happened to the crew? Did you fight with them?'

I stood and shook my head. 'Your man was rather rude to us, then tried to depart at high speed without warning the crew. Two fell overboard and the other two sustained injuries from falling back against the outboards. There was no safety cut-out teether, so the boat ran up on shore at full throttle. That's what caused the damage to it, and also further injuries to the two men left aboard. We don't have a doctor aboard, so we applied first-aid to the best of our limited knowledge, and here they are.'

He barked some orders and davits for the RIB were lowered, a sailor jumping down to attach them. Then the whole RIB was hoisted aboard and stowed in a shaped cradle on the stern deck. Several men then set about extracting the four comatose men from the RIB. They gave me some strange looks when they unstrapped Sunglasses' arm from the canopy strut, but I kept playing the role of the bumbling, wealthy yachtie.

Sunglasses might remember our initial exchange, but too bad.

The tall man stepped back to the rail after examining the wrecked boat and the bashed-up crew.

'I thank you for your assistance. I will question these men when they recover. My doctor says that two of them are in a state of advanced hypothermia and may have trouble recovering. But you have been of great assistance. May I ask if you are remaining at the island for much longer?'

I shrugged, 'Don't know yet. We might stay until a decent weather window opens again and we can head for the Australian mainland. What about yourself? Staying long?'

He shook his head. 'No. We just needed to make some repairs after the storm, so will probably leave soon.'

I saluted him and said in my best bumbling manner, 'Jolly good, Captain. We'll be off then. Cheerio!'

Alex took the cue, fired up the engine and we roared away in a curve to the north-west. I turned to give a parting wave which naturally wasn't answered, allowing me to take a better look at the mother-ship, which was a lot bigger than I'd expected, looking more like a small freighter. Over the roar of our engine, I heard some faint clicks and saw Alex with a small camera firing off frames.

He gestured, 'Bree's idea.'

'Bloody good idea. I don't suppose you happened to get any of the catcher?'

He grinned smugly, 'Only about 50 frames. Including close-ups of the crew and Captain.'

'Excellent, young man!'

We had an easier run with the wind and swell behind us and were soon back on-board *Firebird*, where we were peppered with questions and hot drinks. Finally, into the silence, I said, 'I don't believe those guys are going anytime soon, so neither are we. We'll probably get another visit from them and it could be a night-time one. If Sunglasses can talk, he'll tell them we're armed, at least with pistols.'

'What about the pair we pulled aboard?' Corrine asked. 'I flashed the Mini-Uzi to keep them quiet.'

I smiled, 'The captain suggested they probably wouldn't pull through, although he didn't seem too concerned.'

Sandy, Kelly and Bree looked briefly unhappy about that, but mentally moved on when I told them, 'For the rest of our time here, we'll post full two-person watches. Those on watch will monitor radar, the masthead camera and generally keep a lookout as if we were at sea in a busy sea-lane. I'll set the camera to motion detect so if a raiding party comes by sea or land, we'll pick them up early.'

Everyone was in accord with that, so watches were set and we settled in to see what developed. At afternoon tea, I told everyone of my latest idea.

'I'm still a bit slow after my swim this morning, but I'm going to call Alan Stallman to tell him about these whalers. He'll know who to contact since protecting the Australian Economic Exclusion Zone is the Navy's job.'

'Good idea', was the consensus, but then Bree spoke up.

'A girlfriend of mine did volunteer work for Sea Guardian for a while and I still have her number. I think they should be told as well.'

I shrugged, 'I suppose it can't hurt. The more pressure we can put on these arse-holes the better. How about you call your girlfriend to tell Sea Guardian, then I'll call Alan. He'll want to hear about how the boat's going anyway.'

Bree immediately called her girlfriend Nina in Sydney and passed on the information. Apparently Nina was still closely associated with Sea Guardian and promised to call immediately since she knew their boat was in Melbourne making engine repairs, recruiting new crew, and loading supplies and fuel.

With that under way, I called Hillary and after an exchange of pleasantries, she put me through to Alan who was having a quiet day at the office.

'Hi Harry. Great to hear from you. How's the boat going?'

'Really good, Alan. I hate to say it, but you would have loved the run across from St Francis Bay. It's a bit cold and the winds did get rather strong at times, but the sailing was brilliant.'

'Hang on. What's this cold business? Last time I spoke to one of my skippers who's just two days out from Fremantle, he said it was bloody hot! So... where are you?'

I laughed, 'Well...we had a little change of plan. I thought seeing as we were going to use the top of the Roaring Forties for a boost eastward, we might as well dip into the fifties and visit Heard Island.'

There was a stunned silence of a moment.

'Harry. Heard Island is down near Antarctica! What the bloody hell are you doing down there?'

'Freezing my arse off this morning, when I had to jump in the water for a few minutes, but that's a story for later. Suffice to say, we're presently in Stephenson Lagoon on Heard Island. Go on, look it up on Google Earth. Anyway, the boat goes beautifully. She's fast and comfortable. We routinely cruise at 20 to 25 knots and can usually equal or even beat wind-speed. Even Dave, the die-hard powerboat junkie, is enjoying hand-steering.'

'Man, I'm really envious! If you weren't so damn far away, I'd come and join you. Provided the open invitation still stands?'

'Of course it does, mate. Always. But there's another reason for the call, so you might want Hillary on the line.'

'Already here, thanks Harry. Go ahead.'

I passed on the story of the Japanese whaler's visit, including the unmistakable smell of whale oil. I included the circumstances of our visit to Sealer's Cove and reported the sighting of what we thought might be a mother-ship.

'They claimed to be recovering from the storm we came in on, but we think they are actively hunting and killing whales, using Australian Territory as an operating base. There's a mother-ship and three catchers, with the mother-ship tucked in the northern corner of Atlas Cove. She's hard to spot in there.'

'Okay, thanks Harry. That's what we need to know. I've got a frigate, the Ballarat, nearly at Fremantle, but she will need re-fuelling before she can head your way.'

'Excuse me Dad, but we could speed up that deployment if Sirius got underway from Fremantle immediately. They could do an Under-Way Replenishment with Ballarat while heading south-west. If Ballarat can maintain 24 knots, she could be on station in 92 hours or 3.8 days.'

'Thank you, my lovely daughter. Well, Harry. Do you think the Japanese will remain there for that long?'

'Yes, there's a good chance they will. Especially if we bug out soonest, like maybe tomorrow morning. They might relax a bit if there's no one around to watch them.'

'Okay. Leave the rest to us. You get safely away from there and go back to doing what you had planned to do, before you got the bug to go and freeze your collective tits off.'

CHAPTER 16

HEARD ISLAND, SOUTHERN OCEAN, FRIDAY

I passed Alan's news onto the crew and to my surprise, no one objected to bailing out of our near-Antarctic adventure. The intimidating visit from the four whalers had the desired effect and even though they had made fools of themselves that morning, I felt I owed them one for spooking my friends. Especially the one we'd dubbed Sunnies.

Therefore, I took the pussies ashore for a last run on the rocky beach and to be able to say I had walked on Heard Island. Back aboard, we secured the RIB with all the extra safety straps and went around checking the rest of the boat, but everything looked good. Even the weather looked like it might co-operate for a day or two, before the next low-pressure system came blasting through.

We kicked off the watch plan that evening, and just on dusk, as expected, an RIB made a fast pass outside the lagoon entrance. Despite our heightened vigilance, the night remained quiet without any unscheduled visits. Therefore, with everyone feeling well rested, we were up at first light, breakfast prepared and eaten as I hauled in the anchors. The narrow channel was running fast with the incoming tide, but by running the quad motors at full throttle, we made enough headway. It was un-nerving to have heavy breaking waves within a few metres of either side, but the deep channel looked after us and we passed safely into deeper water and set course to the north-east.

The endless west-wind certainly did blow, but with it on our port quarter, we fled into the dawn with reduced mainsail and jib set and drawing hard. The swell was also moderate and even George

145

was able to hold a reasonably steady course, but for safety at the speeds we were hitting, we hand-steered. We saw 30 knots a few times, which was a new and exhilarating experience for everyone.

The next day just as we were finishing lunch in the comfort of the saloon, the radar traffic alarm sounded its soft chimes. The clever thing gave a gentle alert if the traffic wasn't going to run into us, but if it was likely it would, then the tone changed dramatically to something much more attention-getting. On this occasion, it showed a fast-moving target on a reciprocal course, with the closest point of approach being five miles.

'This has to be the *Ballarat*,' Dave commented. 'No one else would be driving at that speed on this heading.'

I agreed, and with a sense of mischief, looked up the Navy ship-to-ship, short range radio frequencies and found *Ballarat's* normal in-port, non-secure channel.

Dialling it up on my multi-band radio, I called them.

'*Ship on Navy UHF channel, say again callsign?*' came the swift response.

'This is *Firebird*, Navy. Departed Heard Island 06:00 yesterday for Fremantle. Your targets were still in place as of that time. We're the whistle-blowers.'

Silence for 30 seconds, then a different voice came back,

'*Copied that* Firebird. *Can you give authentication?*'

'Roger Navy. Try Stallman and Stevens.'

'*Copied that Commander. Any additional info updates?*'

'Targets are one mother-ship with three black-hulled catchers. Mother-ship appears to be established in Atlas Cove, while the catchers are rafted up in Sealer's Bay. Aggressive crews and probably armed.'

'*Thanks Commander. Safe travelling,* Ballarat *clear.*'

'You too. *Firebird* clear.'

It was barely an hour later, when the SatPhone sounded off with a message for Bree from her Sea Guardian girlfriend, to say the

George Ambrose was presently re-fuelling in Christchurch, and would be heading for the island by the evening.

'It's about to get crowded down there,' Sandy commented. 'I'm glad we bailed out. Those Japanese are going to be a bit pissed with both the Aussie Navy and Sea Guardian on their case.'

'Well, we won't have to worry about tripping across those guys again,' I said cheerfully, 'so we can put this down to an interesting experience and go have some relaxation. I might tell Alan we spoke with *Ballarat*.'

With Alex and Dave taking turns at the wheel for now, I called Hillary and was passed straight through to Alan.

'Glad you were able to talk to Ballarat. *Jim Sanders is a good operator. What's your next port of call?'*

'That'd be Fremantle to clear into Australia. Dave and Corrine want to fly back to the Gold Coast on business, so we'll carry on from there.' I had an idea of what was behind his question, and he didn't disappoint.

'Great! How'd you like two replacement crew for a couple of weeks? We could meet you in Fremantle.'

I chuckled, 'Sure Alan. I'll be a pleasure to have you and Hillary aboard. We were just going to poke around the Tasmanian west coast for a while, so you can bail out whenever you need to. We should make landfall on Tuesday afternoon, but I'll update you when we're closer in.'

'Thanks Harry. I appreciate that and look forward to seeing the new Firebird. *Talk soon.'*

I terminated the call, then told the crew what was happening. The ever-practical Sandy, in housekeeping mode, suggested, 'Alan can take over the port midships cabin and Hillary could have the port bow cabin. They both have an ensuite.'

'Yep. That should spread everyone out nicely. I should have known he'd arrange his schedule to get aboard. It'll be good to have them back - they're good crew and good company.'

The next three days produced some exciting weather and ocean

behaviour, but thankfully nothing else. As we left latitude 50°
south behind, and climbed up through the 40s, it seemed like the
Southern Ocean was reluctant to loosen its grip on us. The main
feature was a powerful train of small, but intense low-pressure systems which came blasting at us from the west, with very little time
between them.

At first, we tried to make best use of the conditions to work
north as quickly as possible, but the increasing size of the swell and
the wind strength, demanded a more prudent approach.

Therefore, the Jordan drogue was heaved over the side again, sail
dropped and a weary crew took some rest. Deployment was just in
time since the seas quickly rose to alarming proportions, many with
a short breaking crest. But the now-familiar feeling of a huge hand
gently, but firmly holding the boat back from accelerating down a
steep wave face was hugely reassuring.

The downside to running with wind and waves meant we didn't
make much progress toward Fremantle, so I called Hillary to advise
we'd be a day or two late.

*'Actually, the delay will work out really well,' she said. 'Dad decided
to make a semi-official visit out of this, so we're staying at HMAS
Stirling on Garden Island. He's having a lovely time visiting all
the ships in harbour and causing a lot of overtime as skippers and
crews prepare for the unexpected inspections, but even though it's
low-key for him, he's stirring things up. I think the CO will be
happy to see you, so you can take him away!*

*When you arrive, Dad has organised for your inbound Cus-
toms and Immigration clearance inspection to take place here on
Garden Island, so just come straight to the small-boat docks in
Careening Bay, on the inside of the 'L-shaped' wharf. All supplies
will be brought out by delivery van from the mainland, if you let
me have the list I'm sure Bree has already made up.'*

'That's very generous and helpful, thanks Hillary. It'll sure save
messing around in Fremantle; that harbour gets a lot crowded at

times. Anyway, we should be there Thursday morning and I'll call you for final instructions when we're close.'

'Fine Harry. Looking forward to seeing you all. Cheers.'

Two days later on Thursday at 06:30, we were rounding the northern tip of Garden Island in shallow water, with a brisk west-south-west breeze whistling through the rigging and the odd lick of spray lifting onto the decks. The whole crew, pussies as well, were on deck to see real, un-frozen Australian soil again. The temperature was 18°C with the promise of 26°C later in the day, and not a minus in sight.

As we turned south-south-east for the run down to Careening Cove, a grey, angular shape loomed out of the sea haze ahead of us. Initially, all we could see was a broad, flat stern which was obviously a helideck, with a clean, minimalist superstructure ahead. She was bigger than a Armidale-class patrol boat, but smaller than the ANZAC-class frigate like *Ballarat*. As we closed rapidly on her, the clean, sweeping lines of her hull shape became apparent. There was a decent size gun in a turret on the foredeck and I thought it might be a visiting foreign Navy ship, but as we drew abeam, holding 28 to 30 knots in the calm water in the lee of the island, I saw she flew the White Ensign but had no bow number.

As we scooted past in relative silence at about three times her speed and I admired the beautiful rake to her bow, the marine VHF radio cleared its throat and a dry female voice announced, *'Some people just can't help showing off... can they, Commander?'*

It took a few moments, then the voice recognition kicked in, 'Good morning Lieutenant Stahall. What are you doing on that over-grown stink-boat?'

The familiar, throaty chuckle came back with perfect clarity, *'Thanks to you and a certain action further north of here, as well as the one in the South Pacific, some of us scored a promotion, but more later. We've been told to look out for a private sailing craft heading for Navy territory, but it seems to have grown a bit since our last visit. Please explain?'*

'As you say, more on it later, but for now this is a new *Firebird*, 23 feet longer, much faster and this is the shakedown and delivery trip. We're ex-South Africa.'

'*My goodness! You do lead an interesting life, Commander. We'll let you go find a space for the monster, and catch up shortly. Our Skipper is keen to see you, as are some of the crew.* Arafura *clear.*'

'*Firebird* clear.'

Everyone had heard the exchange and all knew the crew of the *Glenelg* but what Clare Stahall was doing on what seemed to be the protype of the new Offshore Patrol Vessel was a mystery. And that mystery was put aside because we had to find our way to the correct berth in an all-Navy collection of boats and ships. As we approached the final point before the harbour, the boat's mobile phone rang and Alan was briefly on the line.

'*Morning Harry. Just to advise your marine band VHF channel will be 07, and the Harbour Master will tell you where to go. I'll see you at the wharf. Cheers.*'

Hastily, I dialled up the channel as Alex pushed the various buttons that furled all our sails and woke up the motors.

The Harbour Master was all business and noted, as per standard operating procedure, we were flying the yellow 'Q' for quarantine flag from our shrouds.

'*I have Customs waiting for you, Commander. There is a work-boat approaching if you'd follow it to the wharf.*'

'Copy that. Follow the work boat, aye.'

Ten minutes later, we were berthed just ahead of one of the small-boat floating pontoons designated for personnel transfers to and from the Navy ships which lay at moorings in the bay. A jovial Customs chap and his young female assistant were quite intrigued to be called out to process a private yacht at one of Australia's main Naval bases, but the hovering presence of a Rear Admiral in full dress regalia forestalled too many questions. The presence of the two cats put them in a bit of a predicament, until I offered to sign a Stat Dec to say that since leaving Australian waters, they hadn't been ashore.

I didn't actually sign the document, merely offered to do so, thereby avoiding perjury, but it did the trick, especially when I solemnly promised the cats would serve a two-week quarantine period on board. Customs had a cursory look around, but were more interested in the boat itself than looking for contraband. Finally, they stamped and signed various papers and we were free to go.

Alan and Hillary were then able to sit and chat over morning tea served in the cockpit, with a parade of curious sailors finding excuses to check out the big cat and wonder why the Fleet Commander Australia was so cosy with the crew. At least we'd had time on the run into harbour to do a fresh-water hose down of the upper works to get rid of a serious build-up of salt, so our new girl looked reasonably presentable.

Naturally, Alan wanted to hear the story of our voyage in reverse, starting with the whale boats at Heard Island.

'*Ballarat* has arrived on station and reported the whaling mothership and three catchers are still there. Jim Sanders also reported they weren't happy to be challenged about their movements and intentions. He said to pass on his thanks for the heads-up about their attitude. It saved him a bunch of drama.'

'I'm glad they've been sprung. I hate what they do – it's a filthy business!'

'True. Anyway, he's going to hang around the area for a while, doing the normal patrol which we share turn-about with the French at Port-Aux-Français. They won't dare do any whale catching while the Navy's in the area, so hopefully, they'll move on. Now. What are your plans, Harry? How long do you want to stay here?'

'Really, only long enough to re-supply and top the small amount of diesel we've used, but Hillary seems to have the food side organised with Bree, and we can re-fuel over at Fremantle. Then it just depends on when you're ready.'

He shook his head, 'I think the Navy can spare a couple of hundred litres of diesel for the Fleet Commander's transport. Say the word and I'll have a fuel barge brought over. And as for me, I've inspected everything which opens and shuts and had all the fun I wanted to have. I reckon the base has seen enough of me for a while, so once you're re-fuelled and re-provisioned, we could go. I'm in your hands from here on.'

I grinned, 'Actually Alan. The fuel barge might be a bit of an overkill.' I looked at Alex who smoothly said, 'About 45 litres would be enough, thanks Admiral. Most of that was used by the diesel heaters.'

Alan looked confused. 'I know you sail a lot, but you've come from South Africa. You must have used a lot more fuel than that?'

'Fortunately, Alan, electric motors don't use diesel. Our batteries and capacitors are fully charged thanks to solar, the wind generators and sailing re-generation.'

'You've gone fully electric? This I've got to see!'

Over-riding Hillary's objections, Alan peeled off his dress uniform jacket, heavy with gold braid and ribbon bars and was shown one spotlessly clean engine room. It was used more for storage and water-makers, since each twin motor stack, sitting atop the two sail-drives mounted side-by-side, was no bigger than a small oil drum. This led into a full tour and explanation of the how and why of all the electric systems, until Hillary forcibly had to drag him away for his last official duties.

Before they left, I asked Hillary about the supply lists we'd emailed through.

'Be here in one hour,' she said briskly, 'including a few extra items Bree just thought of.'

'Okay. We could leave this afternoon if it suits. What do you think?'

Alan beamed, 'That'll be perfect. But does your crew want more of a rest?'

Sandy answered for Kelly, Bree and Alex by saying, 'Nah! Now it's not snowing, and the temperature is in positive double-digits, we can lie around anywhere. Let's get to Tassie first.'

Hillary dug her mobile phone out and started making arrangements for some jerry cans of fuel and their personal gear to be brought to *Firebird*.

'OK, that'll suit me and the *Stirling's* CO. I'm really looking forward to seeing if this thing lives up to its promise of speed.'

I laughed at his enthusiasm, 'Just ask the crew of *Arafura*. They were doing about 10 knots coming down the island and we passed them doing 30. But I meant to ask you; that's the new OPV, but I didn't think they were even built yet, let alone ready to enter service?'

'They aren't, but *Arafura* is the first-in-class and is one of two to be built here in Western Australia. In an unusual but sensible move, the Naval Acquisition Board decided to build the first one well ahead of the others. Australia wanted a lot of changes from the original German PV80 design. Therefore, to make sure all the planned mods work as intended, they decided to build a test mule first. It's also to see if we needed to make even more changes before we built the rest. Either way, this is the most sensible thing the Navy has done in years, but I didn't say that!

And to prove the idea, we've been told to do as much real-world stuff with her we can. She's been patrolling off-shore up past Ashmore Reef and along the coast to your old stamping grounds, just shaking everything down or trying to see what's going to break. There's a long list of stuff to change, but not much has broken, so in a few weeks, after all the minor changes are made, I'm going to send her over to the East coast to hang about for a while.'

'She's a pretty boat, but I was surprised to hear Lieutenant Stahall aboard.'

He chuckled, 'You'll be even more surprised when I tell you the rest. I needed to do something good with Paul Davy; he's turned out to be my top patrol boat skipper. Then this opportunity came to do some extended beta-testing on the first of the new *Arafura*-class, and it was perfect. Now we have an ideal stepping stone where a good skipper can move fairly easily from a patrol boat with 25 crew, to a 40-crew Offshore Patrol Boat.'

'I presume he took Lieutenant Stahall with him?'

Alan laughed again, 'He took most of his crew with him. It made good sense so I didn't grumble too much.'

'What about Barbara Peters? That is one competent lady!'

'You're right. Much too good to keep backing up Paul. I gave her *Glenelg* and a fresh, but experienced crew. They're up north at the moment, and doing well.'

'Really good to hear! We all like Barbara.'

Just then, there was a hail from the wharf, and there was Paul Davy, Clare Stahall, Jane Glen proudly wearing Lieutenant's stripes on her rather smart-looking blue Disruptive Pattern Navy Uniform, Terry Boone now a Petty Officer, as was Gillian Smith, and Richard Jackson, still a Leading Seaman.

Alan took the opportunity to leave and say his goodbyes to the Base CO, while we caught up with Paul's doings. But first, there was a teary re-union with Jane, Gillian, Terry and Richard who struggled to express their gratitude for the massive increase in their personal worth, courtesy of the Indonesian operation.

Paul took over, raving about his new boat, then demanded to be shown around *Firebird*.

'You were fairly scooting when you went past us!' he exclaimed with a grin. 'What was she doing?'

'Thirty!' I replied proudly. 'And as quick as it was, we saw well over it a couple of times on the way down to Heard Island. It's magical stuff.'

He pulled a face, 'We're flat out at 22 knots with the wind up our arse. After the first sea trial, I raised the possibility of fitting a booster turbine driving a water-jet, just like *Seeker* has, except we'd need something like 10,000 KW to get 1600 tons moving much quicker. Still, this is what we're supposed to do; work out if the design needs modifying and make proposals.'

They stayed and chatted for another 30 minutes, also getting re-acquainted with Jasper and Krazy who remembered them and were delighted to see their old friends. Just as they were leaving, the delivery van with our supplies arrived, stacked high with what Bree and Kelly had deemed 'essential' stuff. I know it made a large dent in my black Visa card, lowered the waterline and clogged up the saloon until the girls got everything stowed. Lucky we had the extra space!

It was then time for Dave and Corrine to leave to catch their flight back east, and the van driver kindly offered them a lift to the city. The large tip I handed over might have helped bring out his generous streak.

Alan and Hillary's gear arrived, keeping Hillary busy stowing it away, delighted with the size and comfort of the spacious cabins.

A workboat turned up with three lonely jerry cans of diesel with a cheerful crew of young sailors offering to top-off the relatively small diesel tanks for the heaters and back-up generators. After promising not a drop would be spilt on *Firebird's* glowing red decks, I let them aboard where they peppered me with questions about the boat, until Hillary signed the docket and then it was lunch-time.

It was 14:00 before Alan re-appeared, still in uniform, although I wasn't prepared for the departure ceremony accorded to the Australian Fleet Commander, regardless of what vessel he chooses to depart in. There was much saluting with horns and sirens blowing which was very moving as we silently motored across the bay before hoisting all sail and heading north to round the top of Garden Island. I noted in the log, that we'd been in port just eight hours.

CHAPTER 17

It was good to be back in Australian waters, with Australian weather I could interpret for myself, and where it wasn't snowing most the time. Our brief time in port at *HMAS Stirling* had been productive, but hardly restful, so in many ways, it was good to be back at sea again. A cold front was due in a day or two, so the normal pattern of north-westerlies ahead of the change were in place.

Those winds forced us to tack right over to the breakwaters of the huge shipbuilding yards of Austal and Civmec where many of Australia's navy ships are built. Then a very close reach which tested Alan's ability as helmsman, finally allowed us to bear away enough to clear the tip of Garden Island, while dodging the many patches of shoal water. I was pleased the new boat actually pointed higher than the old *Firebird*, a good thing for a catamaran which traditionally weren't much better than a square-rigger for going to windward.

Alan was in his element, having taken the wheel as soon as people stopped saluting him and we cleared harbour. He couldn't stop praising the SIF 80, especially when he was able to tack and make the fast run across the top of Garden Island. The call of, 'exceeding wind speed', became a bit repetitive and thankfully, he soon got over it.

Hillary confided that Alan had been heavily involved in the new Offshore Patrol Boat project from the start, and to an extent, it was his neck on the block if it turned into another submarine fiasco. This was why he'd come up with, and got approval for, the build of the first boat as a test mule. They'd both been putting in long hours and even ahead of my call, had been at *HMAS Stirling* for several weeks going on the sea-trials and making sure the necessary changes were done properly.

'He needs this break so badly, and he's been talking about it non-stop, because there's just one major problem with the boat. Paul made note of it after the first sea-trial, and that is the lack of speed.'

I nodded, 'Yes. He told me and I agree. Twenty-two knots isn't enough, but he said he'd raised the possibility of fitting a gas turbine with a water jet as a booster engine, the same as *Seeker* has. Is the Navy flexible enough to let you do something like that?'

'Yes, we could, although it's a big change. Dad has already had talks with the designers in Germany and apparently, the problem occurred when the basic boat design was discussed and needed to be changed to suit Australian conditions and operational requirements. Someone in Defence Acquisitions rated long range as far more important than being able to sprint at high speed occasionally. Therefore, lower-powered diesels which were more economical were specified. But you should talk to Dad about this, if you can prise him off the wheel!'

I grinned, 'Easily fixed. I'll just talk to him there.'

Alan confirmed all Hillary had said, but then I had one question, 'If you have a fair amount of discretion to change things as needed, what would it take to go ahead and fit a turbine and water-jet? I mean, apart from the financials, is there space? Maybe the factory has already made provision for something like that on the centre line. The boat does have a wide bum.'

He looked thoughtful. 'Now there's a thought. An aftermarket fit-out to an existing boat. When I talked to the designers, they just went straight to the story of the lower-powered diesels. I didn't get to discuss fitting a turbine, although they did say one customer had done it.... Hillary!'

She was by his side in seconds, notebook in hand. 'Yes, Dad?'

'Would you contact Lurssen in Germany and ask who has fitted a turbine booster engine and waterjet to one of their OPVs? Then ask if there are any provisions already in place to accommodate those units. When I talked to them last time, I forgot you have to be very precise with your questions.'

'I thought you *were* very precise,' she countered, 'but I'll send an email to the factory asking for Herr Langer to call ASAP.'

'OK. That'll have to do, although I hate wasting time.'

I showed her where the radio, SatPhone and computer set-up was, then Hillary sent the email. Surprisingly, not five minutes later the phone rang, and when I answered, a man's voice, in perfect English, announced himself to be Dr Martin Langer of Lurssen Shipyards, Bremen Germany.

'You're working late, Herr Langer,' I commented, 'but Admiral Stallman will be happy to talk to you. Please stand-by.'

I passed the phone to Alan, left him to his discussion and stood with Alex who had taken over the wheel.

We were heading south, the brisk nor'westerly whistling up our skirts from the right rear, and sending us slicing through the backs of the low swell waves at 20 knots. It was a warm wind, so it wasn't long before the girls had retired to the trampolines to doze in the sun, memories of the snow and ice of the far southern latitudes quickly fading.

'Everything feeling okay?' I asked Alex.

He gave a big smile, 'Extra good, Commander! She flies like a freed bird. This really is a beautiful sailing boat.'

We sat in communal and comfortable silence as the miles slipped past, Alan and Hillary in the saloon had their heads together whilst Alan had the SatPhone in almost continuous use. Finally, they come out and Alan updated us on the latest drama.

'Bloody Treasury!' was his opening remark. 'We have the money, we have permission to do whatever it takes to get this prototype working properly before the others are constructed, but they insist on taking it through a Committee. Anyway, I'm working on short-circuiting that one.'

'Did Lurssen's have any helpful suggestions?'

'Yes, Dr Langer was most helpful and said it has been done by another customer although he wouldn't name them. He said the units could be retrofitted to the *Arafura* quite easily as the basic mountings are already in place. That sort of encouragement is all I need to try to ram this through. Apparently, Rolls-Royce have both the engine and the Kamewa water-jet units available and are so keen to fit them to a RAN ship, they're offering a big discount. Anyway, I've placed a number of calls to several high places, so we'll see what shakes down.'

Alan retired to the saloon and continued to plot strategy with Hillary, and make further SatPhone calls, leaving a contented Alex on the wheel. By 16:30 we were off a town called Augusta, located right on the south-west corner of the continent, where we turned to the south-east for the evening run down to the city of Albany with its large, sheltered port. As everything was functioning well aboard, there was no need to stop. The north-west wind continued, bringing the scent of the desert and the occasional dust storm which even reached out to where we sailed at speed, 50 miles off-shore.

The forecast was for a particularly vigorous cold front to be chasing us, and it became a race to see if we could gain the excellent shelter of the beautiful East Telegraph Bay just off north-west Tasmania in time. I'd planned to hug the coastline, but reports of wide-spread damage on land behind us and several ships needing rescue after encountering the storm, made me change course to make a direct run at the islands. Sandy was the only other person aboard who'd seen these beautiful un-spoiled islands with me on my first operation.

Naturally, there were many other bolt-holes to dive into if we looked like getting caught, like Port Lincoln, Kangaroo Island, Portland or the picturesque Apollo Bay with its very small harbour. However, it became a challenge and the whole crew were behind the effort as we kept driving hard, day and night, with the front gaining on us from the south-west. We saw well over

30 knots of boat speed on many occasions before the swell built up to uncomfortable heights. In the end, it was down to hours, as we rounded up into the familiar surroundings of East Telegraph Bay, on Three Hummock Island – dropping two anchors in the shallows right up in the little cove at the north end of the bay at 15:00 on Saturday afternoon.

I dropped our lightweight stern anchor as we motored gently in close to shore, releasing the two main anchors in the shallow water near the beach. The island was covered with low scrub and a small headland just behind the beach offered some protection from the worst of the expected blow. Behind us, the bay was open water all the way across the top of Tasmania to Flinders Island, but tucked into our protected little cove, there was no swell and just the strong north-west wind carrying the scent of the Manuka Myrtle and Banksia, while bringing the rattling sounds of the Swamp Paper-Bark trees, thrashing in the gusting wind. As the radar showed the main squall line still about an hour away, I asked Sandy, Kelly and Bree to take the RIB and the two pussies ashore to run wild for a little while on the clean, white sand of the long, curving beach which stretched more than two kilometres to the south. I didn't bother warning the other two girls about the large and active population of tiger snakes on the island; Sandy would definitely remember! Luckily, they didn't stay long since the light was quickly fading.

When the strong north-westerly wind dropped to fitful gusts, then died away to an oppressive, uneasy calm, I consulted the radar to see where the leading edge of the storm actually was. Although the sun had long been blotted out by a sharp-edged wall of green-black cloud, boiling upward in massive billows more than 20 kilometres high, it was what was coming at us at ground level like a runaway train which concerned me most. Daylight was a distant memory by the time we secured the RIB and double-checked the deck for any loose items.

Then with a strange, whooshing sound which quickly grew in

volume, the gust front swept across the island. Roaring down off the scrubby higher ground, it lifted a stinging cloud of sand off the beach, turning the water off our bows into instant foam, then slammed into *Firebird* like a solid wall. The boat was shoved bodily back against the restraint of the twin anchors, the rigging giving out an eerie, whistling scream, while the carbon mast made its usual impression of an bass organ pipe and droned loudly somewhere around lower 'G'.

The storm raged for the next four hours with howling winds and driving rain, which was quite deafening as it pounded the decks. Stabbing fingers of lightning with the accompanying crash of thunder made everyone flinch since some were very close. We luckily didn't cop a strike, although the instant crash of thunder following the flash told of their closeness. I'd learned a trick pilots use, which was to turn all lights up to maximum brightness to de-sensitise our eyes in storms like this and it helped keep vision intact.

Morning dawned by reference to the clock only. It was pitch black outside, and a chill wind still made mournful noises through the rigging, but nothing like we had experienced. A tour of the upper deck by the light of the spreader lights, showed *Firebird* covered in a thick carpet of green, composed of thousands of sandy leaves and assorted bits of plant matter stripped off the trees and shrubs upwind.

The salt-water deck-wash hose was needed to shift all the greenery overboard, but I wasn't in any hurry to head for Wynyard. Although it was our next port of call on this socialising leg of our trip, the cloud cover was only just above the mast-head, and the occasional rain squall marched through, rinsing the salt off the decks and fittings. The air temperature was more like August rather than March, so I was happy to stay inside the warm saloon where the crew had the diesel heaters running and lovely breakfast smells were coming from the galley. At least it wasn't snowing!

Alan and Hillary went back to work the phones again, until Alan finally gave a soft cheer and announced, 'We did it! Treasury caved in and said we could go ahead with the turbine fit-out. There are strings attached, of course, which means my head remains on the block if costs blow-out or if the fool thing makes no difference to the boat's performance.'

He was more cheerful after talking to Rolls-Royce who were so keen to get a RAN order, they waived all shipping and install costs on top of discounting the cost of the units.

'I've told Paul to arrange to dry-dock the boat as soon as R-R have the engine and jet drive in WA, which should be just two days; Rolls Royce are prepared to fly them out on special charter.'

He was tremendously relieved to have the upgrade approved and under way, and looked more relaxed almost immediately

'The lack of any sprint capability has been the main snag in the program so far,' he confided. 'It's a lovely design otherwise and Paul has only had very minor teething troubles. Hopefully, this will turn it into a very useful class of patrol boat.'

In total we spent three days at Three Hummock Island, with the weather improving all the time, although another cold front was forecast for two days hence.

'Let's leave in the morning,' I announced at breakfast on Thursday. 'The nor'wester should be well established by then and from memory, it's only a three to four-hour trip to Wynyard with a good breeze and that was in the old *Firebird*.'

So, we left around lunch-time next day and made the familiar fast run to the pretty little harbour of Wynyard at the mouth of a small creek with the golf course on one bank and the town on the other. I anchored out in the main stream the same as last time, shut everything down and took the whole crew ashore to welcome beers, wine and good company at the pub.

Dear old Mavis, the publican, was the first to recognise and greet Sandy and me, making a big fuss of our return, as well as making the rest of the crew feel at home by setting us up at a big table out the front on the veranda.

While I was ordering drinks, from out of the gloom at the back of the bar area came a familiar gravelly voice, 'That's not that poncy bloke with all the beaut sheilas, is it Mavis? What's he doing back here then? Probably come to poach some of our girls. I'll bet he hasn't brought any of his own lovelies for me to check out!'

Mavis chuckled, 'Sorry about old Ernie, Harry. You remember what he's like.'

'Yep, I do and it's what I'd expect from him, thank heavens. I'm really glad to see nothing's changed. You'd better slip him a beer or two on me for old times' sake.'

She pulled him a schooner first, then did our order.

'It's just as well you haven't forgotten your manners, young fella,' he growled. 'I'll be out to visit you in a few minutes, and I want to see some lovelies. And I'll be watchin' you don't poach any local lasses with talk of adventure on the high seas in a flash boat!'

'Ernie! You behave yourself, you silly old fart! And leave my cus-tomers in peace. They don't want to hear any of your nonsense.' Mavis scolded him as I laughingly collected the tray of drinks and headed for our table out front.

'Of course they want to be bothered by me, you silly old git! It's my job! Checking out the sheilas and drinking all the beers this young fella buys me.'

I warned the crew to expect a visit from old Ernie any min-ute, and he didn't disappoint. I'd barely sat down when his skinny, stooped form came shuffling out through the doors and lurched up to the table.

'Well bless my soul. You really have brought some lovelies for old Ernie to appreciate. Hello ladies. I hope this young fella has been looking after you? Especially you, my red-haired beauty!' he said to Sandy, who jumped up and gave the old fella a hug.

'Ahhh. Thank you. That does me no end of good, me darlin'. I remember you from last time. It's been nearly two years since you came here to brighten all our lives. Did those bikie fellas get upset when you went off with this bloke on his flash boat, instead of sharing yourself around the gang?'

The Admiral spluttered into his beer, and while Hillary and Kelly giggled, Ernie cast a shrewd eye around the table.

'You've got a bit of a mixed bag of crew here this time, Skipper. You aren't heading into strife again, are you?'

Alan looked at him sharply, but relaxed again when Ernie shuffled around and shook his hand. 'I still have a few wits about me and can recognise a military man when I see one. I'm guessing Navy and a senior rank. Welcome to our humble and happy little town, sir.'

Alan was slightly stunned by Ernie's quick assessment and I could see he was also surprised at the strength of Ernie's grip.

'Don't mind our bullshit, sir,' Ernie said quietly, 'we're all quite fond of this young fella and his ladies. We haven't told him yet what happened after he left here last time, but if it helped him avoid some of the trouble chasing him, it was worthwhile. We just enjoy having a bit of a go at each other sometimes... err, well... most times.'

Alan nodded, 'Thanks Ernie, I respect that. I'm quite fond of the silly young bugger myself!'

'Right! That's enough of that there nonsense,' Ernie mumbled, walking around the table, patting Bree, Kelly and Hillary lightly on the shoulder as he passed, 'Old Ernie's got to get home to catch up on some beauty sleep.'

He stopped and pointed a gnarled, old finger at me. 'Seeing as no one is chasing you this time Skipper, I hope you're going to stay around for a few days. I wouldn't mind having a look over that flash new boat you've got out there, and to meet the funny-looking dog what's still peering over the side at us.'

With that exit line, Ernie wobbled his way to the steps and lurched down to the street, with one arm waved over his head in farewell.

'Well,' I said into the partial vacuum left in his wake, 'that's Ernie. Fisherman, pub regular, unofficial town mayor and according to Mavis the publican, a multi-millionaire who owns half the town's commercial real estate.'

'Fascinating character,' murmured Alan, a thoughtful look on his face.

'He seemed to connect with you straight away, Dad,' Hillary commented quietly.

Alan nodded, and said softly 'Yes, he did. Didn't he?'

Ernie's comments about the last visit prompted a chorus of calls for the story to be told, so I gave in and tried to give the short version of the adventure I'd mentally dubbed, 'My Hitch Hikers.' Unfortunately, the short version wasn't anywhere near enough for the crew, so the whole sordid tale had to come out. I wasn't far into it, when Mavis came out to see if we wanted another round. That was a given, of course, but when she heard the tale I was telling, she asked me to hold, went inside and roused out her son, who had taken up residence, to look after the bar. She brought out a round of drinks, pulled up a chair and settled in to listen, for the first time, to what had brought me to her sleepy Wynyard in the first place.

Because the whole story took some telling, there were pee breaks, drink replenishment breaks and as the soft gloom of dusk settled quietly across the little port, a break to order meals. The same pretty young girl who had played guitar and sang for the Saturday night bar crowd on our last visit, was the cook's helper and came to take our orders.

'Tell Beryl to break out the good fillet that's been aging in the cool room,' Mavis said to Wendy, 'and I'll eat out here as well.'

She gave a lovely smile as she went back to the kitchen, and I picked up the tale of my Hitch Hikers. Dinner was a distant memory and the dregs of a bottle of Galway Pipe were being disposed of by the Admiral, before my story came to a close.

Oddly, I found that in many ways, there was great relief in being able to share the terrors and horrors of that time, as well as the wonderful fun we'd had.

'So that's the tale of my Hitch Hikers,' I said in conclusion, 'although only Kelly hasn't had the dubious pleasure of the second encounter with the late Mr Xavier, but that's another story for another time.'

Mavis looked at me. 'I'd like to hear it too, please Harry, but as you say, not now. However, I feel obliged to add a brief footnote to your tale.'

My raised eyebrows invited her to go on.

'After your visitor, 'John' left, we had two hard men come calling asking the staff questions about a person who had been sighted going upstairs that night. I tried to pass him off as being my brother, but they had a photo and wanted more information. To cut the story short, two of them grabbed one of my cleaning staff, a young girl, on her way home from work, blindfolded her, and took her to a local football ground where she was pegged out on the grass. All her clothes were removed and they questioned her for some time. She said they slapped her around a bit, but otherwise didn't molest her. After questioning, she was untied, allowed to dress and to make her way home. Unfortunately, her level of anxiety at the time was extreme, although she managed to get back here without help.'

'Shit! I'm so sorry to hear that. Has she recovered?'

'Yes. It was Wendy, the girl who served us tonight. I have her living here in the hotel and she does whatever she can to help out.'

'But she sang for the bar one Saturday night. She was terrific! The only consolation I can offer is that the man who was organising the hunt at that time has suffered a rather terrible fate.'

Mavis smiled grimly, 'Good to know and I'll pass it on, but we look after our own here and it was Ernie who tracked those two blokes down. The silly buggers stayed on a few more days in a motel on the outskirts of town. He reported that when he found them, they already had a few bruises and black eyes, as though someone else had got to them first, but after he and our maintenance man were done, they weren't really able to walk or talk.

They were taken to Burnie Hospital where there were already two guys from the Saturday morning fracas in the main street. As I say, we look after our own, but we know it was in a good cause, so no blame on you, dear boy. We're just grateful the lady and her two daughters got out of it alright.'

Through the course of the story, the occasional tear around the table turned to disgust, then to happiness, when the bad guys got whopped big-time with some home-grown justice.

Mavis turned to me, 'Well, Harry. I thank you for your story and I hope my little contribution has filled in a few gaps. I'll leave you in peace now and as Ernie said, please stay at least a few days. We like to see friendly, happy faces around and you're now a part of our family here in Wynyard.'

She went back to the bar, leaving Alan, Hillary, Alex, Bree and Kelly to look in wonder at Sandy and me.

'You two really have been getting into some serious trouble,' Alan finally said.

I smiled, 'They mostly are for a good cause, Alan. Although... trouble often seems to find us.'

Sandy lightly punched my arm, 'I hope you aren't having one of your prophetic moments, my dear? We would all like a quiet time for the next few weeks.'

I held out my arms in supplication. 'How should I know? I'm just a trouble magnet and I don't have any control over what happens. Think Karma!'

'Oh dear,' Sandy groaned in mock despair. 'Harry really is getting philosophical on us. This will be trouble!'

CHAPTER 18.

WYNYARD, WEDNESDAY, STRAHAN

On Wednesday we showed Ernie and Mavis over the new *Firebird*; both in awe of the space everywhere. We talked them into staying for lunch and they were introduced to Jasper and Krazy cat. Ernie was blown away by Jasper who in turn, quite took to the old fella.

That night, I took both pussies the short distance across the creek to the Golf Club for a good run on the grass and both had a ball. Naturally, Jasper found some rabbits to chase, finally coming to my whistle, with tongue hanging out, panting from the unaccustomed exertion.

Thursday, the next cold front hit in the afternoon, but nowhere near as violent as the one which had greeted us at Three Hummocks Islands. Still, it blew hard, rain pelted down, and the temperature plummeted, but we stayed warm, dry and comfortable.

Alan was receiving regular reports from Paul Davy regarding the progress of work on the *Arafura* and all was good.

'Knowing how the engine and jet unit is fitted in an OPV,' he reported, 'Rolls-Royce sent a complete wiring harness as well, so Paul says that it's almost a plug-n-play type of installation. That's not including having to cut a hole in the bottom for the intake and another in the stern for the jet nozzle, but they have the templates for that, so the work is going quickly.'

In the end, we stayed five days in the tiny, sheltered harbour, before the winds settled down to a stiff south-westerly. I cautioned the others to expect a big sea to be running, although the winds and swell would be moderate for the first run west due to the proximity

168

of the land.

On Monday we lifted the anchor, the cleaning water-jets ridding it of mud and silt, and motored quietly for the entrance. Some farewell calls echoed across the limpid water as we hoisted sail, turning the corner of the creek mouth and set off west along the coast.

The run to Trefoil Island on the north-west corner of Tassie, was fast, exhilarating and soon put us ahead of our timeline.

Only Alex and the Admiral knew enough to study the Pilot book covering entry into Macquarie Harbour, our next destination, and shared my concern for making entry through the charmingly named 'Hell's Gates'. It was listed as probably the most dangerous harbour entry in Australia; powerful tide flows, a narrow channel with sandbars and rocks, as well as frequent big seas to make it a yachtie's nightmare. Accordingly, if we couldn't arrive off the entrance with at least a couple of hours of daylight, we would have to spend the night in Pilot Bay, which lay right beside the rock wall guarding one side of the entrance, and was exposed to the huge south-west swell. Not exactly a pleasant option.

Approaching Trefoil Island and well before we were due to turn south, we started to feel the effects of the powerful swell generated by the latest cold front, so hatches were dogged down tight as we prepared for a wet and uncomfortable run south. The strong south-westerly wind meant we were on a close-hauled reach with all sails sheeted in hard and the slim bows being driven into the three to four-metre swell. With the different design of the new boat, the bows didn't lift as much as the old one, making the ride more comfortable, but the penalty was the decks were awash most of the time with green or white water. Still, progress was fast and we continued to creep ahead of our timeline.

As we made distance south, the wind and swells came more from the west, meaning we no longer were punching into them, but running almost parallel, making for a better ride, but with a lot more roll motion. The change in wind angle saw the sails eased and speed increased. Unfortunately, there wasn't much to see of the coastline with the dense sea-haze lifted by the wind, so the chart-plotter and radar became the main navigation references.

One feature I picked up was the 17-mile long sweep of sand named Ocean Beach, the southern end of which terminated at Hell's Gates, so it was a most welcome sighting since the time was just 15:00. The down side was that the tide had just turned and the runout started.

Ignoring the advice in the Pilot Guide, we furled the mainsail and genoa leaving the inner staysail in place, stirred the motors into life, and lined up the leading marks for the run up the narrow channel.

It was a bit exciting at times, with sand banks or rocks almost within touching distance either side, and as the tide flow was still picking up, massive, swirling tide boils came surging up from underwater obstructions, keen to push the boat off course. Still, we made it through, earning a salute from a couple of fishermen securely anchored off to the side of the channel.

'Just in time, Skipper!' one called. 'Ten minutes more and you'd be stuck outside for the night.'

I waved to them, and pushed on up the still-narrow channel, until the land folded back left and right revealing the vast expanse of the magnificent Macquarie Harbour. The first impression, apart from the huge area, was the brown colouration of the water from the tea-tree swamps, and the fact the top layer of water was fresh. Away from the disturbances around Hell's Gates, it was drinkable, although with an unusual taste. Just ahead of us, a triple-deck power catamaran with bright red hulls similar to *Firebird's* roared past, heading as we were, for the town of Strahan.

'*Nice colour!*' came the comment on the marine VHF chatter channel 77.

'Thanks Skipper. What's the best channel for the Harbourmaster? I'd like a mooring for a few days.'

'*Channel 72 should get her. There are a few moorings free at the moment, so it won't be a problem. How long are you?*'

Beside me, Kelly giggled as I replied, '25 metres and 11.3 beam.'
.....'*Okay. I've just been talking to her and she's offered a berth at the next wharf ahead of where I'll be parking if you'd prefer to be able to step ashore without playing with dinghies.*'

Beside me, Kelly was nodding frantically, so I replied, 'The crew says take it, so we will, thanks very much Skipper.'

'*Good-oh. Follow me in and she'll wave you in from there. I wouldn't mind a look over your boat if that's okay? We don't see too many of that size in Strahan.*'

'No problem. Tea, coffee or rum?'

There was a laugh, then, '*Rum sounds good! Give me 15 to bed this thing down, then I'll be over.*'

'Done.'

Now we were in sheltered waters and the west wind was still strong, we hoisted all sail including the big code 'zero', and *Firebird* took off! It was pure showing off, but with the speed restrictions placed on commercial vessels, we were a lot faster with over 30 knots showing for minutes at a time. That helped us catch the big 35-metre power cat, then we eased the sheets and kept an easy pace just off her port quarter until we were about to enter Strahan harbour.

'*That looked like fun!*' came another call. '*What speed were you doing to catch up?*'

'30 to 35 most of the time,' I replied casually.

'*My whole crew want a ride! And half the passengers as well!*'

I laughed, 'Bring your crew over if they want. We've got plenty of room, but I'm not sure about the passengers.'

'*I'll do that. Thanks.*'

We were duly waved into a berth at a small wharf ahead of where the cruise boats tied up. One was red-hulled, the other white and otherwise looked very similar. The Harbourmaster turned out to be a short, stocky lady with a sunny disposition and a good tan, who helped with mooring lines and welcomed us to Strahan.

'Where from, Skipper?'

'Last port was Wynyard, the one before was Garden Island, Perth, and before that, St Francis Bay, South Africa.'

She laughed, 'Quite a trip. It's a new boat, I presume by the look of it. Going well?'

'Yes, yes and yes, so far. And thanks for parking us here. The crew will appreciate the convenience.'

'No problem. It'll give the tourists something to look at as well. We don't often get private cats this big in here. But how long did you want to stay?'

'At least a week, perhaps longer if that's okay? We want to explore the whole area, before we move on down to Port Davey.'

She smiled, 'Ah yes. Good choice. Magnificent area. The last of the real wilderness and little intrusion by man, thank goodness. My hubby and I slip down there whenever we get a break from here. Oh...here he comes now.'

I turned to look and saw a pleasant-looking chap in shorts and a white uniform shirt with the four bars of a Captain on the shoulder boards. Three ladies and a young fella in clean overalls trailed behind him, the girls wearing black skirts and white uniform shirts like the Captain.

'Ah...So that's hubby. He expressed interest in my cat and I invited him over. We had a bit of a race heading in, but as the sailing conditions were excellent, we won!'

She pulled a comic sad face, 'Oh dear! Now you've gone and done it. He's always wanted a decent-sized sailing cat just for relaxation. You'd think he'd get enough sea-time doing the cruise 5-days a week, but he reckons he wants more.'

'Who wants more?' he demanded with a grin, and stuck out his hand. 'Craig Wallace. And since she probably hasn't introduced herself, my wife Terri, and my crew Maxine, Alicia, Joanne and Tony.'

I introduced the *Firebird* crew and invited Craig's crew aboard. Jasper had wisely tucked himself away, as he always does when strangers come around unless I invite him out. This time, I thought it might be best to keep his presence quiet. Krazy cat bounded out, however, and was promptly scooped up by Alicia.

I gave them a quick tour of the boat, with Craig asking a non-stop stream of questions, particularly about the electric drive systems. Up on deck again, his crew thanked us, then excused themselves because it was obvious Craig wanted more information.

We settled in the cockpit with rums for the blokes and wine for Terri and our ladies. I had to give a short version of the trip from South Africa, with much detail about how the boat handled the big seas and winds of the Southern Ocean.

Craig and Terri were good company, time flew with lots of talk, and they ended up staying for dinner, a lovely roast lamb with lots of roast vegies which Bree and Hillary had prepared. It was late in the evening, and after several NQ tea's before Terri pried Craig away to head home, promising to see us on the morrow.

We based out of Strahan and did day trips to all of the scenic and historical highlights of the huge harbour including spending hours at the fascinating mining museum at Zeehan. We spent one night as far up the Gordon River as we could go, which was well past the Heritage landing, which was the limit for the cruise boats. Apparently, if the rainfall in the interior was low, the river dropped quickly and rocky shoals prevented progress, but we were lucky and lots of water flowed downstream. It was a magical, mystical experience being so deep in the true wilderness, and when one looked around at the near-impenetrable undergrowth and the endless, rolling green carpet of tall trees, the idea that an animal like the Tasmanian Tiger could be extinct didn't carry much weight.

The whole south-west corner of Tasmania was so under-explored, anything could live and breed there without any human interaction.

For a couple of days, we just stayed in port and enjoyed a leisurely wander around the appealing little village. While the pub served great meals and we normally ate there each day, we chanced on a good source of Tassie scallops at the little Fish and Chip shop further along the waterfront's row of shops. The lovely lady owner gave us extra-large serves of the fresh-cooked, tasty little jiggers, for very reasonable prices. We ate them sitting on the wharf edge just in front of *Firebird's* bows, bare feet dangling out over the water, listening to the comments about our large red baby made by the wandering tourists.

Most knew nothing about boats or sailing cats in particular, but one couple not only knew boats and sailing, but actually knew what *Firebird* was!

I couldn't resist and as I finished the last scallop and risked Sandy's wrath by wiping my hands on my pants in time-honoured fashion, I called out to the bloke. 'How do you know what the boat is?'

He eyed me in a friendly manner and said, 'I enjoy keeping an eye on the latest developments in big cat design, and this Dutch design team have an excellent reputation. Production was supposed to have moved to South Africa, so this would have to be only the second of the 83-footers produced.'

'You're right there,' I said introducing myself. 'We're on the delivery trip from South Africa, and so far, everything has exceeded my expectations.'

He introduced himself as Doug Higgins and his wife Donna. They were visiting from Melbourne and were looking to get a live-aboard cat. 'But not quite as big as this one, Harry,' Doug said with a grin, 'perhaps 45 to 50-foot would be about right.'

'Yes, it's a good size for a couple. I'd recommend a close look at the Antares 44. It's a comfortable and very well thought out cat easily handled by two. It isn't as fast as this beast, but then this is a big boat with normally at least four of us aboard all the time. Still, I spent a lot of extra money to set up the systems so one person can safely sail and manage the whole boat.'

That raised their eyebrows, so I had to take them aboard and show them the powered sail handling systems and the walk-about remote controls, but I wasn't willing to start taking every interested tyre-kicker on a guided tour of the whole boat. Having the rest of the crew file aboard after finishing their scallops decided Doug and Donna that it was time to move on.

'You've given me some good information, thanks Harry. May we come back and pick your brains again?'

I smiled, 'Yeah, sure Doug. No problem. I know what I was like when I was trying to decide what my boat should be. There's a great deal to consider.'

He and Donna did come back the next morning, wandering down the hill from the hotel standing on the bluff looking out over the harbour and the expanse of Macquarie Harbour to the south. They were a pleasant couple and Doug asked a lot of sensible questions. They invited the whole crew up to the hotel for dinner the next evening, even insisting on paying. That in turn made me feel obligated, so next morning when Craig and his crew were scheduled for the late afternoon cruise, we took them all out for a sail, since the winds were still strong from the west.

It was a fun, happy few hours as the conditions were perfect for *Firebird* to show what she was capable of. There was no chance of prising either Doug or Craig off the wheel as the boat speed indicator hovered around the 30 to 35-knot mark for minutes at a time. They both had sailing experience, so after a few minutes of instruction, they were playing with the sheet winch buttons to make fine adjustments.

Also, for the first time, I was able to notice that in the gusts, we were just lifting the windward hull slightly clear of the water. As impressive as the indicated speeds were, the one thing that really got to them was that Bree and Kelly were serving morning tea, coffee and fresh-baked scones on the cockpit table at 35 knots!

Since Craig and crew weren't due out until 14:00, we fed them lunch and were back at the wharf by 13:00; everyone excited and happy.

Finally though, after two weeks in Strahan, we decided to head further south for Port Davey. I asked Alan if he wanted or needed to return to Sydney.

'Not yet, if it's okay with you, Harry. Between your excellent communications systems, Hillary and my competent XO, Lieutenant Commander Zellman, we have the Navy running very nicely. It helps that no one is shooting at us at the moment, so while things stay quiet, I'll make the most of it. This has been one of the most relaxing times I've had since my dear wife passed away.'

Since Alan rarely, if ever, mentioned his wife, I believed he was indeed relaxing as stated.

'Excellent! But if there is a pressing need to return, it would be best to call for a seaplane pickup out of Hobart.'

'Yes, that's a good fallback.'

Doug and Donna had already headed east to Hobart, so we said our goodbyes to Craig, Terri and the crew, and after a small shop to top up a few food items, we headed out on a morning with a nor'westerly blowing. The wind plus an ebb tide, fairly spat us out through Hell's Gates into the Southern Ocean which had a 2 to 3 metre swell. It made for a delightful sail south along the rugged and deserted coastline. There were no refuge bays at all between Macquarie Harbour and Port Davey, and because the distance was only 81 miles, our ETA was about 13:00, making it a really pleasant morning's cruise.

CHAPTER 19

PORT DAVEY, MONDAY

Although the entrance to Port Davey is nearly four miles wide, to the north and south lie clusters of little rocky islets which would be nasty to stumble into during bad weather, so it doesn't pay to cut the corner unless the weather and visibility are very good. Once inside, between the two headlands of North Head and Hilliard Head to the south, we passed by the extensive North Arm area with plenty of sheltered anchorages, opting instead to track in under reduced sail around the south of the aptly-named Breaksea Islands, then headed across Bramble Cove to a small, shallow cove inside Datum Point on the north side of the harbour.

Although the Pilot Guide suggested there were hundreds of good anchorages even further inside at Bathurst Harbour, I thought we'd spend a few days in this sheltered little bay where the rugged slopes of the interior ranges fell steeply to the water's edge. The vista was so different to what we normally saw I couldn't resist, even though Mt Rugby, at 2500 feet or so was just a few miles further up the Bathurst channel.

Someone made the comment that I must have a thing for small bays to tuck into, since this one was barely a hundred metres across, but there were three small beaches close by to go for walks and give the pussies a romp. The anchorage had a good sand bottom and was sheltered from most winds by high ground to the west and north. We didn't see another boat on the way in, although there were normally quite a few, but with the vast area which comprised the Port, they could be easily hidden.

The first job after bedding the boat down was to take the pussies ashore for their romp, which everyone joined in. Alex and I, feeling in need of more strenuous exercise, decided to climb the steep hill just south-west of our little beach and, of course, Jasper insisted on coming too; little Krazy staying with the ladies. It was only about 600 feet high and on this side at least, was mostly covered in low scrub and tufty grass, making for a steep, but accessible climb. Jasper shamed us by easily romping to the top without even breathing hard. Rotten cat!

The view from the top was stunning however and well worth the effort, allowing us to see the whole of the extensive North Arm and the main entrance and channels to the west, south and south-west. I was pleased to see Alex, a giant of a man, was panting as much as I was.

'We're both out of condition, I'm afraid Alex.' I commented when I got my breath back, pretending my leg muscles weren't screaming in agony.

The big man nodded, 'Unfortunately so, Commander. It's an occupational hazard of boat life.'

I scanned for other boats, but still didn't see any. Maybe the weather, with a solid swell and strong west winds might have kept them in port. We were about to head back when Alex nudged me, 'Commander, look at Jasper. He's onto something.'

The big, black cat was standing in a rigid pose, facing west-south-west, his tail well down with just the tip moving slightly. The hackles along the ridge of his back were standing up, adding to the sense that he knew something was wrong, but we couldn't see anything out of the ordinary.

'Blowed if I know what he's sensing,' I remarked, touching him lightly on the back of his neck, disturbed to feel his neck muscles were rock-hard, although he took no notice of my touch, continuing to concentrate on whatever had his attention.

We waited a few more minutes while our breath and muscles recovered, then after calling Jasper away, took the east ridge back down and while it was a bit further, was less steep.

'You ladies should go up there,' I said blithely, 'it's good exercise.'

Sandy bristled slightly, 'What are you suggesting?' she ground out. 'Maybe you think we've grown slack and fat?'

'Ahh.. no way, my darling girl! Merely that it's a magnificent view from up there and you might appreciate the change of scenery.'

I received an emphatic look which said, 'Bullshit!' but she let it go, turned Krazy over to Alan, and with the other three girls in tow, headed up the hill.

'Good lookout post,' Alan commented.

'The best,' I concurred.

'Anything nagging at you,' Alan asked casually.

I admired his perception, but replied, 'Yeah, as a matter of fact. Jasper went weird on us. Did a pointing act to the west-south-west, rigid muscles and had his hackles up. There was nothing we could see, although I did feel a bit uneasy about something. It was nothing I could hang my hat on, just one of those slightly uneasy feelings. There's a bit of a blow expected in a few day's time as a deep low moves past us to the south, but I don't think it's that.'

I shrugged, 'I don't really know, Alan.'

'It's not a bad thing to have, this in-built warning system. I'm sure you had it in the desert, and I certainly had it for my time at sea. Helped me avoid trouble many times.'

'Yes, you're right. It was probably just the way Jasper was behaving. He's always right when it comes to stuff like this. There's something out there which isn't right.'

Alex didn't have much to add, but agreed Jasper's behaviour meant something significant. We kicked around a few thoughts while we waited for the ladies to come back, but nothing was resolved. Jasper sat staring up the hill, even ignoring the attempts by Krazy to make him go for a romp.

All that evening he was quiet and retreated to his isolation perch on top of the cockpit overhead where he gazed out over the bows at the hill. I told the ladies what had happened on top of the hill, so they wouldn't be concerned he might be sick.

The next day and a half were really lovely, although twice a day, someone had to take Jasper up the hill and wait while he communed with whatever was out there. I really didn't mind since this was one of the reasons for being here in the first place, although Jasper resisted any attempts to take him on a walk up the next hill to the north. It wasn't as high as Jasper's Peak as we'd come to call the south-west hill, but was more heavily timbered.

Wednesday afternoon, the synoptic chart showed a very intense low-pressure system moving rapidly in from the west, on track to pass just south of our location. The north-west winds were getting quite strong by midday, and up on Jasper's Peak were strong enough to make standing difficult.

The west and south-west horizon was very dark, so with difficulty, we dragged Jasper away and set about making ready for a few days of bad weather.

Our sheltered little cove was an excellent place to ride out the coming blow, but it had one flaw. Between the hill topped with Jasper's Peak and the lower one, which lay just north of it, was a narrow valley which acted like a wind augmenter. Ten knots of breeze became closer to fifteen or so once it had made the passage, so I shuddered to think what 50 or 60 knots would get boosted to. Still, we were in an excellent position with good holding for the anchors. The main front didn't hit until that evening, heralded by the usual total, windless lull, before the westerly squall line howled gleefully across the port, searching with invisible fingers for any weakness in the puny, man-made floating shelters it came across.

As fate would have it, a large high over New Zealand prevented the low from scooting away over the Tasman Sea like they normally do, so the rotten little thing parked itself about 60 miles south of us and like a spoiled child not getting its way, proceeded to wind up into an absolute fury. What should have been a day or so of wind and rain, turned into a week of hurricane-force winds, low, scudding cloud and driving rain.

There could have been a rugby scrum on the foredeck and we wouldn't have noticed!

Sleep was impossible without ear-plugs, and normal communication difficult, which became tiring.

Apart from those minor inconveniences, we were safe and comfortable in our little cove.

It wasn't until the following Monday, that the low showed signs of moving on, although the difference on Tuesday was barely noticeable. Wednesday morning, however, was a different story, with blue heavens and small, fluffy white clouds scudding along, driven by a still strong breeze. The effect on all of us was remarkable, like the lifting of the cloud of gloom which had hung over us for the last week, had allowed life to return to normal.

Normal to Jasper, however, meant he insisted loudly, he had to go ashore and I knew it meant an immediate trip up the hill to the lookout. Alex and Sandy came as well, and something prompted me to take a pair of binoculars. In this case, I took the hideously expensive, but amazingly good Zeiss 20 x 60 stabilised units, Sandy had bought me for my birthday.

She'd been busting to buy something outrageously expensive and indulgent ever since she became a multi-millionaire, and this stabilised and powerful set suited her desire very well. They were, however, quite superb binoculars and for this task, exactly right. By now we'd worn a path to the top, where the clear, flat area was a perfect lookout. Jasper was still highly agitated and raced on ahead, yowling and yipping loudly back down at us when he reached the top.

'Smart-arse cat!' Sandy muttered as we puffed our way up, slack again after a week off. Finally, we reached the top to see Jasper in his rigid or pointing pose, except that he was pointing south, instead of west-south-west as he had for so many days.

'Hello?' I said loudly over the wind, still blowing strongly at this height. 'Whatever he was worried about has either moved or arrived.'

We scanned around the horizon, quickly at first, then looking more carefully at the local real estate. Sandy was the first to spot the tiny wisp of smoke blowing away from the small bay almost straight south from us, tucked in behind the second little headland up the Bathurst Channel from Turnbull Head.

I turned on the binocular stabilisation and focussed on the area she indicated, amazed when the crystal-clear image of a quite large ship leapt into view. It was tucked close in against the shore, while a couple of other features stood out. Firstly, the shape of the rusty bow was familiar, and the fact she was listing around 15°, with several huge cascades of brown water pouring from temporary pump outlets on deck.

I scanned her a while longer, taking in the ungainly forward accommodation castle and the long, open rear deck with a stern ramp.

Wordlessly, I passed the binocs to Alex, then softly said to Sandy, 'It's that bloody, stinking, rotten Japanese whaling mother-ship. The one that was at Heard Island. It looks like it's hit something and damaged the hull, 'cause they've got several pumps running flat-out and she's still listing.'

Then Alex lowered the Zeiss's. 'Commander! If you look carefully, there's another, smaller vessel tucked in behind the mother-ship and it has a black hull. Would it be one of the catchers?'

I took another look and he was right, of course. The dull, black hull and dirty, stained upper works blended in with the shore. What it was doing in there like that, I couldn't work out.

'Any idea what it's doing in there?' I asked Alex.

'Maybe she's helping to support the mother-ship,' he offered, and it was the only logical explanation.

Jasper remained agitated, but was finally able to be coaxed away from his vigil so we could descend and get warmed again.

Back aboard, we had a round-table discussion when I brought everyone up to date and proposed a response.

'At the moment, he's just another casualty of the storm seeking shelter to repair damage. Therefore, he's not breaking any Australian laws. Would the Navy agree, Alan?'

He nodded, 'Yes. The weird business you told me about at Heard Island was illegal, but as you know, *Ballarat* only saw them sheltering for a short time, then leaving the area, and even though she stayed with them for a day, there was nothing to justify a boarding action. She's back in Perth at *HMAS Stirling* at the moment. I might add that while we were gone, Hillary took a message from Paul Davy saying the retro-fit work on *Arafura* was nearly complete, but would be a few days yet before they might be mobile.'

'Thanks Alan. But I'm not happy about the whalers being here. Mainly because of the fact that we were warned to leave the area twice, by the catcher captain and that Sunglasses yobbo. It was so bizarre, I have to wonder why they were so insistent!'

'What do you make of Jasper's action this morning, and even now?' Sandy asked.

'Well, his attention has definitely shifted to the whalers, so they must have been the source of his upset before the storm. Now he's on the cabin roof, staring south toward them, so between his actions and my feelings, there's something going on.'

Alex and Alan agreed, but Sandy made me promise not to go stirring up any trouble unnecessarily, although she became suspicious when I agreed so readily.

We agreed to make three trips per day up to the lookout to keep a good eye on the whalers, which at least would get all of us fitter than we'd been since we were teenagers.

Alex and I checked the boat over very carefully and also took in the second anchor, which would let us get under way more quickly, should it prove necessary. Then, on impulse, I found the SatPhone and called Corrine.

'Hi ya Harry. How's it all going?'

'Good, thanks Mouse. We've made it to Port Davey and just had our ears blown off by a week-long storm. Even now there are quite strong winds and a massive swell rolling straight into the bay.'

'Yeah. We saw it on TV. Looked pretty bad. We copped a lot of it too, but you were parked almost under it. How are Alan and Hillary liking the new boat?'

'Love it! We can't prise Alan off the wheel, especially since we nearly touched 40 knots surfing a wave the other day. But apart from saying gidday, something odd has come up.'

She instantly came out of relax mode into ready-for-action mode. 'Go ahead. What's the problem?'

'Those bloody whalers have just turned up. The mother-ship has hit something getting here and has a serious list with several deck pumps running flat out. She's tucked into a little bay just into the start of the Bathurst Channel, and has one catcher in permanent attendance. We think they only got in during the last couple of days of the storm.'

'That's bad. They've got no legitimate reason to be up in those latitudes, even damaged. Do you want support?'

'Yeah. I'm thinking it mightn't be a bad idea. These turkeys will know for sure we're here. But it's a long haul for you guys to come down from the Coast when I don't actually have a problem to sort out yet.'

She laughed. 'Two points, Harry. Why don't you launch Dragonfly to go take a look? You guys have it with you, not us. Sandy and Bree know as much about operating it as anybody. Secondly, Dave and I aren't on the Coast, we're in Melbourne. We thought we'd come down and visit some old friends who live on the waterfront at Blairgowrie on the Mornington Peninsula. They overlook the bay just up from where Xavier kept the old Seeker. Dave met them at a pub and used to go visit a lot before I came on the scene. They're lovely, laid-back people. We're moored just out front of their house, but we've been staying ashore with them. Anyhow, the point of all this waffle is that we can be with you in less than a day. Will that do?'

'Ahhh...yes...that would be excellent, thank you Mouse. I just have one of those feelings and Jasper has been acting really upset since before the storm which was before they even arrived.'

'*Oh shit! If he's acting up and you're feeling uneasy, there's something bad going on. We'll see you tomorrow, but meantime, get Dragonfly up and have a look for yourself.*'

CHAPTER 20

Over lunch, I updated the crew about the incoming support, and Sandy metaphorically kicked herself when I passed on Corrine's suggestion about *Dragonfly*, our amazingly competent VTOL drone on semi-permanent loan from the designer.

'In all the rush to transfer all our gear between boats, we just stowed *Dragonfly* in the port bow stowage locker and forgot about it. Do you want a daylight flight?'

I considered a moment. 'Yeah, I think so. After lunch will be fine and perhaps put it up at 2500 or 3000 feet and come in out of the sun if you can. They won't see it at that height unless someone is looking up with good binoculars. Use IR as well. It might show stuff standard colour video doesn't.'

It took Sandy and Bree a while to dig out the coffin-shaped box housing *Dragonfly*, from the messy pile of gear stowed in the big bow locker. But they'd soon sorted things out and put the hybrid UAV together after carefully checking every component. It helped that the storage box was airtight, so the batteries just needed a quick top-up and the fuel tank filled. We hadn't flown it off the new *Firebird* before, so Sandy was keen to try it from the larger foredeck. All we had to do was pull the staysail boom out to the left-side rails, and make the home helipad offset to the other side.

It was about 14:00 when the engine fired easily, then settled down to a warm-up idle. Just minutes later, it lifted smoothly off the deck, moved out to the right to clear the rigging, then steadily gained forward speed into the gusting wind. The flight plan the girls had worked out sent it through the valley to our north-west, then let it gain height still tracking the same direction, before it

186

turned south once it had reached cruise altitude of 3000 feet. We had lost sight of it long before that, and only the telemetry being sent back told us where it was.

At this close range, the video feed was live, was also recorded on-board, and the view on the big screen showed the flight path curving around to approach the start of the Bathurst Channel from the west. The first pass was a straight run west to east, to see if anybody spotted the tiny dot, and Bree had the video zoom at maximum giving an excellent view of the mother-ship. Streams of brown-stained water gushed from three big hoses laying on the broad open stern deck. There was no sign of what had caused the massive leak, although there was a work platform down at water level on the low side and what looked like two black-suited men hoisting air bottles on their backs.

'Ahh...Two divers getting ready to go down. Let's see if they're talking any repair gear with them.'

Three men were attending to the divers who soon disappeared into the brown water, but moments later, two other divers appeared and were helped out of the frigid water.

'Okay. They must be running relay teams to do the work, so she must have hit a submerged container or some rocks, maybe even the ones at the entrance.'

As Bree commanded the UAV to make a very wide orbit around the mother-ship, the auto-track function kept the stabilised lens firmly on the target. We also got a good look at the catcher boat jammed in between the mother-ship and the shore.

It appeared to be undamaged, until *Dragonfly* was on its southern arc, then we spotted the tell-tale streams of brown water also spewing from several outlets on her left side. It appeared she was badly holed as well and probably sitting on the shallow bottom where she could sink no further.

As expected, there was a constant flow of human activity to and from both boats, but still no sign of the other two catchers.

'I don't like those catchers being missing,' I muttered. 'I don't trust any of them and reckon they're up to no good. It'd be too much to hope that the rotten buggers have sunk.'

To Bree I said, 'Break off the orbit on the next westerly heading, and head out on a zig-zag search pattern, two-mile front, with a westerly line of advance. I'd like to see if the other two catchers are close by.'

The video view changed as Bree pulled the zoom back to wide-angle, but even letting the UAV zig-zag west for the next hour, there was no sign of the missing catchers.

Frustrated, I asked the girls to bring it home. They didn't need telling to make the approach from the north side, losing height down between some of the taller peaks. After nearly two hours of flight-time, the splinter-pattern camouflaged tandem-winged form, dropped smoothly on top of the small homing beacon set on the deck between the trampoline and the side rails.

While the girls fussily cleaned and checked their precious aircraft, the rest of us gathered in the saloon to review the on-board video which was of a much higher quality than the transmitted version. It didn't show anything new, but we were able to pause and rewind to double-check scenes.

'Tell me,' I said looking around at my captive audience, 'does anyone deduce anything more than what seems to be just two damaged boats taking shelter from a bout of particularly bad weather in the nearest safe harbour?'

'If they weren't a whaling mother-ship and an obvious catcher boat, I wouldn't have any doubts about the genuine nature of their situation,' Alex offered, 'but as they are what they are, I will always have doubts.'

I looked at Alan, 'They wouldn't be so crass or stupid as to start catching whales in Australian waters, would they?'

He shook his head, 'I just don't know, Harry. Tensions have been high for years over their so-called 'Scientific Research' involved in killing hundreds of whales each year. We, the New Zealanders, Greenpeace and Sea Guardian harass them each year, but they just come back to do it all over again.'

He turned to Hillary, 'How about you see where our closest asset is, my dear? It's only a circumstantial case at the moment, so I can't really justify pulling a frigate off patrol, but if someone was passing, they could drop in without upsetting patrol schedules too much.'

She went on-line, and entered a string of complex pass-words to bring up the patrol schedule. Scanning it with a frown, she finally shook her head.

'Fraid not, Dad. There's no one even close to here for at least a week; probably more.'

'Anyone in port about to leave?' Alan asked hopefully.

She scanned the document again. '*Ballarat* is still at *HMAS Stirling*, but they have an engine in pieces for another two to three days at least... Hang on, what's bow number 38? Oh...Okay. That's *Arafura's* new number. Commander Davy reports he came out of dry-dock just this morning and has already had a successful test run. There were no problems with the new power-pack, so he's refuelling and replenishing. Do you still want him to head east like you first suggested?'

Alan thought a moment, then said, 'Yes please. And have him expedite departure and to track directly here as soon as he clears the south-west corner at best possible speed. Also tell him to have a full munitions load as well.'

She got busy drafting up messages and official orders, then fired them off into cyber-space.

Five minutes later, she announced the orders sent and receipt acknowledged.

I looked around again, 'That's great, Alan! It's good to know a grey boat is coming. I suggest we keep our heads down until Paul arrives with his big gun, although we'll have the support of *Seeker* with Dave and Corrine from tomorrow. Meantime, I think we should prepare for visitors, by keeping *Dragonfly* tucked away, although we will make more flights, perhaps once per day, and at least two climbs of the hill per day to check on any changes across the water.'

There wasn't much to do to tidy the boat up except for stowing the UAV, so with the days noticeably shorter, the bar opened early. Given the low temperature, the preferred drink was NQ tea, and as the chilly evening slowly closed in, we retreated into the saloon.

That night, I thought it would be a good idea to activate the masthead camera, as well as the perimeter defence system and I told Jasper, in the hope he could communicate the danger to little Krazy. In general, he was still anxious, but less agitated than before, and loved the run up the hill twice per day, where he would look across the water at the whalers and make little noises.

THURSDAY

Fortunately, that night was quiet and most got a good sleep, although I woke frequently to stick my head up through the big overhead hatch to have a look around. That in turn disturbed Sandy who threatened to go and get Kelly if I didn't stop jumping in and out of bed.

I failed to see what Kelly had to do with it, and didn't find out, because Sandy was willing to settle for a lovely midnight romp which was more effective than a sleeping pill, and far more enjoyable.

What jarred me awake from a lovely dream, was the screaming sound of outboard engines, and the loud whirring of their props echoing through the hull. Hurriedly pulling on a pair of shorts and an old football jersey, I trotted up top to see two RIBs with four large Japanese gentlemen in each, doing laps around the boat at full speed. Naturally, one boat was driven by a chap with dark sunglasses, despite the dimness of the early hour. One of his arms was still covered in a white sheath.

Alex and Sandy weren't far behind me as I turned off the perimeter defence and tried to patiently wait until Sunglasses got his rocks off. As they continued to roar around us, I had an idea and said, 'OK. Let's go back inside and close the doors, but if it looks like shit-for-brains is going to try to board us, stand-by with the special boathook please Alex, and I'll wave a flare at him.'

'What about flashing some guns? He knows we have them.'

'Yeah, I know, but I don't want to let him know how many. This way, he thinks we only have one and need to rely on flares and the boathook.'

Mind you, the boathook, a 2.5-metre long pole, 55mm in diameter, with a tempered bronze combination hook and point on one end, could be a formidable weapon. In this case, it was especially so, since I'd thoughtfully sharpened the side, back and point of the curved hook. Wielded by the hugely powerful Alex, it could take off a limb or even a head, and in more peaceful times, could even function as a boathook!

Sandy was still the back-up with her Glock 22 tucked into the back of her pants.

The, 'ignore them', strategy worked, as both RIBs quickly stopped just off the stern and a voice called something. I waited a further count of ten, then walked out into the cockpit, a parachute flare in one hand and three more conspicuously stuffed in the waistband of my pants. Alex stepped out behind me and picked up the boathook as Sunglasses eased his boat closer.

He pointed to our make-shift weapons and laughed, 'You not so tough now. You silly man! Perhaps I come aboard to make Haraimodosu.'

I delivered my best sneer, 'You're the fool, Sunnies, for thinking about payback. I didn't wreck your boat or break your arm. You did that all by your stupid self, you bloody wombat! Now fuck off and go break some more boats somewhere else. By the look of the two over yonder, it seems to be the only thing you clowns are good at.'

There are times when I surprise myself with my ability to drive people into insane rages in two seconds flat. It must be an inherited talent I suppose, since I don't even have to try hard.

It certainly worked well this time, as Sunnies bent down and grabbed a pneumatic spear gun off the floor, aimed with rage-affected shaking hands, and fired. The metre-long spear, with its wickedly sharp point, went sailing overhead, but I'd already aimed the parachute flare with a much steadier hand, and yanked the ripcord on the bottom of the tube.

There was a surge of recoil as the ball of red magnesium was propelled out of the tube with a loud, 'whoosh', the magnesium igniting instantly into a blinding red light. Although not exactly a precise device, at twenty metres I could hardly miss as the bright red ball with the rocket motor still burning, shot across the water and slammed into the driver's console, showering Sunnies with bits of blazing magnesium. The main portion, still under rocket drive, bounced down and wedged against the floor and the main side flotation tube. Those tubes are strong and designed to resist most anything, but 2200°C was a bit outside the design range.

There was a flash, a huge cloud of smoke and most of one side of the RIB disappeared. The broken bits of magnesium, apart from re-arranging Sunnies features and burning through his clothes, had sprayed over onto the other side flotation tube where they instantly burned straight through the heavy rubberised fabric, deflating the entire side. Unfortunately, the much smaller bow and stern air chambers were not enough to hold the weight of crew and big outboard motor, so the whole thing sank, leaving four shocked Japanese whalers floundering in the icy water.

It was a farcical repeat of the Heard Island clusterfuck, and we couldn't help but break out laughing, even though the spear would have been quite deadly had Sunnies aim been better. Therefore, I felt absolutely no remorse for dumping them in the water and destroying their boat. Sunnies did fire first. I also realised the masthead camera would still be running from last night, in case I needed to prove who shot first.

To add injury to insult, we made no attempt to rescue them, as their second boat was available, although it was slow to move in, and by the time all four had been dragged on board, three on them looked to be in a bad way.

It must have been Sunnies' intense hatred for me which kept him awake long enough to weakly shake his fist at me and shout abuse. The other driver savagely shoved the throttle wide open and roared off across to the other side of the bay, where the damaged mother-ship waited. In expectation of another visit, I asked Sandy to make a copy of the video of the incident and load it on a PC-formatted flash drive. There was no damage to *Firebird*, and only a spreading oil slick to mark the grave of the RIB.

'What was that word Sunnies called out,' Kelly asked, 'Hara something?'

It was Hillary who answered, 'It means getting even or payback, which in his twisted reasoning, he would think was required.'

The bit of early morning action gave me an appetite which called for a hot, cooked breakfast, so I asked Bree nicely and she set to with a will; Hillary assisting. When we were all eating, I expressed my thoughts.

'I think Sunnies is a bit deranged about all this and losing a second RIB won't help his standing with his Captain. He's taking it much too personally, although I did sink them with the flare. Therefore, I half-expect a more formal visit from a senior officer making a complaint, but tonight, I reckon Sunnies is going to make a double payback raid, so that's the one we have to be prepared for.'

For the rest of the day we took it easy, although the climb up to Jasper's lookout still had to be made morning and afternoon, but there were no obvious changes to either of the Japanese boats. Our perimeter defence system was checked as best I could, given that there was a conspicuous lack of volunteers to test it.

The expected official visit from the mother-ship didn't happen, so we prepared for the next most likely visit by Sunnies later that night.

The real highlight of the day was the arrival in our little harbour of *Seeker*. The long, low royal blue hull of the 100-foot power boat, was first spotted nosing around the tip of Datum Point, not far from where we were anchored.

Although it hadn't been long since they left us in Fremantle, it was a joyful reunion. I then took the opportunity to bring them up-to-date on the situation across the bay.

'You've landed yourself in a bit of a mucking fuddle again, dear Harry,' Corrine said with a grin, 'but don't fret – we're here to save you from the big, bad whalers.'

'Cheeky bitch!' I grinned. 'Anyway, it's twice now that Sunnies has come off second best in an encounter, so he's lost a lot of face. But don't forget; if he'd controlled his temper a bit better this morning, he could easily have hit one of us with the spear!'

'Look on the bright side,' she smiled, 'shooting at you with a spear-gun suggests he doesn't have easy access to a gun of any description.'

'Hmmm...Maybe. But I'm not going to assume that. Tonight, we'll be ready for anything, although I don't think it will be a big assault. I reckon Sunnies will have two RIBs and up to eight men. They will have seen you come in and that might slow 'em down a bit.'

A little later, after we'd enjoyed a lovely steak dinner accompanied by one of Bree's classic tangy potato bakes, we all went over the plans for the night, which would start with keeping a concealed full watch, keeping the radar operating and the masthead camera recording as well.

In anticipation of disturbances, those off-watch went to bed early, which was no real hardship as the twice daily hill climb was giving everyone some badly-needed exercise.

CHAPTER 21

PORT DAVEY, FRIDAY

I woke to Corrine's practiced touch, rolling out of bed in one smooth movement, fully dressed apart from footwear.

'What've we got?' I asked, fumbling for my deck shoes.

'Two small boats on radar, confirmed on IR camera. One headed for what looks like the third beach along from here, the other hanging back just the other side of Datum Point. It suggests the first assault might be by swimmers coming out from shore.'

That report and brief assessment were welcome and reflected her extensive training and our shared experience in the Middle Eastern deserts.

'Goodo, thanks Mouse. Lead on, but I'll shake Sandy first.'

'Don't bother,' came the sleepy reply. 'It's been like a herd of elephants in here, including the trumpeting. You go ahead; I'll be up in a moment.'

I left to find Corrine and Dave in the saloon, all lights out except for a couple of dimmed red night lights. They were checking between the radar and the IR masthead camera, but of the two, the camera was the most informative, showing from the vantage point of 35 metres height, that one RIB was holding station just around Datum Point from us with four bulky men aboard.

Corrine panned the camera around to look north, showing four bright figures moving around the shoreline toward us. 'About ten minutes, Boss,' Corrine informed me. 'It's too soon to tell if anyone's carrying guns, but they'll have something, for sure. Are we staying with Plan A?'

'Yep. Let them all come to us, and if they expect us to be asleep, even better. Apparently, the land group are going to swim the

195

short distance from shore, so they'll take the easy access way via the stern. Hopefully, the safety rail system will take one or two out, then Jasper can have a go at whoever's left. The RIB bunch will probably come over the bows, so wait until the safety rail has done what it can, then the foredeck is all yours. Try not to shoot up any rigging.'

'OK Boss. We're on it.' She and Dave slipped over the railing to *Seeker* which was rafted up alongside as was our usual practice, the Admiral and Hillary going with them. That left five plus Jasper to defend *Firebird*, but we all had allotted tasks, with Bree and Kelly staying together as a team. Then came a soft owl hoot.

'OK. That's the signal the swimmers are almost at the stern and the other RIB is at the bows. Positions, please everyone and no noise.'

Jasper, Sandy, Alex and I crouched in the darkness of the saloon, all lights and displays turned off, the sliding doors half-open.

I knew the girls were poised on the ladder just under the open starboard midships hatch, guns ready for their cue to pop up.

The first sign was a shadowy figure creeping slowly up the starboard rear steps, another close behind. Alex gave an excellent imitation of a sleeper having a soft snore and I could almost see the grin on the first intruder's face. The safety railing gate at the head of the steps was latched closed, so as the first figure reached for it, the third person became visible close behind the second.

Game on was indicated by a flash of blue light, and a weird keening sound from the first intruder as he seemed to jiggle in place, while still holding the railing. Somehow, that performance didn't seem to alarm the second guy, as we saw him reach out to take the first guy's arm. The effect of a couple of million volts on him was similar to the first one for a few brief moments, then they both just dropped straight down to the deck.

Sandy, who was watching the bow, softly reported, 'One guy just coming up to the railing near the port bow. Oopsie...One flash and he's burnt toast. Damn that thing's good! He's fallen in the water,

Harry, but there's another one behind him. Oh look at that. He's doing a happy dance; he must like what he's feeling.'

Back at the stern, the third guy had figured something was going wrong and was hesitating, so I cut power to the hot rail system, and told Jasper. 'Go get 'em, boy. Two bad men. Have some fun.'

There was a blur of blackness that seemed to float through the air and met with the third guy's throat. A brief crunch, a wet sort of a gargle and he slumped from sight. A howl of terror and agony from down near the water suggested the fourth intruder might have lost interest in the splendid murder, rape and mayhem games he'd been promised and was only interested in preserving his own miserable life.

There was a short hammering burst of .50 cal machine gun fire from the upper deck of *Seeker* as Dave and Corrine turned a pair of 150 HP outboards into shredded aluminium. A few rounds also rendered the flotation cells ineffective, since they don't work too well without air. I learned later the fourth guy in the RIB had the bad judgement to try to stop a .50 cal round with his leg, and it was a toss-up as to whether blood-loss or shock ended his misery.

That left the third member of the RIB party and as he made the deck in panic, Bree placed a .22 magnum round through his left knee. That worked well, so to keep him nicely balanced, she repeated the treatment on his right one with equal success.

I did a quick head-count of the bow-boarding boat crew and came up with one semi-live one writhing on the foredeck leaking claret all over my shiny-new fibreglass, one nearly deceased in the rapidly sinking RIB and two fried critters who had already carked it.

The stern steps held two fried, one who had succumbed to breathing difficulties and another currently undergoing Jasper's attention.

I wandered out to peer down the stern steps and shook my head at the mess.

'Dear me,' I remarked to Sandy who had wrinkled her nose at the smell, 'it's a good thing everything is fibreglass and should hose off easily. What a godawful mess. Jasper! That's enough, thank you boy. The thing you're still gnawing on won't be doing any more whaling, I'm happy to say, so maybe there is some justice.'

Alex confirmed that three of the forward boat party were deceased, while the gentleman who had the .22 magnum knee adjustments would survive, but was in considerable distress and had asked if he could have a chat with me.

I smiled at Alex and said, 'Delighted to. Lead on!'

Surprise, surprise, but the pathetic figure writhing on the foredeck with fresh, but already blood-stained bandages wrapped tightly around both knees, and a fibreglass cast on one arm, was none other than our sincerely unloved Sunnies. He was minus the trademark sunglasses, of course, but the sneering voice had only changed to a hoarse croak.

'You in big trouble now, stupid man. My captain make murder charge on you. You kill my men!'

I squatted down beside him, 'Stupid, huh? It would seem that I'm not the one lying on the deck of the boat you made an armed attack on in the middle of the night without warning, and with your knees ruined for life. You're in Australian waters illegally, without clearance, and with a cargo of whale-meat illegally harvested from Australian waters.'

Some of this I had guessed at, but the sudden widening of his eyes suggested I had hit very close to the truth. 'You know nothing. Silly man! You call my captain. He get help. Punish you!'

I shook my head. 'I don't think so, sunshine. I think we'll keep you on ice for a while. Let's see what your exalted captain thinks about that!'

He looked puzzled. 'No ice. Need surgeon and painkiller. You fix!'

Grim laughter was my only answer to that stupid request.

I called over to Dave, who was wiping down the area where the Browning M2 HB-QCB .50 cal machine gun had been mounted, 'Have you still got a small forepeak cabin on that thing? Somewhere we can isolate this piece of arrogant dogshit?'

'Yep! There are two twin bunk cabins for crew, and one is clear of junk. He can go there.'

'Thanks mate. I'll put Jasper on guard duty.'

I looked at Alex, 'Whichever cabin is clear, thanks Alex. Locked door and hatches if you would and Jasper can have his bed moved to outside the door. Oh, and if any of the whaler's crew come calling, gag and strap him down securely.'

Alex grinned and inclined his big head. 'A cabin is way too good for this arrogant piece of scum, Commander, but if it's what you want, it shall be so.'

The big man effortlessly hoisted Sunnies to his feet with one hand, grimacing at the shriek of agony that movement produced.

'Be quiet, small man. You sound like a little girl!' He growled, as, with a tirade of broken English washing over him, Alex carted him to his new home, Jasper padding along behind, his muzzle and head now washed and towelled dry. 'Are you happy now, big cat?'

An expression which passed for a big, cheesy grin crossed his face and his tail was up, the tip curled forward.

'That's what I thought. Okay, watch the bad man. If he tries to escape or make trouble, bite him - hard.'

Alex had halted while I passed instructions to Jasper, and his prisoner looked horrified to hear the big, lethal cat was to be his jailer. 'You no have wild animal attack me. Not allowed!'

Alex and I laughed, 'Not only is it allowed on these boats, but it's what will happen if you cause the slightest bit of trouble. You came here to rape and kill, but now you have two ruined knees and your attack force are all dead. That makes you a very stupid man!'

'My captain he come. You in big trouble fella!'

I smiled gently, 'Of course he'll come to see us, but we haven't seen you since your visit when you fired a speargun at us, trying to hurt or kill me or one of my crew. That's when I'll let him know that I'll be making a claim against the Japanese Whale Research Commission for a million dollars in compensation for being attacked by a crew-member without provocation.'

His eyes widened, 'You mad... he attack you. Make you disappear!'

I shook my head. 'No, no, dear dickhead. You have it all wrong. You're the one who's going to disappear!' I pointed at an attentive Jasper, sitting almost at his feet. 'Just remember...one sound or the slightest bit of trouble and you get a fatal visit from the big black cat.'

He shrieked again as Alex lifted him over the safety rails and hustled him below.

'Interesting,' I said to Dave, 'that he reckons his captain will be willing to attack us if he thinks we had anything to do with the disappearance of his raiding party.'

He nodded agreement. 'That's not exactly the reaction I'd expect from a whaler captain. There's got to be something more going on with this mob. Anyway, we'd better be ready in case. I might leave the Browning mounted for now with a cover over it.'

'Yeah, do that,' I said thoughtfully, 'and quite troubling thoughts you've just expressed, old mate. We'll have to discuss them further. But in the meantime, I was thinking that while it's still dark, we might whizz over and retrieve the RIB that's on the shore. I suppose the one at our bow you shot up has already sunk?'

'Yep. 'Fraid so. But the bloke who was in it is still afloat courtesy of his wetsuit.'

'Okay. How about we drive their RIB out to where the water is deeper. The whaling crew won't know what's happened, and we can plead ignorance, as there's no evidence they were ever here.'

In his best droll manner, Dave intoned, 'I think the seven dead bodies we have scattered around sort of count as evidence.'

I gave him 'the look'. 'I was getting to that. We'll put them in the RIB, tie them to it so they don't float loose, then with you leading in our RIB wearing those neat night-vision goggles you came across, we make a run around the headland and out into the bay a short way, then sink their RIB, bodies and all. That way, there'd be no chance of a stray body washing up on a beach. Is that a plan or what?'

'Yeah, not bad, Harry. Alright, I'll go get the goggles, we'll pick up their boat, and load the bods.'

I clapped him on the back, and being a smartarse, 'Great plan, Dave. Let's do it!'

He rolled his eyes, but went below on *Seeker*, passing Alex on the way. I explained to Alex what we were going to do and asked him to stack the bodies as best he could.

There was only faint starlight to see by, so Dave got to drive since he could actually see where we were going. The third little patch of beach was at the head of a small creek gurgling happily as it fed its tiny contribution into the vastness of the ocean. The whaler's RIB was only pulled up a short way up the beach, not even anchored, so they must have been confident of a quick victory. Or maybe they were just slack. Make that dead slack now.

Dave also used the night goggles to good effect when he found a compact waterproof case in the bottom of the RIB, containing a rifle of some type with a folding stock and a separate box full of ammunition.

'Wow!' he enthused. 'Corrine will go nuts over this. We don't have a long gun at the moment. Plenty of ammo, too!' He transferred the gun case and ammo box to our RIB and with me following closely in the whaler's RIB, burbled quietly back to *Firebird*.

Using a red lensed torch, Alex waved me to the starboard side foredeck where he had the unfortunate seven ex-whalers stacked.

With Kelly holding the bow line to steady the RIB, Alex said, 'Stand back, Commander. I'll dump them in the bow.' Seven huge thumps later, the RIB was a bit lopsided, but it wouldn't matter shortly. A length of old mooring line was tossed down and I zig-zagged it over the bodies with a loop around each unfeeling neck, then tied it off to the rope running around the top of the flotation cells.

Dave drifted up beside me, 'Set to go?' he asked. 'Time's getting on and the chiefs on the mother-ship will be wondering why there's no contact from their boys.'

'Yeah, good point. I'm just about done... there. Just wanted to make sure no one floated free too soon. Okay. You lead again and I'll follow your wake, but keep the speed down to about 15 knots if you would. When you find a good spot, chuck a circle so I don't ram you.'

He chuckled, then fired up *Firebird's* RIB and headed off.

It was a bit surreal to be in such darkness, following a foaming white wake endlessly disappearing into the gloom, but about fifteen minutes later, the reasonably straight wake suddenly curved sharply to the left, so I cut power and waited until Dave quietly eased up beside me. 'We're about 500 metres off the northern tip of the Breaksea Islands in some reasonably deep water, so this would be a good spot.'

I didn't argue, merely scrambled over the side to get in with Dave, after remembering to shut the engines down and shut off the fuel, including the tank vent. Dave had a good grip on the flotation cell rope, so I drew my razor-sharp Gerber knife and commenced stabbing each of the 14 air bladders in each boat. By the time I got to the last one, the RIB was settling fast, so we waited to make sure it and its grisly cargo kept going down before heading back.

In anticipation of some more visitors, we checked our RIB for any traces of foreign bodies, then tied it at the stern. On deck, the crew had been busy with the deck wash hose and all traces of blood and other grisly bits and pieces washed away.

Guessing at one of my concerns, Alex said, 'We only used red torches, Commander. It's hard to see red blood on red gel-coat with a red torch, but we did what we could. I'd suggest another wash at dawn.'

'Good idea, Alex. Thanks for a great job.'

As it turned out, the day dawned grey, cold and windy, with the base of the clouds skimming the tops of the hills around our anchorage and a misty drizzle wetting everything. I checked the decks and sides for anything which could be related to the attack, but apart from a few smudges of smoke from the .50 cal on *Seeker's* upper sundeck sides, which were easily wiped away, all was clear. Dave had left the heavy machine gun mounted, but disguised its distinctive shape with a bucket so it sort-of looked sort of like a searchlight under a lashed-down cover. With everyone awake, Bree and Hillary set to in the galley and soon had a hot breakfast on the saloon dining table since the cockpit was damp and cold.

As we were eating, Dave remembered the gun case we found in the RIB the night before, and presented it to Corrine.

'Now don't say I never give you any presents, princess!'

She grinned, 'Gee Dave, How romantic! A real gun case. Just for me... I don't know what to say!'

Her cheerful sarcasm changed, however, when she saw the Howa Type 89 assault rifle inside. The box of 5.56 NATO rounds sealed the deal, and for a moment, I thought she was going to drag him off to bed! But curiosity overcame lust and she turned to examine the rifle instead.

It appeared to be in immaculate condition, and maybe hadn't been used.

'They don't allow these to be exported anywhere you know. Home use only. Lightweight and very effective. This is a brilliant addition to our armoury. Ta, big guy!'

It was Alex who threw a dampener on her excitement. 'If those carbines are so restricted, why is one being carried by what are supposed to be just a bunch of pissed-off commercial whalers in Australian waters?'

CHAPTER 22

That question remained unresolved as we'd not long finished brekkie and cleared away the debris, when Corrine, who was parked at the nav table still playing with her new toy, announced, 'Incoming visitors.'

I scooted across to peer over her shoulder at the radar which displayed a small white blip tracking straight at us. The masthead camera, zoomed right out, showed a large RIB with centre console and canopy, charging toward us at high speed.

'Okay folks. It's show-time! Alex, Dave and Corrine...please gag Sunnies and lash him so he can't move, then secure all hatches so no one can sneak below. You can use all the force you like to stop these turkeys going any further. We'll do the same here. Be friendly as long as they are, but as we know and saw nothing, we can't help.'

They nodded and left.

'Sandy my dear, perhaps you would like to tuck your Glock in the back of your jeans, just in case, and Alan, maybe have the TAC-14 shotgun close-by. It looks suitably menacing. Bree, Kelly and Hillary...would you mind securing all hatches internally?'

The girls left on their errands, while I dug the TAC-14 and my .44 magnum handgun, out of their concealed lockers. As the drizzle had eased for the moment, Alan and I went out into the cockpit and closed the sliding saloon doors behind us. With the heavily tinted glass, it was nearly impossible to see inside. I fired up the camera display on the steering station panel and saw the incoming boat was about one kilometre out and still moving fast.

It must have been an arrogant whaler's thing, but the RIB roared around us at speed, just like Sunnies did, before slowing and easing in to *Firebird's* starboard stern. Four big men dressed in neat coveralls accompanied an officer in a grey uniform with four gold bands on his shoulder boards, presumably denoting a Captain.

While his crew were big, he was of average height and overweight, but in perfect English, asked, 'Permission to come aboard, Captain?'

I rose and walked to the top of the steps, considered a moment, then nodded, 'Permission granted, but just you, Captain. Your crew can wait in the boat.'

A flash of annoyance passed over his face, but he quickly resumed the previous bland expression as he made his way up the steps, bowed briefly and very shallow, then announced, 'I am Capitan Kurosawa of the research ship *Nissabe Maru.*'

I also made a very shallow and quick bow, little more than a head bob, before saying, 'I am Commander Stevens, Captain of this vessel, *Firebird*. How may I assist you Captain?'

The fact I didn't offer him a seat, caused another flash of annoyance to cross his face, but he smoothly carried on.

'Last night, two boatloads of my crew went out fishing and were believed to be heading this way. So far, they have not returned to the ship, nor reported in by radio. We are concerned for their safety as there are many dangers in such an isolated part of the world. My question is, have you seen or heard anything of them?'

I looked at Alan, standing impassively by my side, 'I can't say I have, Captain. And I know none of the crew would have seen or heard something without mentioning it to me.'

Alan shook his head and gravely stated, 'No, I'm sorry, Captain. All was quiet last night, although the wind did get up around midnight when I went to have a pee over the stern. What time did your men go fishing?'

'They left just before midnight, and were supposed to be gone just two hours. One of our lookouts reported what he thought were flashes of light from over this way about 30 to 40 minutes after they left. Are you sure you saw nor heard nothing?'

'Absolutely, Captain. Unless there was another boat or ship

which came into harbour during the night, but we wouldn't know about it since we were asleep.'

He continued to look annoyed. 'Perhaps I could ask your other crew if they heard or saw anything?'

I shook my head firmly, 'I'm afraid not, Captain. I can vouch for all of them and nobody saw or heard anything to do with your men. Perhaps they decided to go a lot further and ran out of fuel. Or maybe they had another accident like they did at Heard Island, when we dragged them back to the catcher boat.'

He looked like he was sucking on a fresh lemon, and ground out, 'No. That would not be possible.'

Which left me wondering exactly what *would* be possible, but he didn't elaborate, so I rudely forced the issue by saying, 'I regret I cannot be of any further assistance, Captain, but I must return to my duties, if you don't have anything more?'

With what proved to be impeccable timing, a radio crackled on his RIB, the unintelligible voice sounding excited. Whatever was said, the crew became excited or agitated, then one passed the message on to the Captain.

He turned back to speak to me just as Sandy opened the saloon doors and told me quietly, 'We have a visual sighting confirming the missing two catchers are back and both of the rotten bastards have whales in tow! We've got the video recorder running, so I hope this prick is leaving now before I throw him overboard!'

I knew Sandy felt strongly about whaling, but this was raw emotion, so I hurriedly said to the captain, 'I'm sure your radio message has said the same as my crew have seen, that your two other catcher boats are back, and I'm informed they have whales in tow. Your boats have been killing whales in Australian Territorial waters, in a whale protection zone. This is totally unacceptable and illegal behaviour, Captain and is going to bring the full force of the Australian Government down upon your head. Now get the fuck off my boat before I throw you off!'

He made the gross mistake of waving one fat finger at me while saying, 'We will do whatever we want, you silly man. You cannot stop us! We know the impotent Australian Navy has no boats in this area, and we will be long gone before any might arrive…'

I had taken two paces forward and pushed him hard in the chest, causing him to stumble back and turn to avoid falling down the steps. I then took the opportunity to plant my bare foot against his broad beer-fed rump and shoved hard. With windmilling arms to maintain balance, and his gold-braided hat flying off, he awkwardly lurched down the broad steps and fell face-first into the RIB, landing painfully on two of his crew.

There was a sickening crunch as one man's head hit the edge of the solid centre console, and a loud crack which sounded like an arm being broken. Howls of pain suggested my assessment was correct, although the guy with the head injury was unconscious. I followed the hapless captain down the steps, whipped out my knife and cut the RIB's bow line as close to the boat as I could reach.

To make my point even more forcefully, I pushed the needle-point of the Gerber hunting knife hard into the bow buoyancy tank of the RIB, being rewarded by a rush of escaping air and a howl of outrage from the crew. This prompted the driver to fire the engines and back quickly away.

I jumped up and down, cackling insanely and waving the knife at them, screaming, 'And don't fucking come back, you rotten, stinking, whale-killing bastards! We'll show you what happens when you mess with Aussies, you arrogant arse-holes!'

The boat driver shoved the throttles forward rather sharply and with a mighty surge of power, they roared out of the bay.

'Okay…..That went well,' Alan commented tongue-in-cheek, a wry smile on his face, as I regained the deck and reverted to normal. 'You really told them off, but unfortunately, the captain has lost a huge amount of face and that will have pissed him off more than anything.'

Sandy hugged me, 'Don't feel bad dearest, all that stuff needed to be said, and you did it so very nicely.'

'Yeah, thanks, but they'll be back.'

'Oh, yes.' Alan agreed. 'They certainly will. And when they do, they won't be messing around.'

When I'd calmed down, we thought things through and made a few plans, on the basis that the best defence is a strong offence. Corrine was particularly happy since she might get to play with a few of her toys.

'How's our guest?' I asked Dave.

'Unhappy,' he grinned, 'but after Jasper jumped up on the bunk and got a loose mouthful of his dangly bits, he was amazingly docile. We didn't have to tell him the penalty for misbehaving, and he was very co-operative. Unhappy, but co-operative.'

That was worth a laugh, so I said, 'You can untie and un-gag him if you would. I can't think of another use for him at the moment, but we can't afford to have him flapping his gums to anyone about the failed raid.'

Alex came up with another excellent suggestion. 'To cover our collective arses, Commander, how about you put on our Commonwealth copper's hat and formally arrest Sunnies. That way we are legally able to detain him.'

I nodded gratefully to the big man. 'Good call, Alex. I'm not sure what we'll do with him, but if we do keep him alive and process him through the legal system, a formal arrest will certainly help.'

I looked over at Bree. 'How about you get on the SatPhone and call your Sea Guardian girlfriend? We could do with them about now.'

She grinned and went to the chart table, as I looked at Alan, 'Perhaps when she's finished, you could check on Paul's progress? It would be nice to see a grey boat come in here anytime soon.'

He smiled grimly, 'No problem, and I agree, but your plans to deal with them are quite feasible, although the risk of starting a war is high.'

I grinned and shrugged, 'Perhaps. Maybe we should question

Sunnies a lot more closely about what they'd hoped to achieve from the raid last night.'

Alex spoke up. 'Perhaps Dave and me, with Jasper's help, might do the job, if you please, Commander.'

'Thanks Alex. That would be good.'

While that was in progress, Kelly started making morning tea. With two ladies aboard who enjoyed cooking, we were spoiled with lovely food, as well as putting on weight. Kelly found some chocolate cake which hadn't been consumed by the night watch and presented it with the usual teas and coffees.

Bree disconnected the SatPhone and reported. 'My girlfriend Nina told me that Sea Guardian was down at Heard Island, but lost track of the mother-ship and the catchers when another storm hit the island. They said they're heading this way anyway, but are at least three days away.'

'Damn! I was really hoping we could get some support soonest.'

Bree came up with a new twist. 'Why don't we live stream the video from the masthead camera onto YouTube? I'll bet it'd go viral in minutes, and the whalers would get pestered by a whole bunch of concerned anti-whaling persons. It might slow them down.'

I puzzled over her words for a few minutes, before giving up and asking for a translation.

She laughed and replied, 'I've got a YouTube account, so all we have to do is take the current recording from the start of when we first spotted the catchers coming past Breaksea Islands and feed it back to the internet onto YouTube so everyone can watch it. We only have to run 10 or 15 minutes of video to tell the story. We might even speed things up a bit to shorten the upload time. We should get millions of hits.'

Sandy chipped in with, 'But won't that just drag a whole bunch of anti-whalers in all sorts of boats down here? I mean, how many will be properly equipped for living in a remote wilderness, without a supermarket on every second corner?'

'Hmmm. That's a point. I hadn't thought of that.'

'It's a good point,' I said, 'and as much as I like to stir things up, I wouldn't like to be indirectly responsible for some well-intentioned fool losing a life or three by coming around here from Hobart in a 3-metre tinnie and getting caught short in bad weather. Perhaps you can do the upload thingy in a few days. Hopefully, we should have some of this mess sorted out by then...one way or the other.'

Bree nodded, 'Yeah, that might be better. The upload can wait and I can edit it a bit more before we send it. There might even be some more interesting stuff to go with it.'

'Yep. There's a good chance of that if things work out as we planned. I don't expect Captain Kurosawa will take all those insults and the physical abuse to his regal body very lightly, so we may have another late night. Although the continued absence of his entire first party may slow him down a bit.'

Alex and Dave reported back that Sunnies was now a subdued prisoner, although definitely not to be trusted. He had admitted the raid was mostly his idea as face-saving payback for the humiliation he had suffered in the last two encounters with us. The captain was also in favour of any action which might chase away the 'round-eyes' who could interfere with their activities.

'We might check all our gear in that case,' Dave recommended. 'I agree Captain Toad will be a very pissed-off little whaler. He'll want payback, big-time.'

Weapons had already been cleaned and checked, but we did it all over again, because it was the way to make sure at least the guns were reliable... plans certainly weren't. As the Prussian Field Marshal, Helmuth von Moltke famously said, 'No battle plan survives first contact with the enemy.' Or words to that effect; depending on who translated the original statement.

I was still keen to go on the offensive and so were Dave and Corrine, but Sandy counselled a calmer approach.

'Let's see if we can get through tonight without killing anyone. Then see what tomorrow brings. The whalers will be like a stirred up hornet's nest at the moment and you don't really want to stick your head into that just yet, do you my darling?'

Reluctantly I agreed and went back to making cunning plans about how to strike the biggest blow to the whaler's efforts.

Hillary, the perennial quiet achiever, re-joined the group after a session on the SatPhone. After briefing Alan privately about Navy business, he gave her the nod to tell us the rest.

'I spoke with Paul Davy and although he's still on his way here, the weather isn't good so he's had to back off a bit. He says the new turbine power-pak works really well and in the brief trial he's had, they registered over 30 knots. Unfortunately, he can't use it to get here any faster, given the conditions.'

While the group kicked that info around, I consulted the weather situation and saw the front which was giving *Arafura* a hard time, was indeed heading our way and would be pounding us by tomorrow night or on Sunday if the system slowed down. However, I was learning that in these latitudes, with no land in their way, systems don't slow down and often the reverse applies.

Maybe we could use the bad weather to good effect.

As it turned out, the first move by Captain Kurosawa was of mild harassment. He sent three boat-loads of yobbos to race around us at full speed, screaming abuse in several languages, no doubt hoping the noise and wash would drive us nuts. Admittedly, it was a bit tedious, but since we were sitting down to five o'clock drinks, we kept smiling and hoisted our glasses each time one of the drivers got a bit carried away and came closer. It seemed to annoy them quite nicely and the drivers tried even harder to bug us. Several times, a boat would nearly tip over in the confused wash and chop they'd generated.

Dave had a good idea and fetched a coil of well-used polypropylene water-ski rope in a fetching blue colour. He coiled it loosely in one hand and waited until there was a decent gap between the circling boats, then from the stern board of *Seeker* he quickly slung it underarm straight out over the foaming, churned-up water. The next RIB wasn't long in coming, the driver aiming to cut in close to the sterns of our two boats.

Within seconds of running over the floating rope, there were tortured screams from the engines as the prop shear-pins did their job, unloading the engines which immediately over-revved and blew-up before the startled driver could throttle back. The driver looked stunned as the powerless boat drifted away, nearly being rammed by the other two.

We applauded long and loud, called out our own insults and that put an end to Round 1 of Captain Toad's harassment plan.

'I wonder how many of those lovely 150-horsepower Yamaha outboards they have as spares?' Dave thought out loud. 'I mean, if I was their Chief Engineer, I'd be getting a bit terse with the crews by now. It's at least eight they've destroyed or lost by my count, including the two at Heard Island. I wouldn't have thought they would have many spares.'

'Good thinking, mate. In fact, they may be running short of motors and not just spare parts, so it might restrict their plans a bit more.'

As the stricken RIB was taken in tow, we gave another round of noisy cheers to farewell the trio limping back to their base and some difficult explanations.

That night, as I cuddled up to Sandy, I made the comment Kelly hadn't been visiting our bed for quite a while. She giggled, 'You really don't notice girly things much, do you?'

'What's that mean?'

'That means she's taken up with Alan. Really, Harry! I know this is a much bigger boat, but by normal social standards, there are seven people living in a small area. Anyway, I'm happy she's got her head together after all the mess on Lord Howe.'

'But how old is Alan? I suppose I didn't really see him as a potential mate for Kelly, since she's about your age.'

I'd learned my lesson long ago about discussing women's ages, and stayed well clear of the subject where I could.

Playfully, she reached down and tweaked a portion of my anatomy which didn't need any encouragement, but served to make her point.

'Alan's only in his late 50s! It's not too old, and Kelly seems to be happy with what he's doing. Hillary says because of his position, he has to be careful who he has for a girlfriend, but she really likes Kelly and is very pleased for Alan. In her words, 'He's needed to get his rocks off for quite some time and it's doing him the world of good'!'

'Oh...You ladies do discuss some interesting things. Blokes never do. It's all boats, cars and women in general. But what about Hillary? We don't have any more spare guys.'

'Don't you worry about her. I'm working on the problem, and should have something happening soon.'

Without any trouble at all, I turned my mind off the mental picture of a naked Hillary rolling around in bed with Sandy, and focused on the naked Sandy beside me.

CHAPTER 23

It had been a quiet night, apart from the usual happy bedroom noises, with no further attempt by the Japanese whalers to disturb our rest.

After breakfast, I checked the mast-head camera, saw the two seaworthy catchers had gone again, and said to Sandy, 'How about you and Bree launch *Dragonfly*, take a good look at the *Nissabe Maru* and the damaged catcher, then have a scout around to see if you can find the catchers? If they're catching whales close-by, we really need to get video of it for the YouTubey thingy for some government department to do bugger-all with.'

They were enthusiastic about the idea and quickly assembled and fuelled it, checked everything carefully and were ready for take-off.

The flight plan was the same as the other day; climb out away from the whalers, then stay high enough for the camouflaged UAV to avoid visual detection and orbit the damaged ships.

To my dismay, the streams of pump water on the *Nissabe Maru* were much smaller and the list was less. Even worse, there was crystal-clear video of several Minke whales being butchered on the open expanse of the stern deck, the blubber and flesh pieces simply being pushed into a large hole in the deck. The bones and offal were pushed into another adjacent hole until absolutely nothing remained of the 5 to 6-metre whale, the whole revolting process taking less than 5 minutes. It appeared to be the last whale they had for the moment, as deckhands brought out powerful hoses and cleaned every section of the deck. The only remaining indication of the fate of the 'researched' whale, were the two chimneys poking up beside the open holes with smoke pouring from them.

As we watched, covers slid across the two holes which presumably fed the cookers, that being the best way to extract the valuable oil. With the covers in place, there was little to indicate what had happened, although I knew from nasty experience, that to noses not used to it, the smell would be horrific. I wondered why there were whales here at all this late in the summer, but the fact was, they were here and they were being slaughtered by these mongrels!

Sandy, who was guiding the UAV, peeled away from the wide orbit around the factory-ship and headed south-west into the Southern Ocean. Bree programmed in an automatic search pattern, and with target recognition software running, *Dragonfly* was left to look after itself. An hour later, a series of chimes from the Ground Control Station announced the TRS had spotted something matching the parameters already in memory.

On screen were two small ships being tossed around by the huge 8 to 12-metre swells, marching inexorably eastward.

As Sandy hit the optical zoom, it became clear we'd found the catchers and the rotten bastards had been busy! Two smallish whales were tied alongside each boat as they lurched and rolled their way back east, careful of their cargo.

The girls got some good video of the pair, then broke off and hit the return to base button.

'Well,' I remarked ironically to Bree, 'there's some more video for your 'whale-killing' feature.'

'Good name, Harry,' she replied, 'I might just borrow it.'

With no need for further video feed, the camera dome was retracted and the throttle opened until the airspeed telemetry showed 80 knots. Twenty minutes later, the oddly-shaped UAV came to a hover off the starboard foredeck, moved sideways and settled gently onto the deck where the homing beacon had been placed.

'Wrap it up as soon as you can, please ladies, just in case we get inquisitive visitors.'

With that done, Bree was free to get on with making up the video for uploading. The finished result was very impressive, and when the YouTube uploading was done, there was about 10 minutes of action. She had even caught some close-up shots of Captain Toad in his role as 'The Face of the Enemy.' Also, there were the antics of the three RIBs racing around us yesterday.

She had asked Alex, with his deep, powerful voice, to do the voice-over, explaining exactly what the viewer was seeing at every stage, but avoiding any hint of who took the video. Apparently, she had also gone to the extra effort and formatted the video exactly the way YouTube wanted, so when the 10 minute clip was uploaded, it was searchable on-line within an hour.

Bree stayed on-line, watching her upload like a possessive mother, with Sandy beside her getting more and more excited as the hits counter spun up like a turbine starting. Despite myself, I stood by and watched for a while.

Noting my interest, Bree explained, 'To be considered a viral upload these days, a video must register five million hits within a three to five day period. When that happens, YouTube contracts advertisers and they start paying money.'

Intrigued, I asked, 'OK, how much money are we talking? $100... $200?'

Bree grinned. 'If this works out well, it could run into 6 or even 7 figures.'

I stared in disbelief, 'Bullshit! Over a million dollars? Really?'

She nodded, 'Yep! It can and does happen with top videos. We're hoping this gets the right attention.'

Looking at the hit counter rolling up, I got caught up in the excitement, forgetting what the subject matter was. The counter kept spinning and we kept watching, until it slowed momentarily and we saw what appeared to be in excess of one million hits.

Bree and Sandy squealed with delight as I patted them on the back and went to check the safety rail voltage booster.

The rest of the afternoon also remained quiet, until at 16:00, a lone RIB was seen to be approaching us from the direction of the processing mother-ship. In a pleasant change of pace, it slowed politely when still a hundred metres away and idled up to *Firebird's* stern.

There were just two occupants, a seaman in the ubiquitous grey overalls at the wheel and an officer in grey working uniform with two stripes on his shoulder boards, who I presumed to be the equivalent of a Lieutenant or Mate.

He had the driver hold position just off the stern and called out in good English,

'Good afternoon, Commander Stevens. My name is Lieutenant Mitsu, and I am a deck officer aboard the Nissabe Maru. My captain wishes me to invite you and your mate aboard our ship for the evening meal, and to discuss the difficulties and misunderstandings which have occurred between us. My captain is most anxious we should do everything possible to prevent any further arguments, and it is his wish we become good friends. May I say you will attend our ship at 18:00 hours?'

I stepped up to the presently non-lethal railing. 'Good afternoon to you, Lieutenant Mitsu, please excuse me for a moment while I speak with my crew.'

He bowed, 'Certainly, Commander. I await your pleasure.'

I ducked back to the cockpit table and in a low voice said, 'I think it would be foolish to go aboard the ship. Too many temptations for ambush or plain kidnapping, even though it would be handy to get an idea of the layout of the ship.'

There was a chorus of 'No. No way. Don't go!'

Therefore, I was happy with my decision and went back to the Lieutenant. 'Please pass my regrets to your captain that due to pressing duties, I will be unable to accept his most gracious offer. He is, however, welcome to visit here at a time convenient to both of us, to discuss those same matters of mutual concern.'

I could see the Lieutenant struggling to convert all the diplomatic waffle into something meaningful to take back to Captain

Toad. Finally, he bowed and said, 'Thank you for your consideration, Commander, and I will be pleased to convey your apology and the kind invitation to my captain. Good afternoon to you.'

He gave a final bow, muttered a command to the seaman and the RIB idled away until at about 50 metres clear, it sped up and headed back to the mother-ship.

Dave was the first to ask, 'What the fuck was that about?'

Alan summed it up for me. 'That, young man, was pure lies and misdirection. Harry and Sandy almost certainly would have been held hostage in return for information about their missing strike force. It's obvious they only suspect we had something to do with the disappearances, otherwise they'd be here with harpoon guns at the ready. They have shown they have no respect for other countries' laws or rights. They're a bit silly, really, to suddenly act so nice, when they allowed such a large raiding party to attack us. It just puts us on high alert. But consider what would have happened to normal cruising people who weren't trained and armed. They seem to want to eliminate any witnesses and all opposition to their whale killing program, or whatever other dirty deeds they are involved in.'

I made sure everyone was present and laid out options.

'Our choices are to either go on the offensive, or wait and deal with whatever they throw at us next. I might add that the positive side of waiting, is we are closer to having Sea Guardian and/or the Navy turn up. The negative side is, the next attack will probably be full-on. We can't expect the Navy for at least a couple of days and the same with Sea Guardian. The whalers want to eliminate us as witnesses, and also to find out what happened to their crew. In either case, the best we could hope for would to be taken prisoner and to have our boats burned.'

Alan asked, 'Being practical, if we were to take the offensive, what resources do we have to take on one ship and three boats jammed with armed large and angry whalers?'

'Apart from small arms and one long rifle, we have two .50 cal heavy machine guns with several hundred rounds of ammunition, two RPG-7 launching tubes with 20 rounds of armour-piercing, anti-tank, rocket grenades each, and some Semtex, the exact amount known only to Corrine. Oh. Almost forgot. Add a box of hand grenades to that list. I would imagine we could seriously damage all four boats with that lot.... but there would probably be some personnel injuries on the whaler's side.'

'Bloody hell!' he exclaimed, shocked out of his usual genteel frame of mind. 'I guess I shouldn't ask where that lot came from?'

I chuckled, 'No Alan, you probably shouldn't. But we have the resources and know how to use them!'

He showed an excellent tendency toward violence when threatened. 'Okay. In that case, let's think about the best way to utilise the hardware to greatest advantage. I suggest putting everything on *Seeker*, since it is the fastest, maybe leaving two or three crew here on *Firebird* for security, which will still give us plenty of hands to shoot and patch up as required.'

I nodded agreement to his ideas, but playing devil's advocate, I said. 'The only factor we haven't considered is that by initiating a full-on attack, we are committed to making sure they can't retaliate for at least two more days, or we'll have to be prepared and able to defend against serious reprisal.'

That statement got heads nodding wisely, but not a word was spoken for a while, until Alex spoke in his carefully reasoned manner. 'To take the offensive, what you're saying is that we must be prepared to inflict the maximum amount of damage our ordinance is capable of in the initial strike. Even leaving just one of the large RIBs mobile, is to invite a gunboat chasing us all over the harbour.'

'Good point, Alex,' Dave said, 'but what's to stop us from striking, then heading out? We could cripple all the big boats so they aren't seaworthy, then head around to Hobart.'

'Yep! We could do it, except a deep low and a violent front is approaching. It's the same one delaying Paul and probably Sea Guardian as well, so it may well keep us bottled up for a few days at least.'

After a further period of contemplative silence, Corrine said her piece, 'I'm in favour of a hard strike to cripple the four ships. It's been the Sea Guardian tactic for years and the only one which has achieved anything. That way, they won't be going anywhere for a long time, if ever. It would be a hell of a job to make large-scale repairs down here. The longer we play pat-a-cake with them, the greater the chances of one of us getting hurt or killed.

Look at the accidents these idiots have already had, just by fooling around! I hate to think what they'll do if they decided to get serious about trying to stop us. There's a lot of angry whalers over there and I'd rather not get into a hand-to-hand fight with them. I believe we should either get out of here right now, or plan a covert attack using everything we've got. However,' she added, 'if we bail out, they may just do the same, which means they get away with the whaling stuff and whatever else it is they have planned.'

Everyone had a chance to have a say, but in the end I had to summarise their thoughts.

'To sum up, it appears we are in favour of making a strong strike against the whalers with everything we've got or can come up with. However, a delay of 24 hours is also desired. Sound about right?'

There were mostly nods around the table, so I concluded with, 'Therefore, we'll plan for the operation to kick off tomorrow evening, unless the whalers force our hand by acting first.'

Bree and Kelly made another lovely roast dinner for the evening meal, and in case of a call to action, we only had some wine and a couple of beers each. Sandy and I took the watch until midnight, then we went 3-hourly to help the watch stay alert. I checked the progress of the front and it was due Monday sometime.

There were no further comms from Paul Davy, nor from Sea Guardian so we turned the watch over to Alan and Kelly at midnight and went to bed.

With the tensions and concern of the whalers, there was little time or enthusiasm for chasing up Sandy's plan for getting to know Hillary a lot better, so I left the subject alone for now and we enjoyed a peaceful sleep.

CHAPTER 24

PORT DAVEY, SUNDAY

Unusually, I slept past dawn and was woken by a loud knocking at the door leading directly up to the saloon. Sandy volunteered to answer it, but forgot to dress. Sandy just out of bed and naked is a powerful sight for a mere male, and Alan only had to cough and clear his throat a couple of times, before announcing the time was 06:00 and Captain Kurosawa had come calling.

By the time Sandy had thanked him and returned to bed, I was up, dressed and had splashed water on my face. Up top, I greeted Captain Toad most politely and invited him to sit and have a mug of tea or coffee which Kelly was brewing. To my surprise, he did and I was glad Alan had elected to join us.

Kurosawa started out by arrogantly demanding we immediately tell him everything we knew about the raiding party and why they had disappeared. I listened to his list of demands and thinly veiled threats for a few minutes, then decided to prick his ego balloon somewhat.

'You must forgive my bad manners, Captain, but I haven't introduced my good friend here. Captain Kurosawa, please meet Rear Admiral Stallman, Royal Australian Navy Fleet Commander.'

Kurosawa's piggy little eyes bugged out for a few moments, before he shot to his feet, his hand quivering as he held the salute until Alan slowly rose to his feet and returned it.

'Admiral. Please forgive me, Sir. I did not know your position.'

'Perfectly alright my dear Captain,' Alan drawled, emphasising the man's rank. 'You weren't to know and although I am here mainly as a guest of Commander Stevens, my active position in the RAN does put you in an awkward position, does it not?'

'Well, perhaps it does, sir, but I hoped we could move past any unpleasantness. I would like to think any disagreements would be handled by our respective Governments. We are here to do a job; while you are here on holiday, may I presume? There should be no reason why we should clash.'

I gave Kurosawa a stern look and took a deep breath. 'May I remind you, Captain, this 'clash' nonsense was started at Heard Island by one of your crew who came to see us. We had done nothing to you, but he was most arrogant and threatening in his manner and the incident which wrecked his boat was entirely his own stupid fault!

Furthermore, this same individual also came to us here, then carried on with more of the same rude, arrogant and threatening behaviour, which included firing a spear-gun at me and my crew.

Given this incident which put my crew at grave risk, plus your own blatantly illegal activities on an international scale, I cannot find any grounds for further discussion and request you leave my boat immediately.'

Both Alan and I stood, giving Kurosawa little choice but to suffer further loss of face and stand.

He ignored the customary pleasantries and shook his finger at me again. 'You will sincerely regret this attitude and course of action, Commander. That, I can promise you!'

'The only thing I regret, Captain, is allowing you aboard my vessel in the first place. Now get your fat arse back in your boat and out of my sight!'

He drew himself up to his full 5' 6" height and spat something in Japanese. 'I will not forget this insult, nor your previous insults. You will pay dearly for your brief moment of pleasure, and soon.'

He marched stiffly down the stern steps and continued stepping into the RIB, but didn't allow for the double-depth step down to the floor-boards and nearly pitched straight over the far side. He was stopped by the quick hands of his cox'n, but his heavily gold-braided hat kept going and slowly floated out of reach. With no boat-hook handy to retrieve it, and far too proud to ask for assistance, he barked an order at the cox'n who fired up the motors and departed rather faster than he would have preferred.

Naturally, Dave jumped in our RIB and retrieved it for a souvenir.

The whole encounter had to be re-told over breakfast and it was good to see everyone having a good laugh, but I had to deflate their spirits somewhat by pointing out that finally pretence was over, the challenge had been thrown down and the fight was on.

'It means that unless we are willing to bail out and let them get away with their whaling, Corrine's plan is now the only choice and we should hit them hard tonight, before they hit us.'

No one spoke in favour of leaving, but the thought of imminent action sobered up the mood, even though we were mentally prepared. Later in the morning, the girls launched *Dragonfly* again and set it to orbit the mother-ship for an hour, but although there were a lot of people shuttling between the mother-ship and the catchers, nothing which could help us further was seen.

Sandy broke off the orbit and departed the area to the west prior to heading back. Well beyond the heads, she was about to turn north in a wide arc, when she spotted a vessel at the edge of the video scan.

'Harry! We've got company. I'm turning west for a looksee.'

Dragonfly came left in a smooth curve, Bree on the video controls zooming out to get the bigger picture, but there was just one ship coming up from the south-west. For some reason, it was hard to see the shape of it until the UAV got closer.

'It's painted in splinter camouflage!' Bree exclaimed. 'I'll bet it's the Sea Guardian. They bought three ex-US Coastguard cutters. They aren't big, but they are fast.'

'Must be good sea-boats too,' I muttered, 'if they got sent down to Heard Island.'

'Yeah, they are, according to my girlfriend,' Bree said.

Sandy looked at me, 'What do you think? Go down and take a closer look?'

I nodded, 'Yes please. The risk is minimal since it's certainly not Japanese painted in splinter camo. Let's see who it is.'

Sandy set up a 500 ft orbit with the ship as the target, and as the optics locked on, the UAV faithfully went into a tight circle around the boat which was revealed as a pretty and sea-worthy shape with the letters SEA GUARDIAN painted on the sides of the super-structure, and the name *George Ambrose* painted on the stern.

I looked at Sandy, 'I don't suppose that thing of yours could do a radio relay, could it?'

She flashed a beaming smile, 'I never thought you'd ask, darling man. Of course we can, but only low power and on Channel 77 only.'

'Well done! Low power suits me. Take it down to 100 feet please, but widen the orbit out to 500 metres. What mic can I use?'

'It'll have to be this one attached to the console. Just a minute until Bree sets up the link.'

'How far out are they?' I asked while Bree fiddled with switches.

'About 15 miles,' Sandy replied.

'Okay, Harry. The link's open. You can call them, but whether they'll be listening...'

'*George Ambrose, George Ambrose. This is Dragonfly, Dragonfly* on VHF 77. Copy?'

I gave them 10 points for alertness, since the radio crackled into life almost immediately.

'Dragonfly, Dragonfly, George Ambrose. *Go ahead.*'

'We see you approaching Port Davey. If this is your destination, we have information for you.'

There was a longer pause before a different voice replied,

'Dragonfly, *request identification, but be careful this is open channel.*'

'Roger that, *George*. ID is Nina, Nina. I passed the tip about Heard Island and also this one about Port Davey. I'm relaying via a very low-power transmitter, therefore say when ready to copy SatPhone number. There is a hostile reception in Port Davey, so caution advised. Call me soonest. I like your boat by the way. Nice lines. Camo is quite effective too.'

'*ID and warning copied,* Dragonfly, *but I'm puzzled about the visuals. Go ahead the numbers.*'

I passed the SatPhone numbers and signed off. 'Thanks Bree. You can cut the link. Sandy, dear lady, can you safely do a fly-by of George's bridge?'

She had a devilish grin on her face when she replied, 'Of course I can. How about a speed run, followed by a hover?'

'Sounds good, but check for rigging in the way and allow for turbulence.'

'Tell me again how it goes, dearest, do I suck or blow?'

'Ha, ha. Billy Sitch!' I peered over their heads at the screen which showed a view of the bridge of the cutter growing at a ridiculous rate, then flashing past at crazy speed. The view then tilted at a sharp angle, before stabilising in a precise hover, about 3-metres away from the port bridge windows, effortlessly maintaining station despite the turbulence caused by wind and the ship's speed. Two figures, heavily wrapped in foul-weather gear, stepped out onto the bridge wing and examined the UAV from almost touching distance, before Sandy drifted it out away from the ship and made the transition back to forward flight.

Less than a minute later, the SatPhone rang.

'*Is that* Dragonfly?' *a female voice enquired with a hint of humour.* '*This is* George Ambrose.'

I laughed, 'Not at the moment. I've just changed hats to become Harry Stevens again.'

She returned my laugh, '*Well in that case Harry Stevens, this is Jacinta Kennedy, Skipper of* George. *I love your toy, but it was a very cheeky fly-by. Can I have one too?*'

'You probably can, Jacinta, but the waiting list is very long. Anyway, I wanted to warn you that a whaling mother-ship and three catchers are in harbour. The mother-ship is damaged, and is still pumping water, although they seem to be getting on with repairs and one catcher is badly holed and aground immediately inshore of the mother-ship.'

'Copy that Harry. What about the other two boats?'

'They're OK and have been actively catching Minke whales, but with this next storm due, they seem to be staying put. We've already had several run-ins with the crews and the Captain, and now the gloves are off, I'm afraid. We're anchored in good shelter where we can maintain surveillance, so if you'd like to join us, we need to talk face-to-face.'

'Sounds good. Are you a private vessel?'

'Affirm. Although there are two boats; an 83 ft sailing cat and a 100 ft power cruiser. Nine crew in total. There's plenty of water for your draft and good holding ground.'

'OK Harry. We'll do that. Be advised that we're very low on fuel and might need to bludge some.'

'No problem with fuel and our anchorage is just inside Datum Point, position S43.321060 E145.996706. The whalers are at S43.333140 E145.991591. Given their attitude at the moment, they might arc-up a bit if you get too close, so a north-about rounding of Breaksea Islands is strongly advised.'

'Copied all that, thanks Harry, and appreciate the heads-up. We'll come and have a chat. See you soon. George clear.'

CHAPTER 25

PORT DAVEY, SUNDAY EVENING

It was about 90 minutes later, when the slim, raked bow of the ex-Coastguard cutter slid into sight around Datum Point. Even up close, the splinter pattern camouflage in muted blue and grey, effectively broke up the outline of the Sea Guardian boat. The towering superstructure made her look a lot bigger than *Seeker* which was only 10 feet shorter.

Even having normal external propellers for drive, she still only drew 2 metres, and had no trouble nestling in close to the pair of us.

A woman who I presumed to be Jacinta, with a man in tow, ferried over to *Firebird* in an RIB.

We welcomed them aboard and introduced our crew, including Jasper and Krazy. Jasper caused a bit of a stir, as usual, but we finally got them seated with hot drinks in hand.

Jacinta was a lively, competent-looking lady, appearing to be in her fifties, and with her was her husband Rick, who was the Chief Engineer. They were Australian, she told us, but the crew were from many different nationalities, and I was surprised to learn that there were just 15 of them.

'Call me Jacky,' she said with a grin, 'everybody does. Now; who belongs to what boat?'

'Dave and Corrine own *Seeker*, the royal blue Italian phallic symbol, and I own *Firebird*.'

'Cool! Although I like the Italian job better,' Jacky said. 'It looks fast. I was pleased to be given command of *George* and he'll do 30 knots, but yours looks faster. What'll it do, 40 or 45 maybe?'

By way of reply, Dave motioned upwards with his palm.

'No! Really? Faster than 45 knots?'

'Yep. Light load and in calm water, we've seen over 75 knots and I reckon there might be a bit more in it with some careful trimming.'

'No way! What the hell have you got driving it?' By now Rick was interested, being their engineer.

'A pair of MTU V-16s with 2600 hp each and a booster turbine with 5600 hp, all driving water-jets.'

'Shit! We've only got a pair of Paxman 2250 hp V-12s. I suppose you're all carbon-fibre as well?' When Dave confirmed that, he said, 'Now that I'd like to see!'

'Sure, any time.'

To get back to the matter in hand and bring Jacky and Rick up-to-date, I recapped briefly everything that had happened, starting with Heard Island, then the night raid, but without details. Both she and Rick were blown away by the information.

'That's unheard-of, Harry. Whalers never directly attack like that. There must be some other powerful reason why they have made it so personal and want to get rid of you. This changes the situation, but we still aren't supposed to take any action which poses a direct threat to human life, unless we are attacked directly.'

Corrine frowned at Jacky's statement, so I said in a mild tone, 'It's just as well we're not constrained in any way. We'll have to work your restrictions into the plan.'

It was Jacky's turn to look troubled, 'C'mon Harry. Any action you take with us around, will be seen as involving us, whether we do or don't.'

I nodded, 'Yep. I can see that, Jacky, and it's why I said we'll take it into account when planning our strike. You'll have to remain here, out of the way, but having you around makes for a bunch of good witnesses. We're expecting a Navy patrol boat in a few days, but this weather might muck up their schedule even more.'

Jacky looked relieved, 'That'll be another reason to avoid direct action. The RAN can't be involved in any direct action.'

When I introduced the crew, I hadn't mentioned Alan's official position or rank, and didn't now, but grinned ruefully, 'No, they can't, but what happens before they get here is a different story, and really it's a bit late for us to avoid action, I'm afraid. The armed raid they made on us cost them seven deceased and one held captive.'

Their jaws sagged at the news, which for them, was a big step up from egg and flour-throwing.

'Bloody hell, Harry! What the hell did you do?'

I tried to look modest, while my crew all grinned. 'Oh, we shot some, electrocuted others, Jasper bagged a couple, and we have one locked up in Dave's for'rard cabin. There's a range of charges we can lay on him, so the Navy can take him off our hands when they get here.'

Jacky and Rick were stunned. 'But how?...I mean...oh crap!' She looked at Rick, 'We've sailed into an all-out war!'

He patted her shoulder. 'It would appear so, my dear, but remember, Harry and his crew didn't start it. All they were doing was defending themselves. We would have to do the same if we were attacked first. We are allowed to defend ourselves to the best of our ability.'

Jacky looked frustrated, 'Yeah, yeah. I know, but I didn't want to have it happen on my watch.'

'Unfortunately, as Harry says, this mob is aggressive, so we may not have any choice in the matter.'

He looked over at me, 'For defence, we have the usual flares and a rifle, but that's about it for offensive weapons. I don't suppose you guys have much?'

I grinned, cleared my throat and said casually, 'We do have a few items we've collected from various bad guys in times past.'

'OK, I'll bite. Just what do you have which would be useful?'

'An assortment of handguns, two 9mm sub-machine guns, two .50 cal Browning heavy machine guns, two RPG-7 launchers plus 40 HEAT rounds for them, some hand-grenades and a quantity of Semtex, my former demolitions expert here has squirreled away. We figured we should be able to do some good things with all that.'

Jacky and Rick were speechless for a few moments. 'Bloody hell,

Harry!' Jacky repeated, 'You could start a small war with all that!'

'Hopefully, we can stop one in its tracks if we do it right,' I responded.

'Yeah, okay. What do you think you can do to stop these guys killing any more whales, without killing their crew?'

I glanced over at Corrine, who picked up the ball, 'Short of just blowing the bejeezus out of all four boats, my suggestion would be to wrap det cord around each prop and rudder shaft and cripple them where they sit. They might spring a few more minor leaks, but no one will get hurt, if that's your big concern.

But please remember that eight of these bozos came calling the other night, they were armed and weren't dropping in for a midnight mug of coffee. I think it's about time you recognise these clowns for who they are... possible military dudes posing as commercial whalers who won't let anyone stand in their way and who'll go to any lengths to get what they want.'

It's not often Corrine has her say, but this time she really let Jacky have it. To her credit, she took it on the chin and nodded ruefully, 'Fair call, and guess I deserve it. I just don't like violence, especially if it can be avoided. Not all Sea Guardian skippers are blood-thirsty fools. Mostly we can stop a certain activity by just being there and shooting video. It's preferable to shooting people.'

Corrine shrugged, 'I acknowledge your reservations, but if one of these big boys is coming for you, Jacky, I hope you can pull a trigger or something, because he isn't going to be asking for your autograph!'

'Good point, but to wrap det cord around the prop-shafts, you'll have to have scuba gear and a very good wet or better still, a dry suit. Have you got scuba?'

'Yeah, we have several sets and a compressor, although we only have one extra-thick steamer wetsuit,' I tossed in.

Jacky waved dismissively, 'We have plenty of gear, including the best dry-suits designed for these waters. We also have several ex-professional divers who would love to do some hands-on strike-back. They're trained in underwater demolition. If it suits you, of course?'

Corrine smiled. 'Of course it would suit, and thanks very much for the offer. I didn't really relish the thought of paddling around under all those boats in the dark, and if your guys are demo-trained, that's perfect. I have plenty of det cord and waterproof timer-igniters and can tell your guys exactly where to make the wrap for best effect.'

'Excellent! Perhaps you can come over later and brief them? But in the meantime, what's your plan, Harry? I presume you have one?'

Sandy laughed, 'Harry always has a plan and most times, they seem to work.'

'Thank you my dear, for the vote of confidence, and yes, I do have a plan. But to work backwards, when we go on the offensive, the whalers will respond strongly. I count four boats they have lost, out of a possible ten in total, leaving six fast, agile, but soft-skinned boats to attack us. Therefore, we can choose to either meet them head-on, or disappear. The weather is closing in tomorrow and the swell is already up as we all saw today, so leaving Port Davey may not be much of an option.'

'We need fuel desperately if we're going to do anything,' Rick chipped in.

'Good point and I did promise! What can you spare, Dave?'

He thought a moment. 'Would 5,000 litres get you out of trouble?'

Rick grinned, 'What are you, a tanker as well? 5,000 will be plenty...thank you!'

'Okay. We'll do the transfer when we finish this planning brief. Sorry Harry, please go ahead.'

'No problem, mate. We needed to get that cleared up soonest. Now, while we think about whether to stay or go hide somewhere else, I thought tonight, an RIB with your divers aboard, could leave here for the point east of the whalers. The tide will be ebbing at around 22:00, so that's when two other RIBs could make a fast run down past the mother-ship and the two catchers, tossing flares and whatever else you normally would do to annoy and harass them. They would be acting as a distraction for your divers to place the det cord, set the timers for 20 minutes, then get the hell out of Dodge. The tide will carry them well outside any searchlight range, but once picked up, their RIB heads straight back to where we'll be waiting close in on the north side of Tonguers Point, inside of Turnbull's Island.'

Jacky looked at the chart I'd pinned down with empty mugs. 'Why there, Harry?'

'Because if we want to avoid a direct confrontation, it gives us the chance to maybe dodge them when they come here looking for us. The high ground between us and them at Tonguers Point will hide us from radar. The mother-ship still has too much list for hers to be effective, but the two operational catchers will have theirs running.'

Rick offered, 'Seems like a lot of trouble trying to avoid a bunch of RIBs which will probably find us anyway, especially in the morning when it's light!'

Others nodded around the table, so I looked at Jacky and laid it on her.

'I hope you realise I'm only suggesting this half-arsed plan to fit in with your stated wish that no one be hurt. The trouble with your wish for peace is that the whalers aren't following the same rulebook. In fact, they don't have one, so if they come for us, you'd better expect no holds barred.'

Jacky chewed her lip, gnawed a fingernail and frowned at the chart for a while, then finally gave a tight smile. 'Fuck 'em! I've had enough of this pussy-footing around with these fuckers. For years they've called it 'Research'. Now at least they've stopped pretending and are saying openly this is commercial whaling. Let's treat them the same as they've already treated you guys! I know all our crew are dead keen to go bust some heads.'

'Well said,' I congratulated her, 'that makes life much easier. Now we can go back to Plan 'A' which allows for a decent strike to cripple all their ships and we can fight them off properly afterwards.' I looked around the table, with renewed spirits now Jacky's restrictions had been lifted.

'Okay folks, here's what we're going to do. If anybody has a better idea, just chime in.

Dave, how about you and Corrine take *Seeker* over to *George*, do the refuel and Corrine can brief the divers. Mount the second .50 cal on your sundeck, check the feed from the ammo boxes and dig out your RPG and rounds. Alex will take our unit and during the attack, he and I will fire from our foredeck.

For the duration of the attack on the whalers, *Firebird* and *George* will stay anchored on minimum chain with *George's* engines idling ready for an instant move. All good so far?'

Heads nodded and mouths stayed shut, so I carried on. 'Once we have the whaler's retaliation mob on us, we'll use the two .50 cal for most of the work... three-round bursts to conserve ammo, single if you can. Shred any active RIBs to put them out of action, but you need to wound the occupants at least, so we don't have swimmers trying to climb aboard. You'll also have your handguns and the Type 89 carbine, while we'll have the sub-machine guns, handguns and the RPG-7s as last resort.

Alan, you'll be on the wheel of *Firebird*, motors only of course, and Dave on the wheel of *Seeker*. Corrine will have one .50 cal. And...' I looked at Jacky, 'Do you have a spare body who could use the other .50 cal?'

She didn't have to think, 'Mary Jones. She's our electronics tech, but is an ex-US Navy Chief Petty Officer. She loves the big, ugly things and I know she'd love the chance to use it on these targets. Any of them would, but she's the best.'

I clapped my hands, 'Great. Okay people. That's it for the moment. We'll have another brief later this afternoon. I don't expect Captain Toad will do anything before we blow their props, but we'll be watching the camera and radar, so be ready in case he has a rush of blood to the head. We'll send the UAV out later to have a good look.'

The party broke up quickly, with Jacky and Rick heading straight back to *George* while Dave and Corrine fired up one of *Seeker's* diesels and idled the 50 metres to raft up with *George*.

We didn't have a great deal to do, except I shortened the anchor chain to the minimum, Alex stowed the RIB under the overhanging day bed and Sandy dug out our entire supply of weapons and ammunition.

Before they cast off from us, Corrine thoughtfully and reluctantly passed across the H&K MP5-SD6 sub-machine gun, with a handful of loaded magazines. Our best defences were the two .50 cal guns, and the sub-machine guns. I didn't want to waste the RPG rounds as they were a massive overkill against soft-skinned targets like the RIBs.

As Bree and Kelly prepared a simple meal, Alan took me aside, 'This is shaping up to be a bit hairy. Do you really want to go ahead with the plan?'

I regarded him soberly. 'Yes I do Alan, and I appreciate the position it puts you in, but these mongrels have committed a crime against nature and Australia, and have shown they don't give a shit about anybody. Life is cheap to them, apparently. If there was an easy way to stop them I'd take it, but I haven't seen one yet.'

He nodded reluctantly, 'Yeah. You're right, unfortunately. They appear to be a blood-thirsty bunch, so this seems to be the only way. Pity we couldn't bail out and head for civilisation.'

'I agree, but who would keep watch over the bad guys?'

He gave me a sad smile.

The meal was good, but with everyone psyching up for battle, there was little conversation and the only laughter was nervous. The masthead camera and radar were being monitored continually, and I saw Dave and Corrine were sensibly remaining rafted up to *George* for now.

As is usual in the lead-up to an operation kicking off, tension was building as each person mentally rehearsed their duties. Ominously, but practically, Sandy laid out several first aid kits and designated Hillary to be the roving first-aider. All weapons were checked over carefully again, then loaded, with each person selecting what suited them best.

I tucked the Grizzly into a waist holster, and selected the H&K MP5 with the built-in suppressor. Alan had the TAC-14 shotgun close-by the steering station, while Bree, Kelly and Hillary took a PMR-30 each. Sandy had her Service Glock, but also grabbed the Mini-Uzi, a much better choice for night use.

As 22:00 approached, I dimly saw two RIBs leave *George* heading south, a cluster of dark figures in each. I always felt uncomfortable watching someone else leading off on one of my operations, but was able to recognise that professional divers were going to do a much better job than either Corrine or myself could ever do.

We were under black-out conditions, except for the dimmest of red foot lights, with just the masthead camera tracking the boats in IR mode. A fly-over by *Dragonfly* earlier in the evening hadn't shown any special activity on any of the boats, although the water output from the pumps on the mother-ship had slowed a lot more and the list had decreased even more.

CHAPTER 26

PORT DAVEY, SUNDAY–MONDAY

As good as the camera was, 1400 metres in IR mode was stretching its abilities, resulting in a slightly degraded image. Nevertheless, it was still good enough to make out the two RIBs angling to the left of the whaler's cluster of anchored boats to counter the ebbing tide. Both boats held position as four figures in full scuba outfits and cumbersome dry suits, slid over the sides. They drifted off with the current until they were closer to their targets before submerging.

I couldn't see any sort of regular deck patrols shining lights over the side, although there must have been some guards on duty, but there weren't any boats patrolling. The plan I'd discussed and refined with Jacky had a degree of flexibility in it, whereby we left it up to the divers as to whether they needed to stage a diversion or not. The quiet, stealthy option was much preferred if there were no patrols or obvious guards who needed distracting, and that appeared to be the case. The two RIBs drifted silently with the strong tidal flow past the whaler's boats without any alarms being raised, then stopped as they dropped anchors to wait for their divers. I'd worked out rough timings for them to get into position, wrap the prop shafts and rudder posts, set the timers and depart the area to the pick-up point.

It was therefore, with great relief I saw dark figures being pulled in over the sides. Soon after, a small directional green light flashed as the signal all was well. The boats pulled anchor, drifted a bit further away before starting engines, then headed back. As arranged, one boat swung past the stern of *Firebird* and a diver called out, 'All good, Commander. There should be action anytime now.'

'Thanks fellas. Top job. Get ready for the response.'

They waved and headed over to the *George* to unload, while I returned to the camera image which I'd hooked up to the TV screen in the saloon so all could see. It was all a bit anti-climactic as nothing happened for another few minutes, then it looked like there was a slight disturbance in the water at the stern of the mother-ship, although it was difficult to make out. What was hard to miss were the lights which were suddenly turned on over all the boats, and crew running like ants up and down the decks, peering over the sides. Searchlights came on, their stark white beams frantically sweeping the brown frigid waters, in a futile effort to spot any intruders. RIBs were launched and driven in ever-widening circles, until a gangway was lowered down the side of the mother-ship, allowing several black-suited divers with tanks to drop into the water.

Even at 1400 metres, the short, rotund figure of Captain Toad stood out, being the only one encased in a magnificent red dressing gown with a fur collar. There was a disturbance amongst the crew at the foot of the gangway, requiring him to lean over the rail above them, waving his arms. Hand-held radios were lifted to lips and two of the patrolling RIBs broke off and headed downstream.

'Looks like a diver or two have been swept away by the current,' Alan observed.

'I think you're right. Those were just wet-suits they had on, and they didn't have any safety lines attached,' I replied. 'If they're still conscious, they might be able to swim ashore.'

Whatever happened, they weren't coming back to the landing stage, and after a while, the RIBs returned to their futile patrols.

It was nearly 20-minutes later when Captain Toad re-appeared, fully dressed in working uniform, a number of men with him, most carrying rifles and spear guns.

'OK folks. It's game on!' I announced. 'Alan. Fire her up, lift the anchor and move over to the eastern shore, just off Aylen Point, if you please.'

'On it, Harry,' was his crisp reply as the anchor cleared the bottom and our silent drive moved us out. I found the right microphone for the marine VHF and informed *George and Seeker* we had hostile incoming and they were armed.

'Copy that,' came back from both boats, and I was pleased to see Dave had moved *Seeker* behind *George* to hide as long as possible. We tracked four RIBs speeding across the water toward our position, well-marked by the *George* sitting with many lights on and crew moving around the decks.

'Better get your people inside Jacky, these guys may try shooting from a distance.'

'Roger that,' was the laconic reply and moments later, the decks cleared, as the whaler's RIBs came roaring in at full speed, turning at the last second to race around their old enemy.

That was when *Seeker* leapt out from behind *George*, like a moray eel striking at a fat fish, scattering the cluster of RIBs, causing two to collide, spilling their crew into the freezing waters.

The other two RIBs had just ducked around the tangled pair, when both .50 cals zeroed in on them and stammered briefly, chewing into rubberised fabric, flesh and bone indiscriminately. All was quiet for a few moments, before the two RIBs involved in the collision started to regain some crew, managing to get both boats partly functional and headed for the low stern sides of *George*.

'Go Alan,' I called urgently, 'we need to head them off to stop them climbing aboard. Aim to pass down the starboard side, but don't stop.'

'Roger that, Harry.'

Alex was already right up in the starboard bow, but with the Remington shotgun in his hand. I remembered he'd asked me to dig out the special shotgun shells I'd brought from the Gold Coast so long ago I'd forgotten about them. Although a lot slower than *Seeker*, we still accelerated quite smartly to our max-power speed of 16 knots. And we were quiet, particularly from the front, as we swept down on two RIBs in the process of getting men up to the railing around *George's* stern. Alex cut loose with the Remington

12-gauge sending long tongues of white-hot flame out of the muzzle with each shot. Men fell screaming back into the water as the powdered aluminium and magnesium mix burnt straight through everything it touched.

Someone in one of the boats tried to shoot Alex, but I triggered two 3-round bursts from the MP5, and the man and the RIB just folded up and sank on the spot. It left one tenacious whaler who waited until our starboard stern came at him, and lunged up and caught the handhold on the swim platform. I had to ignore him for the moment since I was on the diametrically opposite corner of the boat, and scanning the waters ahead for more targets, while Alex reloaded the Remington 12-gauge.

I screamed a warning to Alan, but it was Hillary who called in our big gun; Jasper.

'Bad man, Jasper. Go get him!'

I had noticed that my big cat doesn't need much encouragement to tackle bad guys; or girls for that matter. In this case, the hulking whaler was just stepping into the cockpit, when a black blur performed a perfect drop-cat off the top of the cockpit roof, planted both sets of front claws in the man's shoulders, and clamped onto his throat.

This had almost become Jasper's trademark means of rapid takedown, although it leaves a god-awful mess to clean-up later. But he does get the bad guys before they have a chance to have a go at us.

The big man tried to push Jasper away, but it was like trying to move a limpet, since he now had both sets of rear claws raking hard into the man's crotch. It has been said the brain cannot process two separate sets of extreme pain at the same time, but whoever came up with that fascinating theory, hadn't taken a Jasper attack into consideration.

If his throat had been functioning, he might have screamed loudly, but it was not to be and he expired quietly, but messily on the top step. Fortunately, Hillary called Jasper off before he made a meal of the man, asking him to sit in place. She reported to me the results of the confrontation and together, we scanned all around for any more starters, but all was quiet. I signalled to Alan to reduce power to idle and to stop alongside *George*, where Jacky and some crew were waiting to have a chat. Several searchlights were carefully sweeping around the ship looking for survivors, but there didn't appear to be any.

As usual, the actual duration of the encounter took barely five minutes, although it seemed to have been much longer.

'Holy crap, Harry!' Jacky exclaimed. 'That was intense! Did we get them all?'

'Yep, I think so, Jacky. There's none left this side, so if your crew don't see any, then we're done.'

'But four boats and sixteen men gone in just minutes. It's just terrible!'

I drew a deep breath, trying hard to avoid having to scream at this woman who refused to face reality. 'Actually, it was just on six minutes, and yes, it was terrible we had to defend ourselves so forcefully. Earlier, we might have damaged their boats, but I guarantee we didn't hurt one person with our attack. As I said before, they chose to come at us, armed and ready to take out both our crews. It's hardly our fault we're better prepared than they thought, and our better planning is due to superior training and past experiences here and in the Middle East.'

'I didn't know you had military experience. What were you?'

'Major. SAS. Corrine was one of my troopers. Sniper, demolitions expert and hand combat specialist.'

'Oh. I see...I think. So, the whalers really were outgunned by taking you on?'

'In general, yes. At Heard Island, they tried to intimidate us into leaving so they could get on with whale killing, but when we looked like staying, they upped the pressure. They're so used to getting their own way all the time, they forget there are a few people like us who are prepared to fight back. I don't regret a single action we've taken, and nor do any of my crew.'

'I do understand, Harry, and I'm not going to make a fuss over it. I'm just not used to the escalation of violence to this extent, but what's done is done. Let's see what they'll do next.'

What they did next was nothing!

Morning dawned with a howling west wind driving solid sheets of cloud so low, the tops of all the hills and mountains around us were totally enveloped. Blinding rain squalls hissed furiously as they marched across the harbour, whipping the choppy waters into foam, and drumming frantically on the cabin tops.

After the excitement of the night, Dave and I had decided to raft both our boats up against *George Ambrose*, in case we had to move quickly again. Given the drag on *George's* anchor caused by the howling wind, Dave and I used our RIB to ferry our main anchors, one per trip, out 50 metres or so, then winching in to set them firmly in the sand bottom. With the load eased on *George's* tackle, the three boats rode more comfortably. We accepted Jacky's invitation to come aboard for breakfast and to meet her crew. Despite not much sleep, everyone was in high spirits and as we mingled, giving and accepting congratulations from *George's* crew, it was clear Jacky was the only one who didn't want to use violence to stop people killing whales.

This mob were all in favour of getting a few shots back.

The opening of the second round came in the shape of Lieutenant Mitsu, the polite but powerless junior officer who braved the elements to make the miserable trip across in what had to be their last surviving RIB. To spare Jacky any embarrassment, I invited him aboard *Firebird*, and took him into the saloon where the heaters were running and Sandy handed him dry towels and a hot drink.

Though reluctant, he finally accepted a large mug of steaming coffee and tried not to slurp too greedily at the fragrant liquid. When his shakes had settled enough to be able to talk, his message was simple.

'My Captain would like to express his regret for the unpleasantness of the past twelve hours. He hopes we will be able to settle any remaining disagreements by discussion and without resorting to violence.'

To Mitsu's discomfort, I started laughing and the representatives of crews from all three boats joined in.

'My apologies to you Lieutenant, we mean no disrespect for you personally, but we regard your captain as a fool of the highest order. His stubbornness in the face of embarrassing defeat is just costing the lives of his crew. So far, by my rough count, he has thrown away the lives of 28 of his crew, at least 8 RIBs and 16 large outboard engines.

For a small whaling fleet, a long way from home, I would think that sort of attrition would be unacceptable and unsustainable. I'd like to hear your personal opinion… your opinion, that is, not Captain Kurosawa's.'

Mitsu looked even more uncomfortable.

'C'mon, Mitsu. You're among friends here. No one is going to tell Captain Toad what you said in your own defence.'

He thought, took a sip of coffee and finally spoke, 'I am pleased with your offer of friendship and your kind treatment. Life on the big ship is difficult under the command of Captain Kurosawa, and it is true he has become obsessed with eliminating the 'Red Devils' as he calls you and your crew, except now there are three sets of Red Devils. There are many who disagree with the captain's policies, but we dare not speak out as all the senior officers are active military. Only Lieutenants and below are civilian rated.'

I mulled over his words, then trying not to show alarm, asked, 'Is your boat driver trustworthy? Or is he one of Kurosawa's minions?'

Mitsu shook his head, 'He is loyal to me personally. He is my steward and comes from my home village.'

I looked at Sandy, 'Sweetness, would mind inviting the Lieutenant's driver inside to dry off and warm up?'

She smiled broadly, 'Delighted to do so.'

The poor man, of quite small stature compared to the hulking sumo-sized forms which had comprised the two raiding groups, was shaking uncontrollably and dripping wet. He was given towels, dry clothes and shown to the bathroom to change. On his return, he was presented with a mug of coffee and a seat in front of a heater blowing hot air, but lacking command of English, he was unable to directly express his appreciation, except through Mitsu.

It was apparent these small kindnesses went a long way to gain Mitsu's trust, for he opened up some more with information about the whaling operation and the fact the senior officers were active military. Alan was most interested and without letting on about his rank and position, asked a few more casual questions.

After which he asked if he could have a word with Sandy, Dave, Corrine and myself.

'Guys, this is getting really heavy. It was one thing to have commercial whaling operations in Australian waters and on Australian soil, but to have the boat's senior officers all military, takes this to a new political level. I have to admit it's above my pay-grade.'

We four of the executive committee agreed, so I suggested, 'Why don't we kick it up to the top? I know just the man to hand-ball this to.'

Dave gave a bark of laughter, 'I love it! Way to go, Harry. It's the only smart thing to do.'

There was general agreement all around, so we went back to the saloon.

'Lieutenant. You have given us some information which may help resolve this conflict without further bloodshed, but we need to consult with other persons. May I ask where does your allegiance lie...with Captain Kurosawa or with Japan?'

'With my home country, Sir,' he replied immediately. 'I do not always approve of my captain's actions, but we are not given any opportunity to voice our objections, or to refuse to accept orders.'

'Good. Two more questions. If we can guarantee protection for you and your man, would you be prepared to stay here and not return to your ship? And if so, would you be prepared to tell your story to some senior people in the Australian Government?'

He looked troubled and spoke in rapid Japanese to his country-man, who made what sounded like an impassioned speech in reply. The Lieutenant thought some more, before saying, 'My companion has reminded me that as Japanese citizens, our primary duty is to the greater good of our country. He also reminded me of all the times I have complained in private to him of many of the wrong things we have done as whalers and continue to do. Therefore, we will do as you ask.'

I beamed with relief and shook his hand. 'Excellent! Two last questions before I must make some phone calls. How many RIBs are left on the whale boats and are all the ships damaged?'

He spoke to his man again, before replying, 'Just two are left, including this one here. But the big ship has three small lifeboats, although they are not designed for long-distance travel. Also, all ships have lost their propellers and rudders. The engineers were discussing plans to maybe make repairs to one shaft on the *Nissabe Maru*, but it would entail using the second shaft for spares and it would take many days of difficult work. The smaller boats, the catchers, are crippled and will need to be towed to a repair facility.'

I gave him a short head bow and said 'Thank you, Lieutenant. Your assistance will be rewarded.'

He gave a grim smile, 'I do hope so, sir. I fear we have taken a course of action that will leave us out of work.'

With some more words to settle him down, I asked Alex, Bree and Kelly to stay with our new guests, took the SatPhone and with Sandy, Corrine, Alan, Hillary and Dave in tow, went down to our stateroom and closed the door.

CHAPTER 27

PORT DAVEY, MONDAY

'*Harry! How lovely to hear from you. Where are you and what's going on? What's the noise in the background?*'

'Hi Charlie. It's good to hear you too. We're having a holiday after collecting the new boat, and are in Port Davey, down in the south-west corner of Tasmania and the noise is wind and rain; a great deal of it and moving fast. I need to talk to the Boss soonest, since we've stumbled across a situation he needs to know about.'

'*Sounds familiar, Harry. Can't you even go on holidays without finding trouble? Just keep talking for a moment or two while the Boss gets off the phone... hang on, here he is.*'

... '*Harry! How are you and how's the new boat? What's going on?*'

'Morning, Andy. We're in Port Davey Tasmania, and the boat is brilliant. You'll love it when you get a chance to join us for a real holiday.'

'*I'll hold you to that, mate. I'm due to have some time off soon when Parliament breaks, so Lara and I were talking about getting away. Charlie keeps shaking her head, but what's the point in being the Boss if you can't make things happen? Anyway, I take it this isn't a social call, so what trouble has found you this time?*'

'Ha, ha! Everyone's a comedian this morning, but regarding the holiday, you organise your end and we'll keep a cabin spare. Regarding trouble, we've tripped across a small group of Japanese whalers operating in Australian waters, with active military guys holding all the senior officer positions.'

'*Geeze, that's a sticky one, Harry. Officially, we protest and carry on about the Antarctic exclusion zone, but in reality, we can't do much.*'

Sometimes Greenpeace or Sea Guardian move in to help, but where did you see these guys? Must have been in the Southern Ocean.'

'Funnily enough that was where we saw them for the first time... at Heard Island which belongs to Australia, the last time I looked.'

'Heard Island? That's being a bit naughty! Were they working?'

'Yep, they were. The catchers were catching and the mother-ship was processing.'

'Right! I remember mention of a frigate being taken off patrol to make a dash to Heard Island to chase up reports of whaler activity. So it was you?'

'Yeah. Afraid so. I called my friend Alan Stallman and he arranged things, but they missed the whalers, although we found them again.'

'You do get around old mate, if you tripped over them again. How is Alan? I haven't talked to him for ages.'

'He looks really well, and he's right here now. You can say hello in a minute, but about these whalers; I'm also looking at them here and now.'

There was a moment of silence...then, 'Well. I suppose if he's there, you must be looking at him, although I'm buggered if I know what he's doing there.'

'Andy! You truly do need a holiday! Now will you shut the fuck up for a minute and let me tell you about the Japanese whalers who are here in Port Davey, which is in Tasmania, and who are still catching and processing whales? As we speak!'

Alan had a scandalised look on his face, but Hillary giggled.

Well, if your good mate happens to be the current PM of Australia, you should be able to tell him to shut the fuck up. I mean, someone has to occasionally, when he starts waffling on and not listening!

'Sorry Harry. Let's back up the bus. I thought you were talking about Alan. What's the bottom line?'

I took a deep breath. 'Bottom line, Andy. An active Japanese commercial whaling operation is being conducted with a processing mother-ship and three catchers based in Port Davey on the west coast of Tasmania, and they'd been doing the same thing at Heard Island. Obviously, both places are Australian territory, but furthermore, I have learned that all the senior officers on the four boats are active Japanese Marine Self-Defence Force officers.

They have tried to intimidate us into leaving both places, and to date have conducted two armed night raids on us, with the total loss of 23 men, 7 RIBs and I have arrested one man on a range of charges, and am holding him captive. Oh, nearly forgot...we have crippled the main four boats by removing their propellers and rudders. We also have two civilian defectors or refugees who have supplied a great deal of information about the whaling operations, so I have also given my promise to this gentleman, that he and his steward would be looked after in return for telling all.'

.....'Crap, Harry! You don't do things by halves, do you? I think I got all that, but if not, Charlie certainly has. Conducting whaling operations on Australian soil is bad enough and warrants a call to their Ambassador, but having active military people in charge steps things up a big notch. Not to mention making armed attacks on Australian citizens in Australian waters. This warrants a call to Japan. Is the guy you have captive in their military?'

'He claims not to be, but I'm not sure, Andy, since we only just found out about the military connection a few minutes ago, which was the reason for the call.

We have some support in the form of Sea Guardian and their boat, the *George Ambrose*, which we called in. Additionally, Alan has diverted the first of the new Arafura-class offshore patrol boats to head this way, but it's caught up in this massive storm that's belting the shit out of this part of Tasmania at the moment. Perhaps you'd better have a quick word to Alan; here he is.'

I passed the SatPhone across and there was a rather one-sided conversation, with Alan not smiling much. Finally, he passed it back and I found Charlie already babbling excitedly.

'Wow, Harry! I was listening in as always, and I can't believe you're *in such a pile of poo again! You were supposed to be on holidays, and speaking of which, is there a chance you could accommodate the Boss, Lara and myself this time next week? It would be for about 10 days, if it's okay? What do you think? Please say yes...he was so excited to think he could get to sail your new boat.'*

I couldn't help but laugh. She was irrepressible! 'Slow down, Princess! Yes, I'm sure we can fit you in next Monday. Alan and Hillary will have to go back to work shortly, if not sooner. We'll probably still be here or in Strahan, but we'll talk again before then for the final arrangements.'

'Great.....thanks. Talk soon Harry and stay safe. Don't get shot, or sushied or anything terrible!'

I disconnected the SatPhone and looked at Alan. 'What's the Boss think about things?'

He gave a wry smile, 'How about, 'Not happy, Jan!' or 'right royally pissed-off PM' which might be closer to the truth. For a politician, he's got a good grasp of the nuts and bolts side of how stuff works. And the guts to say 'No' when he can see bullshit being shoved down his throat. But he's really going to get stuck into the Japanese. Whaling in Aussie territory is bad enough, but intimidating and attacking Aussie citizens to cover up what they're doing is way over the top. Then sneaking the military in as ship's crew looks like spying in anyone's language.

But basically, he's approved of everything we've done and would be happy if more bad luck were to fall on them if we have to defend ourselves again, which I still hope won't have to happen.'

He grinned suddenly, 'He also mentioned Charlie was arranging for them to come down next week and he was asking when we were going, so I said we would probably have to leave later in the week, if not sooner. We've had a great holiday and enjoyed ourselves immensely, but work is calling.'

'Are you still getting Paul to drop in with *Arafura?*' I asked. 'This mess will need sorting out at higher levels than my pay grade.'

He chuckled, 'Yeah. He's still coming and the Navy will clean up the mess... as usual. Don't you worry about that!'

I chuckled at the usual inter-service rivalry, then asked the others, 'Everybody clear on what the situation is? The Navy will take over as soon as *Arafura* gets here, at which point, we might bail-out, resuming our voyage counter-clockwise around Tassie and staying out of trouble. Having the PM aboard will help with that objective, and he, Lara and Charlie will join on or about next Sunday or Monday. Unfortunately, Alan and Hillary will be leaving.'

'What about our new guests?' Dave asked. 'I reckon we need to watch them carefully until the *Arafura* arrives.'

I nodded, 'Yeah, I agree. We don't really know them and their whole story could be a pile of bullshit designed to catch us off guard. I thought if Sunnies stays quiet, we might introduce Jasper to these two.'

Those thoughts were welcome and Dave suggested he might clear out the second forward crew cabin, so Jasper could watch both cabins at the same time.

At that point, we re-joined the saloon group and Sandy went to fetch Jasper, freshly washed by Hillary. It was interesting to see the different reactions of the two Japanese when Jasper was presented and the Lieutenant was informed they would have to be confined to their cabin, and must not leave unless under escort.

The Lieutenant appreciated Jasper's size and obvious ability to interact with humans, but his companion, Yoshi Hideki, immediately dropped to his knees and bowed until his forehead touched the floor. He stayed like that for several minutes until the Lieutenant asked him to sit up again.

'Why is he doing that?' I asked, after the two had a lengthy discussion.

'He says this cat is very special Indonesian jungle cat and deserves our respect and gratitude. He wouldn't say any more, I'm sorry. I was not aware the cat was special.'

'He's a very good guard cat and very special to us,' I observed dryly, making sure the Lieutenant totally accepted they would be watched carefully.

'What is your former captain likely to do if you don't return?' I asked the Lieutenant.

A troubled look passed over his face. 'Ah, yes. He will be extremely upset. But there isn't much he can do about it. There is only one remaining RIB, and I doubt he will risk it in this weather and knowing the losses he has suffered so far. I suspect he will do nothing, except try to repair at least one of his ships. Undoubtedly, he will have called for assistance from any Japanese vessel willing and able to come here. Possibly with the aim of extracting most of the crews back to Japan.'

I considered his words, then asked, 'Do you think Captain Kurosawa is willing to make another assault on us? Even, forgive me for saying so, a suicide run in the RIB filled with explosives?'

He gave my words careful consideration, 'Is he willing to make another assault? He'd like to most assuredly, but with just one RIB and some lifeboats left, his options are limited. However, we do carry a quantity of explosives aboard the *Nissabe Maru* and you should consider that as well. I must warn you sir, my captain feels he has now been made a fool of several times over, and this is a powerful motivator with my people, and Captain Kurosawa in particular.'

'I appreciate that, Lieutenant, and I'll factor it in with our plans.'

While still unsure of our guests' true allegiance, I decided to keep them close, but we needed to discuss stuff, so the for'rard starboard cabin, which had twin bunks and an LED monitor with a media player was their day home for now.

Jacky certainly didn't want them aboard the *George*.

With all our crew plus Jacky and Rick assembled, Bree and Kelly made lunch for everyone, including our guests who were served in their cabin. I opened the conference by saying, 'The Lieutenant has raised some interesting points and I don't think it's too much of a leap to lean toward Kurosawa making some sort of suicide run against us using a lifeboat stuffed with explosives. Any thoughts on it?'

Alex was the first to speak. 'I agree completely, Commander. Everything the Lieutenant has said could be true and it would suit Captain Kurosawa's plans and hatred for us, to set off a large quantity of high explosive in our midst, particularly as we are all rafted together. I would rate that as a highly credible threat.'

Dave, then several others agreed, but Jacky wasn't sure. 'He'd be destroying at least one more boat and I don't think any captain would do that for very little gain.'

Sometimes my mob can be terribly polite, but there is nothing polite about Corrine when she hears either bullshit or stupidity.

'Sorry Jacky, but that's crap!' she stated bluntly. 'We just heard the Lieutenant make a reasoned statement about Kurosawa's state of mind, and it tallied with my own assessment. Both Harry and Dave rate the threat of a suicide run, or something similar, as very high and so do I. It would be a big mistake to underestimate Kurosawa. In fact, I need to ask the Lieutenant one question, so carry on discussing.'

The few who didn't know much about Corrine had raised eyebrows, but as she went below, I simply said, 'Sorry Jacky, but she's right and I'll stand behind her assessment any day.'

Jacky took it with a rueful smile, 'No bad feelings, Harry. You obviously place a lot of trust in her.'

'If you'd seen some of the things she's done in the desert, you would too!' I said emphatically. 'She's saved my neck quite a few times, as well as our whole squad. This is one very capable lady.'

While we waited for Corrine, we kicked a few other thoughts around the table, but nothing of any real consequence arose, except that the weather was too foul to allow even the UAV to go take a look at what the whalers were up to. At which point, Jacky and Rick returned to *George* while the rest of us waited for the result of Corrine's questions.

She returned with new thoughts.

'I asked Mitsu if they had the ability to make a remote-control setup allowing a lifeboat to make the trip across the bay to Datum Point and he thought it possible. He went on to say the suicide concept was an extreme move, but then he suddenly changed his mind and said he doubted even Kurosawa would go that far.

However, I still don't buy Mitsu's story, and reckon we should maintain a 24-hour radar and mast camera watch and be ready with the .50 cal and the RPG-7s. If they send a boat, it could be either the fast RIB or a slow lifeboat. Anything approaching from their anchorage won't be making a social call. If it is full of explosives, we can't afford to let it get close, so 100-metres should be the absolute closest limit of approach. I'd also suggest getting Mary Jones from the *George* to stand a watch tonight ready to man one of the fifties. She really is good with the thing.'

Her thoughts were accepted readily and Dave volunteered to visit *George* to ask for Mary's time tonight, while Alex and I would stand ready to handle an RPG-7 each. The others would take one-hour watches on the camera and radar because of the concentration levels involved.

CHAPTER 28

PORT DAVEY, MONDAY

For the rest of the day, the weather remained foul with low cloud, driving rain squalls and howling winds. The question was asked whether a remote-controlled boat could make the journey if the guy controlling it from the mother-ship couldn't see it visually, but Mitsu suggested an autopilot unit from one of the other boats could quite easily be fitted and programmed to navigate directly to us without any remote-control at all.

After more consideration, this was accepted as the most likely and most scary scenario.

'What about a trigger?' someone asked, and it was Corrine who suggested a simple impact trigger on the bow of the boat would do the job nicely.

'All the thing has to do is run into any one of us and we're all taken out.'

Based on that assessment, we decided to move all three boats to the next cove east, just past Aylen Point, and to separate by fifty metres, in the hopes the move would foil a pre-selected GPS waypoint.

At least all three boats had remote anchor winch controls, so no one had to stand out in what was already a very unpleasant day and getting worse by the hour. The forecast showed a steady deterioration over the next couple of days. None of us liked playing the waiting game and not being able to launch the UAV to check on the whalers was even more frustrating.

I allowed Mitsu and Hideki out of their cabin for a short time in the hope of extracting more information, but Mitsu had nothing else to offer, which was strange, or perhaps I just wasn't asking the right questions. Either way, he simply stopped talking, which increased my feeling that something wasn't quite kosher. Many of the crew also felt the whole thing could be an elaborate set-up, but with the information already supplied, I couldn't see how the enemy was going to benefit unless Mitsu or Hideki had a radio transceiver hidden on them, and Sandy had already checked Hideki's clothes when she exchanged his wet clothes for dry ones.

Still, one off-beat thought often leads to another in the same vein, and the vague idea of Mitsu and Hideki being spies with a hidden transmitter, refused to lie down and go to sleep. But it wasn't the simple idea of Mitsu passing information back to Kurosawa that kept rearing its ugly head, but a more insidious and dangerous one.

I had a quiet word to Sandy, and another to Dave, Alex and Alan, who nodded silently and relocated themselves casually about the saloon.

'Lieutenant. Would you stand up please?'

He looked puzzled at the request, but did so, moving automatically to stand in front of me.

'Yes, Sir?'

'I would like you to remove all your clothes, please, and place them on the table.'

'Sir?' He sounded a little more alarmed when he saw I was serious.

'Yes, yes. C'mon! Take them all off. Chop, chop! Don't mind the ladies. I'm sure they'll appreciate the sight of a naked virile Naval Officer.'

'But, sir. I'm not a Naval Officer. Just Merchant Marine.'

I waved my hand as though this was unimportant stuff, 'Yes, yes, so you claimed. But I'd still like you to take your clothes off. Now if you would, otherwise Alex and Dave might have to help you.'

Nervously, he glanced over his shoulder, to see both those gentlemen were standing close behind him. Facing front again, all expression left his face like bathwater down the drain hole, and he slowly began to remove his clothing. As he placed each garment on the table, Sandy and Kelly went over it carefully, fingering each tiny bump. Once he was completely naked, Dave fetched a simple hand-held direction finder that could lock onto a radio signal being broadcast on a wide range of frequencies. Setting it to auto-range, he pointed it at the Lieutenant and moved slowly around him. As he stepped closer, a 'Beep' repeated itself every three seconds, causing Mitsu's face to fall and ours to rise.

'Well, bugger me, Harry. Our new friend here seems to have indigestion. For sure it can't have been the lovely lunch the ladies served him. It must have been his last meal over on that broken-down hulk over on the far shore.'

'Try his mate now, please Dave. Even though we've changed his clothes, he might've been keen to have swallowed the wrong thing.'

Therefore, Dave waved the tapered cone of the input side of the beacon detector over the alleged servant, and promptly was rewarded with an indignant squawk.

'Ah, ha!' I exclaimed with delight. 'Got the little buggers!'

As I had pre-arranged, Alex silently took the signal detector, hauled on a heavy foul-weather jacket and went out into the cockpit. He was back in less than five minutes and gave me a brief nod.

I looked at the two visitors, and it was Hideki who cringed, 'Gentlemen, what are we to do with you? Hmmm? What would be a suitable punishment for your crime of deception? Let me ponder your fate for a few minutes while my crew render you rather more immobile than you are. No, no, Lieutenant. You needn't bother to dress. Like that will be fine. And Hideki, I'm sure your English is as good as mine, but it won't help you either. Wrap them well, please boys and girls. We want Captain Kurosawa to know we appreciate his gift and we are returning them in the same condition.'

Within minutes, both naked men had been wrapped with gaffer tape to the point of total immobilisation, complete with a gag and blindfold that made them look more like Egyptian Mummies than Japanese Military Officers. It took four of us to manhandle each out into the cockpit and down into their RIB which was still tied up astern. They were laid side by side on the floorboards. I dug out a hand-held GPS unit, an old RIB anchor, 50-metres of rope and tossed it in the boat, as Dave and Alex lowered *Firebird's* RIB into the water.

Alan and I then took the Japanese RIB back to the west toward where we had been and anchored it securely in exactly the same spot, before I shut down the engines. I had to rely on the GPS readout, as visibility was near zero, the rain still pelted down and the raging wind blew the tops off the small waves even in this protected little bay.

Dave nosed alongside, we hopped across without a word and motored back to comfort, and hopefully safety.

Despite the foul-weather gear, we were soaked and were hurried below by the ladies to change, but once back together, Alan was the first to ask, 'Okay, Harry, that was an interesting exercise, but what's the objective? I could see they had some sort of radio device on them, presumably something they'd swallowed, but what information were they passing back? And how did you know they weren't genuine defectors?'

'I'll answer those questions in reverse, if I may. I kept thinking back over how Mitsu and his mate turned up, and what Mitsu said. It occurred to me he volunteered everything they wanted us to know, but then he suddenly didn't know anything more. It was a bit too convenient, and a lot too contrived, even though most of what he said was true. I also asked myself what Kurosawa would gain by knowing what we were talking about, apart from if we were going to attack them again, but there was no real point in us doing that as they were already crippled.

I knew Hideki had nothing in his clothing since Sandy had taken them for drying, but what really tripped the alarm bells for me was the talk about suicide attacks. It took a while for the dots to all join up, but I'm betting what has happened is this.

Kurosawa has hatched the plan to wipe us out purely out of

revenge for the humiliation he thought he'd received. Those radio transmitters weren't 2-way radios, they are simply transmitters.'

'Yes, but isn't it what you'd expect?' Alan interrupted impatiently.

'Not quite, until I joined the dots. Those things are beacons.'

I could see the thoughts suddenly line up in his mind as he blurted out, 'A beacon attracts something. He talked about a suicide run with a lifeboat full of explosives, then dismissed it as something no one would do. But then there was talk of remote-control, then about an autopilot unit. You think they've cobbled up an autopilot unit from one of the damaged boats and hooked the beacon receiver to it so it's like a guided bomb. So it was a suicide run after all, since the incoming boat would track to wherever Mitsu or Hideki was. But why have we trussed them up like that and anchored their RIB back where... oh you cunning bugger! That really is payback! Kurosawa gets his bang and thinks all is well. What a delightfully bent and devious mind you have.'

'Thank you, Alan. I really appreciate the compliment.'

'Hang on you two!' demanded Hillary. 'Some of us didn't follow all of that. Why are those two fellows out in the boat?'

I spoke up, 'If I'm wrong, then we'll just have two cases of severe hypothermia on our hands, but if I'm right, an incoming boat loaded with explosives will soon be sent to track the beacon in the RIB, and which is duplicated for safety in the bodies of two volunteers. By putting them in their boat, away from us, but securely tied so they can't throw themselves overboard, where is the bomb boat going to go?'

The light finally dawned. 'Ahhhhhh, I see. That really is very devious Harry, even for you!'

'The proof will come sometime through the night, although there is nothing to gain by them waiting, and I'm guessing if the bomb is big enough, they won't care where it detonates... it'll still do the job.'

'So, we keep watch on radar and the camera, although there's not much to see on camera, even in IR?' she asked.

'That's the go,' I replied. 'Keep watching for anything moving. In the meantime, I'd love another mug of tea.'

I got my tea, and less than an hour later, Kelly called out, 'Incoming radar contact.'

Even with clutter filtering wound right up on the pulse compression radar, the image was somewhat indistinct, but it firmed up at one kilometre. It was small and moving almost straight for us at 6 knots.

'OK people, this is probably it. In case it doesn't track the beacon, we have to knock it out before it gets too close. I reckon 400 metres minimum, just in case. The .50 cals are most accurate, so they'll be best for it, but Alex and I will have the RPG-7s ready.'

Kelly spoke up, still watching the screens, 'What if we see people aboard this boat? Maybe they want to talk.'

'No Kel. Sorry. The time for talk and fart-arsing around has long gone. Kurosawa has shown how devious and untrustworthy he can be, so this will be proof the gloves are off. We can't take any chances with this one in particular.'

She smiled at me as I prepared to go for'rard to man an RPG-7 with Alex, 'No problem for me, Harry. Just playing Devil's Advocate.'

I made a quick call to *George*, informing them of what we expected, and were wished a heartfelt, 'Good luck and good aim.'

I left her to it and ventured out into the driving rain, where Alex had the launchers under a tarp, fresh batteries installed and was wearing the second set of night-vision goggles we had. Corrine had the other pair on *Seeker*; manning the .50 cal. When she had fresh info, Kelly would open one of the forward saloon windows and call out.

'This visibility sucks, my friend,' I groused.

'With the goggles, it's just acceptable,' Alex commented, 'I can faintly see the whaler's RIB, but if the incoming heads our way there's not going to be much time to attack.'

'Then let's hope it's going to do what we expect.' We were having to talk loudly over the rain and wind noise, so stayed quiet until there was an indistinct shout from the saloon window, I went back to hear and Kelly repeated, 'So far, the target is definitely heading for the whaler's RIB, and has less than 400 metres to run.'

I told Alex and within moments, he picked up the indistinct shape through the shifting curtains of rain. I couldn't see anything, until Alex quickly swept the night-vision goggles off his head and rumbled, 'Targets about to merge, Commander. We should get down.'

We'd barely had time to lay flat on the trampolines, when night turned to day as a pure white flash seared my eyes even through closed eyelids. The light persisted for a few seconds, before the first shock-wave swept across us, slamming *Firebird* hard back against the anchor chain. The sound wave was next, hammering at my ears with a physical force which persisted for long seconds, even over-riding the howl of the storm, before slowly dying away with the light.

If there was any debris from the two boats falling back from the stratosphere, it must have been small, since none of the three boats found anything strange on decks. With our low, streamlined shapes, *Firebird and Seeker* survived the shock-wave without any damage, but *George*, with a towering central bridge structure, had several windows blown out, a number of antennas ripped off and the radar scanner bent. Alex and I packed up the RPG-7s and retreated to the saloon to dry off and warm up again, being joined by Corrine and Dave soon after.

'Bloody good call, Harry,' Dave offered. 'It must have had a ton of explosives in it!'

'Yeah. Some blast hey? I'm just glad it wasn't any closer. We were lucky.'

'Lucky my arse!' Sandy said, giving me a tight hug. 'You called the whole thing, and that's how it panned out. We'd be nano particles by now if you hadn't worked out the plot. But what's next?'

I looked around at my crew, thinking of the operations we'd been through, 'Regardless of the peaceful intentions of our friends next door, I've had enough of this idiot, Kurosawa.

This was the final straw. Even through this storm, he should have seen the flash, so as far as he's concerned, we're toast. Therefore, what we're going to do is this...'

Over the next 20 minutes, I went over my not-so-cunning plan, using our usual method of brainstorming feedback to refine the idea into something workable. We consulted the sunrise/sunset tables to set the timing, then wrapped it up for the night. I set a watch on the radar and camera again, just in case our friends decided to brave the elements to confirm our joint demise.

With that done, Alex and Bree took the first watch, while Alan and Kelly took the second. After the events of the day I was more than happy to have a reasonably undisturbed night in my very comfortable bed with my very comfortable lady, but after I came back from showering, I was agreeably surprised to find Hillary wandering through from her cabin just for'rard of ours.

'I'm too wired to sleep,' she announced, climbing up between us, 'so I hope you don't mind some company. Just carry on with whatever you were doing. I won't look...much.' Her choice of sleeping attire seemed to be the current fashion of just a longish T-shirt, covering up all the nice bits normally, but was quite inadequate when the wearer is crawling around the bed or trying to get under the covers.

In Hillary's case, it seemed to spend more time up around her neck, something I found to be visually pleasing, and didn't seem to bother her at all. Not surprisingly, Sandy was happy to help settle her down. For once, I even scored a cuddle or three, which led to within a gnat's whisker of what promised to be a delightful romp, before Sandy dragged her away, an evil glint in her eye. 'Girlie stuff first, dear man,' was my only consolation.

I got my just rewards later, however, sometime in the wee small hours and Hillary's small, but agile form made the wait worthwhile. It was so good in fact, that seconds were demanded and happily delivered.

Soon after, Sandy's alarm went off giving us time to shower and dress, ready for the kick-off.

CHAPTER 29

PORT DAVEY, TUESDAY

Earlier, before going to bed, Alex had helped me transfer the RPG-7 tube and rounds over to *Seeker*, along with most of our stock of firearms and ammo. With Kelly, Jasper and Krazy left in charge of *Firebird*, six of us transferred over to *Seeker*, where I found while I'd been playing, Corrine and Dave had been busy. In the previous strike against the whalers, Corrine had supplied the Sea Guardian divers only with det cord, so her extensive stock of Semtex was untouched.

Therefore, she and Dave had made up bombs consisting of a ½ kilo block of Semtex with a detonator and a short fuse, the whole thing wrapped tightly in gaffer tape. There were about 30 of the deadly little bundles, sitting ready in a cardboard carton near the gas BBQ out in the cockpit with its lid and metal grills removed to allow the flame to be easily reached with a fuse.

Dave had also made up two catapults for the Semtex bombs, using cups cut from someone's 36C bra, and attached to lengths of bungee cord made from ockie straps. He'd fashioned forks from copper tubing and mounted them either side of the cockpit.

The Browning heavy machine guns mounted on the upper deck had been cleaned and oiled, ammo waiting in boxes, the first of the linked rounds already fed into the receiver. The RPG-7s were ready, the rounds stacked neatly in cartons ready for quick reloading.

Jacky Kennedy had kindly loaned us four crew to man the heavy machine guns, Mary Jones, Sven Pederson, Katey Davidson and Noleen Tarragon. Mary had been deployed before, and although Sven, Katey and Noleen were unknown to us, they seemed good-natured and competent and were cheerfully looking forward to shooting at an antagonist who'd been getting away unscathed too often. With a quick call from *George* saying, 'Good hunting,' we burbled away from the anchorage.

The plan, as such, was to get *Seeker* to the east of the whaler's anchorage under the cover of darkness. We would sneak through the narrow channel between Turnbull Island and Tonguers Point, then hug the northern shore of Bathurst Channel at low speed until the next point. We'd then cross over the channel to the southern shore to wait for enough light to see our targets. Then we'd make a run past the group of ships, cutting loose with the machine guns, the RPG-7s and everything else which would sling a bullet or a bomb. The object was to blow the shit out of these turkeys who had started this bit of argy-bargy down at Heard Island and had escalated the whole thing here in Tasmania.

After passing through the Turnbull Island channel, we turned east with the lights of the whalers intermittently visible through the rain squalls, just 600 metres away. It was then that Alan came up and quietly said, 'There's a problem with the timing of your plan, Harry.'

'Oh? What's that Alan?'

'Even with the rain squalls, we're going to be quite visible to the whalers if we go at first light, so why don't we try this. We've already seen they have plenty of lights on, so why not go as soon as we're in position? We see them but they won't see us coming, and if Dave uses the turbine by itself, I reckon they won't hear us until the last moment.'

I smacked myself on the forehead in disgust! 'Good one, Alan. I really am slipping. Let's do it, but we'd better tell the crew first.'

Everyone agreed with the plan, although little else had to change. We would attack as soon as we got over to the south side of the channel and Dave could do the engine change-over on the run when he was ready.

He must have been ready as soon as he heard the new plan, as he just went through the start routine for the turbine, which was fully automated anyway, waited until the soft, rising whine stabilised, then cut the two big diesels. As their rumbling bass notes were replaced by the soft treble whine of the single turbine, it was apparent even at speed, the turbine was the quieter of the two types. The big MTU diesels had a glorious, thunderous roar at speed which always got the adrenaline pumping, but they weren't conducive to making a sneak attack.

Once we made our kick-off point on the southern shore, it would be just a matter of everyone manning their assigned weapons. The first run would be fairly slow so we could accurately pour plenty of bombs and bullets into the ships, but after that, we'd be taking return fire and Dave would have to keep the boat twisting and turning. The ladies laid out several first-aid kits plus packs of heavier wound dressings.

It was almost an anti-climax when Dave accelerated a little at the southern launch point and the whalers were about 1.5 kilometres ahead, in a tight cluster. He planned to hold the boat as steady as possible for the first pass to give Alex and me with the RPG-7s the best chance to place the deadly armour-piercing rounds low down in the hulls of the three visible ships.

Corrine had given up a place with one of her beloved Browning machine guns, for the chance to toss bombs from the cockpit, ably assisted by Bree and Hillary who were hoping to create havoc on the decks to restrict return fire and maybe lob some down any openings like the funnels on the big boat.

The machine guns were to aim for the bridges and try to take out the radio antennas, as well as any fool stupid enough to stick his or her head up.

Since the cockpit was getting crowded, Alex and I took our two launch tubes and the 40 anti-tank rounds up to the sun deck where Mary and Sven had a .50 cal each, with Katy and Noleen acting as loaders. All four were excited to be involved in the strike.

Everyone's adrenaline was surging through their veins and the approach worked well with the cluster of ship's lights showing clearly from several hundred metres away. The rain squalls were still blasting through which gave us extra cover, so Dave steered in closer to make it easier for all the shooters and bombers. I looked for any sign we'd been spotted, but everything looked quiet. Perhaps my cunning plan to lure the bomb boat away from us had worked so well, they thought we'd been blown up.

Whatever, with the rain squalls, the royal blue hull and the quiet whistle of the idling turbine, our approach didn't attract attention, until Corrine called, 'Fire in the hole,' and the first little brick of Semtex sailed into the blaze of light surrounding the unsuspecting whalers.

The size of the explosion was totally out of proportion to the size of the gaffer-tape-wrapped block as it landed beside one of the forward hatches in the deck of the mother-ship, blowing the hatch up in the air, lazily turning over and over before crashing back down on the top of the bridge, wiping out most of the radio aerials. That was the signal for the .50 cals to fire short bursts into the superstructure, hoping to find thin plating or softer bodies. As it was, with the range only about 100 metres, the armour-piercing incendiary tracer rounds easily chewed holes in the relatively thin steel plating which made up the superstructure, leaving tell-tale puffs of smoke where they hit. The carnage caused inside must have been immense as smoke was soon pouring from every orifice. Both guns continued to fire their three-round bursts into everything which looked like it held something important.

Once the bridge and entire upper works were a blazing shambles, the fire team dropped their aim down to the accommodation areas. They were aided by Corrine and her team who continued to drop their little surprise packages onto every part of the ship, even putting some down the funnel, which belched a very satisfying gout of heavy black smoke, interlaced with fierce red tongues of flame.

Both the .50 cals and the bombing crew soon shifted aim to the two catchers moored close in beside the mothership where a few brave souls had ventured on deck, two of them running to man the big harpoon gun on the bowsprit walkway. I think it was Mary who was warned by her loader, Katy, and adjusted her aim. Two quick bursts and the foredeck was magically cleared of live persons.

Unfortunately, the crew of the other catcher had time to man their harpoon gun and hurriedly fired at us. Their haste was our salvation as the massive steel dart struck *Seeker*'s bow with a gigantic clang shaking the whole boat; the head remaining buried in the bow structure and the shaft poking out sideways. Dave's howl of rage prompted Corrine to drop several care packages on and around the bow of the catcher, and when the smoke cleared, the harpoon gun and its whole mounting system was a twisted mess dangling in the water.

Meanwhile, Alex and I were having immense fun popping a series of armour-piercing grenades into the hulls of all three visible boats at the waterline. As they hit, the RPGs formed a shaped, conical charge, which immediately fired, sending a jet of molten plasma into the interior. The charge also tore a large hole in the skin of the ship. Several struck right on the water-line which rather degraded each boat's seaworthiness factor, but with fuel and whale oil tanks usually fitted against the outer hulls, these were instantly breached and set alight. The resulting huge clouds of greasy black smoke impeded the efforts of the crews to fire back with their rifles, whereas we only had to aim for the centre of the smoke to keep hitting something worthwhile.

Only sporadic return gunfire came our way, was badly aimed and quickly suppressed by the machine gun crews, who worked with deadly efficiency to keep shooting up the upper works of all three ships. The third catcher, who we'd spotted with the UAV, was still nearly sunk just inshore of the mother-ship. We weren't too worried about it, but as we moved on past the first three boats, Alex and I got a clear shot at the bow and some of the right side. We promptly sent several RPG rounds into what we could see and I called for the

.50 cals to aim for the superstructure, particularly the bridge since I wanted to destroy all radio and navigation equipment.

The crews laid in with delight and bits flew everywhere.

Then came the call from Dave that he was turning around to do it again as resistance was so light. Luckily, he'd had the foresight to set up central mounts for the guns, so it was easy for the crews to just swivel around and shift the ammo boxes to cover the opposite side.

Alex and I were down to five or six rounds each, so we waited to see if any more were needed. I also had Corrine's H&K MP-5 sub-machine gun which fired a 9mm round, and while not much good at 100 metres, it was enough to discourage a potential hero.

The machine-gun crews continued to concentrate on the bridges of all boats, adding to the previous destruction. Finally, after a few more circuits, Alex and I pumped a couple more RPGs into the engine rooms and were rewarded with two decent internal explosions as gas or something very flammable let go in a big way, sending renewed gouts of flame and dense smoke out the funnel of the mother-ship and through a gaping hole in the side of one catcher. We put the rest of the RPGs into the water-line of all the boats, just to make sure they weren't going anywhere for a while.

At that point we withdrew, leaving three boats well alight behind us. The half-submerged catcher was the only one not actually on fire, but who knows what might happen next. The only damage we sustained was the harpoon still stuck in *Seeker's* bow, four bullet holes in the sundeck surround, and to my annoyance, a chunk of shattered carbon-fibre or bullet fragment had lodged in my back. I hadn't felt it at the time, but it had bled enough to make a large red patch on my shirt when I took the foul-weather gear off.

Sandy was pissed, but when it cleaned up without needing stitches, she settled down. 'That's three times you've been shot on one of these jobs!' she growled. 'When are you going to learn to keep your fool head down?'

Pointing out that it wasn't my head which got shot didn't earn me any sympathy, as was my smart-arse comment that, 'Maybe when people stop shooting at me!'

Our welcome back at Aylen Point was exuberant to say the least. Kelly was pleased with the way it had gone and said that she'd caught glimpses of the action via the masthead camera through gaps in the rain squalls. Jacky and Rick motored over to pick up their gun crews and wanted to hear the short version, before heading back to hear the full story. When we had told everything we could think of to Kelly, Alan asked, 'What's the likely response from the whalers, do you think?'

'I honestly don't think they can do much. As you know, three of the four boats were on fire when we left, but they may put those out before fire guts each boat. The half-sunken catcher may have some dry accommodation, but I doubt it. But I can guarantee they won't be going anywhere except as scrap, loaded on an ocean-going barge. I don't know how many of the crew survived, but probably most of them, so they're going to be tight for shelter, food and water for a while.'

'They must have reported to a higher authority before you shot up all their comms antennas.' Alan suggested.

'I'm sure they did and probably have several SatPhones to do so, which is what they should be doing right now. But it'll depend on when they called for help and how far away the help is.'

'I see. Therefore, a rescue ship could arrive at any time?'

'Yep. It could. So, what about your movements?'

'I think we'll still bail out Thursday or Friday, if the weather eases a bit more. I'll get a seaplane to pick us up, and we can fly commercial out of Hobart. I'd like to stay until *Arafura* gets here, but there's no guarantee on the timing for that either.'

The unworthy thought crossed my warped mind that both Sandy and I wouldn't mind a few more days to enjoy the delightful company of Hillary, if she was up for a repeat of last night's delights.

'Hang on Dad,' Hillary called, 'I'm just trying to reach them now.'

Three minutes later, she reported Clare Stahall, the XO on *Arafura*, said they'd be in Port Davey by tomorrow about 11:00. She also said they were running with some of the biggest seas they had ever seen, but the boat was handling the conditions really nicely with no problems to report.'

'Oh, that's excellent! I can catch up with Paul before we have to go. I'll have to think about what we do with the mess over the other side of the bay.'

'Maybe it will be more like a political hot potato, best handled by the diplomatic boys and girls? Anyway, the Boss will be good at sorting that one out.' I had a quick chuckle, 'It would be interesting if a Japanese rescue vessel arrives soon. The presence of *Arafura* may be enough to deter the whalers from doing anything else stupid.'

Alan nodded thoughtfully, 'I think you've given me the answer, Harry. I'll leave *Arafura* here until such time as the relief or rescue ship arrives, then she can be officially escorted out of our waters. We'll let them pick up the pieces of their boats at a later date, but that's all.'

Privately, I thought Alan was going to be disappointed if he thought he'd be left alone to put together an operation which had so many political aspects, but I was the last one to understand the ins and outs of international politics.

CHAPTER 30

PORT DAVEY, TUESDAY

After a late breakfast, I had to admit to Sandy in private, that my back was giving me some trouble. She immediately collected Hillary, took me down to the privacy of our cabin and parked me face-down on the bed. Jasper had insisted on coming down as well, and when they took the dressing off, I could feel his whiskers tickling as he sniffed at the wound. He gave a soft merowl to Sandy as she and Hillary had another careful look at the wound, before using what felt like a half-inch wood chisel and a claw hammer, to gouge a mangled lump of bullet out of my back.

Jasper was still sitting on the bed and gave another merowl, before nuzzling Sandy's hands aside as she was about to slap a dressing on the open wound. Then Hillary cried out softly, 'Oh no, Jasper! What's are you doing?'

I felt his 40-grit raspy tongue licking the site as gently as he could, although it still made my eyes water.

'Oh. Yuk! He's dribbling all over it... that's totally gross!' Hillary exclaimed again, before giving Sandy a chance to reply. 'It's pouring out of his mouth.'

'It's OK,' Sandy finally got to say, putting her arm around the younger woman's shoulders to stop her from trying to push Jasper aside. 'He did this last time Harry got himself shot on the job and caused the most amazing healing process I've ever seen! The pain went almost immediately and within 36 hours, Harry was healed.'

I endorsed those remarks, since even now the pain was fading, as Jasper stepped back with a satisfied huff, letting Sandy lay a dressing over the hole and tape it closed.

'There!' Sandy said. 'Despite, or I should say, because of the unorthodox antibiotic applied by our resident feline MD, it should heal properly. But sponge-baths only for a few days, don't you think Nurse?'

Hillary giggled, 'Oh, definitely! But don't you think he should be confined to bed as well?'

Sandy laughed, 'Oh, no you don't, young lady. I want him in one-piece when you leave; not a shattered wreck!'

Hillary pouted, 'You're the one who introduced me to the pleasures of sharing. I've got a lot to learn and catch up on you know.'

'Ha! Early this morning I think it was, it didn't look like you had anything to learn.'

She grinned, 'Maybe I was feeling inspired with the excitement of the coming operation.'

I gave an exaggerated groan as I managed to roll over unassisted and sit up. 'It's alright, ladies. I'll be alright; don't you worry about me. I'm okay. I can do it!'

Actually, my back wasn't feeling so stiff and the pain was fading rapidly, although it was still tender where Sandy had dug out the bullet fragment, but I wasn't going to admit to that just yet, so I patted both bums and went up top.

I spotted Dave wandering around the cockpit of *Seeker* and carefully stepped over the rails.

'I keep forgetting to ask - how's our prisoner?'

He grinned, 'Never stops complaining, so I figured he isn't too bad. He keeps asking when he's going to be released.'

'Good. Next time he asks, say it'll be in two days. He doesn't know he'll be going straight to the brig on *Arafura*, so that might keep him quiet for now.'

With that little detail tided up, I went back to *Firebird* and found Bree just finishing in the galley.

'When you're finished here, how about putting the UAV up, if you think it will handle these winds?'

She nodded, 'Yeah, sure Harry. It'll handle this wind alright, although we might launch from *Seeker* for safety. I guess you want to have a good look at the carnage?'

'Yes please. But still stay covert if possible. They aren't a happy set of campers over there and they have rifles as my back reminds me.'

It wasn't long before she and Sandy had *Dragonfly* rigged and ready on *Seeker's* broad, uncluttered foredeck. While the winds were still strong, they had settled a lot. The cloud base was a little higher and the rain squalls were intermittent, rather than almost continuous. The little UAV fired up easily as usual and sat there warming up, before Bree commanded lift-off and it rose reasonably smoothly into the air, before transitioning into forward flight. The climb to cloud-base didn't take long as I saw on the altimeter tape read-out when Bree levelled off at just under 1200 feet, but with the dull, low-visibility paint scheme of mottled, three-tone grey and blue undersides, it was effectively invisible.

Bree knew to keep the speed down once it had reached the target site, and started a wide orbit; the stabilised camera system zoomed right in showing in graphic detail the results of this morning's action.

With the whole crew crowding around, I put the feed up on the big-screen monitor, and immediately, we saw the three boats which had been dry, weren't any longer. Pumps were running hard as streams of brown water poured overboard, while smoke still leaked out of several openings, to be whisked away by the wind. Already, tarpaulins were being strung in places on deck to form make-shift tents, suggesting conditions below weren't suitable for living.

Still staying in a wide orbit, I asked Bree to drop down to a lower altitude to get a better look at the bridge on each boat, and was gratified to see the destruction was virtually complete on all four. With recordings secured, I asked for a sweep out west to the entrance to Port Davey, as I wanted to see the state of the ocean.

Bree took the little bird back up to cloud base and pulled the zoom back so we could see the whole picture.

Approaching the heads, I was appalled to see giant waves breaking most of the way across the seven-kilometre distance between Point Lucy on the north shore and Hilliard Head in the south. From height, they didn't look too dangerous, until Bree dropped down and the almost slow-motion effect as they humped up, then the towering crests toppled over in a seething mass of white water was the give-away to their extreme height which I could only guess at. They must be truly huge to be forced to break in water that was 70 to 80 feet deep! There was a deeper channel on the north side close to Hilliard Head, revealed by waves which only broke occasionally, but even there, only a large ship would brave those monstrous hills of moving water.

Sobered by the sight of the sea state, we watched as Bree directed the UAV to return home where it made an uneventful, hovering landing on *Seeker*.

Alan shook his head admiringly, 'Bloody hell, Harry! We really did a number on those boats. They won't be usable anytime soon, if ever, and I think camping on deck in this weather won't do a lot for their sense of humour. Any chance Kurosawa will send another boat over here?'

I shrugged, 'Possible I suppose, but after all this, very unlikely. I mean, how many times does he have to get a bloody nose from clashing with us?' It was a rhetorical question, but Dave laughed and said, 'One dead mother-ship and three dead catchers add up to a fair sort of a bloody nose. He's going to have a lot of questions to answer to whoever is overseeing this weird operation.'

Alan had asked a good question, however, and I thought it wise to set a radar approach alarm. Jackie and Rick came over, having seen the UAV flight and Sandy played the recording for them, then burned a copy for them to take back and show their crew.

The Sea Guardian skipper was upset by the level of carnage,

although engineer and husband Rick just grinned as he said, 'Great work guys. Wish I'd been there.'

With a slightly concerned tone to her voice, Jacky asked, 'Are they really going to have to camp out in this weather?'

I could see where she was going with the question, so before somebody threw something at her, I said casually, 'Nah! It'll just be until they put the fires out, which has nearly happened. Then they can move back below. The generators should still work, so they'll have heating.'

Rick flashed me a look that said, *Bullshit!* But Jacky missed it, choosing to placate her overly protective nature by accepting my lame explanation.

'What are your plans, Jacky?' I asked.

'Well, thanks to Dave letting us have the fuel, we're good to go. We might stop in Strahan to re-stock the pantry but after that, there's a job chasing beche-de-mer poachers on the outer parts of the great Barrier Reef.'

'Why is it a problem?' Kelly asked, crinkling up her nose. 'They're horrible-looking things and feel awful to tread on.'

Jacky laughed, 'You're right, they aren't attractive, but because they're purely herbivorous, they eat algae and decaying matter on the ocean floor and the reefs. They keep the coral environment clean and healthy for everything else living there, so they're natural cleaners and help to look after the reefs. Essential really. The Asian poachers collect them by the tens of thousands, so there are some areas where there's hardly any at all. That's why we'll go and try to chase these buggers away before they do too much more damage.'

I drew Jacky's attention to the breaking seas over the entrance to the Port. 'Yeah, good point. That's not so good. We've been here before and for seas to break there, they must be huge. We might wait until tomorrow, but the channel on the north side is generally okay to get through, being a bit deeper. We might have to give Strahan a miss though. Hell's Gates will be impassable.'

I nodded, 'Yep. That's what I told the Navy. They're expected tomorrow morning.'

Her eyebrows raised, 'Really! How did they find out what's going on? Do you have friends in high places?'

I sidestepped that question by replying, 'I know the Skipper of the boat quite well and suggested it could be useful if he were to stick his nose in here seeing as he was sailing passed anyway.'

'Oh, nice. It's good to have powerful friends.' She didn't look at Alan or Hillary who, in her eyes, appeared to be an odd couple, although now that Kelly was sharing the Admiral's bed, the situation looked more normal. 'Anyway,' she went on, 'we'll bailout early in the morning if the seas back off a bit, so I'll say goodbye and thanks for the fuel and the experience. It's been...enlightening!'

It was Rick who said the right thing, 'That goes likewise for me, Harry, and from the crew who loved having the chance to lash out at these buggers. We're usually on our own, so it's really good to have some serious muscle behind us for once.'

Hugs and handshakes were dutifully exchanged, before they returned to *George* and we settled down to see if Kurosawa did anything else stupid.

One thing occurred to me, so I said to Alan, 'Any chance *Arafura* might have shot off a few thousand rounds of .50 cal in a training exercise? Gun shops carrying that calibre are a bit thin on the ground around here.'

He looked appropriately thoughtful, 'I'm sure I told Paul to make sure he exercised all weapons carefully as part of the shakedown, so I guess the crew could easily have been a bit too enthusiastic with the .50 cals.'

He smiled at Hillary, 'My dear. Perhaps you'd better pass that thought verbally next time we talk to them.'

She grinned back. 'No problem, Father dear.'

The rest of the day passed peacefully, with no movement from the whaler side of the bay, so we sent the UAV out again and the appearance of the cluster of broken ships was the same, apart from a few more make-shift tents strung along the side decks of the

Nissabe Maru. Pump water still poured from deck outlets, although the amount of smoke oozing from below decks was less. There was no movement at all on the three catchers, suggesting maybe they were effectively abandoned.

CHAPTER 31

PORT DAVEY, WEDNESDAY

In general, it was a peaceful night with no disturbances from the whalers, although Hillary had definitely got the sharing bug and was in our king bed before Sandy and I were. Not that either of us complained as she tried to make up for years of zero social life in just a few days.

'Being the Fleet Commander's PPS, is a 24/7 job,' she explained during a rare pause in her voyage of personal exploration. 'I've not had a social life since I was 16. I was supposed to go to Uni, but when Mum died, Dad needed support at home, so it just seemed natural to take over the house-keeping duties. Then when his long-term PPS retired soon after, I took that job on as well, since I was already across most of what was going on as Dad was in the habit of using me as a sounding board for ideas and problem-solving.'

'Consequently,' she added, idly stroking a tender and surprisingly responsive portion of my anatomy, 'dating and having a normal social life just didn't happen. Goodness me, Harry! That's very impressive! Sorry Sandy, I do hope you don't mind me being just a little bit greedy. In my wildest dreams, I didn't ever imagine I would be in this situation, but you guys are just so comfortable and easy to be with, it feels natural. Oh, yes! And that does too...thank you very much, kind sir!'

Nobody was in a rush to do anything next morning, although when we finally surfaced and disposed of a very late breakfast, I asked the UAV crew for another fly-over to check our whalers progress, or lack thereof. However, things hadn't changed since yesterday, although there were more tarpaulins spread along the side decks of the *Nissabe Maru* suggesting conditions below were worse, not better, so it was just as well Jacky had bailed out early.

Sending the UAV on a sweep to the west showed the seas had settled somewhat from yesterday and there was only the occasional breaker at the entrance. What we did pick up, after *Dragonfly* had climbed to two thousand feet, courtesy of the largely broken and higher cloud cover, was a medium-sized ship rolling very heavily as it approached from the south. Its progress was slow in the large swell, and Bree sent the little spy-craft down to meet it which only took about 15 minutes. We weren't surprised to see it was flying the Japanese flag and on closer inspection, appeared to be a part tanker and part cargo carrier.

It was labouring heavily in the beam seas, which broke with awesome regularity right over it.

'At that rate, they'll be several hours getting here,' I commented, 'provided they don't break something on the way.'

Bree brought the UAV back to the port entrance, then ranged out to the west-north-west, until we spotted the welcome sight of a long grey hull heading our way. She was running with the big seas on her right rear quarter, and was being careful the larger ones didn't turn her into a surfboat.

I asked Bree for the VHF marine radio repeater again, and hailed the *Arafura*, getting an instant reply. I passed on the information about the incoming Japanese support ship, the occasional breaking sea at the entrance and recommended the north side approach, the location of the crippled whaler fleet, and our position. I also mentioned the whaler crew were hostile.

'Interesting times again, Harry. I can't wait to hear how you fell into this one. According to the chart, you look to be in a good position to keep an eye on things, so we might join you there and let our friends sort out their troubles. I'll get a full update when we get in. Arafura clear.'

'This port's getting busy.' Alan commented dryly. 'We'll need traffic control next!'

'At least we won't have to worry about Kurosawa acting up, not with a 40mm gun backing us up,' I added with a laugh. 'Paul's getting a bit pushy. He must be frustrated he wasn't here earlier.'

'Just as well he wasn't,' Alan growled, 'knowing him, he'd have been right in the middle of the action. It's bad enough I'm here, but at least I can pretend to have been uninvolved.'

I let that one slide through to the keeper without comment!

With the UAV retrieved, I suggested the girls leave it rigged, because it might have to go out again in a couple of hours to let us all have a close look at what the supply ship was going to do.

It was after 11:00 when the grey, beautifully-raked bow of the *Arafura* poked around Milner Head and aimed straight for us. We were anchored in deeper water off Aylen Point, so Paul could safely park his shiny new toy close to where *Seeker and Firebird* were rafted up. He dropped his anchor where he could see across the bay to where the whalers still smouldered.

Close-up, the new Offshore Patrol Boat had clean, handsome lines and looked very impressive. Paul lost no time in getting the smaller RIB launched over the side, and was delivered to us along with Jane Glen's familiar and happy face as Weapons Officer. Obviously, Claire Stahall as XO, had to stay with the boat. We'd been through all the promotions and catching-up chat at *HMAS Stirling* off Fremantle, so initial talk was of the severe storm.

Paul was surprised to again find Alan and very pleased to see Hillary aboard, but wisely held back questions.

'We took a good look at the remains of the whaling boats as we came in,' he commented, giving me a grin, 'and it's amazing how easily whale oil catches alight and burns so hot!' he said. 'Those whalers must have been terribly careless to allow the fire to spread to all four boats like that. It doesn't look like they'll be able to repair the mess anytime soon.'

With the official bit out of the way, I had to tell him the full, real story and as Alan had suggested, he was jealous to have missed the main action.

'What's my tasking, Sir?' he asked Alan.

'Well, Hillary and I will be leaving tomorrow by seaplane, if the weather keeps clearing, so I want you to stay to make sure that lot over there behave themselves. The PM and the Diplomatic Service have made due and proper complaints at all levels, up to and including the Japanese PM. The gist of the order is they must come and remove all traces of their presence ASAP. The supply ship will probably just collect what's left of the crew and bugger off, but I believe a much larger cargo ship with its own cranes and a crew of workers will be here within the week to patch the *Nissabe Maru* sufficiently to allow it to be towed away and the catchers will either be towed or cut up into scrap and stacked on deck.

So you'll be here for two to three weeks, I'm afraid, unless I can find a patrol boat or a frigate to relieve you. What's your supply situation?'

'Quite good, sir. Although after two weeks we'd be scratching the bottom of the pantry.'

I looked over at Dave and he nodded, so I cleared my throat. 'I know this is Navy business, but since we are working together for now, Dave needs fuel, having given a heap of it to Sea Guardian's patrol boat. So, how about we make a run up to Strahan tomorrow to pick up a supply order. If there's stuff the local IGA can't supply, then there's time to have it trucked over from Hobart. Between both of us, we can carry everything you'll need. Will that suit?'

Alan, Hillary, Paul and Jane had a quick confab before Paul said, 'Great, thanks Harry, although you might have a few extra passengers. I want to see how that thing sails in a bit of heavy weather, and we might take a couple of seamen to help with the lifting.'

I checked with Dave again, but he said the same as me, 'Sure. If we get away at first light, we should be able to get back the same evening, but even if we can't make it, then between us there are plenty of beds.'

The Navy said, 'Excellent!' and Jane called the *Arafura* to tell the galley crew to make up a list of supplies they'd need to fully re-stock... ASAP.

'How are you off for fuel?' I asked Paul.

'About 50% at last count.' was his succinct answer.

I looked at Dave, 'Do you want to off-load some and re-fill up there as well?'

'Yeah, no problem. I could sling you eight or eight and a half thousand litres, if that'd help?'

Paul looked delighted, 'Hell yes! It'd make Engineering feel very comfortable again; just in case something comes up in a hurry.'

Alan nodded, pleased with the arrangements being made to resupply his newest patrol boat and keep it on station, especially now the whaler's supply ship had arrived.

He turned to Hillary who, as usual, had her notebook out and pen flashing, causing distracting images of her in a totally different condition and environment to flash across my mind.

I stopped smiling and forced myself to concentrate.

'Regarding the local supermarket, and on reflection, when we were there recently, it is quite small, so I suggest you truck everything over from Hobart. They can probably put an order together quickly with what's on hand at your base. That'll save us time in port.'

The Navy readily agreed with that suggestion too, so Alan nodded to Hillary, 'Make it happen, please my dear.'

'Yes sir,' was her correct response in front of other Navy personnel.

Our next item of business was to arrange for the transfer of our smart-arse prisoner, Sunnies, from his cell in *Seeker's* bow.

'Now,' I said to Paul, 'are you able to take this clown off our hands? He's officially charged with staging an armed attack upon my crew and that of *Seeker* and assault with a deadly weapon. Sandy's got the details.'

I had been so impressed with him, I hadn't even bothered to learn his name, but Paul readily agreed to take him into custody.

That was based on my official Commonwealth Police arrest, and backed by Alan's approval that he was to be taken back to the mainland to face charges for numerous crimes against Australia and Australian citizens.

When he was brought on deck, he was pale, thin and still squinting in the relatively bright daylight, despite the cloud cover. What hadn't been subdued was his desire to complain about everything.

Finally, Paul had enough of his whinging, and called his RIB crew aboard to take Sunnies and toss him in the brig.

Two large sailors climbed the steps, saluted the Admiral, then turned their attention to the loud-mouthed Japanese who still hadn't shut up. Handcuffs were improvised from cable ties and Sunnies was frog-marched down the stern steps. Unfortunately, he seemed to slip just as he went to step into the RIB and fell straight into the freezing water. It would appear the Navy men didn't want to get wet this day, so they waited until he managed to surface under his own power, then took their time hauling him out of the water before roughly shoving him into the RIB.

On its return, the RIB sat a lot lower in the water, with a bunch of large boxes stacked up on the floor-boards.

'Compliments of the XO,' one seaman said cheekily, as he and his mate made many return trips up and down, carrying the heavy boxes, all marked .50 cal.

Corrine's eyes lit up as I thanked Alan.

'No problem. It's the least we could do, seeing as you did all the hard work. It must have been quite a surprise to old Kurosawa when we started chewing his boats apart with the .50 cals, then the RPG-7s, and the Semtex bombs. I wouldn't imagine they expect civilian boats to kick back so hard.'

Dave left shortly after to move the short distance to snuggle up beside *Arafura* and transfer some fuel. Good-natured sailors made light work of the hoses and pumps, careful not to spill a drop on the decks of either boat. While that job was underway, the RIB was busy ferrying white-suited galley staff back and forth amending lists, but finally, Hillary was able to send an email through to Anglesea Barracks in Hobart, comprising a very long list of food and other supplies to be assembled and trucked to Strahan, to be there by midday tomorrow.

Finally, as the afternoon was drawing to a close, along with a sharp drop in temperature, I happened to overhear Hillary speak quietly to Alan.

'I guess you don't want me to ask for a car to be sent over with the truck, to take us back to Hobart?'

I only caught the chuckle in his voice, 'No, not really. I'm having way too much fun, which always seems to happen on this boat and with this crew.'

There was a slight pause, before he went on, 'And I gather you would rather stay a while longer, too? I must say I've never seen you looking so relaxed and happy.'

'You too, Dad. She's such a lovely lady and I'm so happy for you both!'

At that, I slipped away unseen, pleased we had brought some happiness into three people's lives.

Before he left to go back to *Arafura*, Paul invited all of us to a buffet dinner with their entire crew to be held in the aft RIB storage area, which had been suitably tided up for the occasion. Both cats were invited as well, Jasper in particular, because he was so popular with the old *Glenelg* crew. Sandy wasn't sure how Krazy would get on in the crowd on a strange boat, but I assured her Jasper would look after his little sister.

It turned out to be a terrific night. The cooks had really outdone themselves with food choices, Paul had allowed a reasonable ration of beer only to be issued to the off-watch crew, and the sailors organised several sorts of after-dinner games. Notwithstanding the presence of the Fleet Commander, Jasper was the guest of honour and happily visited every table in turn, with little Krazy cat perched on his muscular shoulders, claws dug in when he walked. Each table fed both pussies bits of food, until even Jasper could eat no more.

One of the highlights for Paul's crew was when one of the braver seamen ventured to the table we shared with Paul, Clare, Jane, Alan and Hillary. He must have been put up to it, because an instant hush fell across the room when he asked for a demonstration of how Jasper could understand me. It had become a sort of party trick for my big cat, and Jasper seemed to enjoy the extra attention.

It consisted of me asking the person who made the request to place a distinctive object like a piece of coloured cloth, tucked into a waistband or on someone's lap, except Jasper wasn't allowed to see what went on.

I would then tell Jasper in normal words, what the object was and where it was. Proving he was a born show-off, he usually huffed at me first, which always got a round of laughs, then went to where the object was and gently retrieved it in his mouth.

I'd learned to be careful where the object was put, since a girl once jammed the handkerchief into the back pocket of her tight jeans, but when Jasper wants something, he has long, sharp claws as well as long sharp teeth.

On that particular occasion, the girl ended up with the entire backside ripped out of her jeans.

As Jasper was receiving attention after another successful demonstration, the same young sailor asked, 'We've heard Jasper has killed several people while on operations, or defending you, Commander. Is it true?'

While I didn't like advertising the fact Jasper wasn't all soft black fur and startling green eyes, with this group it was perhaps appropriate, so I replied, 'Yes, it is true. But only if he thought my life, or any of my nominated friends were being endangered by some bad guy or girl. Lucky he considers you lot our friends! On a job he always watches our backs, so he's the perfect partner.'

'Excuse me, Commander,' came another voice, that of a young lady sailor, 'would you mind telling us how many he has killed?'

It was the sort of question I didn't like, but I also don't like being evasive with people I respect, so I answered, 'I think it's ten so far and many more just wounded.'

There weren't any gasps of shock and/or horror from these people, but some looks directed at Jasper turned thoughtful and perhaps more respectful.

To lighten the mood, I said, 'However, have you heard about Jasper and the giant crocodile?'

That grabbed their attention as I told the full story about the first encounter, including the bit where Jasper made me keep the croc company by sitting with my knees almost touching his snout while he, Jasper, went to pee, poop, eat and drink.

I think there was an element of disbelief amongst some of the crew, until I held up a DVD in its case and handed it to the Chief Petty Officer. 'This is a recording of the entire episode from when the croc first climbed up on the old *Seeker's* stern-board. Which, I might remind you, is the full beam of the boat which is 4.95 metres or 16 feet 3 inches. I'll let you work out the total length of the croc from that when you watch the video.'

There was a question about other animals Jasper had befriended, so I answered, 'To date the list has been seals, orcas, the giant croc, a wandering albatross, dolphins and several whale species. I don't know how he does it, nor do several animal behaviouralists who made a study of him for their Masters thesis.'

CHAPTER 32

PORT DAVEY, THURSDAY–FRIDAY

It was well we only drank sparingly the night before, since we were up before dawn preparing for departure to Strahan. With the Japanese supply ship in port, Paul decided to stay with his boat and keep a high state of readiness, but kindly lent us three well-built young seamen to help with the loading, one of whom stayed on *Firebird*, and the other two going with Dave and Corrine on *Seeker*.

The big seas were still rolling in from the west, with nothing in their way since Africa, but at least they'd stopped breaking across the port entrance. The howling winds of the last week had finally dropped to Force 5 or 6; a fresh to strong breeze.

It was still sufficient to give us a lively ride with the beam seas and wind, and 18 knots seemed to be the maximum which was comfortable, although *Seeker* was riding remarkably well for a monohull, and not rolling anywhere near as much as I would have expected. I made a mental note to ask Dave if he'd fitted stabilisers. Our slim bows and hulls sliced through the waves with little disturbance, making for a fairly pleasant and fast sail.

The 81 miles to Macquarie Harbour took just on 4 hours of speed-sailing fun, and Alan wasn't to be pried off the wheel for a moment. Our loaned sailor divided his time between marvelling at the speed we sometimes hit under sail and playing in the saloon with Jasper and Krazy.

We were first to front Hell's Gates, where we found the tide just starting the run in, otherwise, we would have had to wait for the change. The ebb tide with strong onshore winds was a very dangerous combination and automatically closed the narrow, treacherous entrance. Once inside, I called the Harbourmaster, Terri Wallace, and requested re-fuelling for *Seeker* and a tie-up to the wharf to load supplies.

'I've got two ten-tonne Navy trucks already parked on my wharf, with a bunch of sailors saying they're waiting for you two to arrive. You can take turns at the fuelling wharf; it's further down near the slipways.'

'Thanks Terri. We don't need to re-fuel so we'll start loading supplies first. My mate will take a lot of fuel.'

'No problem, although the Sea Guardian mob took a lot yesterday. Were they with you?'

'Well... we did see them down that way,' I said evasively.

We went straight to the wharf in front of the cruise boats, where Alan tried to avoid being recognised, but a Lieutenant with a good memory for faces spotted him, and insisted on saluting and saying 'Sir' every second word.

I could see Alan getting annoyed, so before he chewed this guy to bits, I took him aside and explained the Admiral was on leave and would very much prefer to stay low profile. The young man got the word and shut up, letting his sailors do the hard work.

It seemed by chance, the heavy stuff was in one truck while the lighter, bulkier stuff was in the other. Therefore, we started loading all the light items as quickly as possible, since I hoped to be able to get back to Port Davey before last light. The other truck I sent down to the fuel wharf because there wasn't room at the loading wharf for both boats. There seemed to be a lot more stuff to go into *Seeker* than what we'd taken, but finally the job was done and I called Terri on the VHF.

'How's the tide looking for departure Terri?' I asked.

'No problem, Harry. Just be careful of the big seas.'

'Thanks Terri. Catch you next time.'

The run out through the Gates was certainly exciting, but we both made it unscathed and headed south. We were rolling more than usual and that kept the crew busy relocating items before they toppled off a stack. We had boxes and bags of every shape and size effectively filling every cabin and taking up most of the saloon, with only small walkways left for access. Alan stayed on the wheel the whole way again, and we were back in our sheltered anchorage right on sunset.

Paul had draped *Arafura* with fenders on both sides so we could raft up simultaneously to speed unloading, and both watches turned out to help. It really sped things up and we were able to move away to anchor after just 30 minutes.

As usual, we rafted up with *Seeker*, not far from the comforting presence of the sleek, grey ship.

During the unloading, Paul reported to Alan that all was quiet with the whalers, although they couldn't see much. After we'd had our meal, and acting purely on a whim, I asked Bree and Sandy to launch the UAV for an IR look-see at what the devious buggers were up to.

The only lights showing were on the supply ship, and the IR was particularly useful since it was able to show the heat signature of internal fires. In this case, there was almost no heat left inside any of the original four boats. It also appeared the make-shift tents along the mother-ship decks were gone, suggesting all the displaced crews were relocated onto and inside the supply-ship.

One curious item was the presence of a lifeboat floating at the end of a gangway lowered down the side of the supply ship.

I looked at the others, clustered around. 'They wouldn't; would they?'

Dave shrugged, 'Maybe. They haven't done anything clever so far.'

I called Paul and got the girls to stream the video over to him.

'I can't believe they'd be stupid enough to try the exploding-boat trick again, but who knows. We'd all better keep a close radar and camera watch tonight and keep your guns manned.'

'How about you keep your fancy UAV toy over them? Didn't you say it has an 8-hour endurance?'

'True. I did say that and it has. Perhaps we could borrow two of your crew to help out with watching the video feed through the night?'

'*No problem. Half the ship will volunteer, but I'll choose a couple of good ones.*'

'Thanks, Paul. We'll refuel it and launch shortly.'

While the girls serviced *Dragonfly*, I asked Dave about stabilisers.

'Oh, yeah. I forgot to tell you. After we got back from Fremantle, we ran into this bloke who had the agency for a mob called Side-Power. They make stabiliser fins and thrusters. Since we already had their bow-thrusters, we took a look at their powered stabilising fins and the data was pretty amazing about how effective they were, and how their design makes them much more efficient than fixed fins or gyro-stabilisers.'

'I hope you asked around?' I asked cautiously. 'You know what salesmen types are like. Everything they sell is the best, according to their brochure bullshit.'

'Yes, Dad! I did ask around and those who had them said they were bloody marvellous, at rest or underway. Anyway, once I was sure they were the real deal, I got a set fitted. They made a huge difference today with the beam swell.'

I nodded, 'Yes. I noticed how much you weren't rolling. But how much do they add to your draft?'

'About 250mm more, and the drag at speed means we lost about 10 knots off our maximum, but we thought about how often do we do 70 plus knots? I'll show you the manual later on. They're good value.'

'Of course, if you had a catamaran, you wouldn't need stabilisers.' I added rudely.

He ignored me, the unenlightened bugger!

The ladies launched a fully-fuelled UAV at around 21:00 and pro-grammed the autopilot to maintain an orbit around the whalers at 1500 feet, because I figured the brisk wind would render even the soft purr from its engine inaudible from 200 metres away. The video was set to IR mode and the UAV left to look after itself.

All the crew had to do was keep an eye on the UHD video feed for any suspicious activity on the supply-ship associated with the life-boat.

The two crew Paul sent over were our old friends from the Indonesian adventure days, Gillian Smith and Terry Boone.

They both gave us huge hugs and thanked us all over again for including them in the sale of the pirate treasure that had made them both millionaires, and said they had decided to stay in the Service until they become used to the idea of being wealthy. In fact, neither had touched the money, currently happily earning a few percent in a numbered Vanuatu bank account, nor had they told anybody except for some discussion with Lieutenant Jane Glen and Leading Seaman Rick Jackson who were on the same operation and had received the same bonus. If the other crew speculated what connection caused the Weapons Officer, two Petty Officers and a Leading Seaman to hang out together so often, like old and dear friends, then they were left to wonder.

Paul offered their services for the duration, so Dave gave them a cabin each on *Seeker*. Sandy took the first watch with Gillian, letting me relax and get some sleep. I was able to relax knowing that three radars, the UAV and the masthead camera system were on the job, plus several sets of trained eyes.

All the preparation led to an anticlimax because nothing happened and Friday dawned with clear skies for the first time in over a week.

During an early breakfast, Alan announced they would have to leave this morning. 'I've tried really hard, but I can't put it off any longer,' he said, with a rueful glance at Hillary.

'Apparently some things require my physical presence, so Hillary has organised a Cessna Caravan amphibian from Hobart to pick us up at 09:30. The flight drops us at the airport so we can catch a direct flight to Sydney.'

'We're all sorry to see you both go,' I said sincerely, since they were undemanding as guests and fitted in perfectly as crew. 'And you know you're welcome anytime. You only have to let us know where to pick you up.'

He was getting misty-eyed when he replied, 'I will hold you to that, thanks Harry. This boat and crew have had a magical effect on both of us. When we're aboard we seem to be able to relax like nowhere else. It's incredibly therapeutic!'

Hillary added her thoughts, echoing Alan's, then said, 'The Caravan pilot said that when there's a big sea running, he prefers to land in the bay just north of Opossum Point. Can you run us up there please?'

'Of course. It's too choppy to go in the RIB and will only take 15 minutes in *Firebird*.'

'Thanks, Harry, and I really mean for everything. You and Sandy are very special people to us and I can't wait to come back.'

While they packed their minimal amount of gear, I let Dave know what we were doing, and unhitched from our raft-up. There was plenty of time, so I motored at half-power. We entered the Bathurst Channel just opposite the cluster of Japanese vessels, although all was quiet, with only a few personnel on deck and no one shot at us.

Ten minutes later, I dropped anchor just off Opossum Point and switched on the air-band VHF radio. Just before 09:30, the radio leapt into life with an all-stations Port Davey call from the Caravan amphibian.

'Tango, Tango, Zulu, this is *Firebird* base just off Opossum Point with your two passengers.'

'*Good morning* Firebird *Base. I have you visual and be advised I have three incomings for you. I presume you will accept them?*'

'Cheeky bugger! As if we'd knock the PM back,' I remarked before pressing the mic button again. 'Roger that. Three incoming, expected and welcome.'

There was a chuckle from the radio, '*Thought you might. See you in a minute or so.*'

The familiar soft, buzzing whine of the single PT6 turbo-prop grew louder as the utilitarian lines of the red and white striped Cessna Caravan, made a low pass over the water to check for floating debris, then made a neat turn and dropped feather-light onto the water just 150 metres away. I'd forgotten how quickly seaplanes decelerate once they touch-down on water, and the pilot had to power up to get to our stern. He went through the shut-down procedure before the turbine whine faded and the feathered propeller whooshed to a stop, letting the aircraft drift the last few metres until the port float tip was just touching the stern boarding platform.

The young pilot was quickly out of his seat and passed me a mooring line attached to the float. He walked back to the passenger doors set further back and helped first Lara, then Charlie, then a grinning Andy, who shook the pilot's hand before making his way carefully along the wide float top to the safety of *Firebird's* stern steps. Several soft bags followed, our new guests remembering the advice I'd given them on the old boat.

There was a lot of hugging and handshaking going on in the cockpit as I passed Alan and Hillary's bags to the pilot, then it was their turn to say goodbye and make their way along the float and into the cabin.

The pilot gave a cheery wave, closed the rear doors and climbed into the cockpit through his own forward door. I untied the mooring line and pushed him clear as the starter motor began winding the engine up, the spine-tingling whine kicking in as the RPM rose.

The prop turned slowly at first, then spun up quickly once the engine lit off and accelerated.

I could see the pilot scrolling through a checklist, then the engine sped up to full power and the Caravan roared off across the water, before lifting cleanly and clawing for height over the rugged mountains.

There was another round of hugs and handshakes from Lara, Charlie and Andy. Charlie was especially fierce with her hug and said softly, 'Thank you so much for letting us come down on such short notice. We all really appreciate it, but especially Andy. He badly needs this break.'

'No problem my dear lady,' I replied gallantly, making her giggle and attracting an amused glance from Andy who was in the process of hugging Sandy. Bree and Alex were comfortable with Andy from the Indonesian excursion, but it was a very emotional brother and sister reunion between Andy and Kelly.

When Andy got to me, he gave me a big man-hug and said, 'I can never thank you enough for sorting out the Lord Howe problem and looking after my little sister. Anything I can ever do for you, I will. Thanks Harry.'

'You're welcome Andy. I won't say it wasn't a problem, but it had some high points as well. Anyway, the bad guys got what they deserved and a lovely lady was rescued. That's the way it should be.'

Alex took control of getting us back to the anchorage, while I showed Andy around the boat, and Sandy showed Lara the cabin she and Andy would share, and Charlie to hers, just ahead of Sandy's and mine.

As I'd pre-arranged, just before we made the right turn to pass between Turnbull Island and Tonguers Point, Alex called Andy and me up top. I wanted Andy to get a reasonably close look at the whalers, and five hundred metres was certainly close enough. Although the supply ship dominated the other boats, he got a brief look at the disabled *Nissabe Maru* and the catchers, then a closer look through the Zeiss binoculars.

He shook his head in wonder at the destruction. 'So, all four of those boats are without props and rudders, as well as being burnt out internally?'

'Yep. The props and rudders are courtesy of Sea Guardian's divers, while the holes and the burnt-out stuff was our work. If asked officially, I would speculate that someone got careless with a welding torch near the whale oil storage tanks.'

'What about these raids you and Alan were talking about? Like who started what?'

'Okay. Let's start at the beginning.'

Once again, leaving the very capable Alex to look after getting us the rest of the way back to Aylen Point and rafted up beside *Seeker*, I sat Andy, Charlie and Lara down and went through the whole series of events with the whalers, starting with the first aggressive visit by 'Sunnies' at Heard Island.

Andy was incredulous until we showed him the video of the raids taken from the masthead camera which had been left running throughout each event. We also brought out the Howa Type 89-F assault rifle in its waterproof case, which Dave had salvaged from one of the raiding party's RIB.

'I've heard of these,' Andy said, 'but they aren't supposed to be released outside the country unless on a military vessel.'

I shrugged, 'That tends to prove the officers on the whaling boats are all military personnel. The suicide bombers told us quite a lot.'

He looked startled, 'Suicide bombers? What suicide bombers? Where do they fit in?'

'Damn! Sorry Andy, so much has happened in a very short space of time, I forgot to mention them. Although I did tell you we had two defectors.'

'Yes, I remember that.'

'Well, it turned out, they were actually on a suicide mission with radio locator beacons inside them.'

I went through the elaborate plan of deceit where the two 'defectors' came to us having swallowed homing beacons to guide the lifeboat full of explosives straight to us.

'I'm stunned by the level of aggression shown by these people toward you,' Andy said, 'but going back to Heard Island and this Sunglasses fella. What happened to him?'

I chuckled, 'He led the final night raid, was the only survivor, and was wounded. I arrested him on a string of charges and he's in *Arafura's* brig at the moment, until we can turn him over to my people. Unless you want to do something else with him?'

He pulled a face, 'It's a messy situation, although the Japanese did say they were stopping 'Research' whaling. However, a private company came out and said they were going to start commercial whaling, but only in home-waters. This activity goes against every treaty currently in play and the attacks on Aussie citizens in Australian waters with Self-Defence Force officers aboard is tantamount to a declaration of war. I'll have to think closely on this and maybe phone a friend.'

He, Charlie and Lara went down to their cabin where Charlie said that this time, they'd brought their own SatPhone.

CHAPTER 33

While Andy, Charlie and Lara conferred in private, I joined the crew in the cockpit where they were making the most of the sun and scoffing down piles of fresh pikelets with jam and cream.

My dear Sandy had set some aside, although Dave, Alex and Krazy cat were eyeing them off.

Claiming my share of the lovely tucker, I filled everyone in on what Andy was doing. It sparked a parallel discussion about how the situation should be handled, and in the middle of it, Paul was ferried over to us.

With a mug of his preferred coffee blend in hand, and a few pikelets that Bree had tucked aside, he was curious about the latest with the whalers and wanted to know that Alan and Hillary had got away alright. I told him they were safely away, but was a bad boy yet again by not mentioning our new guests, but I did enjoy seeing the look on his face each time he got caught out by my juvenile 'gotcha's'!

As was the case when Andy wandered out from the saloon and with his trade-mark boyish grin on his face, stopped in front of Paul, held out his hand and said, 'Commander Davy, I presume? I'm Andy Friar.'

I choked back a laugh as Paul shot to his feet, coming rigidly to attention, before belatedly taking Andy's hand. 'Delighted to meet you, sir. I also believe I have you to thank for the recommendation for my promotion and my new boat.'

Andy laughed at Paul's discomfit, and sat down. 'You deserved all that and more, Commander. However, I'm sorry to laugh, as obviously our host chose to forget to tell you I and my two lovely ladies had joined his crew for a couple of weeks.'

That got Paul to his feet again to shake hands with Lara and Charlie, who felt obliged to say with a laugh, 'It's not as bad as you're thinking, Commander. I'm just his PPS; Lara's the lovely lady.'

Paul regained his seat with a disgusted look at me. 'Any more surprises, Commander Stevens? You haven't got Queen Elizabeth stashed away down below as well, have you?'

I stopped chuckling long enough to say, 'Sorry Paul... couldn't help myself, and I know I still owe you for the Lord Howe gee-up. Anyway, it's good you're here, because we need to discuss the best way to handle this messy situation. Over to you, Andy.'

'Okay. Basically, to cut a long story short, my colleagues are less concerned about the illegal whaling, than they are about the covert presence of the Japanese military on Australian soil and waters without due cause or permission. It could, in conjunction with the two armed attacks they've made, be classed as an invasion of Australia. I know it's a bit of a stretch, but that's the case we can make to the Japanese Government.'

'It'll cause a furball,' I observed dryly. 'I suspect the higher levels of the Japanese Diet don't know they've invaded Australia.'

That raised a laugh, but it was a serious subject, so Andy went on. 'Anyway, the advice we got was that somehow, we have to provoke the Japanese military guys into showing themselves. I have no idea how to achieve that, so it's a handball back to you guys and girls for one of your well-known cunning plans.'

Discussion ran back and forth while a germ of an idea festered and grew in my warped mind, until Sandy said, 'Uh oh... Harry's got that famous stare going. This could be the making of a cunning plan. Come on dear, cough it up. It's just like a furball...you'll feel much better afterwards.'

I poked my tongue out at her. 'Well, yes. I do have a bit of an idea which might work. See what you all think of this.'

I explained my rough plan and while it raised a few eyebrows, there weren't any serious objections. A few refinements were tossed on the table and worked into the plan until nobody had any more to offer.

I looked at Andy and Paul. 'As the two most senior responsible persons here, do we proceed?'

'Go from me' said Andy immediately. 'There's nothing to lose by trying it. If they don't respond; no harm, no foul.'

Paul nodded agreement, 'Yep. No real problem from me either. Just be ready with the radio.'

'Okay, Harry. It's your show,' said Andy. 'Carry on.'

It was just going on for 11:30 when I nodded and said to Paul, 'Alright. How soon can you launch?'

'Pretty well straight away if we go out on the turbine and let the diesels warm up gradually like they're supposed to. It'll be a good exercise in quick response. Might help the case to justify fitting more turbines.' The last was offered with a cheeky grin at Andy who waved him away with a chuckle. He unclipped a small radio from his belt and called the bridge watch.

'XO! Rapid deployment exercise,' he announced. 'I'm on my way back, and want to be moving in three minutes from now. We go out on the turbine only while the diesels warm up. Sound action stations. Clear!'

He was already climbing into the RIB while finishing the call and his boat crew hustled. From what we could see, the crew were superbly trained; there was no panic or screaming of orders and as the anchor was clanking in, a rising whine told of the turbine already spooling up. A crew were ready with the boat hoist on the starboard side and the boat crew hooked the falls on as they swung in against *Arafura's* side. The moment the anchor cleared the surface, there was a boil of water at the stern which quickly grew as the patrol boat gathered way rapidly, while the RIB was still being hoisted.

'That's an impressive response,' Andy observed. 'He's trained them well.'

As the boat accelerated away from us, heading for the open ocean, twin puffs of black smoke told of the diesels being started.

'So, the normal response time would be another five or ten minutes while the diesels warmed up?' Andy asked.

'Yep, at least that. There's no way they could be started, then run up to speed straight away.'

The plan called for Paul to make a speed run straight for the southern tip of the Breaksea Islands, before turning to run out through the heads. The course took him within 500 metres of the collection of Japanese shipping, so they'd have to be blind, deaf and dumb to miss him. But to make sure, as he passed just west of their anchorage, he cheekily sounded off his horn, which was a set of massive brass trumpets fired by compressed air. The deep bass notes scared thousands of seabirds into flight and despite the stiff breeze still blowing, the echoes rolled back and forth off the hills around us.

'Damn!' I said admiringly, 'I'd love to have a set of those.'

Sandy patted my knee. 'Maybe for Christmas, dear.'

'So now we wait?' Andy asked.

'Yep! Paul can sit in comfort down in Cox Bight for the next day or possibly two, until the whalers make the move I think they will. Then he's only 90 minutes away.

'Sandy, my dear, would you and Bree mind putting *Dragonfly* up so we can have a look at these people? Fuel it fully and we'll leave it up for the day. If nothing happens, we'll retrieve it before sunset and rely on radar and the camera in case they take the late-night option.'

We did our best to relax, but even with a BBQ lunch and one of Bree's tasty salads, the tension hung like a dense fog over the two boats.

Lara and Charlie took towels and stretched out on the trampolines, although the breeze was way too cool to strip off.

Andy wanted to chat and kept coming up with more questions about the last few weeks, from Heard Island onwards.

'I'm sorry this mess is cutting into your holiday,' I said at one point.

Andy laughed, excitement flashing in his eyes. 'It's not, actually.

I'm telling the staff back at the funny farm this is hands-on work, and my holiday starts after this is cleaned up.'

The rest of the day was quiet with no movement from the mob across the water. The UAV didn't spot any unusual activity, so was brought back just after 17:00. I told the girls to prep it for the morning and leave it ready for launching. After a tension-filled day, everyone was tired, so after a simple evening meal, I set two-person watches of four hours each, and took Charlie with me for the first watch to midnight, then Sandy and Andy were to take over, then Alex and Kelly, who was a bit down over Alan leaving.

'It looks like this has become fairly serious between Alan and Kelly,' I said to Sandy as she got ready for bed.

'Oh yes,' she replied, 'they've hit it off extremely well. Alan's only 55, Kelly's 39, so the difference isn't too extreme and they've got a lot a good living ahead. I wouldn't be surprised if she leaves the boat at some point on the way back. They seem well-suited to each other, and she's never been happier than in these last few weeks.'

I grinned, 'Yet another match *Firebird* is responsible for. Must be in the name!'

Our watch passed quietly, if one discounted Charlie's almost non-stop chattering. Still, she had different things to chatter about and I gained a fresh insight into the devious and murky world of Australian politics. Lights continued to burn on the supply ship, but even with the camera on full zoom, there was nothing of any significance to see.

Sandy and Andy, sounding like an old vaudeville stage act, took over at midnight, by which time I was ready for sleep.

Charlie wasn't, however, and wandered in just as I was climbing into bed. She wore her usual T-shirt in lieu of PJs and with the weight she'd lost, looked rather appealing, but I behaved myself and we just chatted for a while, before she gave me a long kiss goodnight, then went to her cabin on the other side of our bathroom.

I presumed nothing happened for the rest of the night, since I awoke feeling refreshed at 06:00, to find a sleeping Sandy in bed beside me, and Alex and Kelly on watch.

'All quiet, Commander,' Alex reported, 'no activity from our friends at all and the lifeboat is still tied to the gangway landing stage.'

'Hmmm. I really thought they'd have seized the opportunity by now.'

'Maybe they're being cautious?'

'Yeah. Maybe. We'll give it another day.'

However, we didn't need to wait that long. At around 11:00 Bree called out from the chart table where she was maintaining watch on the UAV's camera feed.

'Better take a look at this, Harry. We've got movement at the station.'

I hurried over and sure enough, several figures were on the boarding ladder steps and the landing stage. Without being asked, Bree was already carefully zooming in on the figures.

The first two were plainly men in uniform and Bree coaxed a bit more zoom out of the lens to show what appeared to be four gold bars on the shoulder boards of the first man. This suggested it was Kurosawa. The second man was interesting in that he had what appeared to be gold shoulder boards.

'Well fuck me!' I said rather crudely without thinking. 'Kurosawa is entitled to wear four stripes as Captain of the *Nissabe Maru*, but this next character has come off the supply ship and no Merchant Marine rank has gold boards. Only the Military have them and it denotes an Admiral of some level. It looks like they're really showing their true colours. What the fuck's an Admiral doing on a whaler's supply ship?'

'This is getting interesting,' Andy observed, 'these blokes are digging their hole deeper all the time.'

The men went from sight into the lifeboat's cabin and two seamen followed them, plus a coxswain who took up the open steering position near the stern. They shoved off and headed our way.

I sat back and blew a long-held breath. 'This appears to be just what we wanted,' I said to Andy and the others crowding around, 'but we might take a few precautions just in case, although two officers and three sailors hardly constitute a raiding party. Still, let's get everything we can on tape in case they're trying the decoy thing again.

'Bree, would you mind dropping *Dragonfly* down to around 1,000 feet. They won't see or hear it, and we'll get a much better look at these blokes. I want good close-ups of faces, please people. Sandy, would you mind getting our hand-held video and shoot from inside here? They won't see you though the tinted glass, but leave the door ajar so you get all the audio as well. Also, Kelly, can you drive the masthead camera, recording the approach, as close-up as you can?'

The lifeboat wasn't fast and bobbed its way toward us at about 8 knots, so there was plenty of time to get the video set up. We got some good hi-res shots when the Admiral climbed up beside the cox'n to have a good look around. I must admit he looked like a fairly typical senior Naval officer, and the way the cox'n had stiffened to attention when he appeared, suggested he was the real deal.

I took the precaution to arm Alex, Dave and myself with the MP5, the Mini-Uzi and the TAC-14 shotgun, simply because they really looked menacing. I arranged Andy on the far side of the table, with Lara and Charlie on either side. Because the cockpit was out of the breeze, I asked the ladies to wear bikini tops in the hope they might be a distraction to the officers.

As the lifeboat came closer, I fired a red parachute flare above it, then a second one lower, which fell into the water beside it. Immediately, a white flag of truce appeared beside the cox'n, looking like a grubby bedsheet tied to a boat-hook being waved madly.

'Are the .50 cals ready?' I asked Dave.

'Corrine's ready but she's kept them covered,' was his answer.

'OK. Any suspicious actions by these blokes, we shoot first, ask questions later. On second thoughts Andy, would you mind waiting in the saloon until I call you out? Just as a safety precaution. You can still see and hear everything.'

'Sure thing Harry,' he replied amiably. 'Good idea.'

Taking Lara and Charlie with him, they went inside, leaving the door ajar. My other second thought was to have Jasper, minus Krazy, come out into the cockpit and sit on the stern daybed. When he was up there, a dopey grin on his face because he was the centre of attention again, I said to him, 'Bad men coming, boy. Growl when they come aboard, and if I say so, attack.'

He immediately stopped grinning, huffed in response, and turned to look at the approaching lifeboat, just 50 metres away. Two heads popped up from the middle hatch, one of them unmistakeably Kurosawa. The bowman was in position, as the cox'n expertly eased the big boat alongside the right-hand boarding platform. Significantly, the bowman was dressed in a smart, pale grey uniform with yellow on black shoulder patches, with an anchor over branches, a star-shaped device above and a single horizontal bar on top.

'Commander,' Alex softly said in his deep rumble, 'it is interesting that the bowman is a Petty Officer and it would appear the cox'n is a Chief Petty Officer. Not only are they way over-qualified to be driving a small boat, but those are Naval ranks, not Merchant Marine ones.'

'Thanks Alex. That's further confirmation, and suggests the entire crew of the supply ship are Naval.'

Andy's voice sounded from the saloon, 'We're getting all this, Harry. Good detail. These blokes must have thought they were safe to come and scare the civilians again, now the patrol boat has gone.'

I grinned, 'Yeah. Would you make the SatPhone call please Sandy?'

'Roger that, on it now.'

'Damn! Don't you hate it when my plans work out?'

'You're being a smart-arse again, Harry.' came Sandy's voice again. 'Knock it off!'

'Yes dear! Knock off the smart-arse. Copy that!'

'You're pushing it, boyo. Pussy can get locked up for a while you know; and I don't mean Jasper and Krazy.'

Several muted giggles and a masculine chuckle drifted out of the saloon as the tones of the SatPhone connection sounded.

Captain Kurosawa was the first to step out of the lifeboat mid-section, and he marched up the steps without asking or being invited. A second bulky figure stepped out behind him, both dressed in the naval winter uniform of black coat and trousers, white shirt and tie. Kurosawa's four gold rings gleamed on his sleeves, while the newcomer wore the two broad and one narrow sleeve bands of a Rear-Admiral.

The bowman and the other seaman started to follow the Admiral, but I stepped forward and racked a shell into the TAC-14 shotgun, the loud clack-clack sound unmistakeable and threatening – as intended.

'Back up the bus, Captain.' I said with a nod to Jasper who immediately let loose with a deep rumbling growl that even sent a shiver down my spine, causing Kurosawa to freeze in mid-step.

'You have ignored basic marine courtesy by not asking permission to come aboard, so you can leave your goons back on the boat. The three of them can sit on their hands on top of the cabin where we can see them. Come on ladies, up on top now, quick-time.'

Kurosawa immediately blustered. 'You no threaten Captain and Admiral of Japanese Marine Self-Defence Force with weapons!'

'I can and I have. Now – tell your Petty Officers to sit on top of the cabin, or get your grain-fed arses out of here.'

After a glare in my direction, he tuned his head and barked an order. I waited until all three hefty men were sitting cross-legged on the cabin top, hands uncomfortably under their backsides, before saying, 'Alright, Captain Kurosawa. Despite your appalling lack of manners, you and your Admiral may continue up to the cockpit.' I flicked the safety on the Tac-14 with an obvious click, and stood in front of the table, while Alex and Dave moved apart to be able to cover the three sailors as well.

Jasper had stalked to the back of the day-bed where he could reach either the sailors on the lifeboat or the two officers with a single bound, and certainly held the attention of the three sailors who apparently hadn't seen anything like him before. Even the Admiral looked a bit pale since Jasper was less than a metre away and growling continuously, mouth open to show his long white fangs to ominous effect.

'State your business Kurosawa, then get the fuck off my boat!' I said rudely, my tone and words bringing a flush to his face. I watched the Admiral's face as I spoke and saw the slight change of expression which suggested he at least understood vernacular English.

Kurosawa's reply was, 'You arrogant man and very stupid. You kill my men, ruin my boats for no reason. I make official complaint through my Embassy to the Australian Government. Admiral Kimura wanted to see Australian rebel with own eyes. He most displeased! He....'

'Why don't you let Admiral Kimura speak for himself. Stop being everyone's puppet for once,' I interrupted him rudely.

'You very rude man! Admiral Kimura no understand English,' Kurosawa countered, 'I talk for him.'

'Oh, bullshit! He probably speaks it better than I do.'

'No. Him no speak.....'

CHAPTER 34

In a deep, resonant voice, Admiral Kimura said, 'It is alright, Kurosawa. I will speak for myself as this man says. Perhaps he is not as much the fool you have suggested he is.'

The last was delivered with a dark look at Kurosawa, before he turned to me and made a short bow, to which I responded in kind.

'I am Rear-Admiral Kimura of the JMSDF.'

'And I am Commander Stevens of the Australian Commonwealth Police.'

Kimura's eyebrows rose, 'So! Were you at Heard Island and now here on official business, Commander?'

'That really isn't your business, Admiral, but since you are being polite, unlike your arrogant and ill-mannered captain here, I shall do you the courtesy of a response. No, I was not on official business. My friends and I were on a holiday voyage when we were accosted by one of Kurosawa's crew at Heard Island and ordered to leave the island. That man and his colleagues were incompetent seamen and caused themselves and their boat a lot of damage. We had nothing to do with causing their problems.'

Kimura nodded, 'I am inclined to believe you, Commander. Some things are obviously not the way they have been represented to me.'

'That is frequently the case, Admiral, but before we proceed further, I would like to let my crew and guests join us. They have witnessed the unprovoked aggression of your captain and his crew on several occasions.'

Without waiting for a reply, I waved the saloon group to come out and it was interesting to see the effect the ladies in their brief bikini tops had on the two officers since Sandy, Bree and Kelly had changed as well.

Andy resumed his seat at the head of the table, but said nothing as the girls sat. 'Now, Admiral. Your captain has accused us of killing many of his crew and says your Government will be making official complaints to our Government. These are very serious accusations which cannot be dismissed lightly. Would you care to explain further?'

Kimura looked a bit discomforted. 'What Kurosawa has said is the current view of my Government, after we received reports of the confrontations my people have had with you and those Sea Guardian fools. Our Prime Minister is upset our citizens could be attacked so viciously, while taking shelter from a bad storm. I was sent here to see the situation for myself and am appalled to see the destruction wreaked upon my country's shipping.

Our Prime Minister will be making the strongest protests directly to your Prime Minister, demanding reparations to the whaling company and the relatives of all those you have killed.'

I got a tight smile on my face, one that Sandy recognised, causing her to say clearly, 'Down Harry! Softly, softly.'

Kimura glanced at Sandy, then insultingly said, 'Your woman speaks good sense, Commander. Perhaps you would do well to heed her, although in my country, we don't have many female advisors. It is obviously different here.'

I could see Sandy was on the verge of forgetting her own advice, so I jumped in with, 'You appear to have accepted Kurosawa's story without any attempt to find out how true it is. Maybe we should be discussing these accusations in more detail, Admiral. I invite you to take a seat at the table and hear our side of the situation.'

I pointedly didn't invite Kurosawa to sit and he didn't dare move as Jasper had moved closer, but I could see he was fuming with the humiliation I was dishing out.

Sandy visited the galley and returned with a mug and a small teapot of green tea which she placed in front of Kimura with a neutral look on her face.

'Thank you, Commander, most civilised.'

'We try to be, Admiral. Which reminds me - it is unfortunate you missed meeting one of our Navy Admirals who was also here as a guest on holiday. He flew out just yesterday and is a two-star Rear-Admiral. He would have enjoyed talking with you, and might have been able to correct some of the misconceptions you seem to have. He has been with us for nearly three weeks and witnessed everything which occurred here in Port Davey.'

Kimura forgot about his green tea and looked even more disconcerted. 'That would be Admiral Stallman? And he was here all the time?'

I nodded happily. 'Yes, he had a wonderful time, apart from being attacked by Kurosawa's men.'

'I know Alan well. He spent time with me in Japan and I regard him as a good friend. The fact he was a witness to all that happened is interesting.'

'Well, I'm glad you find it interesting. And even more so that you know and respect him. Perhaps you should talk to him and ask him what he saw? He can tell you all about when your Captain's raiding parties came to attack us twice in the night, armed with.... where is that rifle, Dave, that what-ever it is?'

'Oh, you mean the Howa Type 89-F assault rifle firing NATO 5.56 mm we turned over to Commander Davy of the *Arafura*? His people said it looked a very good weapon and they were going to recommend that our Military should maybe buy a hundred thousand or so from you.'

I beamed at Kimura, 'But I have a photo I took when your raiders ran off and left their RIB and the rifle in the bottom.'

I dug out my phone and dragged out the hunt for the right photo, before showing it to him, complete with an identifiable Japanese RIB.

Kimura had gone pale again. 'You cannot have that weapon. It is for Japanese use only.'

'Oh dear. It's too late now. He's long gone.'

Kimura turned to the hapless Kurosawa and berated him in Japanese, long and hard. Turning back to me he apologised for his lapse. 'You say the raiding party ran off. Where did they run off to? There is nothing here.'

I grinned at him, 'That's correct. There is nothing here except un-tamed wilderness, and a lot of it. There are no towns or villages. They cannot have survived unless they've returned to Kurosawa's ship.'

'No. They have not been seen since. But this weapon is secret. You cannot just take it. This is theft and I will have my Government take it up with yours very soon.'

'Oh, what a great idea, Admiral. But I think we can short-cut that long, involved process. You like to short-cut red-tape, don't you Admiral?'

He looked a bit wary at my words, wondering where I was going with all this waffle. 'Yes. Of course. All military leaders prefer to act rather than waste time endlessly talking like diplomats.'

I beamed at him. 'Excellent! Now, earlier, you made all those accusations about us killing all your men without provocation, and causing damage to your boats, also without any provocation. You say you have passed all this information on to your Diet to debate, before they call our Prime Minister to sling some abuse our way. Is that a fair summary of what you said?'

Cautiously, he nodded. 'Correct. My Government feels strongly about the immense damage you caused to our boats and your involvement in the disappearance of twenty-six of the Captain's crew.'

I clapped my hands sharply together. 'Great! In that case, allow me to present the Honourable Andrew Friar, Prime Minister of Australia; and even better, you don't have to explain yourself again. He's heard it all.'

The hackneyed phrase, 'his face fell' is rarely accurate, but in this care, his facial skin seemed to slump, before training kicked in and he jumped to his feet, prompting a sharp growl from Jasper, then gave Andy a deep bow.

'Please forgive me for not recognising you immediately, Prime Minister. I have followed your career and am well aware of your rise to power and the plot to assassinate you last year. I am deeply embarrassed by my lapse of manners, and also for presenting my information so badly.'

Andy waved it all aside. 'Thanks for the explanation, Admiral Kimura, and it was useful to hear your side. I note, however, you haven't offered an explanation why 26 of the Captain's men, who it seems were all full-time members of the Japanese military, were making an attack on Australian citizens on Australian soil in the first place.'

Andy forestalled Kimuras response with a raised hand, then continued.

'First and foremost, these are the main issues I'll be discussing with your Prime Minister, who I consider to be a close friend. However, another excellent question is whether my good friend, Shinzo Ito, actually knew about the Japanese Military manning commercial whaling ships in Australian waters. What do you think of that for an opening question to my discussion?'

Kimura looked stricken at the thought of that conversation and failed to find suitable words.

'In fact,' Andy continued, 'I think your response, or lack thereof, encourages me to have that conversation shortly. We have all the facilities aboard this boat and I'd like to be able to settle this matter immediately. I'm sure you would also like to see this matter swiftly resolved.'

The Admiral, now sweating profusely, tried to rally. 'I can assure you, Prime Minister, there is a perfectly valid explanation for all of this. But to receive a proper explanation, you would have to talk to the Lord High Admiral of the Japanese Empire, who is the man who authorised this operation.'

Andy's eyes lit up, 'Ah, ha! So there is an operation which

apparently requires the covert infiltration of Japanese military personnel into Australia. This gets more interesting all the time. I think I must ask you and your Captain to stay right here until I have spoken with Prime Minister Ito.'

Kimura hastily stood, 'I regret it will be impossible, Prime Minister. I have to return to my ship to consult with my superiors.'

With a regal gesture, Andy waved him down. 'Nonsense, my dear fellow. We need to get to the bottom of this, dare I use the word...conspiracy.'

Andy looked thoughtfully at Kimura. 'It's a particularly nasty word, conspiracy, don't you think, Admiral? Especially in the military, which is why the penalty for those caught indulging in it is so high. Death by firing squad is the current method in your country, I believe. Still, that could change. Can't have the military, especially the senior officers, acting on their own against the national interest. Particularly when it involves invading a friendly country. I cannot believe that Mr Ito would sanction such an operation. He is an honourable and decent man.'

Kimura collapsed back into his chair, pale, shaking and gasping as though he was about to have a heart attack, so Captain Kurosawa tossed his ten cents worth onto the table.

'You no dictate to us. We go to ship, now! You cannot stop us!'

Andy just smiled and as he motioned for Charlie to fetch the SatPhone, I said mildly, 'I don't like having to disappoint you yet again, Captain, but if our PM says stay, then you stay. You both have a few questions to answer.'

He stood, hands on hips, glaring defiantly. 'What you do? You stupid! How you keep us? You not shoot JMSDF Captain and Admiral.'

I nodded ruefully, 'You know what? You're right. We won't shoot you two. But we could shoot those three Petty Officers you brought over as strong-men.'

'Pah! You no do it! You kill too many my crew already.' He grinned triumphantly; certain he'd faced me down.

'Hmmm.... Are you right, or am I right? Although perhaps the question should be... are you feeling lucky? I wonder what can I do?' I asked him rhetorically, as the arrogant toad continued grinning.

Flashing a quick look at *Seeker's* upper sun-deck, I saw that Corrine was seated behind the closest .50 cal and the cover was off. I briefly pointed at the lifeboat, then held my hand in the 'wait' signal position, to which she nodded, way ahead of me as usual.

'Eureka!' I cried out, hamming it up like a pro. 'I have the solution. Watch closely, Kurosawa, you're going to love this.'

With that, I jumped up on the day bed, strode to the rear edge and looked down at the lifeboat tied up close astern, the three petty officers still sitting uneasily on the cabin top, clearly wondering what I was up to.

'You blokes might want to think about moving aft sometime soon,' I said loudly, before lifting my left hand. The thunderous noise of the .50 calibre being fired at close range was painful, especially as the stream of half-inch bullets was passing a few inches away from my right shoulder. Corrine's aim was perfect as the heavy bullets carved their way like a sabre-saw, from the deck down to the waterline, allowing the entire bow to fall away from the rest of the boat, in a choking cloud of smoke and fibreglass dust.

The three seamen, who'd magically teleported aft as the first bullets rained destruction down beside them, looked very worried as they clustered in the stern where the cox'n started the engines to activate the high-volume bilge pumps. It didn't work for long since Corrine's next burst chewed away several metres of waterline, which was enough to defeat any bilge pumping system.

With a tired sigh, the chewed-up lifeboat slowly settled, flooding the engines and giving the terrified sailors only one sensible choice. They chose to abandon ship by jumping onto the stern boarding platform, where they cowered in front of a maniac waving a shotgun, a heavy machine gun at his command, and a very large black cat which hissed and growled at them non-stop.

I beckoned the sailors to come up to the cockpit where Alex

cable-tied their wrists and ankles, but Kurosawa still wasn't giving up, saying, 'Very clever, silly man. Now you stuck with five prisoners. You make more problem for you. What you do with us now? Ha, ha!'

I was sick of this arrogant fool, so I stepped up to him and with the barrel of the shotgun shoved hard up against one nostril, I forced his head around so he faced the south-west. 'I don't have a problem, dickhead! I'm just going to turn you over to our Navy; they just hate whalers!'

Coming into sight around the heads was the sleek grey bow of *Arafura*, her bow wave arching up level with the foredeck and obviously under maximum power of all three engines. His arrogance fled as I produced my warrant card and formally announced that he and Kimura were under arrest for conspiracy to plan and despatch teams to commit armed attacks on Australian civilians in Australian territory.

Arafura saw we were still in one piece, so she slowed her approach, as Charlie handed the Satphone to Andy. 'Prime Minister Ito is on the line, Boss, and the call has been authenticated.'

He nodded thanks, took the handset and after informally greeting his friend Shinzo, proceeded to tell him all that had happened. I listened closely in case of a mistake, but Andy was well-practiced in the art of gathering facts and condensing them into a concise, cohesive story. Part-way through, I noticed one of the Petty Officers wriggling his bound hands a bit more than seemed necessary to maintain circulation. Looking up at Alex, I said, 'Alex. I know you searched these turkeys, but would mind checking this dude again, please?'

'Certainly, Commander,' he rumbled, placing the MP5 on the table. Roughly, he dragged the man into a more upright position and starting with his wrists, worked carefully up from there.

'This might be what he was trying to reach,' he said, expertly flicking a thin and flat double-edged throwing knife onto the table. It still had a scrap of electrical tape sticking to it from where it had been bound to his inner wrist. 'My apologies, Commander. I should have found it earlier.'

I shrugged, 'No harm, no grief. But maybe go over the others as well.' He and Dave examined every square centimetre of his body and clothes, then started on the other two, the whole episode only taking a few minutes. Before long, there were four knives and three throwing stars, piled in an untidy heap on the middle of the table.

The winter season hadn't officially started, but already the daylight hours were becoming shorter, as I turned back to Andy's conversation with the Japanese Prime Minister. However, he seemed to have finished, as he held out the phone to me.

'Just explain the encounters with the whalers, please Harry.'

He was offhand about it, so I presumed that while my attention was distracted by the seaman, the phone had been passed to an assistant.

'This is Commander Stevens,' I said, 'what did you want to know?'

A smooth, cultured voice replied in perfect English, 'And this is Shinzo Ito, Commander. Your Prime Minister speaks very highly of you, so I would appreciate you telling me of the series of encounters you and your crew have had with these whaling crews.'

I poked a face at Andy for dropping me unprepared into a conversation with Japan's Prime Minister, but he was busy trying to contain a fit of the chuckles.

'Certainly, Prime Minister. It started shortly after our arrival at Heard Island in the midst of a blizzard.' I briefly stepped him through the Heard Island events, then covered the Port Davey encounters. He wanted full details and was particularly interested in the two suicidal persons, Lieutenant Mitsu and Yoshi Hideki who had swallowed marker beacons for the explosive boat.

'So, this Lieutenant Mitsu told you all the officers were JMSDF personnel?'

'Yes, sir. His defection story was quite convincing, but as several of my crew had doubts, we kept the two of them in isolation. We were fortunately able to detect the marker beacons inside them and on their RIB'

'*Today, you received two officers, this Captain Kurosawa and Rear-Admiral Kimura and they were accompanied by three Petty Officers. They were all in uniform?*'

'Yes, sir. The two officers are in winter dress uniform, and the Petty Officers are in working coveralls with rank badges on their sleeves.'

'*And Admiral Kimura claimed the whole crew of the supply ship were JMSDF personnel?*'

'That's correct, sir. Captain Kurosawa hasn't said if all his crew are the same, but we suspect so. Their statements were all recorded on video with audio.'

'*Very well, Commander. I thank you for all you have done. It seems you have rendered my country a great service, but I will find out more in the coming days. Thank you again and may I speak with my friend Andy again, please?*'

'Goodbye Sir. It's been a pleasure talking to you.'

I passed the phone back to Andy, sitting back to let a breath out. While he wrapped up the discussion, Alex finished checking the seamen for weapons and re-checked their wrist and ankle ties.

'Well, Harry,' Andy said, sitting back with a frown on his face, 'it would seem you have stumbled into some particularly dark and nasty business which goes way beyond simply whaling. I'll go through it with you in private, but in the meantime, Mr Ito has requested these five gentlemen, and the entire crew of all the whaler vessels are to be detained in custody, pending the arrival of a genuine Japanese Maritime Self-Defence Force vessel which is on its way as we speak.'

Dave and Alex brought their guns up as they heard those words, so I rose and collected my TAC-14 as well.

'Does that mean the supply ship is to be seized as well?'

He nodded happily, 'Yep. The whole damn lot!'

'Okay, let's get Paul and some lads over here now.'

I went inside to call *Arafura* on the SatPhone, as the VHF radio was too easy to monitor by the Japanese, and gave Paul a brief explanation. He promised to send a detail immediately, and at my suggestion, had another detail start to clear out the large storage bay on the rear deck and convert it to a lock-up.

Kimura and Kurosawa suffered the indignity of being searched, then bound securely, before being sat on the deck beside the sailors.

A large RIB arrived with several hefty RAN sailors and they managed to get the five Japanese into it without any accidents.

'The Skipper will be over shortly, Commander Stevens,' a Petty Officer said. 'He mentioned there were a few things he wanted to discuss.'

I chuckled, 'Yes, there are a few, and thanks for taking these characters off our hands.'

He fired off a quick salute, 'No problem, Sir.'

CHAPTER 35

PORT DAVEY, FRIDAY

'Ito is still trying to put the elements of the operation together,' Andy briefed us, 'but it appears there is some sort of power struggle or revolt happening within the military. A bunch of senior officers have disagreed with Ito's plans to cap the size of the JMSDF at current levels. They wanted a massive increase in funding to build more ships and acquire more aircraft.

The Diet are fully supportive of Ito, so the trouble hadn't spread outside the JMSDF, but that's bad enough.'

'But what's the go with the whaling thing?' I asked.

'It was all just a cover. Heard Island, being so remote, was to be the rally point for ships as they were progressively taken over by the rebelling crews. You arrived just as they were settling in and it seems the hostile reception you received was a lame and misdirected attempt to chase you off quickly. The whale-catching operation was a lucrative cover, but when they intercepted your message to Sea Guardian, and then the *Ballarat* turned up, they decided to move to Auckland Island, south of New Zealand.

It has a much better harbour for a large number of ships, although the risk of detection was higher as it's close to New Zealand. After leaving Heard Island, they were on their way there when they ran afoul of a savage storm. The *Nissabe Maru* was bounced off a reef leaving the area, tore the hull and her Captain decided to put in here to make repairs, Port Davy being the closest shelter.

Admiral Kimura was one of the lead officers in the plot, and he made the supply ship, *Riku Maru*, his flagship because it also was good cover. He was on his way to Heard Island when the message came through about the change in base location.

317

What Ito can't work out is the end objective of the rebellion. Ordinarily, what they're doing wouldn't make sense.'

'Additionally, Ito has asked Australia to help shut this thing down quietly, before the rot has a chance to spread any further. To that end, we, in the form of *Arafura*, are directed to seize all the ships associated with the whalers and to hold their crews in custody until we can hand them over to a JMSDF ship which should arrive here tomorrow or Sunday.'

'That's handy,' I commented, 'one must have been close.'

'It was. Since the rebels made so much fuss about their objections, Ito has had warning that something was brewing for some time. He positioned the rest of his Navy, the ones he knows are loyal, close to the more remote areas where it was considered likely Kimura and his buddies might gather. Therefore, we are to be graced with a visit from one of their largest ships, the *Izumo*, a 27,000-tonne aircraft carrier. She's a big bugger at over 800-feet long.'

My eyebrows climbed up my forehead as Dave asked what I was thinking. 'Was that just lucky? Or was there another purpose in having one of their big ones close by?'

Andy laughed, 'No luck about it! Ito's planners had decided that the rebels might use a remote southern island as a rallying point, so the best choices were south of Australia or New Zealand. They've had the *Izumo* and one of the smaller ones, the 19,000-tonne *Ise*, hanging around our east coast and New Zealand, playing at good-will visits for the last few months. Both ships are well-equipped to take on a batch of prisoners and have additional security personnel on board like their Special Boarding Unit guys. Sort of like Special Forces. They'll sort these people out, so we don't have to, thank heavens.'

'Boat coming over from *Arafura*,' Bree called out. 'It looks like Paul and another officer aboard.'

'Sorry Andy,' I said, 'you'll have to repeat some of this briefing to Paul and, I presume, Clare.'

He waved dismissively, 'No problem. Used to it.'

Minutes later, Paul and Clare, his XO, were seated in the saloon, mugs of coffee in hand and scoffing down some sweet little cakes that Bree had been experimenting with. In short order, Andy laid out the situation.

Paul summed up his instructions. 'Therefore, our mission will be to formally seize the *Riku Maru, the Nissabe Maru* plus the three catchers, then to arrest and hold in temporary custody all their crews, in the name of the Japanese Government. Is that correct sir?'

'Yep, that's about it. It's a bit unorthodox doing it that way, but this ensures that custody appears to pass directly to the Japanese military. We're hoping there won't be any opposition, but just in case, that's why we pay you the big bucks, and gave you that 40mm attitude-adjuster mounted on your bow.'

Paul risked poking a face. 'Very funny, Prime Minister, but point taken. I don't suppose we have anything in writing to make this highly unorthodox exercise official?'

In response, Charlie wordlessly slid a photocopied sheet of paper in front of him. Under the letterhead of the Office of the Japanese Prime Minister, was a formal request to the Australian Government to assist in the short-term detainment of certain elements of the JMSDF, who had acted against the best interests of the Japanese Government. There followed a detailed list of assets and personnel which covered all the vessels and personnel on the other side of the bay. The signature of Shinzo Ito was under all that, and further down was a stamp of the Australian Prime Minister's Office, marked 'Authorised' and signed by Andy Friar.

'A copy for your log, Commander,' Andy said, 'and I think we should act as soon as possible, if you don't mind? Just in case someone on the supply ship decides to be a hero or go walkabout on shore. Dave – we might come over on *Seeker* to watch the fun, if that's okay with you and Corrine?'

Paul nodded, 'That's a good idea, sir. And if you don't mind Dave, I'd like to put two .50 cal crews on-board to man those devices as a back-up to mine. I don't want to have to use the 40mm cannon if I can avoid it. It makes such a huge mess up close!'

Dave nodded, 'No problem on both requests. We'll be ready when you are, Paul.'

That broke the party up as there was a general scramble on *Firebird* to get ready and get over to *Seeker*, leaving Jasper and Krazy to mind the store. The RIB ran Paul and Clare back, then a few minutes later, returned to *Seeker* with the same crew who'd manned the machine guns previously. Dave had the diesels warming up and with all aboard, idled out to hang about while Paul got moving.

To reduce the alarm factor, we travelled at the relatively slow pace of 15 knots, angling for the Breaksea Islands, before turning at the last moment directly toward the whalers and accelerating hard.

Paul's concerns about opposition weren't realised, or maybe it was the fact that Clare parked the patrol boat alongside the *Riku Maru* with the 40mm cannon trained around to point directly at the bridge, less than rock-throwing distance away.

A detachment of heavily armed sailors trotted up the gang-plank laid between the two vessels and disappeared into the bowels of the supply ship, with the Lieutenant in charge giving a running commentary on their progress over UHF radio.

With four .50 calibre heavy machine guns pointing at them as well as the 40mm cannon, it only took a couple of brief bursts to convince the crew that resistance would be both futile and painful. Finally, in ones and twos, they slowly emerged from the superstructure to be met at gun-point by a strip-search station. The icy-cold deck and the near freezing wind provided all the urging necessary for the task to be completed quickly. Only one feisty young buck objected and he was smartly dealt with by being dropped overboard. A cargo net was belatedly dropped to help him back up, and the additional delay in getting him stripped and wrapped in a blanket, was enough to remove all thoughts of further resistance.

The presence of a surprising number of young ladies among the crew provided a minor distraction as without favour, they received the same treatment as the males. A growing pile of handguns, knives in a bewildering array of styles, tiny radios and other nasty weapons like throwing stars, was testament to the belief amongst the crew that they still had something to fight for.

All received cable-tie handcuffs and ankle hobbles, while Paul's crew hastily setup another two toilets when they saw the number of prisoners.

There were around 90 prisoners once the boarding party had scoured all five ships and they were jammed into *Arafura's* aft work and RIB storage space, with armed guards present to prevent interference with what they could reach of the ship's systems.

Paul stood on a ladder to briefly address them, an interpreter standing beside him.

'I'm sure you all know why you are here, but in case you doubt the validity of being held in custody by a Royal Australian Navy warship, let me read a letter from the Japanese Prime Minister's Office.'

As he read Shinzo's words, many shoulders slumped in defeat. Many more did the same when Paul announced good news, bad news! This bit of levity went straight through to the keeper with most of them. The good news being that within 24 to 36 hours, they would have a lot more room. The bad news being the extra room was on one of their own ships, crewed by unsympathetic sailors.

One change of plan was that, with the number of prisoners to feed, Paul's catering Petty Officer suggested they remain rafted up to the *Riku Maru* and use her galley and stores. Two prisoner cooks, who were delighted to be free of restraints and with the prospect of being warm again, were taken under armed supervision to activate the ships galley and provide a suitable menu.

SUNDAY

Two uneventful days later, and before the overcrowding discontent amongst the prisoners had a chance to fester too much, we were treated to the majestic sight of a large, grey aircraft carrier nosing into the confines of the inner harbour through the misty curtains of rain of yet another cold front.

'She certainly is a big bugger,' Dave commented dryly, echoing Andy's words of several days earlier.

Maybe it was the limited visibility, but the ship seemed to totally dominate the Port as she dropped anchor just a few hundred metres away. A ship's boat ferried the Admiral's aide, Lieutenant-Commander Takada, across to see Paul and when told of the presence of the Australian Prime Minister aboard *Firebird*, immediately presented his Admiral's invitation to come aboard for the midday meal and a briefing. Meanwhile, Paul signed a release and all the prisoners, including 'Sunnies' who had not been treated well by his fellow crewmembers, were ferried under guard across to the towering steel cliff which was the side of the *JS Izumo*.

I was asked to accompany Andy and Paul, and we were met by *Izumo's* Captain Maeda, who turned out to be a well-spoken, pleasant chap. He took us to his Admiral Kondo, who made us very welcome and expressed his personal gratitude for our assistance in catching what appeared to be the ring-leaders of the revolt. He didn't go into details of the punishment which could be handed out to the senior officers involved, but hinted it might be terminal.

'You might be interested to know,' he said during an excellent lunch which consisted of a parade of small servings of various forms of sushi and other delicacies, 'the person you referred to as 'Sunnies' is the only one who did not belong to the JMSDF. He is a member of one of the major Japanese Yakusa gangs, which introduces a new and very sinister aspect to the whole affair. We are trying to find out if the plot originated with the Yakusa, or were they merely brought in to help and advise.

We know many Yakusa factions have a large and quite legitimate financial stake in the industries which have done very well from Defence Force spending over the years, so this might be the missing connection we're looking for.'

I lifted my eyebrows interrogatively.

'Ever since we first uncovered evidence of this plot, my fellow Admirals, together with the Prime Minister, have been working together to find a logical explanation why the rogue personnel of our JMSDF have gone to such extraordinary lengths to oppose the proposed defence spending cap. They have literally put their necks on the line, so the Yakusa connection might be the reason we were looking for. Therefore, you and your crew have done most of the hard work for us, and earned the gratitude of the Prime Minister and the JMSDF.'

I bowed my head and said, 'Thank you for saying that, Admiral, but while initially we were just defending ourselves, we did wonder why Kurosawa kept attacking us. Even after he lost a lot of men and RIBs, he still kept at us like a dog gnawing a bone.'

He smiled, 'Kurosawa is well-known for taking offence very easily. I suspect that each time you beat him, he grew more determined to take you down.'

I nodded, 'That makes sense, but what are the plans for the disabled ships?' I asked.

He and Captain Maeda grinned at us, 'That was an extremely effective way to disable ships, I must say, Commander. I didn't know Sea Guardian had explosives. If it were only the propellers and rudders blown off, they could easily be towed, but there are also too many holes in the hulls and many repairs will be needed first. Fortunately, the *Izumo* has all the expertise and facilities necessary to carry-out those repairs. It is the order of the Prime Minister that we repair those ships as quickly as possible, and remove them from this amazing wilderness area. I have not been privileged to walk through such pristine forest, but I hope to before we leave.'

I smiled agreement. 'It is a wonderful place and you should take the opportunity to do so. But speaking of repairs, we saw the *Nissabe Maru* must have had a lot of patches put on underwater and her list has been corrected by pumping, so maybe she will be okay to move.'

He acknowledged that. 'Our engineers will look at it. Although the catchers are holed along the waterline in many places, Captain Maeda's divers will repair them enough to tow them away from here.'

'It will be good to clean up this mess as quickly as possible,' Andy said, 'and I will be grateful for it. I'll arrange to have Commander Davy with the *Arafura* on stand-by here while the work proceeds, just in case any problems come up.'

He looked at Paul, 'Will that be in order, Commander?'

'Yessir. If you contact Admiral Stallman, I'm sure he will raise new orders for me based on that. Thanks to Harry and Dave, we should have sufficient fuel and supplies, depending on how long the repairs take.'

'If it would help,' Admiral Kondo said, 'I'm sure Captain Maeda can arrange for the *Izumo* to re-fuel your patrol boat and re-supply you as well. It's the least we can do to make up for all the trouble our internal problems have caused.'

Captain Maeda agreed unreservedly, and said to Paul, 'I will get my Executive Officer to contact your XO when you would like to make a replenishment run.'

'Wonderful, Captain, thank you.'

Admiral Kondo picked up a sheaf of papers in front of him. I knew what it was since I'd dictated it and Charlie had speed-typed it.

He waved the pages vaguely, 'This report on the entire series of incidents that started at Heard Island; is the dialogue accurate?'

'The best that I, and those who were present at the time can recall. They are also backed up by a video of the initial encounter with Kimura.'

'Excellent. I say that because there are several statements made by Kimura and Kurosawa, which are effectively admissions of complicity. If you and the appropriate persons are prepared to sign that the statements are correct, then under Japanese law, we have a much stronger case against them.'

'No problem doing that, Admiral. It'll be a pleasure.'

CHAPTER 36

PORT DAVEY, MONDAY

With the *Izumo* dominating the seascape, we moved *Seeker* a few hundred metres away from the whaling fleet as a bunch of engineers, divers and assorted support personnel descended onto the *Riku Maru* with a mass of gear. Following the transfer of prisoners, Alex and I had made the trip across the bay to collect *Firebird* and reassure the kitties that they weren't abandoned after all, before bringing it back to raft up to *Seeker*. The noisy work carried on well into the night, as Admiral Kondo honoured his promise on making the damaged boats seaworthy as quickly as possible.

One surprise was the invitation from the Admiral to join him on a bushwalk after lunch.

Corrine and Sandy decided to join me and I was amused to see Paul there as well. We were picked up in the captain's gig, a 35-foot power boat which dropped us all ashore east of the fleet site where a valley promised much easier access to the higher ground to the south than the steep and barren slopes adjacent the collection of boats.

Admiral Kondo and his cheerful aide, Lieutenant Commander Takada, were dressed in proper hiking gear, making the four of us look like refugees in our hastily cobbled-up selection of gear. A cold wind still blew from the west, cooling the sweat collecting on our brows from the steep climb up.

The view of the Southern Ocean to the south and south-west from the top, was fantastic, once we had got our breath back. The Admiral set a cracking pace back down, the descent proving much harder on the legs than the climb. The exception, of course, was Corrine who out-paced everybody and showed no side-effects.

Back aboard, Charlie, Lara and Andy grinned to see Sandy and me hobbling off the Admiral's boat and Charlie offered to do the leg massage bit on both of us. I didn't complain as she was quite expert at loosening knotted muscles and after a steaming hot shower, I felt almost human.

Leaving Sandy and Charlie working out who was going to massage whom, I joined Andy and Lara who were playing chess in the saloon.

'What's the plan, Harry?' Andy asked.

'Not much more for us to do here,' I replied. 'Paul can supervise, so how about we bugger-off tomorrow?'

They both sparked up at that, so I asked, 'Not that I want to over-organise this trip, but is there anywhere in particular you'd like to visit or take a look at?'

'Well,' Andy replied, 'we thought it might be really nice to just take our time and have a look at some of the smaller places one doesn't normally visit. I know we can head home quickly if necessary, but there's another 10 days or so we don't have to rush anywhere. Does that sound okay with you?'

I grinned, 'Actually, that sounds perfect. What if we anchor up each night, and go ashore at some little village? Have some pub-grub and chat with the locals. We'll get Bree to do a bit of a disguise on you again Andy, so you don't get pestered by your adoring public.'

He laughed, 'Now that sounds like the real holiday I was counting on you to provide!'

'What were you looking forward to, Boss?' Charlie said, coming up the aft companionway, flexing her hands and fingers and smelling of sweet oil.

'We're going to do a pub crawl back to Sydney... by boat!'

'Yay!... That's my style of boat trip. Maybe we can talk the Skipper into dropping us off at the back door of your second residence?'

'Now there's a thought. How 'bout it Harry?'

I shrugged, 'Sure. Why not – anything's possible. It's your place after all.'

Andy was almost fizzing with excitement, as he exclaimed, 'Great! Where's a map? What's your first choice, Harry?'

'Well...a good mate of mine once lived in a village just the other side of Tassie from here. It's called Dover, as in white cliffs and all that, except there aren't any at this one. Apparently, his father built the slipway there, but he got the sand and cement ratio all wrong, and it started to break-up, so he got the sack. Anyway, the remains are still there, right beside the main jetty. But we can park further along the bay, near another jetty and walk across the road to the only pub in town.'

'Perfect. Should be fun.'

We said our goodbyes to Paul and the *Arafura* crew, and sent a message to Admiral Kondo and Captain Maeda. With plans in place for a relaxing trip back home, we indulged ourselves by opening the bar early at 16:00. Andy proved once again to be able to hold his booze well, however Charlie and Lara quickly got a bit out of control, but were funny at the same time. They were rolled into their respective beds by 21:00 and started snoring as soon as their heads hit the pillow.

Next morning, we made an early start with a clear sky and a light southerly breeze for a change as a high-pressure system was momentarily passing through. Not being in a hurry meant we sailed at a steady 12 knots, with Dave and Corrine idling along off our stern quarter as usual.

Hilliard Head, being the southern rampart of the entrance to Port Davey, drifted past to port and once clear of the numerous rocky outcrops, we turned south for the run to South-West Cape. This was the magnificent face of the true Tasmanian wilderness, with no tracks, where steep hills fell directly to the crashing waves of the Great Southern Ocean smashed relentlessly into the black rocky feet of the ranges. Only occasionally was a small, heavily forested valley allowed to penetrate the rugged coastal hills, generally cradling a small creek at its base, pouring the results of the abundant rainfall back from whence it came.

While the lower slopes were heavily timbered, the upper reaches were scoured by the ever-present salt-laden winds down to twisted, low bushes and hardy grasses. Our turn point was the long, jagged finger of South-West Cape, pointing mutely toward the Clarie Coast of Antarctica, some 1,372 nautical miles to the south.

Giving this stunningly rugged and hostile piece of land a wide berth, we turned left again for the short run across the bottom of Tassie. A group of deserted islands named the Maatsuyker Group lay on our direct track and provided a good reason to duck and weave a little, before resuming course for the aptly-named South-East Cape.

By lunch-time, we had turned the other corner and were heading north-east. Deciding to by-pass the village of Southport, Australia's most southerly town, with its population of 135 persons, we headed further north. We passed to the inside of the large, irregularly-shaped Bruny Island, and by early afternoon, had turned Lomas Point into the spreading bay of Port Esperance, guarded by Hope Island. We stayed close to the island to give the multitude of salmon-farming pens plenty of clearance. It seemed like there were dozens of them floating close in against the southern shore, with small boats coming out to regularly pump clouds of feed pellets to their voracious inhabitants.

The small town of Dover lay at the head of the bay, a lush, green valley behind it with encroaching hills squeezing the town sideways along a kilometre or two of narrow coastline. As dedicated pub-crawlers, we bypassed the main jetty and headed for an anchorage near a distinctive L-shaped jetty conveniently located almost directly opposite the only pub in town, The Plover Inn.

With our shallow drafts, both boats were able to anchor close to shore, so we tied the two dinghies to the head of the jetty and walked over the road.

Bree had done her usual subtle make-up disguise on Andy,

making him look a lot older and suitably scruffy since he hadn't shaved since they'd arrived a week ago. With a ball-cap on his head, he didn't rate a second glance, especially surrounded by six ladies looking particularly attractive. As a party of ten, we nearly doubled the number of customers, causing the locals to pause their conversation momentarily, but once we had two tables pulled together and everyone seated, they resumed muttering to each other, while casting assessing looks at the unexpected newcomers.

The owner was behind the bar, a cheerful fellow who was absolutely delighted at the prospect of a decent increase in the takings for the evening. I made him even happier when I asked if an evening meal was available.

'Yeah, mate. No problem. The wife's out back with the daughter, so whenever you're ready, just sing out.'

'Thanks, mate. No rush; we might have a few cold ones before we think about tucker.'

'Good on you mate. Now. What's the drinks order?'

I passed over $200, 'Let me know when it runs out, please.'

He grinned, 'Yep, sure will. It looks like you're off those two boats. They're bloody big to be in such shallow water aren't they? Especially the powerboat.'

'Yeah, that's us. The powerboat has water jets and only draws 1.3 metres, whereas the cat draws 1.5 metres. I hope we're not in anyone's way if we park there for the night?'

'No worries! You'll be right. Where are you heading?'

I almost grinned, knowing the question was coming, so I said, 'We've been over at Strahan and Macquarie Harbour, so now we're heading north, everyone wanted to visit some of the small places for a change.'

'Well, you've picked a small place here all right, but she's a friendly little town if you want to stay a few days.'

'Yeah, I'll see what the troops think. How's the fishing?'

'Bloody brilliant, mate! Just out from the jetty here or the one further up, you can score barracoota, salmon, flathead and mackerel at any time. Can't miss!'

I laughed, 'Yeah, I've heard that one a few times, but we'll see what happens.'

'Good oh, mate. You'll stay. Bet me shirt on it. She's a beaut little place.'

While we'd been chatting, a very pretty girl had come from the kitchen and carted all the drinks over to our table.

'Thanks, Sheila.' the owner called to her.

She grinned affectionately at him, 'You'd talk the hind leg off a donkey, Dad. Fair dinkum! Now let this gentleman go, so you can serve Joey down there. He's been hanging out for a refill for five minutes.'

He looked around guiltily. 'Oh, yeah. Sorry mate,' he apologised, 'can't ignore my other customers. Sing out when you want a feed, or just go out to the kitchen and see Sheila or Margie, the wife. They'll fix you up.'

CHAPTER 37

PUB CRAWL, DOVER, THURSDAY

It turned out to be a very funny night with everyone relaxing properly, since there were no pressures or foreigners trying to shoot at us. Sheila was very attentive and joined in the joshing and carrying on. In a flash of déjà vu, she came out after dinner was over, with a guitar and sang a variety of songs, mainly Irish folk songs, in a beautiful, clear voice that would have gone over well in any club or stadium, for that matter.

It was late when we wished Geoff, Margie and Sheila goodnight, promising to stay at least another night or two, and we'd come back the next afternoon. We all were a bit wobbly getting into the RIBs, but as no one fell in, that was a bonus.

It was a late start next morning and I was wakened by a voice hollering, 'Ahoy *Firebird*!' in a strident tone and banging on the stern railings. Jasper and Krazy tag-teamed me to make sure I was awake and after fumbling my way into a pair of trakky dacs, I stumbled up top to find a beautiful day and a bright-eyed Geoff in an 18-foot open fishing boat, hanging onto the swim steps.

'Ah, there you are, Harry,' he said cheerfully. 'I was heading out to get some fish for the kitchen and thought I'd drop in to see if you wanted to join me.'

'Ah...Yeah. I will, thanks Geoff. Two minutes.'

Dressed and armed with some tackle, I joined him and we headed for his favourite spot. An hour and a half later, we had two esky's full of a mixed bag of barracoota, salmon and flathead. We stayed on the fishing ground to clean and fillet the catch, then instead of heading back in, Geoff said, 'You seem to like animals,

Harry. I've got something to show you that I find fascinating and I hope you do too.'

He seemed keen, so I said, 'Yeah, sure Geoff. Lead on. It's a lovely day to see fascinating stuff.'

We'd been fishing near the first of three islands out from the jetty called Charity Island. He took us to the second small island called, naturally enough, Faith Island. The fish farms were about one kilometre away to the south, but Geoff stopped the boat about 50 metres out from the island shore. With one of the emergency paddles, he splashed at the surface of the water a few times before there was a gust of fishy breath and a be-whiskered face with a mouthful of gleaming white teeth poked up beside the boat. It was followed by a second, then a third grinning head as the small family of fur seals came to say hello. Geoff rewarded them with the fish carcasses and guts in what was clearly a well-established routine.

He turned to me, his honest eyes shining with childish delight. 'Isn't this the most amazing thing you've ever seen? I've been meeting up with this family for six months now and they brought the baby out just two weeks ago to meet me.'

I was more than happy to share his delight in such a charming interaction between man and animal, despite having been involved in many similar encounters with Jasper. However, I didn't want to be a smart-arse for once, so I asked quietly, 'I think it is brilliant, but would you mind showing them to Andy and his lady Lara as well? I know they'd be blown away by this.'

'Yeah, sure mate. I'd be pleased to. I don't tell too many people about this little family. Some of my customers are workers on the salmon-farming pens and they hate seals with a passion.'

'Why?'

'Oh, sometimes the seals tear through the nets surrounding the pens to get at the salmon, so the fish escape and the netting has to be repaired. Very costly. Even though the seals are protected, the fish guys still kill them when they can catch them near the pens.'

'Bugger! That's bad. Can't the Fisheries Patrol do anything about it?'

'Nah,' Geoff replied in disgust. He started the engine and waved to the seals as they splashed us with their flippers, before darting away. 'The salmon farms are big money for the town, so blind eyes are common. That's why I've got to be careful. But enough of my waffle; let's go fetch Andy and Lara. They seemed like nice people, the little I saw of them last night. What's Andy do for a crust?'

'Oh...He's a business administration consultant to large corporations.'

'Oh. I thought he looked smart.'

'Yep. He certainly is.'

Minutes later, we coasted up to the stern of *Firebird*, where I called out for Andy and Lara. They were keen to come and as we waited, I said casually to Geoff, 'I reckon my cat would like to see the seals too. Would that be okay with you? He'll behave himself. He likes sea creatures too.'

Geoff looked a bit puzzled, but politely said, 'Your cat? Really? Sure, I don't mind if he doesn't.'

'Great! Thanks mate. He'll love it.' I whistled and Jasper's sleek black head promptly poked over the stern railing. 'C'mon boy. Boat ride.' I called.

I didn't have to repeat myself; he was down in the boat in two bounds. Geoff was a bit shocked at seeing Jasper up close and personal for the first time, but covered up well.

'Jasper. This is Geoff and he is a friend. He wants to show you some of his friends I know you'll like.'

My big, black cat huffed, shook hands with Geoff, then sat on the bow seat looking forward.

Geoff touched my arm to get my attention, 'Ah... Harry. I thought I was showing you something amazing with the seals, but Jasper is way beyond that.... just what is he?'

'Who? Jasper? He's mostly Indonesian jungle cat, supposedly bred down with domestic cats, but something went wrong with the process and this is how he's turned out. He's legal and I have permission to keep him.'

'He's magnificent! I've never seen anything like him outside of a zoo.'

I laughed, 'Don't praise him too much. He'll want better meals and bedding.'

'You make it sound like he understands us.'

'To an extent, he does,' I replied, playing down Jasper's abilities to avoid giving too much away, and was grateful for the distraction of Andy and Lara. 'Ah, here they are. C'mon you two. We've got places to go and things to see.'

With Andy and Lara seated, we buzzed back out to where the seals had been.

'I don't know if they'll stay around without being fed,' Geoff said, sounding worried. 'I'd hate to disappoint Andy and Lara if they don't show.'

'Don't worry. I reckon they'll show alright.' I reassured him, as we slowed at about the right spot and Geoff went into the water-slapping routine. Still up in the bow, Jasper became excited and started mewling softly. Then when the three sleek heads popped up right beside the dinghy, he simply jumped in with them.

Geoff nearly had a fit and yelled the seals would kill him to protect their baby, so I just smiled and said, 'No. They won't do that. They'll get on really well.'

Andy and Lara were delighted at the spectacle, but Geoff was nearly speechless to see the black cat and three seals playing together so well. There was no sign from the parents that they feared for their pup, with Jasper using his big paws to advantage as paddles although way outclassed by the seals. Finally, he tired and the big male seal gave him a boost up with his snout to scramble back into the boat where a vigorous shaking anointed everyone with cold seawater.

I thought Geoff might be annoyed at the upstaging, and said, 'I only experienced this interaction with the seals after I was given Jasper, but you've done this by yourself. That's magic!'

In reply, Geoff couldn't stop telling me how wonderful Jasper was to play with the seals like he did. The object of all this adulation lay stretched out on the bow seat, letting the warmth of the sun soak his black fur, his head hanging over the side where the seals still splashed about, making soft barking sounds as counterpoint to Jasper's mewling.

It was a magical time, but was ended by a fast boat approaching from the direction of the fish pens. 'Here's trouble!' Geoff muttered, as he hastily started the motors, which sent the seals diving away, and pretending not to notice the other boat, he headed back toward *Firebird*.

'What's going on?' Andy asked, looking concerned as the other boat roared up behind us.

'Barry's with the fish-feeding crews and they suspect I feed seals. They haven't caught me at it, but they can see when I come out here. They always try some sort of bullshit intimidation stunt.'

It was intimidation alright as the other boat, driven recklessly by a large red-bearded man, came up close alongside, spraying us with water and yelled, 'Stop the boat, ya' useless fuckin' prick!'

Geoff had little choice as Barry eased across in front of us, forcing a turn, so he cut the throttle.

'What's up with you, Barry? You sprayed us with water and could have caused a crash. That's bloody stupid stuff!'

'Oh, I'm stupid, am I?' came his belligerent rejoinder. 'How about I come over there and show you what stupid feels like, you fuckin' seal-lover?'

Lara was cringing; Andy stood in front of her; and Geoff didn't know whether to flee or fight, so I said mildly, 'I fail to see what the problem is, friend. Geoff has been kind enough to show us around the bay and we caught a glimpse of some seals. What's the problem with that?'

Barry had hauled his boat alongside, and standing up, grasped

the hard-top of Geoff's boat with one meaty paw, making Lara cry
out as it tilted alarmingly, so I spoke again.

'Please don't do that; you're scaring the lady.'

'Butt out, city boy!' he said rudely. 'This arse-hole knows what
I'm talking about. Do you know how long it takes to repair just one
of those pens after some of ya mates have had a feed?'

As well as having a nasty attitude, he was a very big man with a
very big beer gut, had a serious BO problem and I noticed his boat
was tilted even more than ours as he braced against Geoff's hard-
top. So, as soon as he focused back on the hapless Geoff, I lifted
my leg and gave the side of his boat a gentle shove.

That upset his precarious balance enough to dump Barry into
the water. He must have had his mouth open when he hit face-down,
since he surfaced a while later, coughing and spluttering.

Before he fully recovered, I said quietly to Jasper, 'Bad man, boy.
One bite please, but don't eat anything.' That instruction earned
me a look from my weird black cat, but he slid over the side like a
seal, disappearing under the dark water.

Moments later, Barry let out a howl of pain, a look of panic in his
eyes as he looked around for what had attacked him, but a black
cat in dark water? I don't think so!

While he was distracted, I leaned over the opposite side of the
boat and when I splashed my hand Jasper appeared, letting Andy
and me haul his dripping mass from the water. Meanwhile, Barry
was still trying to climb back into his boat, looking fearfully around
for the mysterious attacker.

Finally aboard, he glared at me and shook one huge fist, the other
holding his left bum cheek, where a red stain was rapidly spreading
across his torn shorts. 'I'll get you for this, smart-arse city boy.' he
threatened. 'I don't know how you did it, but that bloody dog of
yours had something to do with bitin' me arse. It's bleedin' real bad
and all that there then!'

I looked impassively back. 'I don't know what you're talking about. If you're clumsy enough to fall in when I tried to hold the boats apart, you get to take your chances with the creatures who live there. I reckon you were bitten by a barracoota. There would be lots of them hanging around those fish pens.'

'That was no fuckin' barracoota what bit me bum!' he declared furiously. 'I'm going to see the coppers about this. Youse can't just attack somebody like that.'

'Perhaps you shouldn't threaten violence to other people, either. Three of us heard what you said to Geoff and we were all endangered by your reckless driving. You could have caused a bad crash. If anyone's going to the police, it'll be us.'

He glared again, 'I'm not finished with this, Mr Smart-arse-whoever-the-hell-you-think-you-are. I'll be seein' all youse again real soon, so just youse watch your fuckin' backs.'

With that parting threat, he fired up his engines and roared off back to the fish pens.

Geoff shrugged helplessly, 'I'm really sorry about all this. I normally try to feed the seals before those guys come out for the first morning feed, but we were a bit late today.'

Lara jumped up and hugged him. 'Andy and I loved seeing your seals. Thank you for a wonderful experience. That man is just a really bad person.'

Mollified by Lara's kind words, Geoff stopped frowning and took us back to *Firebird*, where Bree fed us hot tea and coffee and freshly-baked scones. I washed Jasper down with the warm stern shower, and Sandy managed to smother him with a towel before he had the chance to shake his coat over the whole crew as usual.

We kept just enough fillets of fish to do a couple of meals, then Geoff had to go and open the pub for the day, with our thanks and promises to see him that evening echoing in his ears.

CHAPTER 38

DOVER PUB-CRAWL, THURSDAY

Round two of the seal encounter occurred early the same afternoon when a small boat motored across the anchorage with a uniformed Senior Constable aboard from the Dover Police. He politely asked to come aboard, and as is usual with visiting strangers, Jasper took to his bed tucked away in an open locker in the port bow cabin. After an appreciative look around, Senior Constable Marlow happily accepted Bree's offer of coffee, and once a few sips were taken, got to the point.

'Mr Stevens, we've received a complaint from Barry Wishart, one of the supervisors at the fish farm complex, that he was attacked by you, pushed into the water, then your dog bit him. Can you shed any light on this situation?'

'Certainly Senior, although it doesn't quite sound like what actually happened.'

He dug out his notebook and made ready. 'No problem, sir. Let's hear it.'

'Well, for a start, I'll say I don't have a dog, nor is there a dog aboard either of the two boats. I do have a cat, however. Just a minute.'

I called Krazy and the irrepressible little bundle of black fur shot out of the saloon to see what the fuss was all about.

Senior Marlow was quite impressed with her name and the little flecks of white hairs scattered throughout her coat, and scratched her chin and back for a few minutes.

'That's the cat,' I said with a grin, 'and she loves going for rides in boats, but no dog I'm afraid.'

He made a brief note, before I went on to describe exactly what had happened, including the seal encounter, but leaving Jasper entirely out of the story.

'So, that's it. Mr Wishart behaved in very antagonistic manner and could have caused a bad crash. Mr Gardner tried to reason with him, but Mr Wishart seemed to be looking for a fight. He was making a move to board Mr Gardner's boat when I tried to steady the boats with my leg. That's when he overbalanced and fell in.'

'He claimed my non-existent dog bit him, but he must have gashed his bum on a sharp fitting on the side of his boat when he fell in. We didn't see any sharks or seals in the water at the time. Mr Wishart left, after making a lot of threats of physical violence to come, which made my friends and me very uncomfortable. Really, we don't know why he was so upset with Mr Gardner or myself. It was a lot of fuss about nothing and we'd be happy for the whole incident to be put to bed.'

'Yes. That would be the best solution, Mr Stevens. What was your last port of call and when do you plan to leave?'

'That would be Strahan and we're leaving on Saturday morning. This is a pretty place and we all like being here, but we have many other places to visit.' Sandy was hovering back in the saloon, so I waved her out.

'I'd like you to meet my partner, Sandra Thomson. Sandy, this is Senior Constable Marlow.'

As they shook hands, I mentioned, 'Sandy's an Inspector with the Queensland Police at Southport.'

I suppressed a grin as his back automatically stiffened to attention. 'It's a pleasure to meet you, Ma'am. May I presume you're on holidays and not on official duty?'

She gave him her best beaming smile, 'Holiday only, Senior. Enjoying the quiet life on the water, which makes these nasty threats of violence very unwelcome and unnecessary. Anything you can do to defuse the situation would be greatly appreciated.'

Senior Constable Marlow almost tripped over his tongue assuring her he'd do everything possible to settle things down and that we should enjoy the rest of our holiday.

'It's always a pleasure to welcome members of an interstate force to our area Ma'am, so I'll leave you in peace now.'

With that, he returned to his boat and headed back to the small marina at the main jetty.

I patted my dear lady's bum. 'Well done, Inspector. He seems a good fella, so hopefully he'll sort out Mr Wishart. I wouldn't like any fallout to affect Geoff's business.'

'Difficult, when he's the only pub in town, but I do agree with you,' she replied.

The rest of the crew had been wandering around the town and returned shortly after.

I told Andy the police had been calling, but all appeared to be okay.

'That's good, because this is a nice little town and I wouldn't want to have to rush away on account of some guy with a thing about seals. Or have a nice guy like Geoff be adversely affected by it.'

By 17:00, we were cleaned up, Andy subtly disguised, and leaving Jasper and Krazy in charge, were soon heading ashore in the two dinghies, which we again tied up to the head of the jetty. The bar looked to be populated by the same characters as last night, but this time, we scored a few, 'gidday mates' and 'howyagoin, awright?' greetings from them.

One old character went so far as to say, 'Hear you had some fun out fishin' this mornin'.'

''Yeah,' I replied, not sure which side of the fence the old bloke was on, 'it was a bit different. Must be some real bitey fish out there in the harbour who don't like humans.'

I'd made the right response, since there was a round of hearty laughter at my remark, and the old fella pointed to a big table close by, saying, 'Why not grab this table? Then we can all have a chat. We don't get too many visitors this time of year, or any time for that matter.'

The social ice was well and truly broken when I included the old fella and his mates in the shout, which had them turn their stools around and start chatting to our crew, turning the evening into a loud and happy one.

That was until one of the locals came in from out front and called out, 'Have you blokes got your dinghies tied up at the head of the jetty?'

'Yeah, mate. What's up?' I said, walking up to him.

'I just saw two blokes messing around there with a torch. When they saw me, they jumped in a ute and took off heading outta town.'

'Thanks mate. I'll go have a look.' I called Dave and Alex out, got a torch from Sandy who always thinks of these things, and headed across the road. At first glance, there was nothing wrong, then Dave noticed the dinghies weren't sitting on the water properly. Closer inspection showed the front three buoyancy chambers on each boat had been slashed open with what must have been a particularly sharp knife. They must have been interrupted by the guy from the pub, since the motors were still above water.

'Rotten bastards!' Dave cursed. 'I reckon it's your mate from this morning having a bit of payback.'

'Yeah. I'm inclined to agree. Who else would do this? Bugger it!' I felt like kicking something in frustration, preferably the clowns who'd ruined two good RIBs.

We pulled the ruined dinghies up amongst the reeds bordering the shoreline and were about to head back to report to the rest of the crew, when there was an agonised scream from the boats, moored just 40 metres out. Another yell followed, until it faded to an uneasy silence.

I turned to Alex, 'Get Geoff and his boat and follow us out, please.' He took off at a lumbering run, quick for such a big man, while Dave and I stripped down to our jocks and carefully entered the cold water. It almost took our breath away, but then we hardly noticed as we swam strongly for the boats where a torch light shone crookedly down the port boarding steps on *Firebird*.

Quietly, we eased out of the water on the other hull and crept up the steps, hearing odd, distressed sounds from the cockpit. We needn't have been quiet, for kneeling on the cockpit floor was indeed our redneck mate, Barry Wishart, with Jasper's jaws locked onto his forearm. Jasper looked to have a damaged ear, with a bunch of matted fur around it, but kept up a steady growling rising in intensity with every movement his captive made.

Blood was pouring from Barry's badly lacerated arm and more from both legs. Deep gashes adorned both his cheeks, and they added their share to the puddle of claret gathering on the deck.

He turned his ruined face to us and cried, 'Oh shit! Please mister! Call your dog off, won'tcha? He's killing me!'

I could almost handle the 10-litre can of petrol, with a bunch of rags sitting on the cockpit floor, and the barbeque lighter sitting beside them, but what sent me into a towering rage was the sight of my beautiful cat with a damaged ear. Despite bare feet, I pretended Wishart's rib cage was a football to be sent into the next state. To his credit, he had the grace to pass-out after the first two well-aimed kicks crunched into his ribcage, but I'd managed two more before Dave physically pulled me away.

'Harry! Harry! C'mon man! The arsehole's not worth it. I heard at least four ribs go.'

As the red mist slowly faded, I realised he was right and there'd be more opportunities to square accounts with this ignorant prick. Accordingly, I composed myself and identified the items on display, being the petrol, rags for fuses, a lighter, a pistol and a decent knife with a double-sided blade.

I stepped aside with Dave and said, 'We can't cover this up by losing the body overboard, unfortunately. Therefore, it's going to become official with Senior Marlow running the investigation. We have to protect Andy first, and Jasper next. I heard shit-for-brains call him a dog again, so I might try to pass him off as your dog. I told him earlier I didn't have a dog, so I don't know if this will work. The only other thing to try is to flash my credentials and suggest I'm undercover on the job, but Sandy isn't part of it.'

Dave looked thoughtful, 'I like the second option better. Lying to coppers makes more trouble than it's worth.'

I patted his arm. 'You're right Dave. Leave it with me for the moment. I'll come up with something when I settle down a bit.'

'You always do Harry, you always do,' he replied.

'Yeah,' I nodded wearily, 'but you know mate, I'm really getting tired of having to think up ways to outsmart a constant parade of shit heads, or do cover-ups like this one. It would be so nice to be able to live a straight life for a while, at least, where I didn't have to practice the art of deceit so often.'

'I'm with you, mate. But your training and experience has helped keep all of us alive for quite a few years now. And we're all tired and need a good rest without tripping over any more bad guys.'

'Amen to that brother and thanks.'

By the time Alex arrived in Geoff's boat with the rest of our crew, I'd asked Jasper to unclamp from Wishart's arm and turned on some lights to examine my beautiful cat. With the blood washed away, it didn't look as bad as it had at first, although there was a large lump on his head which seemed tender.

When Sandy arrived, I was sitting on the cockpit floor, propped against the side, cradling Jasper's head in my lap, while Dave had wrapped a towel around Wishart's arm to staunch the bleeding. Luckily, Sandy and Corrine took over first aid duties and after she had looked closely at Jasper, informed me that he just had a small tear at the corner of his ear, plus the lump on his head from something solid.

Corrine's real first-aid kit was put to good use and while I was still sitting on the floor planning what to tell Senior Constable Marlow, Sandy came out to tell me that Corrine had stitched Jasper's ear, finished cleaning him up and had given him a tranquiliser. They had put him to bed in our cabin to get some rest, with Krazy cat snuggled up for company.

The girls had a much more difficult time with Wishart, but finally got him cleaned up as well. His tally of injuries were deep lacerations to his arm, but no break; deep scratches to his face, arms, back and legs, none of which were too serious.

All his wounds were smeared with normal antibiotic paste and bandaged.

By the time the work was finished, he was in more pain than when Jasper had him clamped, but was at least conscious.

I stood in front of him where the girls had propped him up in a chair.

'Can you hear me, you miserable piece of shit?'

He nodded sullenly, 'Yeah. I hear you.'

'You destroyed two RIBs, hurt my ca... Dave's watchdog and were going to burn both boats. This has made me particularly upset, and I feel like doing something suitably nasty in return. However, wise advice has prevailed to the extent that I've given myself the choice of turning you over to the police with a bunch of very serious criminal charges to answer, or I can take you out now in my borrowed boat and drop you into the nearest fish pen. From what I've seen, those young salmon are so hungry, they'd have the flesh off your bones in a few minutes.'

From the look on his face and the involuntary shudder which ran through him, I knew falling into a pen would be the ultimate nightmare for all the pen workers.

'Now here's my dilemma. The second option is for me, by far the easiest and simplest. You disappear and there's no fuss, no paper-work. Whereas turning you over to the police will tie us up in paperwork for days. I'm sure you'll understand why I reckon the fish pen is the best way to go. But I'll be fair, and ask you what you think of those options?'

He gave me a look that defied explanation, but finally replied. 'I'll give you a third option. Give me two days and I'll scrape up fifteen grand. That should replace the RIBs and cover the vet bills for your dog. Wadda ya think?'

I pretended to think long and hard on his truly excellent sugges-tion. 'It'll have to be twenty grand. Where's the money?'

'Twenty's a bit stiff, so I'll have to do some ringing around, but I'm good for it.'

'Okay,' I said abruptly, 'but because I don't trust you, the deal is you stay here, locked up until we have the money. You can use your mobile to call in sick and organise the money, but that'll be under supervision and you'll get fed occasionally. Try to mess me around, then I guarantee it's straight back to option #2.'

He nodded, 'I won't mess you 'round.'

I explained to Dave the new plan and he was pleased.

'Brilliant! That's a great way around the official exposure concern. Only our crews heard the screams, or we could pass them off as Krazy pouncing on some bird having a sleep on *Firebird*.'

'Yeah, something like that. In the morning, I'll talk to Geoff about who could've slashed the RIBs. Now, let's get boofhead settled in your lock-up and get some sleep. I'm buggered.'

CHAPTER 39

DOVER, FRIDAY

The rest of the night was quiet and I had a really deep sleep for once, not waking until 10:00. The boat was quiet, Jasper was dozing on the bed beside me, so I drifted off to sleep again, my arm draped around him. I woke feeling refreshed at 11:30, with Jasper absent, so I cleaned up and went to see what the world was up to.

There was a collection of crews in the cockpit, including Geoff who announced, 'Good news on the pair who slashed the boats.'

That got my attention, so he went on, 'It was Wishart's dopey sons. Either he sent them or they dreamed it up between them that they should do something to lash out on Dad's behalf. They've both got a few rungs missing from their ladders, so they were dopey enough to go home straight afterwards. A few of the blokes from the pub went around there last night and found a knife on the kitchen table, still with some shreds of rubberised fabric stuck to it. Anyway, they both got a pretty good sorting out; something that was badly over-due. They've been responsible for a lot of minor mischief in the district, but Barry has always protected them. Not this time, however, so there'll be no come-back. Anyway, I've gotta go, but Sandy's got the name and number of the best agent for RIBs in Hobart. He can deliver whatever you want within two days. See you tonight.'

Dave ran him ashore in his boat which he'd graciously loaned us for the duration.

With that settled, it was nice to know we had some allies in the pub regulars, so I turned my attention to Jasper who looked normal and was back to his usual self. It was difficult to see where his ear had been torn and he didn't seem to be in pain.

'We spread the tiniest bit of Green Gold on the lump and his ear,' Sandy said, 'so he seems fine now.'

'I hope you didn't waste any on Wishart?'

'Hell, no! He got a Panadol and the usual first-aid dressing. I fed him this morning and he needed to call in sick, so I sat there and listened, but all was straight. He also wanted to call a bank and some other guys about the money, but I said he'd have to wait until you were available.'

She sat beside me with Andy, Lara and Kelly across the table and asked, 'We don't need the money Harry, so why are you doing it this way?'

'He needs to pay for what he did to Jasper, the threats he made to us, slashing the two RIBs and for trying to burn our boat. Some tit for tat is the only thing he understands, plus at the moment, I'm a bit tired of having to use violence against all these idiots who try to bully us and everyone else into doing what they want. Maybe I just needed to apply the non-violent solution for once.'

Nobody mentioned the broken ribs Wishart had suffered in addition to the lacerations from Jasper, although Sandy and Kelly understood. I could see Andy and Lara were puzzled, so for once I took the time to explain something every trained soldier who has seen action has to live with.

'I was in the military for nearly eighteen years and most of the time was spent training for the few other times when serious bad guys were trying to kill my troops and me. The more I was promoted, the more people I became responsible for. If you're going to keep your people alive in that sort of environment, you have to learn very quickly how to out-think the enemy so you can be prepared. It isn't rocket science, but if you can get inside your enemy's head, it makes a huge difference to the outcome of skirmishes. I was also lucky early on, and got away with making mistakes until I learned better.

In a war-zone, violent response to a serious threat has to be an automatic mind-set, or you're dead. Unfortunately, the same can apply on the so-called peaceful civilian streets, so I've been trained at great expense to react to violence or the threat thereof, with violence in return. And exactly like the bad guys in the war-zone, the bad-guys on the street often don't know any other response, which is why soft-talking rarely works. When someone I care about or have to look after is threatened, I usually react quickly to shut down the source of the threat before it develops further. It is actually that simple, although shrinks try to analyse the whole subject to death.'

After such a long-winded speech, I sat back and sipped at my nearly cold tea. Andy stood, gave me a man hug, then shook my hand. 'Thanks Harry, for all you've done and are still doing. The fact is, with the flawed justice system we have, people like you are needed occasionally, so you'll get no grief from me or anyone else in a position of power.'

It was an unusually emotional moment and all three girls were teary by the end, so I said, 'Thanks, Andy. I'd better go and listen to our prisoner raise twenty grand.'

Barry Wishart was a much-subdued person after a night locked up with multiple wounds; especially his savaged arm. Before he made his calls, he asked, 'What sort of a dog was the thing that bit me? I couldn't see very well once I lost the torch.'

'He's a bit of a mixture, but he has the Doberman slim head and sharp teeth. He's also awfully keen to defend his territory.'

'A bit too fuckin' keen,' he grumbled, then made a couple of phone calls to mates who could lay their hands on a lot of cash. None of them seemed to be surprised at being asked to dig thousands of dollars out of the biscuit tin and each promised to drop a package off at Geoff's pub that afternoon.

'There. Will that keep you happy?'

I shrugged, 'Sure. Provided you are too and forget about any more of this retaliation crap.'

He looked sullen, 'Yeah, yeah! I got the message. Those drops should be done by four, if you like to check it out. Then I'd like to get outta here.'

'No problem with that. If the money's there, you're gone.'

For a change, things worked out as planned. I went ashore at 16:30, and with a big grin, Geoff handed me two supermarket shopping bags each holding several weighty bundles wrapped in newspaper.

'Thanks Geoff, I'll be back shortly with the troops.'

'Good work, Harry. See you then.'

The count was accurate and I tossed Dave one bag with ten grand, before grabbing a bundle of notes from the other. 'I'll just run Mr Wishart over to the town jetty, then we'll all go ashore.'

Our captive had a hard time walking, with his wounds stiffening his legs, but he finally made it into Geoff's boat. I returned his phone, and on the way over, he called someone, presumably one of his sons, to come and pick him up. He got out of the boat without a word so I returned to load our crew and head for the pub.

The bar was unusually crowded; we were welcomed by the locals like heroes and were introduced to the four guys who'd made the house call on Wishart's sons. Geoff had apparently been storytelling, with suitable embellishments of course, which meant we hardly bought a drink all night. There was a bit of a moment when one of our new best friends told Andy he looked somewhat like the Prime Minister.

Andy laughed and waved his hands dismissively, 'I get that all the time. Sometimes I think I could make money hiring out as a double.'

With plenty of good food, some more songs courtesy of Geoff's daughter, Sheila, and an excess of drink, it was a roaring, happy and un-eventful evening.

One of our drinking mates ferried us out to the boats, wished us well in our travels and left.

Alex and Bree headed for bed, but everyone else wanted tea and coffee and to talk the day through from a quieter perspective. No one had any regrets about what had gone down with bloody

Barry, and I told them we'd skip the next village I'd planned to visit. Instead, we'd go straight to Hobart and pick up the two new RIBs directly from the dealer.

SATURDAY

It was an easy and picturesque run up to the Tasmanian capital, with a brisk breeze out of the south helping the nautical miles slide smoothly past.

We stayed inside Bruny Island which translated to smooth water and fast sailing, with no pitching or rocking. Around 11:00, we were running fast up the famous harbour and by 12:00, were being allocated outside berths at Franklin Wharf, right in the middle of the city.

A phone call to the RIB agent produced an enthusiastic response and he promised to be at the wharf with two new boats within the hour. True to his word, a smart-looking RIB motored up to *Firebird's* stern, with two brand-new, 4.6-metre Australian-designed and built RIBs in tow. He had two crew to help fit the salvaged 40-horsepower Yamaha outboards to the new hulls. We swapped some papers for a shopping bag full of cash, much to the dealer's delight, before he took his crew and headed off with a cheery wave.

Although small by the standards of the mainland, Hobart is still a city with a degree of rush and bustle, which was at odds with the peace and calm of the small-town anchorages. I spent an hour with Alex setting up the davits to lift the new RIB out of the water.

Dave didn't have that problem, since his RIB lived in a garage under the cockpit and just slid on rollers through the transom door.

We stayed aboard until 17:00, then ventured out to Irish Murphy's pub in Salamanca Place. It's a grand old pub, and the varnished woodwork has a soft amber glow which looks beautiful.

The beer was good; the company around our group were all lively, and the food excellent. Afterwards, we went for a walk around, and as we were passing a narrow alley between two classic old sandstone block buildings, heard the sound of live acoustic music. To me, it was like a homing beacon, so I headed the charge down to the source. The Salamanca Whisky Bar had all we needed; a bluegrass band, a vast variety of sipping whisky, a happy crowd and fingerfood snacks for those still hungry.

We wandered out after midnight, very happy, relaxed and with our wobbly boots firmly in place.

SUNDAY

Definitely a day of rest with a late rising, then brunch in the cockpit, chatting to an endless parade of tourists who had come out to wander the docks looking at the boats. Although not unpleasant, after a while we felt like being in a zoo, but on the wrong side of the fence. The girls wanted to go and do some shopping, so they wandered off for a few hours, returning happily laden with armloads of parcels. We went looking for a different pub for the evening drinks and a feed, but ironically, ended up in a delightful Japanese restaurant that served a wide range of traditional foods; all of which were wonderfully tasty.

Sandy was caught out by the wasabi; putting way too much on her first succulent piece of kingfish sashimi. Luckily, my bottle of Kirin beer was close at hand, but she soaked three tissues mopping her streaming eyes. Lovely beer and an excess of sake made for wobbly boots again as we weaved our way home, everyone in another happy mood.

I discovered the mood continued when we drifted off to bed, since Charlie came in just as Sandy and I were getting into bed. She wore her usual sleeping T-shirt, but it must have been washed in hot water too often, as it managed to stop enticingly short of being decent. It became even less so when she crawled up the bed between us and sat up, cross-legged to have a chat. I would have been content to let Sandy do all the chatting, but I was required to make a few intelligent responses occasionally.

My interest produced the usual bodily response which was difficult to hide, and made Charlie giggle when I tried.

The girls chatted on for a while, so I had just rested my eyes for a moment, when I felt the covers lift and Charlie said, 'Oh my goodness! Will you look at that?'

She did for a while, before snuggling down between us, proving to be a such an active little bundle that we didn't get a much sleep. But we certainly had a lot of fun!

MONDAY

Another slow start, but that's the point of a pub-crawling cruise. Charlie was still in bed when I woke and refused to get up without a some more fooling around, so that delayed things a bit further. Finally I got the girls out of bed, and when I went topside, I found a lovely day with a stiff breeze ruffling the small chop out on the harbour and making the flags along the waterfront snap and flutter. Tourists were still wandering the dock area and a couple stopped to have a chat for a while.

Over dinner last night, I'd suggested we could pass up our next scheduled pit stop at St Helens, 170 odd nautical miles up the coast, but as everyone had heard of it and wanted to have a look, that was severely howled down. So, St Helens it was for tonight.

After finishing my cuppa and a chat with an English couple, I checked the drive motors, and with Alex untying and retrieving the lines, let the breeze drift us away from the dock, then motored out through the narrow entrance to the dock.

CHAPTER 40

PUB CRAWL MONDAY/TUESDAY, ST HELENS

The run up the scenic coast to the pretty little town of St Helens was fast and very comfortable with a stiff breeze up our tail although it still took most of the day. We dropped anchor off a beach bordering a park, with the main hotel-motel just the other side of it.

'I don't suppose another mate of yours came from here?' Dave asked sarcastically with a big grin.

'Nah... No mate this time. Just me. I was here about ten years ago on a bike with a bunch of other SAS guys. It was a wild two weeks, and great fun.'

'Bloody hell Harry, I didn't know you rode bikes! You're supposed to tell your mates a few things like that. Anyway, what sort of bike was it?'

'Yamaha FJR1300a,' I replied. 'It was a big bike, but with the alloy frame and aftermarket mufflers, it was fairly light and more than enough power for this little black duck. The other guys used to knock the shaft-drive, until I regularly rounded them up on their drop-barred, café racers. We stayed at the motel part of the pub over there. It was fairly basic, but comfortable enough. Bloody good tucker at the pub.'

'Sold! That's where we can go for a feed. All this fresh, salty air has made me hungry.'

Corrine poked him in the ribs. 'You're always hungry!'

It didn't take us long to freshen-up and head for shore, where the beer was cold, the wine acceptable to the ladies and the food excellent. After a long day sailing, it wasn't a late night.

Next morning was a slow start and it wasn't until close to lunch o'clock before we were wandering the streets. Sandy sidled up, batting her eyelashes. 'Darling! Is there somewhere we can get some fresh crayfish? I've got a bit of a craving for a decent-size one.'

With last night's activities still fresh in my mind, I started to make a rude remark, but somehow restrained myself. 'Maybe. There's a fish and chippery down past the pub. We could go see if they have any, but it's difficult to get big cray's locally. They all go to the export market.'

'Good,' she said, 'I want the biggest one.'

I laughed, 'Don't get your hopes up, but we'll try.'

After that, the whole tribe decided to tag along, so we retraced our steps back past the pub. The fish and chip shop was still in the same place, a happy, hard-working Greek family doing their usual excellent job. It had been through a face-lift since I was last there, with white tiles lining the walls and floor, so with the blue stripes on the edges, it looked very nationalistic.

The old man, Stavros, looked the same and naturally he didn't remember me, although I couldn't forget his cheerful greetings and nicely-cooked food and the shop was as immaculate now as it was back then.

Sandy got excited to see a large fish tank against the wall, occupied by the biggest crayfish I'd ever seen. The thing was the size of a small dog, and even with his tail curled, was more than a half metre long! His long front feelers poked inquisitively out over the end of the tank and twitched in our direction.

'Hello my friends. You come for some of Stavros's beautiful food? Yes? Best seafood on the east coast! You like my crayfish, eh? He live here for ten years. Eat too much, now tank too small. What you like today?'

'Actually, Stavros, my lady wanted some big crayfish. Do you have any?'

He happy grin slipped as he shook his head, 'Alas, my friend. No big crays sold locally. They all go to South East Asia. We just get baby ones.'

'What about the one in the tank?' Sandy wanted to know.

Stavros looked unhappy again, 'Five, mebbe six year ago, I would have happily sold him, but now he a member of the family. Granddaughter would cry, wife would cry, daughter would howl, son would kick my shin if I sold him. His name is Hercules and he weighs 8 kilos.'

Although disappointed, Sandy was delighted by the story and the fact that they had a pet crayfish called Hercules.

'That's okay, thanks Stavros. No crayfish today, but thanks for the chat.'

'No problem my friend. You come back later and I make you special souvlaki to go with some of my beautiful fish and chips.'

'Sounds good, Stavros, we might just do that.'

After walking around for a while, the others marvelled at the number of bikers riding, parking and checking into or out of accommodation.'

'At any given time, year-round, there are hundreds of bikers over from the mainland, just tripping around. It's a great way to see Tasmania, but with the unpredictable weather, you have to love bikes. When I was here with my mates it was early April, and we left Strahan right in the middle of a howling cold-front. After climbing the slippery roads to Queenstown in pouring rain, we rode through sleet, then snow, across the top of the high country on the way to Hobart. With the wind-chill, it was the coldest I've ever been, and the roadhouse half way across never looked so welcome! I was busting for a pee, but with numb hands and about six layers of clothing to fight through, I could hardly find the bloody thing, let alone pull it out!'

After a good laugh at my story, everyone decided to go back and get a feed of souvlaki and fish and chips and it was as good as promised. We ate while perched on the wall surrounding the Remembrance Park like a flock of seagulls. As we ate, I wondered why Andy was copping a few searching looks, then realised we'd become so used to him just being one of the crew, that Bree hadn't done any makeup that morning. I pulled my cap off and offered it.

'Sorry it's not clean, Andy, but someone's going to spring you any minute.'

Thankfully, he pulled the cap down low and put sunnies on, which helped a lot. When we finished we drifted around town checking things out, before somehow ending up at the pub for a post-lunch beer or two. Naturally, it became a happy, extended session so we opted for an early pub meal, then back to the boats. Over tea and coffee aboard, Andy asked, 'What's the plan from here?'

'The next port of call will be Lakes Entrance, but since the run across the strait is about 13 hours, and the bar crossing can be nasty, I'd rather tackle it in daylight. I thought we might bail out of here early tomorrow and stop at Erith Island half-way across Bass Strait for tomorrow night, then head for Lakes on Wednesday.'

He smiled, 'Sounds good to me. Looking forward to it.'

WEDNESDAY

It was a fun sail up the remainder of the east coast, before we ducked around the bottom end of Flinders Island, and set course for pretty little Erith Island, which was part of a group of three islands; Deal and Dover being the others. I had spent a couple of days in the sheltered bay here when I was helping my hitch-hikers, a runaway abused wife and her twin daughters, to escape the clutches of an insane husband who qualified as a professional bad guy. It was the scene of some terrible violence, but there were good memories too, and I focused on those.

Fortunately, Sandy had been with me on that occasion and talking things over with her always helped put the bad memories into correct perspective.

The southerly breeze was steady, so we held a good speed,

passing through the channel between Dover and Deal Islands at 15:00, and dropping anchor in the beautiful and sheltered West Cove soon thereafter. First impressions can mean a great deal and Erith Island made marvellous first impressions. The green, rolling hills, the gin-clear water over a white sandy bottom and the air of peace was just what we needed. Everyone wanted a walk, especially Jasper and Krazy who'd had to stay aboard over the last few days and were bursting to have a run around.

I must admit it was very relaxing to scuff my bare feet through the soft, white sand of the beach, and to see the two pussies having such a wonderful time. To give everybody a good night's sleep, I dispensed with keeping a watch, relying instead on the electronics of the masthead camera and the radar to warn if there was anyone coming too close. Charlie was up for a return bout of lovely fooling around, so I slept occasionally and lightly.

THURSDAY

Although there was no hurry that morning, Jasper delayed things further by calling in a pair of seals. There was no pup like last time, but they were just as friendly and happily accepted some bait-fish while splashing around the sterns of both boats to everyone's delight. We finally departed at 09:30 and because the stiff southerly was still blowing, we were driven at a good pace to the north-east; a course taking us straight through the busy gas and oil fields. It meant a lot of helicopter and boat traffic, although in the seven-hour journey, we only saw two rigs, both at a distance. Once clear of the islands, the swell was quite large, making me glad I hadn't decided to brave the Lakes Entrance bar at night. As it turned out, the tide was ebbing when we arrived, creating a potentially dangerous situation with the outflowing water making the incoming swells stand up in the shallow water, then breaking heavily right across the bar. Via the VHF radio, the Coastguard warned the bar could be considered closed, but I said we accepted the risk and were crossing anyway. I had everyone put on life-jackets, and to help maintain the extra speed necessary to run in safely, I left all plain sail up and ran the motors as well. With her power and speed *Seeker* had no trouble initially running in on the back of a breaking wave, but I used a smaller one to surf in on.

It was good all hatches and doors were closed, because we took a lot of broken water aboard, but otherwise, the narrow hulls tracked perfectly straight and what could have been dangerous was just an exciting and safe ride in.

'*Gutsy call,* Firebird!' *came the Coastguard radio call.* '*But well handled.*'

Dave made it look easy, sitting on the back of the biggest wave he could find, and didn't even get wet. I called the harbourmaster and told him we were only in for a couple of nights, and since it was mid-week, he kindly offered us the use of the Cunninghame Jetty as a berth, but we'd have to leave by Saturday morning. Even though I usually prefer anchoring for security purposes, being able to step straight ashore onto a wood jetty was a luxury I decided not to pass up.

Due to *Firebird's* extreme beam, I took the outside of the end arm, while Dave took the inside section. I must admit the royal blue and red boats made a strong visual statement, especially *Seeker* with her long, low Italian lines and it wasn't long before tourists started drifting out to check the new arrivals.

There were no special plans for our time there; just wander around, eat at the pub and on Friday night, at an Italian Restaurant in the main street which was excellent. Just east of our berth was a sand beach which was very popular with tourists, and I told the story of the orthodox Jewish family who went kayaking. They did so, still fully dressed in their best formal wear, although it was only big Poppa who managed to flip his boat with his granddaughter up front. The younger ones were far more graceful and had a ball.

From the time the first kayak was launched, the couple of hundred spectators were crying tears of laughter at the family's serious antics, but gave them a round of applause for persevering.

SATURDAY

It had been a great visit and Andy managed to avoid being recognised, although when the Harbourmaster came around just to say gidday, I got the feeling he knew who he was, but didn't say anything.

We left at 06:30 on a warm morning with a blustery, north-west wind blowing 25 to 35 knots ahead of a vigorous cold front howling across from Adelaide, where it had wreaked massive damage as it headed our way. If it were any closer we would have had to stay, but the advantage of a big cat is speed and I figured we could use it to get clear of Lakes and head for our next stop, the beautiful port of Eden where my maritime adventuring life had really started.

The bar was blown flat as we left, with the good wishes of the Coastguard sending us on our way. I don't know if they were impressed by my recklessness in sailing out of the town arm and over the bar with engines off, but *Firebird* made it easy. Once clear of the bar, we hauled up the Code C gennaker and the boat really took off! Within a minute, we were seeing 28 knots with occasional higher bursts. We stayed inshore where the offshore wind had beaten the swell flat, and Andy grabbed the wheel and refused to hand over. He had a manic grin on his face as he carefully felt the potential of the bigger boat when we scooted east, our twin wakes lifting behind like small rooster tails.

Seeker managed to go fast enough to just get up on the plane, prompting a series of rude radio calls from Dave. We continued to stay fairly close to shore and our course slowly bent left as Point Hicks lighthouse was passed. The small town of Mallacoota came next, and then we bore left again as we rounded Gabo Island late morning. The island with its pink granite lighthouse is home to the world's largest colony of the beautiful and inquisitive Little Penguins. The border between Victoria and New South Wales was a few miles further on, and at 13:30 we entered the vast expanse of Twofold Bay, one of the finest deep-water harbours in the southern hemisphere. I called the harbourmaster on VHF radio requesting a berth for two nights for both boats.

'Harry? Is that you?' came the non-procedural reply.

'Gidday Johnny. Yeah, it's me. New boat and some great friends. Can you squeeze us in? We don't mind slinging the pick over if you can't.'

'I'll squeeze you in, good buddy. Don't you worry about that! Main jetty, eastern side, moor inshore from the tug. I'll see you there.'

'Thanks mate. There's some dirty weather chasing us and it's not far behind.'

'Roger that. It's about two hours away, according to the weather radar, so don't mess around. Triple up all lines; she's going to be a screamer.'

'Copy.'

Accordingly, I left all sail up until we were nearly up to the main wharf and a few other boat owners were starting to look worried at our reckless charge. But with electric motors running silently, and all sails furled at the same time, we slowed rapidly and pivoted sideways into the berth, our bows just a couple of metres from the stern of a large ocean-going tugboat, one of the two which made the port home.

The familiar, lanky figure of Johnny was waiting to take our lines, an attractive girl ready to do the same for *Seeker*. A few minutes later, we were secured to the wharf by a spider's web of heavy nylon ropes that deliberately had stretch characteristics, with the same happening just astern of us with *Seeker*.

Only then did Johnny jump down onto the deck and grab me in a bearhug.

'Harry Stevens, you old bugger! Look at you and this bloody great cat! What bank did you rob to afford this thing? Hi folks, sorry to ignore you, but I've not seen this bloke for years.'

As a way to shut him up, I introduced him to everybody and when I came to Andy, he didn't miss a beat. Just shook his hand and said, 'Pleasure to meet you, Sir. You're doing a great job, although how you got tied up with this degenerate character, I'm buggered if I know.'

Andy glanced at me, but relaxed when I gave a thumbs up. I was a bit perplexed myself as this was a new Johnny; one who really had his act together and was more self-assured and worldly, and I suspected a female behind it all.

The question was answered momentarily when we were joined by Dave, Corrine and a lovely lady I recognised as Molly, who used to own the newsagency in the wharf shopping village. Unusually, when extra people are around, Jasper and Krazy made a joint appearance, Jasper going straight to Johnny, then Molly, shaking hands with each in turn.

They made the expected fuss over him which he considered to be his due, before Johnny resumed the bombardment of questions. 'Hold on!' I commanded. 'There's a lot to talk about, so how about you let us get cleaned up, then join us here for dinner. I'm sure Bree and Kelly can whip up something great in the next couple of hours. I'd love to take you to the Fisho's Club, but with this storm coming, we'd best be with the boats.'

Johnny looked at Molly who nodded, so he replied, 'Good call, mate. How about in an hour?'

'Done!'

CHAPTER 41

PUB CRAWL, EDEN, SATURDAY

There was plenty of room for everyone in *Firebird*'s mini-ball-room-size saloon where the girls had made some finger-food nibblies to keep grumbling stomachs happy while the lamb roast was cooking.

Although the storm hit in the middle of all this story telling, Johnny just raised his voice and kept asking questions. Over drinks, then the main course, we caught up on how he and Molly got together, then I told the short version of some of my adventures since I last saw him, and had agreed to assist Janice and her two girls get away from her deranged husband.

Later that evening, I reflected on the vagaries of fate and how close I'd been to not taking on the task of looking after Janice and the girls. With the drumming rain washing the salt off boat and sails, I drifted off to sleep, Charlie's lovely, rounded form tucked in against my back.

SUNDAY

Next morning dawned cold and windy, with a hard driving rain which encouraged nothing more active than to stay in bed, so I gave in to common sense and did just that, enjoying the company of my lovely companions. By 10:00 the weather was even worse, if anything, so a leisurely breakfast sort of rolled into lunch as the two boats tugged fretfully at their mooring ropes. I noticed one of the tugs had departed through the night, apparently gone to help some ship in distress.

362

The rain eased up by mid-afternoon, so I called on Johnny and arranged to meet him and Molly at the Fisho's Club for the evening meal.

It was a fun evening and there was a lot more talk and catching up before we made our way back down the steep hill to the boats, where the pussies were happy to have company again and get fed.

Monday was a clear, sunny day encouraging everyone to get active and wander the wharf and then up to the town, poke around, check out the Whale Museum, then have another great feed at the Fisho's.

TUESDAY

We were up early at 06:00 and motoring out of the harbour by 06:30. The wind had veered to the south-west following the cold change, and it drove us north up the coast at 25 knots plus. With 215 miles to cover, we could be in Sydney by around 16:00. We stayed around 3 nautical miles off shore and once again, Andy laid claim to the steering wheel, obviously having a ball.

The seas were low with the off-shore wind, so the ride was flat, easy and fast.

Montague Island off Narooma was the only free-standing obstacle to be avoided, so Andy took us inshore of it so we could check out the pretty town of Narooma. If we had more time, I would have liked to call in and stay awhile, but tucked the thought away for next time.

There was a lot of ship traffic, both north and south-bound, which made the use of radar essential. Even close to the coast, the bigger cargo ships were terrible at keeping a good lookout, so we did; having to change course several times. The wind stayed strong, which meant at 15:30, we were rounding South Head into Sydney Harbour.

The remainder of the run up-harbour was a matter of dodging ferries and a constant stream of ships outbound.

Charlie had phoned ahead as we left Eden to alert the staff at Kirri-billi House to expect guests and to make sure the ACP guarding the private wharf, didn't shoot first when we pulled up. Andy had already invited us to stay for a day or two because he was still on leave and wanted to invite Alan and Hillary over for an evening meal.

There was quite a welcoming committee when we eased along-side, and since it was a small wharf, Dave parked *Seeker* against our outside hull. The sight of two large boats tied up there attracted a flock of private and media boats, who ended up being shooed away by the Water Police.

Dinner that night was a grand affair, mainly because the catering staff were used to serving large gatherings of VIPs, so taking care of a bunch of degenerate boat bums was easy. It was a superb feast of five courses, and talk flowed freely and happily as adventures were dissected and foes vanquished by the time dessert was served.

We were a happy band of pissed possums who meandered back to the boats, past the grinning ACP patrol on the wharf.

WEDNESDAY

Andy wandered down to have an early coffee and scoff some of Bree's fabulous fresh scones. Just before leaving, he casually said, 'We've got a couple of official visitors for dinner tonight, so if you wouldn't mind dressing up a bit, I think you'll enjoy yourselves. I know you don't have suits and cocktail dresses, but if you are willing, there will be a minibus here at 10:00 to take you to an excellent outfitter in the city where there is a terrific variety of suits and dresses, including shoes. There'll be no charge, so get whatever takes your fancy. Cocktails will be served from 17:30 and the meal will be served at 19:00.'

'Christ! We'll be pissed by then Andy,' Dave threw in.

He grinned, 'Don't worry. Just enjoy yourselves.' Before leaving, he took Sandy aside and had a few quiet words, but in the rush to get ready for the trip into town, I forgot to ask what they chatted about.

The outfitter was essentially a government hire shop, with the most amazing array of male and female formal wear. We were expected and a team of men and women gave individual service. I headed for the Armani suit section, but a very smooth gentleman intercepted me and I was gently steered to another section where uniforms were on display.

When I expressed surprise and admiration at their range, he said, 'We pride ourselves in being able to either have, or to create in a short time frame, any uniform, from any country and any era. In your case Commander, the Prime Minister has issued particular instructions for you to wear your ACP dress uniform with all your Commander rank insignia. You are also to wear your military service medal ribbons.'

I was surprised. 'What sort of a party is this this we're going to?'

He smiled as he expertly ran a tape measure over my vital bits. 'I'm afraid I really don't know, Sir, except my orders came direct to me from the PM. 'He who must be obeyed' and all that!'

'Oh... okay then.' I gave way with good grace as he quickly sorted through a rack of ACP uniforms, finally extracting a complete dress uniform, already fitted with Commander stripes and badges. I'd never had occasion to wear one, being permanently undercover, so when I tried it on, I had to admit it all looked very smart, even if I do so say so myself. My attending gentleman made a few notes about fit, then said some small alterations would be made immediately, and it, and any of the other outfits needing alterations, would be delivered to the boats by 14:00.

The ladies were terribly excited at the prospect of a dress-up party, and all had found some really special dresses that suited them beautifully. Less than 90 minutes after leaving the boats, we were back at Kirribilli House for lunch. As the taxis dropped us off in front of the historic old building, I saw a very welcome sight through the trees on the east side of the point, in the form of a long, grey shape that looked like HMAS *Arafura* anchored close in to shore. That was confirmed when we ran into Paul and Clare at lunch and found they were invited to the evening party as well. I also learned *Arafura* had been relieved by the *Ballarat*, the ANZAC-class frigate skippered by Jim Sanders who I'd spoken to briefly on our way back from Heard Island.

After lunch, I fiddled around planning our return to the Gold Coast, deciding we didn't really need any more pub-crawling, so we'd take-off in the morning and run straight through.

A strong south-easterly wind had set in and the seas were rising again, so because I didn't want to be trapped in Sydney for any length of time, a morning departure would work well.

I called the Southport Yacht Club to advise my mooring and Dave's berth would be required from tomorrow evening on, and felt better about having committed to finally going home, even though in one sense, I already was home. At afternoon tea, Kelly announced she'd been talking with Alan and had decided to stay in Sydney with him and Hillary. They were coming to the dinner tonight and she'd go home with them that evening.

I was annoyed with myself for not considering her situation a lot sooner, but we were all happy she'd found a home with good people. Of course, there were hugs all round, so I looked fondly at Bree and Alex. 'I hope you two are staying?'

Alex nodded vigorously, 'Absolutely, Commander. This is our home and we are well content for now. I would never say forever, because attitudes and situations change, but for now... all good!' Bree enthusiastically backed that up, much to my relief.

By late afternoon, the ladies were getting ready, doing all the mysterious things ladies do when there's a chance to get dressed-up for a change, and even my Sandy who usually only wore shorts and a cut-off T-shirt, was having a lovely time fluffing about. The fluffing bit included laying out my hired uniform, ironing the shirt and making sure all my medal ribbons were in the right order.

With the ladies fizzing with excitement, and we males feeling awkward in dress-up gear for the first time in ages, we trooped up to the house to find the main guests hadn't arrived yet. In the small ballroom, we were pointed to the bar flanked by several tables groaning under the weight of plates of lovely little snacks. I was intrigued by the sight of a huge TV at one end of the room and was looking to take my coat off, when Andy appeared, looking very Prime Minister-ish for the first time in weeks.

Lara, Charlie, Kelly, Alan and Hillary followed, but that was all.

'Great to see you, Alan and Hillary,' I said with a cheeky grin, 'but getting us all dressed up just for that was a bit over the top. Still, congratulations on you and Kelly getting together; I suppose it's a good enough reason for a celebration.'

'Oh, do belt up, darling Harry!' mild-mannered Lara said with a disarming smile, as tyres crunched the driveway gravel outside, followed by the measured slamming of car doors. Moments later, the doorman announced the entry of the Japanese Ambassador. He was accompanied by two aides who fussed around his tall frame.

Andy quickly strode forward to greet him and from the laughter, it would seem they were good friends. He brought him forward and introduced him as Sakura Ito, cousin to the Japanese Prime Minster, Shinzo Ito.

'Commander Stevens,' he said in a smooth, deep voice that held not a trace of accent, 'what a pleasure to meet you after all I have heard of your adventures.'

I took his proffered hand, smooth and with a powerful grip. 'Mr Ambassador. The pleasure is all mine. You appear to enjoy representing Japan in our country.'

He chuckled, 'Indeed I do. Shinzo and I attended your National University which was where we met Andy. We've been close friends ever since.'

I nodded, several dots joining up as we spoke. 'Ah... that explains a lot.' As I stepped back to let Andy introduce Sakura to the others,

I noticed a couple of the staff messing with the giant TV screen and cursing quietly, until it came to life with a strange symbol centred on the screen. I felt really hungry, so while everyone was occupied, I snuck back to the buffet table and found some sushi. I'd just taken a mouthful of the succulent filling, when the face of a Japanese gentleman appeared on the screen.

The same staff members who had fixed the TV, were now messing with a small camcorder mounted on a tripod. Then another smaller screen popped into life in the lower left corner of the big screen, showing the interior of the room.

Andy appeared at my elbow and moved me in front of the camera. 'What's the go Andy?' I asked quietly.

'You've got about twenty seconds to finish your mouthful, before the Prime Minister of Japan appears on the monitor to award you the Order of the Rising Sun, the highest award which can be made to foreigners. Sakura will pin the medal on your left chest on behalf of Shinzo and the Emperor.'

I hurriedly cleaned myself up. 'Emperor? Bloody hell! What's he got to do with this?'

'The highest powers in Japan have come to the conclusion that by taking out their ships and so many of their men, you broke the back of the plot to overthrow their Government. The Emperor was terribly impressed a foreigner would fight on behalf of Japan.'

'Personally,' he added with a cheeky grin, 'I think the whole thing is overstated, but they are terribly keen on the honour bit and love some pomp and ceremony.'

'I'll get you for this one day,' I muttered, looking for something to wipe my sticky fingers on, as Shinzo Ito appeared on the screen, and Sakura stepped up, an aide holding a velvet cushion with a finely-crafted wooden box on it.

I forgot what his words were, focused as I was on the large and ornate medal that he lifted reverently from its case and hung on a clip already in place on my chest. It was a silver star of eight points, each point having three alternating silver rays, with a central red stone to symbolise the sun.

He then draped a broad red and silver sash across my chest, and with a deep bow, presented a scroll.

'These words are from my Emperor to thank you for helping to preserve a lawful and peaceful Government.' He bowed deeply and I was obliged to do the same, before he stood beside me and bowed to Shinzo who said a few more words, then with a final round of bows, it was over.

One of Sakura's aides produced a camera and took shots of me shaking hands with everybody, showing off my decorations.

Another aide approached, bowed, then held out a mobile phone. I took it, saw that it was live.

'Hello. This is Harry Stevens.'

'Good evening again Mr Stevens,' came the deep, measured voice of Japan's Prime Minister. 'Apart from thanking you again, I wanted to privately to warn you that your actions in Tasmania, while they helped to preserve the integrity of the Japanese Government, have incurred the wrath of a dissident faction within the Yakusa, who were jointly behind the scheme in the first instance. They have put a price on your head, but it is considered unlikely they would do anything outside Japan. Nevertheless, my advice is to be careful and maybe keep a low-profile for a while.'

'Thank you sir, for the honour of receiving this award. As for the bounty, I'll live with it. How much is it?'

He chuckled, 'You presently top Japan's list, even ahead of myself, Mr Stevens, at the princely sum of 150 million yen, which I believe is just over 2 million of your dollars.'

'That is a slightly sobering thought, Mr Prime Minister. In the past I've had bikie gangs after my head, but not a major criminal organisation in a foreign country. I shall indeed watch my back.'

'Excellent. So I'll say goodbye Mr Stevens and thank you again on behalf of my Government. Ambassador Ito has a small gift from us, should you ever be in need.' With that enigmatic statement, the phone went dead, so I handed it back to the aide and thanked him.

As he bowed and stepped back, Sakura appeared, smiling, as he handed me a small envelope.

'This contains a card which, should you find yourself in need, will gain you the fullest possible support of any official Japanese department, including the Self-Defence Force, anywhere in the world. It is written in Japanese characters, but there is a separate translation as well, including a telephone number. Good luck with your future endeavours and may they be as worthy and successful as this one.'

He bowed, then shook my hand and went to re-join Andy and the others.

CHAPTER 42

SYDNEY – GOLD COAST

After the bombshell of the Japanese award and Shinzo's warning, we stayed another day, saying our heartfelt goodbyes to Andy, Lara, Charlie, Kelly and all. Andy thanked us all once again for the rescue of Kelly and the quality time he had spent with her. We were hopeful we had successfully closed another operation which we'd been caught up in entirely by being in the right place at the wrong time. Or was it the wrong place at the right time? Someone a lot smarter than me could figure that out!

Charlie had arranged for a Navy re-fuelling barge to drop around and fill *Seeker* to capacity, so at dawn on a bright and breezy Friday morning, we headed off up the coast for the Gold Coast and home.

As usual, Dave made the most appropriate comment when he radioed, *'Next time you go on holidays old mate, we might stay behind. OK?'*

We had planned to stop at Port Macquarie to break the trip into easy day sails, but with the brisk southerly pushing us along at well over 20 knots, we were further up the coast and decided to drop in at the quiet and very picturesque South West Rocks on the Macleay River. The bar was a bit of a challenge with breaking waves either side of the channel, but once in calm water, we motored up river where we anchored just off the friendly Riverside Tavern for the night. Good company, great food and friendly locals were a perfect way to settle down after the Sydney experience.

Saturday morning, we headed off again and gratefully sailed in through the Southport Seaway late in the afternoon. After bedding both boats down, we met up in the Boathouse Tavern for home-coming drinks and tucker.

ONE WEEK LATER

After Sandy came home from work one afternoon, she told me she'd taken a phone call from Hillary who reported all was well and the clean-up in Port Davey was complete. The *Ballarat* had returned to its normal patrol duties and *Izumo* had escorted a very motley collection of boats out of the harbour, all under tow by two powerful salvage tugs.

She also mentioned that she and Paul Davy had become an item and were getting on very well. Unfortunately, she and Paul could only get together after each deployment rotation, since she remained her father's PPS.

TEN DAYS LATER

Although when moored at home base we didn't eat out every night, we did tend to hang out at the Boathouse Tavern a lot. On this occasion, my friend, Ellie the bar supervisor, came over to our table as we settled in and handed me a postcard.

'This came yesterday, Harry. I thought you'd all be in tonight so I hung onto it. I hope that was alright?'

I was puzzling over the card and absently said, 'Yeah, sure thing Ellie. No problem.'

The picture on the front of the card was a busy street scene in Tokyo. Nothing remarkable about it and produced in millions. On the back, however, was a strange symbol with a curved knife beside it.

Ellie was spoiling us by taking the drinks order, so I asked, 'I don't suppose you know what this symbol is, do you Ellie?'

'I didn't until one of the kitchen girls freaked out. She used to have a Japanese boyfriend who fancied himself as a tough guy, and always talked about joining the Yakusa. That's the symbol or trade-mark of one of the biggest clans. The knife symbol means an enforcer.

Why would someone send something like that to you?'

THE END

ALSO BY THE AUTHOR
BOOK ONE IN THE FIREBIRD SERIES

Harry Stevens, a Middle Eastern war hero, thought that recovering in Eden with his huge and mystical cat, Jasper, after his catamaran is bashed around by a storm, would be a delightful break from his sailing voyage around Australia. However, the finger of fate in the very pleasant form of an abused, runaway wife and her two lively, wilful and beautiful teenage daughters lands Harry in more trouble than he could ever imagine.

Harry's hopes for a quiet time in this beautiful and peaceful town are shattered as he learns that the psychotic, vengeful husband is pulling out all stops in an effort to locate, not just his wife, but even more so the girls for his own, much darker purposes. Suddenly on the run, Harry is forced to fall back on his natural inventiveness and SAS training to combat an increasingly resourceful foe who shows that there is truly no limit to human lust, greed, depravity and treachery.

Barely staying one step ahead of his pursuers, Harry forms some most unlikely alliances to try to defeat his many opponents with their limitless resources.

"It is always a pleasure to read a new and entertaining series from a first-time Australian author. This novel will take you on one hell of a ride where the goodies are okay and the baddies are really BAD."
—John Morrow's *Pick of the Week*

"The hero, Harry, when asked what he has been doing lately, answers "Boats, bad guys, bullets and old friends." What he fails to add is — beautiful women, sex, a bad-ass black cat, and Bond type cunning to overcome the bad guys. Piqued your interest? This is a great fast paced read and I am looking forward to the next phase of Harry's life as promised by the author.
—Judith Flitcroft, Author of *Walk Back in Time*.

ALSO BY THE AUTHOR
BOOK TWO IN THE FIREBIRD SERIES

Harry Stevens, the Middle-Eastern war hero from Hitch-Hikers, the first book in the *Firebird* series, thought that having dinner at the pub and chatting up the waitress was a safe and pleasant way to pass an evening, but circumstances conspire to dump the delivery of a new super-drug as well as a large bag of bikie gang cash in his lap. Assumptions are made, confusions are leapt to, shots are fired, people are dead and Harry finds himself in the middle of a bikie gang war with both sides looking to take him out. And that's not to dinner!

Being on the hit lists of all the Outlaw Motorcycle Clubs in SE Queensland, Harry is forced to run for his life, but not before stocking up on lovely girls, rum and a few select close friends. Harry's mystical giant cat, Jasper once again proves that he's more than worth any two humans in a fight.

Harry, the floating trouble magnet, discovers that being shot in Afghanistan was nothing like being the focus of attention of all the OMC's in South East Queensland. His inventiveness gets the workout of a lifetime as he tries to stay one jump ahead of the bad guys as they form strange alliances to find him.

"This is Book 2 in the Firebird Series, and *Backpackers* leads us on another adventure with a maritime background. All the drama and action we have come to expect from Ian, we are left with just one question... when can we expect book three?"
—Alison Lewis, author of "Missing"

Praise for *Hitchhikers* (Book 1 of the Firebird Series)

"The hero, Harry, when asked what he has been doing lately, answers "Boats, bad guys, bullets and old friends." What he fails to add is — beautiful women, sex, a bad-ass black cat, and Bond type cunning to overcome the bad guys. Piqued your interest? This is a great fast paced read and I am looking forward to the next phase of Harry's life as promised by the author.
—Judith Flitcroft, Author of *Walk Back in Time*.

ALSO BY THE AUTHOR
BOOK THREE IN THE FIREBIRD SERIES

An Eco-terrorist organisation formed with lofty ideals...a ratbag wealthy industrialist egomaniac...a plot to overturn the entire Australian political process...a major natural gas processing plant at risk...a giant crocodile...RAN patrol boats...an assassination contract targeting the PM. All the ingredients for a Firebird cocktail...definitely shaken, not stirred!

Book 3 in the Firebird series sees the Special Marine Strike Force (SMSF) head for the Pilbara to deliver their own special brand of mayhem and retribution on the bad guys.

ALSO BY THE AUTHOR
BOOK FOUR IN THE FIREBIRD SERIES

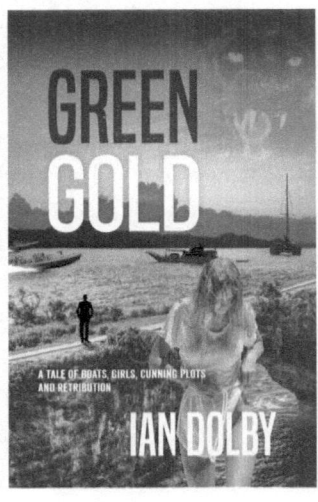

Driven by intense personal interest, including a shoulder with a bullet hole in it, Harry takes the Special Marine Strike Force across the Timor Sea to Indonesia in pursuit of the escaping Earth Care principals. Retribution and reward follow in the best Harry Stevens tradition, before the Strike Force take some well-deserved R&R and head for West Indonesia to keep their promise to their friends, Roger and Jill, in the search for the highly elusive and remarkable Green Gold.

Greedy islanders and pirates plying their age-old trade, do their best to complicate the process, but more treasure, along with the body count, keep piling up for the crews of the two boats, before some seized papers reveals details of an assassination plot against the Aussie PM and names the shadowy figures who were financing the EarthCare debacle!

Harry's not the only one with cunning plans - the special envoy who arrives to collect the papers comes up with a hare-brained scheme to safeguard the PM, but more strange alliances are formed as an old adversary unexpectedly re-surfaces.

A final round of havoc brews up that attracts Harry's particular brand of retribution, but who wins...who loses, and is the job really finished?

ALSO BY THE AUTHOR
BOOK FIVE IN THE FIREBIRD SERIES

With former Australian SAS Major, Harry Stevens and the Firebird crew heading home from their harrowing, but lucrative Indonesian operation, a call from the Australian PM sees the crew despatched to beautiful Lord Howe Island to investigate some disturbing events.

How can a beautiful and tranquil sub-tropical paradise have such a rotten core? Harry's disconcerting habit of attracting trouble strikes again as he encounters:

+ A wife-beating police officer.....
+ A homicidal maniac terrorising young female tourists.....
+ A major international smuggling operation, involving stolen uncut gemstones.....
+ A very profitable smuggling operation dealing in protected Australian reptiles.....
+ Are any of these linked?
+ Is putting two of Harry's favourite ladies in serious harm's way justified?
+ Can Harry's passion for coming up with complex 'cunning plans', save the ladies?
+ And what does one do with a homicidal Police officer in the absence of witnesses and 'smoking gun' evidence?
+ Who guards the guardian?

Doubts and misgivings plague Harry's waking thoughts as the darkest side of humanity increasingly shows its ugliest face.

At least with the diminutive, but deadly Corrine helping Harry and Jasper, there is possibly a way.